A love story for when Christ walked the earth. *A Certain Man* is a celebration of love, devotion, persistence, and faith so needed in our uncertain world. Author Linda Dindzans crafts a suspicious death into a tale both harrowing and inspiring—a story about the power of prayer, never-ending love, and ultimately, salvation. A must-read.

— Peter Van Sant, Correspondent, CBS News

Linda Dindzans captures the passion of the woman at the well like no other retelling of this Gospel story. Beautiful writing coupled with solid research makes this novel both thought-provoking and emotionally stunning. I so empathized with the Samaritan woman before Jesus walked into her life at the well that when He spoke of her five previous husbands, I knew without a doubt He must have felt even more compassion and sorrow for her than I did. Her zeal and faith in the Messiah was so well grounded because of all this novel portrays, and I'll recommend it to every biblical fiction lover I know!

— Mesu Andrews, Award-winning author

Linda Dindzans takes us on a transformative journey from heartbreak to restoration, establishing herself as a promising and vibrant voice in Biblical Fiction.

— KD Holmberg, Award-winning author

Linda Dindzans hits the nail on the head with her inspiring and moving book, *A Certain Man*. Set in ancient Samaria and Judea, Mara is a young Samaritan woman who waits to marry the love of her life, Samuel. In an unexpected turn, her father's greed leads him to devise a marriage to the son of a wealthy High Priest, making Mara's future unsure. Written beautifully, with characters that grip the reader, Dindzans spins an endearing story of love that survives the trying events placed before them. A well-done must-read that should be on every bookshelf.

— Cindy K. Sproles, Award-winning author of
This is Where It Ends

Linda Dindzans' debut novel, *A Certain Man*, is a must-read. Based primarily on two familiar Bible stories, she has woven a tale of good versus evil that will keep you on the edge of your seat until the last page.

— Deborah Sprinkle, Awarding-winning
author of the Trouble in Pleasant Valley Series
and the Mac & Sam Mysteries Series

A Certain Man breathes life into familiar gospel stories we too often skim. Characters come alive, giving us deeper insight into the hope they find in their world, a world with Jesus in it.

— Marilyn Malcolm, author of *The Disciple's
Wife*

Hearing Bible stories at the knee of my devout grandmother, I wanted to know more about the people in those gospel stories. *A Certain Man* weaves the tales of Mara and Samuel into a captivating connection of several Bible stories. An engaging story that twists and turns, yet has a satisfying ending – a book that I believe my grandmother would have enjoyed. I certainly did and think you will also.

— Nancy Martin, writing instructor, co-author
Patton's Lucky Scout

Readers who might shy away from a novel labeled Biblical fiction shouldn't with *A Certain Man*. They would be missing a beautifully written book with rich characters, a powerful and surprising plot, and a strong woman's point of view, all set against the backdrop of the well-researched and detailed history surrounding the period of Jesus' life.

— Susan Taylor-Boyd, author and columnist

Mara, the heroine of *A Certain Man,* finds herself in the warming presence of a stranger-turned-prophet. And quite unexpectedly, she becomes one of the blessed few who experiences love in its purest distillation. Author Linda Dindzans creates an ancient world that gives voice to the women of first-century Palestine under Roman rule.

— Michele Merens, author of *Inside Our Days*
(Muriel Press)

A CERTAIN FUTURE: BOOK ONE

A CERTAIN MAN

Blessings
Linda Dindzans

LINDA DINDZANS

Scrivenings
PRESS
Quench your thirst for story.
www.ScriveningsPress.com

Paperback ISBN 978-1-64917-403-1

eBook ISBN 978-1-64917-404-8

Editors: Amy R. Anguish and Michael Ehret

Map design by Lena Cass and Suzanne Edstrom

Cover design by Linda Fulkerson - www.bookmarketinggraphics.com

Some scripture quotations are taken from the Holy Bible, New International Version®, NIV®. Copyright © 1973, 1978, 1984 by Biblica, Inc. Used by permission of Zondervan. All rights reserved worldwide.

Some scripture quotations are taken from the New King James Version®. Copyright © 1982 by Thomas Nelson. Used by permission. All rights reserved.

Unless otherwise mentioned in the list of characters, all characters are fictional, and any resemblance to real people, either factual or historical, is purely coincidental.

To my husband, Vincents.
I am my beloved's and my beloved is mine.

Song of Solomon

The Land at the Time of Yeshua of Nazareth

PHOENICIA

GALILEE
Ruled by Herod Antipas

Sea of Galilee

Tiberias

Mt. Carmel

Nazareth

The Great Sea

Caesarea

Megiddo

DECAPOLIS
Ruled by Philip

SAMARIA

Mt. Ebal

Shechem

Jordan River

Mt. Gerizim

JUDEA
Ruled by Pontius Pilate

Winter Palace Garden

PHILISTIA

PEREA
Ruled by Herod Antipas

Jericho

Jerusalem
Mt. of Olives
Bethany

Bethlehem

Salt Sea

IDUMEA

Hebron

Machaerus

Lena Cass and Suzanne Edstrom

KEY
Blacksmith
Jacob's Well
Ampitheatre
Village
Temple
Altar
Inn

APPROXIMATE SCALE IN MILES
5   15   25
0   10   20

A Certain Man: List of Characters

*Historical figure in first-century Judea

Abram: Samuel's father

Achor: youngest son of High Priest of Shechem

Barid: innkeeper at Jericho inn

Caiaphas*: High Priest of Jerusalem

Dan: Daveed's younger son

Daveed: Mara's fifth husband

Delilah: wife of Dan, gave Mara pagan herbs

Dex: blacksmith at forge in Jericho

Enosh: middle son of High Priest of Shechem

Herod Antipas*: Tetrarch or "King" of Galilee and Perea at the time of Yeshua

Herodias*: Herod's wife, after she divorced his brother, also Herod's niece

Jareb: oldest son of High Priest of Shechem, rightful blood avenger

Johakim*: High Priest of Samaria at time of slaughter of the innocents in Bethlehem

John the Baptizer*: prophet in the wilderness of Judea

Joseph of Arimathea*: wealthy merchant, member of Sanhedrin

Judith: Johakim's wife, deceased for many years.

Lyra: Samuel's daughter with Zosi

Mara/Tamara/Shamara: Young girl who loves Samuel

Miriam*: mother of Yeshua

Misha: Daveed's oldest son

Naomi: mother of Johakim high priest, respected matchmaker

Okpara: Egyptian slave, camel driver

Ozri: apprentice at Abram's workshop

Pil-i: twin of Okpara, camel driver

Pontius Pilate*: Prefect of Judea

Prima: first harpist at Herodias' court

Pyrce: Greek stonecutter who hides Samuel

Rivkah: Mara's mother who died in childbirth

Ruth: Samuel's mother, expert weaver, healer with herbs

Salome*/ Yonah: princess, daughter of Herodias. Not named in the Gospels

Samuel/ Didymus: young man who Mara loves

Sarah: midwife, present at Mara's birth

Seth: Mara's fourth husband, conscripted into the Roman Army

Sophia: wife of Dex, wet-nurses Lyra

Theo: victim of bandits on Jericho Road, named by Barid

Tobiah: Mara's greedy drunken father

Yeshua the Nazarene*: Jesus, The Messiah, The Promised One

Zosi: Samuel's comfort woman, Lyra's mother, favorite handmaid of Herodias

1

The Samaritan City of Shechem
During the reign of Emperor Tiberius Caesar
Spring, Nisan 14, Day before Passover

Mara

Mara ran deep into the field of barley, arms spread wide, embracing smells of fertile earth, ripening grain, and a few stolen moments of solitude. Having suffered thirteen years in her drunken father's house, more servant than daughter, soon she would be deemed mature enough to marry. Motherless since birth, only the Lord knew what type of match her father would broker.

Samuel. Her heart fluttered like a fledgling sparrow ready to take flight. Last night when he watched her weave, he called her *Mami. Sweetness.* Memory of his chiseled cheeks, sculpted form, and sun-bronzed skin set her feet dancing, weaving a path through the barley stalks. The rising sun warmed her back and face, her head-cover spilling to her shoulders, setting her hair free in the soft wind.

Samuel. For a moment, she allowed herself to imagine what her life could be if he came to love her—if she came to love him.

And, for just a moment, she allowed herself to dream. She spun, hands reaching for the sky, feeling beautiful and blessed and beloved.

Humming a wedding dance, Mara set aside her troubles and scampered toward the road, her heart singing Samuel's name.

Mara burst onto the dirt path and slammed into the chest of a man. She stepped back and gaped at the pitch-black eyes of Achor, son of the wealthy High Priest of Shechem.

"A thousand pardons." Mara fumbled, failing to secure her head-cover.

He seized her chin.

Warm sweat beaded on her neck, and searing heat crawled onto her cheeks.

Everything about Achor was dark. His eyes, his hair, his cloak. His soul.

"Those blue eyes must harken back to some pagan temptress in your bloodline." He leaned his head back and his eyes crept over every new curve of her body. "Such an enticing blush. You are ripe in time for the Festival of First Fruits. Ripe for early harvest."

Mara's heartbeat hitched like a startled doe. She sidestepped him and started to run.

He seized her arm and hauled her into a crushing hug. One hand slid into the hair at the back of her head. "Tresses the color of copper." He twisted her hair around his fingers. "The sign of a fiery woman." He leaned in, lips pursed.

Achor's breath reeked of last night's savory stew and well-aged barley wine. Both gone rancid.

Mara angled away from him. "Let me go."

"Who will hear you in this out-of-the-way place?" Achor's slurred speech flashed a familiar warning of violence.

He was still besotted.

She shoved against his chest with all the might she could muster.

He licked his lips and pulled her closer.

Her skin skittered with the feet of a hundred scorpions.

"Release her." Samuel stepped through the barley, looking more warrior than woodworker.

Achor yanked her hair tighter. "Ah, the toolmaker's son. This time of year, the fields are full of creatures coupling. Perhaps that is why you are here." He looked from Mara to Samuel. "Surely you are old enough to have a woman."

Mara's eyes blurred with tears of pain and shame.

"Release her." Samuel raised his voice and widened his stance.

Mara drew in deep, slow breaths, striving to slow her runaway heart and mind. Samuel had tamed the quick temper that marred his youth, but Mara was sure he would not hesitate to defend her honor. She studied the two men.

Achor was a few years older than Samuel's eighteen, and a fist taller. But he did not have hard muscles forged by long hours of heavy work. He lived a soft life of luxury. If it came to blows, Samuel would prevail.

"I will share her with you." Achor let go of her hair and ran his hands down her body. "No one need ever know."

A bitter taste filled Mara's throat. She batted his groping hands away. *Lord, strike this demon dead.*

Achor clutched the neckline of her tunic, ready to rip it open.

"Release her." Samuel grabbed and squeezed Achor's wrist — his large hand a vise. "I will not warn you again."

Achor's fingers uncurled from her tunic.

Samuel's face was frozen in bare-teethed fury. His temper must not explode.

"You have won." Mara tugged at Samuel's sleeve.

"You only think he has won." Achor's face flashed revenge and he kicked Samuel's knee.

The blow dropped him. He clutched his leg, face the color of ashes.

Achor seized Mara around the waist.

Samuel reached up. "Let her go." He yanked Achor's robe.

Achor staggered. "She wants me."

Mara wrenched away, but Achor stepped on her long tunic. Trapped—her pulse raced, her hands shook, her blood boiled. She rounded and rammed her knee hard into Achor's loins.

Samuel yanked harder at Achor's robe and toppled him.

She pulled free.

"Run, Mara, run."

She ran faster than she had ever run before.

"I will ... kill you." Achor's threat was edged with an evil she had never heard.

Mara stopped and turned. Achor straddled Samuel, pinning him to the ground. Both hands on his throat. Cutting off his life-breath. Samuel's face purpled.

Achor's lust for her been exchanged for a lust for blood.

She picked up a stone and hurled it at Achor. But the stone glanced off his back. He leaned into his chokehold.

Mara spotted two men on the road and ran, waving her arms above her head. "Help." She pointed toward the brawl. "He is killing him."

The two men hurried closer.

Mara knew them. Achor's elder brothers. Her stomach dropped and twisted. "Stop him."

They must save Samuel.

They eyed each other and something unreadable passed between them.

"If Achor kills Samuel, you will be called before your father as witnesses against your brother's sin."

Jareb grabbed Achor around the middle and heaved him away from Samuel. "Rein in your temper."

Achor gained his feet. Spewing curses, he headed back toward his eldest brother.

"Fool." Jareb shook Achor by the shoulders. "Kill him and you will be stoned."

Achor might have fought Jareb were he not a hand taller and half a talent more weight.

Sucking air, Samuel lurched to a stand, lame knee bent, weight on the other leg.

Enosh, near as wide as he was short, folded his arms across his chest. The look settling on his face was one of perverted pleasure. He seemed to relish his brothers' discord.

Achor straightened his clothes. "This lout attacked me."

"He lies." Both brothers ignored Mara's shout of the truth.

"Should we teach this brazen woodworker's son a lesson?" Enosh, the lifelong victim of insults, seemed to savor the chance to brutalize someone else.

Jareb turned to his brothers. "Samuel may survive, but he will not soon forget. He has dared to assault a son of the high priest."

Achor shot Mara a lecherous look. "Then, I will take you as mine."

Bolts of horror surged through Mara's veins. The three brothers closed in and surrounded Samuel—a pack of wild dogs.

Samuel's eyes locked with hers. He mouthed, "Run."

Mara could not breathe, she could not scream, she could not move.

The three brothers shoved Samuel to the ground. Fists and feet flew at him, landing vicious blows.

Mara's mind was overrun with fears. Samuel could die. No witnesses. The words of women were worthless. She would be defiled, violated by all three brothers.

Above all, she must save Samuel. A newfound courage quickened her legs. She raced toward town, screaming for help.

At the crossroads, she rushed past Jacob's well. Too early for the village women. She ran past the forge. Fire stoked but no smithy in sight. A stitch in her side stole her breath. But she dashed on. At the edge of town, her father sprawled in their yard. Useless sot. The humble home of Samuel's parents was next door. She shouted inside. "Help! Priest's sons. Thrashing Samuel."

Mara picked up the striker and hit the cymbal hung in the front tree to call Abram from his workshop.

"Where?" Ruth bolted from the house.

"Near the priest's field."

Ruth rushed to Mara and took the striker from her hand. She kept banging and shouting for help.

Abram came running. His apprentice, Ozri, trailing by a few paces.

Ruth pointed. "Trouble. Samuel. High Priest's field." She ran to meet her husband and looked back, eyes wide, mouth pulled tight. The flicker of fear on her face faded and changed to a squint and set jaw of determination. She waved Mara toward her house. "Bring hyssop, wine, oil, and towels."

Mara darted inside, shoved what they needed into a woven sack, and ran back to help Samuel.

Abram and Ozri rushed to the road where the men had attacked Samuel.

But they were gone.

Every trace of the brawl had been covered by the brush strokes of a nearby barley bundle fashioned into a broom.

Off to the side, Abram picked up a handful of darkened dirt, sifted it through his fingers, and sniffed. "Blood, not water, has soaked this ground."

"HaShem, save my son." Ruth gasped and fell to her knees. "Where is he?" She pressed a fist to her heart.

Mara forced herself to stay calm and study the scene. "Samuel must be alive. To touch a corpse would make them unclean to sacrifice the lambs for the Passover."

She knelt and took Ruth into her arms. "They must have dragged him into the barley field."

Abram looked in every direction. "Nothing stirs."

Ozri touched Abram's shoulder. "Master, you go east. I will go west."

Abram looked at his wife. "You stay here with Mara. We do not know if the priests' sons are still nearby."

The men went into the field, their calls for Samuel sounding across the land.

Ruth wrung her hands. "We must find him. His time is sifting away."

Mara hugged Ruth. "Abram and Ozri will find him."

Ruth pushed away, a wild look in her eyes. "Samuel's time is short. His blood leaks away. His life fades away."

Mara buried her face in her hands. "No. No. No."

"Yes." Ruth gently took Mara's hands from her face. "Look at me."

Mara met her worry-filled eyes.

"I am his mother and I know in my bones, his heartbeat slows. Time is short."

Mara grabbed Ruth's arm. "We must search too."

Ruth rose. "We will stay where we can hear each other."

Mara headed into the field, prickling barley snagging her robe. Time seemed both too long and too short.

"Come back to the road." Abram's shout hitched with disappointment and despair. The exhausted search party met and traded looks but not words. Abram offered each a drink from his waterskin.

"We cannot stop." Mara plunged back into the field. Ruth flanked her right.

"Judging by the overhead sun, it must be midday." Mara wiped her brow with her head-cloth. "Samuel." Her voice was hoarse and failing.

Several paces away, Ruth stopped and tilted her head. "Shh. I heard something."

Time crawled in circles.

Ruth shrieked and dropped out of sight.

Mara ran toward the place where Ruth had vanished and found her kneeling next to Samuel, her ear pressed to his chest, grief etching wrinkles around her eyes.

"Those beasts almost buried him alive." Ruth cleared dirt away from Samuel's face.

He lay unmoving and bloody. Eyes closed. Face gray. Mara began to dig with both hands. "Over here. Help me."

Ozri and Abram crashed through the barley and unearthed Samuel's body.

Mara studied Samuel's still face. This was her fault. Memories of her father's relentless taunts ripped at her soul. *Mara can turn a moment of blessing into a curse.*

HaShem, please. Will you hear the prayers of a woman? I have no father, no brother, no husband to pray in my stead. Lord, let him live.

Mara held her breath.

Silence. A far-flung silence. A silence clinging to a shred of hope.

A Certain Man

A gasp broke the silence.
And her buried Beloved began to breathe.

2

Nisan 22

Day after Feast of Unleavened Bread

Samuel

amuel fidgeted at the low table and looked out into the courtyard where the women were cooking and baking bread. "After only a short walk outside, I slept for hours."

"You were senseless until the third day." Ima dumped vegetables and lentils into the pot Mara stirred. "Praise HaShem. Death has passed over our door. For today, I am content to see my son leave the sleeping mat."

Samuel broke the last *matzoh*, but the unleavened bread did not satisfy his hunger. "I long for the sweet, yeasty smell and taste of a leavened loaf slathered with honey."

"I am glad your hunger has returned." Mara slipped him a shy smile. "The feast is complete, and my father has agreed to sup with you and your father this very night. We are preparing a special meal." Mara's voice trembled with what sounded like both excitement and worry.

Perhaps Samuel was hearing the echo of his own worries in Mara's tone. Hopefully, Mara's father would remember the supper meeting. He blamed Mara when her birth took his cherished wife's life. Seeking solace in strong drink, he so often crushed Mara's spirit with broken promises, belligerent words, and more recently, bruising blows.

She tried to hide the marks of her father's attacks and ran for refuge into the arms of Samuel's mother. When their betrothal was confirmed, under the Law, Mara would be his wife and he could and would protect her. His stomach knotted —into a double twisted Solomon's knot. To secure a betrothal was one thing, but it was quite another feat to secure the bride-price.

Mara scooped a small portion of lamb stew into a bowl and set it before him. "Taste. Does the stew need more salt? More leeks? More wild garlic?" She wiped her hands on her apron and returned to Ima at the cookfire. "Do not worry. My father never forgets the promise of one of your mother's meals."

Ima put her arm around Mara. "Your mother taught me to cook."

Mara rested her head against Ima's shoulder "I never knew. My father never speaks of my mother."

"She would have been so pleased with you."

Samuel dipped the matzoh in the stew and took a mouthful. "Beloved, this is wonderful." The stew was bland, but at least not burnt. "Ima, you taste."

His mother ladled a sip. She would show Mara how to make a meal fit for the table of the high priest, all the while offering the gentle encouragement she so desperately craved.

"When I was your age, cooking was merely a chore." Ima

turned to Mara. "For your mother, meals were an expression of deepest love."

Ruth wiped tears with the edge of her apron. "I miss her so." She sighed. "Come, Mara, let me show you some of your mother's secrets for a savory stew."

"Show me all of her secrets." Mara bent over the stew and wafted the fragrant steam toward her nose.

"Not tonight. We will have a lifetime to share them." His mother and Mara huddled over the pot, taking turns spicing and tasting. "After your betrothal, you may call me Ima. HaShem knows you are already a daughter to me."

An evil foreboding slithered up Samuel's spine. "Abba will be home soon. Mara, you should make sure your father is on his way." His tone sounded more unsettled than he intended. This evening, nothing must go awry.

Mara flashed him a look full of mischief. "Do not fret. When I was home earlier, I hid the wineskin and left a pitcher of cold well water on the table."

Samuel could not keep the astonished look from his face.

Mara moved to him and touched his cheek. "Beloved, let there always be plain speaking between us. My father is a drunkard."

Ruth handed Mara a linen-wrapped parcel. "Here, tempt your father, Tobiah, with this warm matzoh."

"I will not linger." Mara scurried past Abba returning from his day's work.

"Wife, cover yourself. A messenger came to the woodshop. The high priest and his sons are on their way here to make amends."

Ima arranged her veil. "They have tarried for many days and many nights. Why should this night be different from all the other nights?"

Her mother-lion eyes flashed warnings toward the door.

She would not readily forgive or forget the beating her wounded cub had suffered. "The high priest offered to pay lost wages, but no recompense for Samuel's suffering."

Abba placed a hand at the small of Ima's back. "This dispute must be concluded quickly. We cannot stand against the House of the High Priest. We must seek peace."

Samuel rose and brushed away the matzoh crumbs.

"Husband, meet them at the door, but please do not invite them in, for then we must feed them." Ruth took a short paddle outside, lifted the bread loaf from the hot cook-stone onto a platter, and returned inside. "This evening we settle Samuel's betrothal. This supper is far too important to allow evildoers to interrupt our plans."

The mutterings of a gathering crowd outside were pierced by the braying of an angry donkey. The high priest had arrived.

"Come, Samuel, son of Abram. My sons would speak with you." The high priest's voice carried through the door.

Samuel grabbed his walking stick and hobbled toward the threshold. Sweat beaded his brow. He ground his teeth against the lightning bolts of pain blazing down his legs.

Samuel set his walking stick in the shadow of the doorpost. His father took a place behind Samuel's weak side. "Lean against me. They will not see." Abba reached for the latch and swung open the door.

The high priest's sons stood clustered at the threshold.

"Your father remains out of earshot on the road, seated on his donkey." Abram's level voice betrayed no anger, no judgment. "He expects you to act for yourselves."

Jareb nodded. "Abram, you spoke rightly to our father. We are men not boys and though fury flared on *all* sides..." Jareb turned, played to the gathering crowd, calling to mind Samuel's well-known hot temper. "We must make settlement for Samuel's injuries."

All the townsfolk were here, and Samuel knew every face. Some pretended to pass by. Some pretended disinterest. Others were openly curious. Secrets were never safe in a small town such as Shechem.

Samuel watched Jareb check the faces of those gathered. As eldest son, one day he would be put forward for the position of High Priest. If he wanted to be confirmed, he must keep the people's favor.

"Our father has pledged fifty days wages to compensate for Samuel's lost work. An expense we three will divide."

Achor's face was the embodiment of compassion. A mock expression that did not read true in his cold-blooded eyes. "In addition, I personally will offer thirty pieces of silver." Achor's tone dripped with the pride of privilege. Not a drop of repentance in his voice.

Ima gasped. "Praise HaShem." Her whisper carried across the tense silence. "Thirty pieces of silver." She clapped. "The bride-price."

Samuel cringed. One more private matter unveiled before all of Shechem.

Achor turned toward the crowd. "The additional coin will also ease the burden of any *ever-lasting* infirmity."

Enosh laughed. That strange giggle.

Samuel's memory of his beating flooded in. *Enosh's high-pitched giggle. "This beating may put Samuel off women altogether."*

What a strange thing for Enosh to say.

Samuel's sour stomach burned and churned. Achor had brought Samuel's ability to provide for a wife into question. "There will be no lasting injury. I will not take one silver coin beyond the fifty-day wages. And no payment is required for my defense of a young woman's honor."

Achor's expression was more disdain than denial. "Of

course, you were not present when the girl and I met in the field, so you have no certainty she did not offer herself."

"She pushed you away. I saw." Samuel clenched his fists, barely keeping himself from lunging at the liar.

"Everyone in Shechem knows of your quick temper and your quick fists. Always ready to defend the poor against the wealthy, the weak against the strong. This time you mistook the scene. The girl's push you saw was playful ... a challenge for me to pursue."

An awl bored into Samuel's stomach, and a vise clamped his chest. "You lie."

Samuel took a step toward Achor. "You would destroy the honor of an innocent girl. You would sully her name."

Abba gripped the back of Samuel's robe. A warning to hold his tongue. Further protest would spark the town gossips and feed the fires of doubt.

Achor clasped Samuel's shoulder as if he were offering friendly advice. "Who will believe the drunkard's daughter against the word of a high priest's son?"

Samuel twisted away from Achor's grasp and spoke to the people. "HaShem knows the truth and He will not let Achor's false witness go unpunished."

Abba pointed a finger at the three brothers. "One day your sins will be laid bare."

Uncertainty flitted across Achor's face. He shrugged. "Jareb, Enosh, bring your shares to me."

The two brothers added their coins to Achor's money sack and stepped back into the crowd. Achor handed the sack to Abba.

Samuel turned a shoulder to Achor. "Your debt is paid."

Achor took a small pouch from his bosom and dangled it in front of Samuel's face. "Thirty pieces of silver." He dropped the pouch at Samuel's feet. "Enough for a bride-price."

Samuel's jaw clenched, his blood boiled. He wanted to beat Achor as he had been beaten. The growing silence felt heavy with hate, heavy as death. "I will not take your silver." He took a deep breath and bridled his temper. "Never. Ever."

Mara's father pushed through the crowd and headed for the money sack. "But I will."

Mara

Mara's father stretched out his hand to take hold of the money sack Achor had dropped at Samuel's feet. Horror surged through her veins.

"The silver is not yours." Mara grabbed her father's arm, but he flung her away. She could not let him take the money.

Her father held the edges of his outer robe and stood tall. "Samuel lost wages, but Achor owes me for the sullied name of my daughter."

Mara wished her father loved her. "I told you. Samuel preserved my honor. If you take the silver, it seals the suspicion I was defiled."

Her father's eyes changed, alight with greed and need. His lips smacked as if he could taste the barley beer the coins would buy. "You are right, daughter." He pointed his finger at Achor. "This must be a bride-price. You must marry my daughter."

"Nooo." Mara sank to her knees.

"Never," Samuel shouted.

"Nooo," Ruth whispered.

Abram's lips tightened. Mara knew that look—he was harnessing his temper. The well-known temper of his youth rivaled Samuel's.

Achor flashed her a look of hatred. "Old man, bring her to me."

Her father hauled her to her feet, closer to her attacker. Once again Achor took her by the chin, but she pushed away and refused to meet his eyes.

"She is comely enough." The lust in his voice made her arms prickle as if a thousand dung beetles scurried toward her neck.

Achor crossed his arms. "If my father approves the match, I will marry her."

Samuel stepped up next to her. "But I was going to speak to her father this very evening."

Abram nodded. "It is true."

"And where is Samuel's bride-price?" Achor pointed to the sack of coins on the dirt.

Mara clutched the back of her father's robe. If only her father would consider her heart. "I beg you, *Abba*. Do not do this to me."

"Now, for the first time in your life, you call me Abba, not Father, feigning you are a dutiful, loving daughter." He flung Mara to the ground.

The crowd began to stir, snigger, snipe.

The high priest dismounted his donkey and approached Achor. "What goes here?"

"This woman's father demands I marry her to restore her reputation. If you approve, I am willing."

Father crossed his arms. "I demand the tradition to delay betrothals during the counting of the weeks of Omer be set aside. My daughter's honor must be restored."

Achor leered at Mara. "And the wedding must take place before the third full moon."

Mara knelt in front of the high priest. "Mercy, sir. I am not willing."

The high priest motioned for Ruth to help Mara. She moved Mara a respectful distance away from the men and whispered, "Do not speak."

Samuel glanced at her, then turned to the high priest. "Sir, Mara is yet a girl. She is too young to marry. In two years, I will have the bride-price. She and I both want to be wed."

"Under the Law, the girl's will is nothing." The high priest glared at her father. "Only Tobiah can, and should, consider her heart."

Mara turned pleading eyes to her father. If this abomination of a betrothal was sealed, she would never again call this selfish man father. If she spoke of him at all, he would be Tobiah.

"As a dutiful father, my place is to negotiate a fortuitous match." Tobiah lifted his hands and moved them as if balancing scales in the marketplace. "The woodworker's son, or the son of the high priest. The bride-price now, or possibly in two years. Possibly never."

Mara's stomach sickened at the wheedling in Tobiah's voice. All her life this sot had craved attention, be it for gain or for shame.

"A word." Ruth approached Tobiah. She leaned close and spoke with quiet strength. "Remember. Your betrothal to Rivkah was a love match. Your beloved wife would not want you to bind her daughter in a loveless marriage."

"Rivkah is not here to object." His voice curdled with bitterness. "Mara's birth stole my wife from me. You were there. I will never accept your son as a suitor for her."

"Then, I will speak for Mara in her mother's stead." Ruth's tone was edged with iron. She looked back at Abram.

He ushered Mara and Ruth before the high priest. "Before you confirm this contract, I would ask that you hear my wife. It is customary the mother has some say bargaining for the bride.

My wife was the closest friend of this young woman's dead mother."

"Speak, woman, in her mother's stead." The high priest's face was gentle, open, as if he craved a voice of reason in the midst of the burgeoning chaos.

Ruth bowed her head, eyes lowered with respect. "Please, if this marriage is to be allowed, my *daughter...*" Her voice faltered. She took a deep breath. "My daughter is too young. Would you allow your son to take a child to the marriage bed like the pagans?"

Achor rushed forward. "I will not take a child to my bed."

"She has not yet seen her first moonblood. By that time, Achor may be taken with another, and Mara would no longer be first wife or first favored."

Achor loomed over Ruth, his chin almost touching her brow. "That is no reason to delay the betrothal."

Tobiah stepped to Achor's side. "Or to delay the payment of the bride-price."

Abram edged Ruth behind him. He looked at Achor, then the high priest. "A betrothal span shorter than one year will suggest a child may be on the way."

"Her father has already admitted that likelihood by requiring me to marry her."

Snickers and snatches of vicious gossip buzzed around Mara. She did not look down, did not shrink. She stood tall and met the eyes of each woman who would dare defame her. Then she shot Achor a look full of defiance.

Ruth spat at Tobiah's feet. "Rivkah would forswear what you have become." She turned to the high priest. "Please, sir, the bride-price coins, *the mohar,* should not be held by Tobiah. Everyone knows he is never to be trusted with money. If Achor would ever divorce Mara saying *Return to your mother with your mohar,* she would have neither mother nor mohar."

Mara pressed her hands to her cheeks. Ruth. Well-spoken and valiant. Mara's mother would have wept with pride.

The high priest nodded. "Her bride-price will be held in the city treasury."

Her father yelped. "I must have compensation for the cooking, cleaning, and other chores my daughter does now and will do in my old age."

"If you agree to an immediate betrothal and a wedding two weeks following her first moonblood, you will be given a generous sum each year we are married." Achor negotiated her *ketubah* as if he were haggling over a contract for a slave, not a wife.

"And if you divorce my daughter?"

"If she displeases me, she will be given her *mohar* and sent back to you." Achor leered at Samuel. "But I assure you, in time, she will anxiously await my visits to her chambers. She will give me many sons."

"Good. Grandchildren are a blessing." Tobiah clenched forearms with Achor and turned to the high priest. "We are agreed."

Samuel wedged himself between Achor and Tobiah. "It will not go well for either of you. This betrothal will bear the fruits of false witness and a frightened, unwilling bride."

The crowd grumbled, loud and long. But Mara was not sure if they were with or against Samuel. With or against her.

"Silence." The high priest lifted his hands. "The ketubah will be drawn up but remain unsigned until the sun sets tomorrow. If Achor and Tobiah are still in agreement, I will witness the wedding contract and the betrothal will proceed."

The high priest turned and walked away. The crowd slowly parted before the high priest. No one greeted him. No one bowed. He mounted his donkey. Achor and his brothers joined their father, readying themselves for the walk home.

Abram drew Mara and Ruth close to his sides.

"The bride-price." Tobiah raced forward and reached for the money sack on the ground.

"Leave it." The high priest's command cut across the gathering. "The marriage contract has yet to be sealed."

"But the silver might be stolen." Tobiah's hand edged toward the money.

"Who would risk the loss of his hand?" The high priest mounted his donkey.

Tobiah stepped back.

The high priest rode away.

Achor approached Mara and stood much too close. His vile gaze traveled from her sandaled feet to her burning cheeks.

He kissed his fingers and flicked them toward her. "You will be a woman soon enough."

Samuel shook both fists in the air. "If you persist with your evil plans, you will not escape the wrath of the Lord."

Achor mouth twisted into a cruel smile.

A wave of hot dread ran through Mara, draining all warmth in its wake. She crumpled to the ground. Pebbles pressed into her cheek. The sack of coins lay just in front of her face. Her world went black. Black like Achor's sin.

3

Samuel

S amuel's slow, lopsided pacing across the common room did not ease his worry or anger. "Baal's Blood. If I had set aside my pride and taken the extra silver, Mara and I would have been planning our betrothal." He turned toward his parents. "Look at me." Pain drilled like an auger into his stiff knee. "I am a cripple now and may be forever."

Abba took a fig from a wooden bowl on the table. "Let us reason together."

Ima stopped kneading the dough, wiped her hands, and drew near. She lowered herself onto the bench next to Abba and sighed. "What is done is done."

His father covered her small hand with his comforting one. "We can only pray Achor will withdraw his offer. The high priest did not seem pleased. Perhaps he will have some sway?"

Samuel sat and pressed his throbbing temples. "None of the high priest's sons seem to afford him the respect due a father."

Abba tugged his beard. "Surely the elder brothers will not want Achor to sire the first son who may become the favored heir." Samuel knew that tone. Abba always saw the good, the hopeful. He was trying to reassure himself.

Ima clicked her tongue, shook her head. She was the one to worry. "The high priest's wife was a righteous woman. Perhaps if she had not died mere days after Achor's birth, he would not have been so coddled."

As if a yoke had been lowered onto his neck, Samuel struggled to find hope from any quarter. "What of the high priest's mother?"

Ima leaned in and pushed the bowl of figs closer to him.

"When I was drawing water at the well this morning, gossip shot through the air—a volley of poisoned arrows. The high priest's mother came with her handmaids. I was standing far off, but she seemed to weigh the mood of the women. I pray she will speak with her son against Achor's marriage."

"And..." Samuel gestured with a beckoning hand.

"Not one woman was in favor of a forced marriage. When Mara arrived, they not only embraced her, but offered advice."

Abba turned to Ima. "What could they possibly suggest?"

Ima's face brightened. "One told Mara to over-salt and burn-to-black every meal she served Achor during their betrothal. Another suggested she leave her clothes among the hens at night so she will reek." Ima's lips pressed back a laugh. "The most bold proposal was that Mara turn her back to Achor every time he approached her in public."

"Women can be very cunning." Abba grinned. A grin that hinted he had been the target of at least one cunning woman.

Ima flushed and lowered her eyes. "Yes. Woman can be ruthless."

"Did you hear something that could save Mara?" Samuel longed for a way to deliver Mara from a loveless life.

"One foolish girl pulled Mara aside, but I overheard." His mother fisted her hands, knuckles white as bone. "She offered to bring Mara a pagan potion to stave off her moonblood."

"Such a potion exists?" Samuel balked at the eagerness in his tone.

Abba pulled at his silver-flecked beard. "Wife, perhaps the potion would be a means to bide time. Mara is so young."

Ruth crossed her arms. "It is a dangerous practice used by pagan priestesses to banish babies from their rightful wombs." She shuddered. "Wombs that are often left barren for life."

Samuel pushed back from the table. "Mara loves children, she would never—"

"Not today. Not tomorrow." Sadness seeped into Ima's voice. "But alone and desperate? Without a mother's wisdom or warning?"

Samuel's stomach twisted, and a sour-sick taste rose in his throat. "You must keep that vile girl away from Mara. How does someone so young learn of such evil?"

"Is it any wonder when for generations our men took pagan wives and gave their daughters to other nations in Babylon and beyond? She learned from her mother, and her mother's mother, and all the mothers of all her generations." Ima headed to the threshold. "The sun is high in the sky. I will go to Mara."

"Please tell her no matter what happens today, my heart is hers. Always."

"Have faith, my son." Ima arranged her veil, gazing at him with such tenderness. She opened the door, walked to the path, and stepped wide around the half-open sack of silver that remained in the dirt. Coins covered with filth. Filthy money.

Samuel turned to Abba, determined to save Mara, heedless of the consequence. "Before Mara is betrothed, we could run. We should run."

"Never." Abba leapt to his feet. "I forbid it."

He shook a warning finger.

"You are lame. You would be caught before the next sunset and accused of adultery." His face was as red as the blood of a Passover lamb. "Both your lives would be in the balance. Even if you denied coupling, Mara would be forced to consummate the marriage with Achor without delay. And if your lives were spared, Mara would be set aside. Shamed. Divorced."

"I would take her to wife."

"No." Abba grabbed Samuel's arm. "Mara's father would be enraged at the loss of his yearly allowance. He would declare her a disobedient daughter and drag her to the stoning pit."

Samuel dropped his head into his hands. A grindstone of sadness weighted his shoulders and crept onto his chest, binding his breath.

"The ways of HaShem are not our ways. We must trust Him." His father's deep voice was filled with grief. "To run is to die."

Samuel looked up. "To stay is to die slowly."

Mara

Mara swept the packed dirt floor of the hut she shared with Tobiah and looked through the front window. The morning was as gray as her spirit. Tobiah, fury contorting his face, knocked the broom from her hands and herded her into a corner with a shepherd's staff. She pressed her back against the rough wall, hands behind her back, ready to push off and dodge the blow.

"Daughter, you will obey me as the Law commands." His words were blurred from his early morning barley beer.

"I will never go willingly to the house of Achor."

Tobiah raised the staff.

Heart racing, Mara took a deep breath and slowly rose onto her toes.

"Willing or not, you will go." Tobiah swung the staff.

Mara pushed off, darted under his arm, and the staff swished past her ear. Defiance pulsed through her veins.

Tobiah turned and lifted the staff again, rheumy eyes glinting with drunken madness.

HaShem, help me.

Mara's mind stilled. She needed a clear path to the door.

He swung the staff again.

She faked the same dodge but sidestepped the other way and broke for the door, rushing headlong into Ruth.

Her father grabbed her shoulder from behind.

"Tobiah, you attacked your own daughter." Ruth's glare could have scorched stone. "The staff is meant to rescue a lost sheep, not beat it to death."

"Woman, do not meddle with a father's discipline." Tobiah brandished the staff.

Ruth curled her hand around the staff and edged Mara behind her back. "If you mark her, Achor will take back his silver."

Her father slowly surrendered the staff and shook a fist at Mara. "If you do not obey me, you will be stoned."

Rage erupted from deep in Mara's soul. "Then I would be happily dead, freed from the torture of a loathed wedding bed."

Ruth gasped and wrapped Mara with a motherly embrace. "Child, never despise the life HaShem has given." She stroked Mara's hair. "HaShem has promised one day the ashes of mourning will be traded for joy."

Mara let hopeless tears spill down her cheeks. Today she was a captive. A captive to Achor's lust. A captive to her father's greed. And a captive under the Law of the Lord. But one day, the Taheb, the Promised One, would appear. One day, He would set every captive free.

"Tobiah." The high priest's shout rang across the village center.

Tobiah pushed past Mara and Ruth and ran outside. "I come. Let us confirm the marriage contract."

The high priest rode his donkey up to the sack of silver, now tainted with dung. He glanced toward his sons, who walked beside him.

Tobiah scuttled up to them.

Mara veiled her hair and lower face. She and Ruth went outside. The heat was scorching, windless. Mara felt she drew breath through a burial face cloth. She searched for Samuel. He stood behind his father but had not crossed the threshold of his home.

The crowd gathered quickly, still as death.

Ruth touched her arm. "My son is no coward. We have commanded him to stay inside. For his safety and yours. His rash words or deeds would only bring disaster."

The high priest raised a hand. "Tobiah, you have had the night to consider. What say you?"

Mara's chest tightened, her hands trembled, and her heart tripped over its racing rhythm. "Please, father." She threw herself at his feet and clung to his robe.

He kicked her in the side, yanked free, and looked up at the priest. "Let the wedding contract be signed."

Abram stepped forward. "Priest, what think you of the dung clinging to the silver offered for an unwilling bride?"

The high priest seemed to study the coins glinting from the dung heap. "It is peculiar."

Abram moved even closer. "Do you think the dung is an evil sign?"

Mara's stomach twisted around a kernel of hope. She rose and Ruth squeezed her hand.

Achor snorted, lifted the coin sack by its strap, and shook it free of the dung. "There is no evil sign—merely a sign someone nearby owns a goat."

Nervous snickers came from the skittish crowd.

"We will sign the contract one hour before sundown." Achor glanced toward Samuel, bounced the bride-price sack in his palm and raised an arm, gloating in triumph. "The whole town is invited to a feast this very night. We will rejoice."

The crowd murmured. Some offered hollow blessings. Others slung quiet curses.

Samuel. Mara watched him try to plow past his father. Ozri, Abram, and two others held Samuel back.

Achor approached Mara and lifted his fingers toward her face as if he would unveil her. "Until sunset."

Mara stepped back and sniffed. "The smell of dung has clung to you."

Achor's look changed. His eyes flashed cruelty and his lips pulled back revealing perfect teeth. Bone-white teeth. Sharp teeth. The bared teeth of a dog gone mad.

She glanced at the sun, past its peak.

At sunset she would be forced to surrender a lifetime with her Beloved. A lifetime filled with laughter and love, exchanged for a lifetime with Achor. A life of days serving a cruel man. A life of nights at the mercy of his lust.

Samuel's righteous bloodline would have been blessed.

Achor's bloodline of bad seed would be cursed for generations to come.

Shadows cast by the sinking sun stretched toward her like the talons of a circling vulture.

Mara trembled.

The looming shadows closed in, darkening the edges of her sight. The sun was sinking fast—and suddenly, so was she.

Ruth rushed to Mara's side and put an arm around her waist, bolstering her knees turned-to-water. "Come *Ta*mara, you must rest inside, out of the scorching sun." Ruth angled toward Tobiah's hut.

Mara pushed away. "Tobiah has sold me like a slave. He is no longer a father. And I am no longer a daughter."

Ruth clicked her tongue. "Shh. To be overheard is dangerous."

Mara's father was dead to her. Slain by a demon of drunkenness. She was an orphan without name, without protection, without hope.

"Tamara, my *sweet* date palm." Ruth drew comforting circles on her back. A touch Mara always craved. A touch that never failed to calm her.

Until now.

"Be at peace, my Tamara."

Mara pulled away from Ruth's comfort.

"Your *sweet* Tamara is dead."

Any sweetness in her had been killed by a bitter root planted in her bones when her father sold her to her attacker. A bitter root that spread through her veins and threatened every tender shoot that might sprout from her heart.

Mara heard sounds of a struggle. She turned.

Samuel broke free of his restrainers and ran toward her. "My Mara. *Mami*, my sweetness."

She halted him with an upraised palm. "Do not call me *Sweet*. For I am not yours. Call me *Bitter*."

Samuel fell to his knees and beat a fist against his heart.

"Call me Mara."

Achor stepped between Mara and Samuel.

"Mara." Achor's tone was a sickening sneer. "Until sunset." His look was an ugly leer.

Until sunset.

Until the end of the light of day.

Until the dawn of an unending night.

4

Mara

Ruth finished the long braid binding Mara's copper curls and placed the golden circlet on her head. Each dangling coin seemed to brand her brow, marking her as Achor's chattel.

Mara's chin trembled. "This crown is meant to be a promise of hope, not of horror." She grabbed the gold band, ready to toss it from her head.

Ruth reached up and uncurled Mara's fingers. "Child, from this moment you must play a part, surpassing even the best Hypocrites who perform before Herod."

Mara reached again for the circlet that felt like a crown of thorns stabbing her head. "I would cast off Achor's gold and the honored station as his wife. I would cast away his lust disguised as love."

"You would cast away not only your life ..." Ruth firmly grasped both Mara's hands. "You risk the life of my son."

Mara shrunk back from the scathing rebuke. "Samuel's life is not at risk."

"Tamara, you must appear willing to obey your father and free Samuel from any hope of marriage." Ruth clutched Mara's shoulders. "Otherwise, evil minds will twist the pure love between you and my son into an accusation of adultery."

Dread dragged through Mara's chest and down her legs, buckling her knees.

Ruth pulled her into a hug. "Samuel must believe you have set him aside."

Ruth's loving whisper stirred something in Mara's soul. She must protect Samuel. "No one will believe I go willingly to the betrothal."

Draping Mara's veil so the loosely woven window rested over her eyes, Ruth moved to face her. "You must convince everyone that you go, not with joy, but with acceptance."

Ruth knelt and flung her arms about Mara's waist. "Above all, you must persuade Samuel. If you fail, I fear for what my son will say, what he will do, how he will grieve."

Pulling Ruth to a stand, Mara nodded. She would save Samuel from himself. She willed her heart to slowly harden to stone, encrusting all feelings of love, and fear, and shame. "I will play the dutiful daughter. The sacrificial dove."

Ruth reached inside her robes, drawing out a small pouch looped on a leather cord around her neck. "This was given to me by your loving mother on the day you were born, for the day of your betrothal." Ruth tipped a small gold coin into Mara's palm.

An image of a dove in flight, olive branch in its beak. She turned the coin over and stared at the symbols, tracing the largest with a finger. "I will treasure this always."

Ruth placed the pouch around Mara's neck. "Keep the coin

well hidden. One day it may secure you the freedom to fight or to flee."

"How did my mother come by such a rare gold piece?"

Ruth's eyes dimmed, drifting into remembrance. "Rivkah and I spoke often of the Magi who passed through Shechem when we were very young girls. We never forgot the large caravan, the silk-draped camels, and the treasure chests. The foreigners entered our village under the light of a wondrous star. If stars are windows to heaven, this star was a gate."

"You once told me the Magi were on a quest to find a babe born King of the Jews."

"The Magi made a great journey following the Kingstar until it hovered over Bethlehem. One night, your mother asked them if this newborn they found was the Taheb, the Promised One, we Samaritans await."

"And their answer?"

"The Magnus Magi went silent and studied the sparkling star. A light in the darkness that rivaled the moon." Ruth's voice softened to a gentle whisper. "After a long moment, he said the mystery would one day unfold. Perhaps the babe they had worshipped was also our Taheb. Just before they left, the Magnus Magi wondered if the path they chose, home through Samaria, figured into some greater plan."

A small, unexpected sense of wonder seeped into Mara's hardened heart. She would cling to the hope that there was a greater plan at work. That hope would strengthen her resolve to reject Samuel. "And then?" Mara closed her hand around the coin.

"The next morning at dawn, we were awakened by the sounds of the departing caravan. Your grandmother, mother, and I slipped out to bid farewell. Even the bright rising sun did not blot out the light of the great star. The Magnus Magi handed your mother this coin and blessed her with words heard only by the three of us. I am the only living witness."

"Ruth, tell me his blessing."

"The Magnus lifted his eyes to the shining star. I remember each of his words."

> *Last night wisdom came to me in a dream that was more than a dream. The Taheb you watch for has been born. Let this coin be a sign and promise to you. The dove on one side portends he will be a sacrifice for many. The other side bears the symbol of the savior to come. Whoever possesses such a coin will know Him when He comes.*
>
> *Through the daughters of your line, the people of Shechem will be saved.*

The coin warmed Mara's palm. The Taheb would come to Shechem. A promise of salvation. Sealed with a sign.

"Bring the bride out to me." Tobiah's call from the road cut through the tender moment. "Her bridegroom awaits."

Mara took a deep breath, gathered her courage, and linked arms with Ruth. "No tears. You must play your part as well so I will have the strength to shatter the heart of my Beloved."

Ruth went to the door and leaned outside. "One moment more to speak for your beloved Rivkah to her beautiful daughter."

"Must I barge in, bind the wrists of my wayward daughter, and lead her to her betrothal with a rope in one hand and a cane in the other—more disobedient than a worthless, stubborn donkey?" His words piled upon one another in a drunken heap.

Ruth led Mara onto the road into the waning light of day. Mara, clinging to Ruth's hand, took her place next to Tobiah.

They trudged up the hill toward the House of the High Priest. Since Mara had been old enough to walk, she had climbed this hill every feast day. This path marked the only way to Mount Gerizim, the holy place for sacrifice. Villagers joined the solemn procession.

She must feign calm, acceptance, obedience.

Her chest tightened around a sudden insight. The path sharply split beyond the House of the High Priest. The steep path she had never taken led to Mt. Ebal. The mount of curses. And the stoning pit.

Footfalls behind her brought her back to the moment. She glanced over her shoulder. Abram and Samuel followed close at her heels.

Tobiah sneered at Ruth. "Why are your husband and son here?"

Ruth stopped and faced Tobiah. "I am here in Rivkah's stead to protect Mara. And my husband and son are here to protect me."

"Neither of you need protection. I am within my rights under the Law of Moses."

Samuel rushed forward and grabbed the neck of Tobiah's robe. "Under the Law, the bride must consent."

"Peace, Samuel." She must make Samuel believe her words. Her full veil was a blessing. He could not read the lies in her eyes. "Samuel, I beg you ..."

Samuel relaxed his grip but did not release Tobiah.

She would not risk the rumors of adultery that might have Samuel stoned. Once before she watched Abram scoop up earth soaked with her Beloved's blood. Once before she witnessed grief gouge deep into the hearts of Ruth and Abram.

She would never witness that again. Never suffer that again.

Never. Never. Never.

She pushed down a sob, a sob that sunk into her chest and shackled her soul.

Never. Ever.

HaShem, gird my heart.

Mara turned to Samuel and adopted a haughty, distant tone. A tone her tongue had never spoken. A tone Samuel's ears had never heard from her lips. "I obey my father. It is the Law. I will be Achor's wife."

Samuel stumbled back as if struck full force in the chest.

"You must wed another." Mara turned from Samuel's agonized face. He would never forgive her. She would never forgive herself.

Samuel

Samuel took his abba's arm, steadying himself. His ima and Mara continued up the hill toward the House of the High Priest. Samuel called after Mara. "I do not believe you agree to be wed to Achor." Samuel hated that his voice was a strangled croak.

"Your words say one thing, but Mara if I, I ..." His voice stuttered, stalled. "If I could see your face, you could not shroud the truth behind your veil."

Mara stopped and turned as if she would relent.

Tobiah grabbed her arm. "Betrothal is as binding as marriage. Within the hour Mara must wear the head-covering of a married woman."

"Yes. But her eyes will never lie." Samuel glared daggers toward Tobiah.

"Be still." Abba's tone was a cutting command. "The bride has spoken."

Mara turned, walked away. Somehow Mara's bridal trappings made her seem smaller, younger. Barely more than a child.

"But Abba surely—"

"Respect Mara's request." Ima raised a hand. "Would you make this night worse for her?"

Samuel covered his face with his hands.

Abba took his arm. "Son, you must gird yourself for battle. Mara has already done so."

"Battle?" Samuel dropped his hands and searched his father's face.

"The fight against the desires of your heart."

"But HaShem intended Mara for me."

Abba urged Samuel forward. "His ways are not our ways."

Ima dropped back to walk beside Samuel. "Achor can only host the wedding feast and consummation under the huppa after Mara's first moonblood bears witness to her womanhood."

"Why torment me with these things?"

"Much can change in a year." His ima's tone was tense and sad.

Samuel quickened his pace to stay close to Mara. "What, Ima?"

"Achor's desire may be captured by another and he may set Mara aside with a *get* of divorce."

"Or Tobiah's heart may soften, and he may relent."

Samuel could no longer abide his abba's calm. Resentment raged across Samuel's tongue. "Or Achor may die."

Tobiah spun toward Samuel. "You dare to call down death on the high priest's son? Your father is second witness to the curse you have spoken over Achor."

The hairs on Samuel's neck bristled and stood guard like a Roman regiment.

His mother raised a finger to her lips. "Shh. We have arrived."

The group climbed the stone stairs that led up the cliff face to the House of the High Priest. Passing under the stone arch, they entered through the iron gate into the outer courtyard. All stood in readiness for the betrothal ceremony.

Mara and her father took a place at one end of the long table.

Achor, his father the high priest, and his brothers stood at the opposing ends.

Abram and Ruth tugged Samuel back into the crowd swarming the edges of the courtyard.

Achor, triumphant, waved toward the parchment displayed on the polished cedar table. "Surely, the bride will be pleased with the gilded edges and the exquisite script of her wedding document."

Tobiah stepped forward and stroked the gold edges, looking eager to complete the sale of his hapless daughter.

"Silence." The high priest's command doused the trills of excitement and wonder from the womenfolk. "The bride must agree." He turned to Mara. "Do you come here of your own will?"

Mara stood statue still. Her stillness weighed heavy on Samuel's chest. Not one soul shifted. Not one soul spoke. Not one soul breathed.

After what seemed a lifetime, Mara dipped her head.

Tobiah picked up the quill, ready to make his mark.

The high priest cleared his throat, halting Tobiah's hand. "The bride must speak her agreement."

In that moment, Samuel no longer knew what he wanted to hear. No matter the cost, Mara must be safe from her father's threat of stoning.

"I do my father's will."

Mara's whisper lanced Samuel's heart. Her voice sounded sure, but her hands were clasped before her, as if one hand clung to the other for comfort.

"But you must declare your will." The high priest crossed his arms, his expression unreadable, but his voice was sad, solemn.

Tobiah glared daggers at the high priest, then shot his daughter a threatening look.

"It is my will ... to obey the will of my father."

This was Mara's surrender, not her consent.

The high priest turned to Tobiah and unleashed a look of disgust. "It is your duty to honor your daughter, to enrich her future, not line your purse."

Tobiah half-bowed, but his face was full of disrespect. "It is your duty to carry out the letter of the Law, not what you judge to be its intent." Tobiah pushed forward and made his mark.

Achor scrawled an elaborate signature.

"Let it be so." The high priest's tone was also one of surrender, not consent.

The two scribes witnessed the wedding contract.

Achor poured a glass of wine and brought it to Mara.

Ruth helped Mara take the cup under her veil and sip. She handed the cup to Achor who downed the wine and wiped his mouth with his white sleeve, leaving a stain of blood-red wine.

The scribes rolled the parchment and sealed it with hot wax.

Achor handed the contract to Mara. "Everyone is invited into my inner courtyard for my betrothal feast."

The villagers proceeded through elaborate colonnades into the inner courtyard.

Samuel nudged his parents forward. "We must stay close to Mara."

Abba turned. "Be steady. Bridle your temper for Mara's sake. Remember she is now under Achor's cruel control."

Mara passed under the entry arch, cried out, and sank to her knees. She pointed. "Look ..." Her voice quaked and faltered.

Ima rushed to her and lifted her to her feet. "It is nothing child. It is meant to torture Samuel and terrify you, but your contract shields you."

Samuel rushed through the archway to see. Near the house stood a white huppa. The wedding tent. The place of consummation. His heart flapped like a fish dying in the sand. "If he tries to take her tonight, I will kill him."

Tobiah turned. He heard Samuel's threat.

Samuel lunged forward.

Abram threw an arm across his son's chest. "Do not utter such evil. The contract will protect Mara."

More villagers flooded in behind him, anxious for the promise of a rich meal. Spotting the huppa, snatches of confusion rippled through the crowd.

"*Not* our tradition ..."

"Not the time for the wedding feast ..."

"Not seemly..."

Samuel looked toward the high priest and the hostess, Naomi, mother of the high priest. Their anxious eyes kept returning to the white tent roof fluttering in the breeze. The yawning door flap awaiting the entry of the bride and groom.

The men were directed to low tables to one side, the women to the other. Ruth guided Mara to a place of honor, but one that did not face the huppa.

May Ima be blessed for her compassion.

Servants brought platters laden with fruits and olives. Trays of roasted goat and lamb were placed on the banquet table. Large pots of lentil stew were ladled into finely turned wooden bowls, which Samuel and his father had fashioned in their shop.

The men were served first. Samuel's stomach roiled rebellion and rage.

Ima served Mara, but she trifled with her food and did not bring one bite to her lips.

"My dearest, you must partake." Achor's strident tone stifled all speech.

Mara looked down. "The excitement has stolen my hunger."

Mara sounded weak, on the verge of collapse.

"Think of the vigor of our future heirs." Temper edged Achor's taunt.

All eyes turned to Mara, who dipped flatbread into the lentil stew and took a meager bite.

The sun sank, gilding the black clouds of a gathering storm. The gilded cloud brought to mind Mara's loathsome wedding contract. Torches were lit, but a pall hovered over the wedding feast like a miasma ushering in a plague.

After several moments, Mara took Ima's arm. She motioned to the women nearby and they scurried, surrounding her in a distant corner. The wall of women did nothing to block the sound of the new wife retching.

Gossip flared, singeing Samuel's ears. Platters were loaded with rich food. Conversations were loaded with wicked words.

"Will the couple enter the huppa tonight?"

"Does the brief betrothal hide the bride's shame?"

"The bride must be with child."

Samuel's cheeks blazed. Such cruel murmurs would leave his Beloved shaken and shamed.

Mara returned to the table.

Samuel stared at the woven window in her veil below the gold coins banding her brow. If only he could see her eyes, then he could be certain she kept faith. Faith in his pledge of honor and love until they were parted by death.

5

Mara

Mara sighed with the chill wind that soughed through the betrothal feast. The wealthy reclined on couches, dining in the manner of the Romans. The villagers lounged on their cloaks spread on the ground. Some guests were loud, some lethargic.

Ruth leaned close. "See how the fruit of the vine magnifies joy or deadens sorrow."

Mara felt neither. She was numb. "I want nothing more than to return to my own sleeping mat, far from Achor."

"Be patient and still. Achor calls for more fine Syrian wine, which he shares with Tobiah. Let us pray both fall into a stupor and we will slip away."

The silken roof of the wedding tent snapped in the gusty wind. Achor swayed to a stand and staggered over to Samuel. "Is my bride not beautiful? Is she not worth every shekel of the price I have paid for her?"

Samuel's face did not change. He did not concede he even heard Achor's slurred jeer.

Achor's lips pulled back baring his teeth, his angular face tightened around his evil eyes. Eyes locked on her. He crossed the courtyard, trespassed into the place set apart for the women, and extended his hand. "Come wife, now we enter the huppa."

Terror nailed Mara to her seat. Her chest tightened around an unseen stake that ran her through and robbed her of breath.

Samuel leapt up.

Abram gripped Samuel's shoulder and pushed his son back down.

Ruth stood and waved her arms to silence the gathering. "Mara is too young for the wedding tent. And Achor has sworn to wait. I will notify the high priest when she becomes a woman."

A vicious gleam flared in Achor's eyes. "Ahh ... but within the contract Tobiah signed, there is no such *safeguard* recorded."

Mara's gorge rose. Safeguard. She was anything but safe or guarded.

Tobiah ran toward Achor. "This was not our agreement."

"Our agreement is what was signed. A prudent man who could not read would have hired a scribe to confirm the particulars." Achor was a jackal howling his triumph over fallen prey.

Tobiah yanked the contract from Ruth's hand. "My yearly portion? Is it written here?" He shoved the contract under the nose of the high priest.

The high priest opened the scroll. "Yes, your portion is recorded."

Achor had rightly guessed Tobiah's main concern was shekels. He would raise no further objections.

"Please." Ruth looked directly at the high priest. "Permission to speak in the stead of the bride's mother."

"Granted."

"Every soul here heard the terms agreed upon by Tobiah and Achor. Is a man's word not his bond? Should not the sons of the high priest be held to the most rigorous rules of righteousness?"

The high priest shook his head, pain and shame etching his face.

"Pagans take children to their beds." Abram's complaint started others grumbling.

Achor's grandmother, Naomi, rose to speak.

Mara held her breath, hopeful Naomi would plead for her.

"My son, remember Judith, your late wife. Would the mother of your sons abide Achor's deception? For as surely you are Achor's father, you must weigh what his mother would have wanted included in the contract."

The way Naomi said 'Achor's father' hinted at something hidden.

Achor lifted one hand. "Perhaps I protect my bride's honor from vicious rumors." He lifted the other hand. "Perhaps, she came to me in the fields and offered herself as would a grown woman. And perhaps she already carries my child."

"You lie." Mara remained seated, but her angry voice rang off the stone walls.

"Peace, child." Naomi covered Mara's hand with her own. She approached the high priest, as a mother to her son. "Surely this young girl is not the only one to ever have been accosted in a field. By her word, she is not defiled. Other girls may not have been so fortunate. Should she not be believed? Should her innocence not be protected and preserved? What if she were your daughter, your Beloved, or your Betrothed?"

The high priest's face turned ashen. His short beard did not hide his trembling chin.

Mara looked from Naomi to high priest. A secret simmered in the silence.

Achor grabbed Mara by the arm and dragged her toward the wedding tent.

The villagers' murmurs festered to loud grumbles.

Several paces before the open tent flap, Mara dug her heels into the ground and yelled, "Remember the wedding lies of Leah. And her daughter, Dinah."

Mara's shout sent a lightning bolt of horror through the crowd. They gasped and fell into superstitious silence.

A little girl tugged at her mother's skirt. "What does Mara mean?"

Naomi stepped between Achor and Mara and turned to the little girl. "Leah was a veiled bride exchanged for her sister Rachel. Misery followed that notorious wedding lie."

The little girl glared at Achor. "And the other one?"

Ruth joined Naomi and Mara. "Dinah was taken by force by the prince of Shechem. He married her, but her brothers murdered every man in this city. Death followed that wedding lie."

Naomi knelt before the high priest. "My son, consider. What curse will befall Achor if he is allowed to consummate this wedding lie?"

Achor crossed his arms and turned to the high priest. "My bride. My huppa. My right under the Law. The Law you hold so dear, Father."

Ruth removed her right sandal and threw it. The sandal skimmed by Naomi and struck Achor in the chest.

Mara smothered a scream. What had Ruth done? She could be flogged, or worse.

Naomi glared at her grandson. "You are well named. For

you will bring *trouble* on this house." She also took off her sandal and flung it at Achor's head.

He threw up his hands to shield his face.

Mara wished the sandal had struck his lying mouth.

Every woman gathered around Ruth and Naomi. Suddenly, a volley of sandals and curses rained about Achor.

How Mara wanted to add her sandal and her curse to the heap strewn at Achor's feet. She lifted her foot and reached down.

Fear not. Hold onto your sandal and your faith.

A still, small voice. A voice she had never heard. A compelling voice that spoke to her heart. A voice meant only for her. She placed her sandaled foot back down.

A hag leaned against the banquet table. Deep into her winecup, she peered over the rim. "If the bride enters the wedding tent tonight ..." Her croak cut across the courtyard. "No man will be welcomed to his wife's bed for more days than he can reckon." Her cackle seemed to embolden the women.

The women linked arms and barred Achor's path into the wedding tent.

The men shrugged at one another and laughed, looking uncertain how they had lost all marital rights in less time than needed to down a barley beer.

The high priest took up the contract and walked through the women to the threshold of the huppa. He unrolled the scroll. "By custom, the contract is drawn in good faith and given to the bride for safekeeping." He tore the contract into twelve pieces. "I do this to safeguard a child-bride."

Mara's heart fluttered with hope.

The contract was forfeit. Was she free?

Tobiah pointed at Achor. "Draw up a new contract, in accord with what we agreed, and I will sign it." He turned to

Ruth, mouth twisted around his snarl. "You kept the bride-price from me. You will not deny me my allowance."

"Old man, do not be troubled, you will have your silver every year." Achor threw a lecherous look at Mara. "Every year until she ceases to please me." His expression changed to something darker, more dreadful, more demonic. "Every year until she is no longer fair or fails to bear an heir."

Tobiah came nose to nose with Ruth. "You have spoiled the feast and shamed me before all of Shechem."

"You shame yourself." Ruth placed a protective arm over Mara's shoulder. "I would do anything to protect Rivkah's daughter." She pulled Mara closer.

"You declared me untrustworthy." Tobiah glared at the high priest. "But Ruth is not trustworthy either."

Ruth did not retreat.

Tobiah shook a fist at Ruth. "Neither my daughter nor this woman can be relied upon to report her first moonblood. And I forbid Mara to sleep in Ruth's home. A home shared by a suitor I have rejected."

Mara's stomach heaved, threatening another rebellion. She swallowed carefully, coaxing her stomach to submit. She would not add fuel to the gossip fire that whispered she was with child. Mara threw her arms around Ruth and looked at Tobiah. "Where would you have me live?"

The loose-lipped hag lifted her winecup toward Mara, blood-red wine splashing onto the table. "I have no leaning to either side, so I will house the girl." She grinned. A grin laden with gaps and rotting teeth. "For a price."

HaShem, please, anyone but this crone. She is a sharp-tongued souse worse than Tobiah.

Other village women called out bids as if she were a slave stripped naked on an auction block.

A deep note from the banquet cymbal rang out. Every eye turned to the startling sound.

Naomi wielded the leather-padded striker like a battle axe. "The bride will be safely housed with me." Naomi's gentle face changed. Suddenly, her gaze was stony. The gaze of a powerful queen who would brook no defiance.

The high priest stepped forward. "Let it be so."

Naomi waved toward the head scribe. "Let the new contract read that I will certify when Mara is no longer a child and fully fertile."

Mara looked toward Achor's chambers and shuddered at the thought of him sleeping nearby.

Naomi's eyes, sharp yet sympathetic, seemed to read Mara's face. "My quarters are well away from any of the men. They are spacious and comfortable and secure." Naomi's voice was soft yet steady.

Mara clung to Ruth tightly, seeking the courage to let her go.

Ruth dabbed her brimming eyes with the edge of her head-covering. "Each morning and each evening at the time of sacrifice, you will be in my heart and my prayers." She placed her hand on Mara's brow. "May HaShem's hand be upon you."

Naomi approached and leaned in close. "My girl, one should always treasure a blessing, but Ruth's blessing is not one of parting." Her voice was a whisper. "Ruth, you are welcome to visit your *daughter* at any hour, on any day." She squeezed both of their hands. "I have but two requests. First, come as would Mara's mother, by the back gate."

"And—" Ruth eyes flashed joy, mingled with her tears.

"I speak this second condition only as a kindness." Naomi's sigh carried the misery of every Shechem wedding lie. "Never speak to Mara of your son Samuel. In the minds of all, Samuel must no longer be Mara's Beloved. He must be Mara's *brother*."

Mara cringed. Though she was betrothed to another, she would never think of Samuel as brother.

6

Summer
Day after the Feast of Shavuot

Samuel

Samuel checked the sky through the open door of the sweltering wood shop. Abba, Ozri, and he had been working since first light. He wiped the sweat from his brow and finished sharpening the final sickle.

"Seven weeks since I was buried alive in that field." Samuel's tone was bitter and brazen.

A look crossed Ozri's face. One Samuel knew well. A look warning him to tame his temper.

Abba raised a hand to heaven. "Praise HaShem, you are very much alive."

Forty days since he last laid eyes upon Mara. Surely, he would see her today when every man, woman, and child was needed to bring in the harvest.

Ozri rose from his workbench and went to Abba. "I propped my last rake in the corner."

"Good." Abba poured water and set a basket of barley bread and a bowl of honey on the table. "Come, both of you. We must eat before the villagers come for their tools, and we join them in the fields."

Ozri sat on a stool. "I, for one, must drink water and wash away the fog from last night's merrymaking. Shavuot is my favorite feast. No tedious rituals, simply a celebration of the harvest." He dipped bread into the honey and took a large bite. "Samuel, if you do not come quickly, there may be none left." Ozri grabbed another chunk of bread.

Samuel leaned his new sickle against the wall apart from the others and hurried to the table.

"This harvest is especially joyful. Samuel's strength is restored." Abba reached for a piece of bread.

Samuel would not worry his father with the aches that wracked his bones and the cramps that seized his muscles. Or the flashes back to the brutal attack that haunted his sleep, jolting him awake in terror. He would never confess the heart-longing loss of his beloved Mara that plagued his nights and days. The loss that threatened to rend his soul and rob him of his faith.

Sounds of the villagers coming to the wood shop broke into his thoughts. Achor and his brothers burst through the doorway.

"Payment." Achor tossed a heavy coin sack on the table in front of Samuel, making his bread bounce.

Samuel did not trust his tongue. He waved toward the corner and the brothers retrieved their sickles. More villagers filed in, taking rakes and sickles and sieves for the threshing floor.

Achor lingered, testing his sickle. "This handle is too short for me." He spotted the new long-handled sickle Samuel crafted for himself and grabbed it with his other hand. "I will take this one."

Samuel could not keep the urge to charge at Achor from his face.

Abba shot Samuel a stern look and pressed his shoulder. He chose to submit to his father's will, but he could almost feel Achor's disdain.

"You take the one I have rejected." Achor drove the point of the short-handled sickle into the doorpost. "Pray Mara does not please me." He waved toward the sickle hanging by its blade. "When I divorce her, you can once again partake of my leavings." Achor laughed—half snarl, half snort.

Samuel wanted to grind Achor to ashes.

Ozri grabbed the back of Samuel's tunic and held firm.

"Achor, leave." Abba's face took on the wrath of a prophet. "Do not cross the threshold of my woodshop again. Such talk dishonors your betrothed, your father, and your entire House."

Achor sneered at Samuel. "Hurry to the fields if you expect to be paid a full day's wage." He and his brothers left.

Samuel pried the sickle from the doorpost, hoping the blade would not bend or snap. "The tip is nicked, but this sickle should serve."

"Check the haft."

"Yes, yes." Samuel barely felt the joining of the blade to the handle, his mind a whirlwind of worry.

"If you wish to win the high priest's prize for the best reaper, do not let that cur distract you from your labor." Ozri gathered small tools for repairs that might be needed in the field. "Make haste, Achor will have an early start." He crossed the room, tool sack slung over his shoulder. "Your father and I will tie your bundles."

A sly look flickered across Abba's face. "Since only the first day bundle count determines the prize, we will tie each sheaf loosely, and leave less on the ground to glean."

"But gleanings are meant to be generous and left for the poor." Samuel had never seen this conniving look on his father's face. Abba was ever-honest.

"Ozri and I will leave excess gleanings for the poor tomorrow."

Ozri walked outside with Samuel. "Keep your father and me in sight. Stop to drink water only when one of us is free to sharpen your blade."

Samuel swung the sickle Achor rejected. "A sharp blade and a wide sweep will vanquish Achor in the harvest contest."

Mara

Mara watched Samuel from a distance. He traded Ozri his sickle for the waterskin.

Samuel drank and stretched while Ozri sharpened the blade. Samuel's standing sheaves leaned together on end to form stooks. Across the fields, stooks stood in rows like soldiers on guard. Achor's stook was the only one that might present a challenge for Samuel.

Cain, the village strongman, and his twin bundled for Achor even though they detested him. They must have been offered extra wages.

Samuel took the sharpened sickle from Ozri and resumed his reaping.

Mara drifted toward Cain, extending a water cup.

He knelt to tie a bundle.

She leaned close. "Jareb and Enosh are sneaking their sheaves into Achor's stook."

Cain stood and watched Jareb and Enosh harvesting. "My brother and I will make certain that not one more rogue sheaf is added." Cain sidled close to Samuel and spoke from the side of his mouth.

Mara headed toward the next man to offer water.

Achor blocked her path. "Give me some water, beloved." He spoke too loudly. Mara filled his cup.

Cain walked between Mara and Achor, grabbed a sheaf from Achor's stook and threw it toward Enosh and Jareb. "You will not add sheaves to your brother's stooks." Cain's angry voice drew the attention of nearby bundlers.

Samuel kept working. He could not chance wasting precious moments.

The high priest turned, the accusation of cheating loud enough for him to overhear.

Achor's flushed face twisted into a sneer of pride and privilege. "There is no proof. Where are the witnesses?" The humiliation that heated his cheeks did not lessen the disdain in his voice.

The high priest pointed an accusing finger at Achor. "Move to reap just ahead of Samuel so everyone can watch over both rows of stooks."

Ruth arrived with full waterskins. "Mara, why are Samuel and Achor working so close to one another? Abram warned Samuel to keep his distance."

A smug satisfaction simmered in Mara's stomach. "They are the main contenders for the prize, but I saw Jareb and Enosh slip some of their sheaths into Achor's stooks."

Ruth studied the two contenders. "Samuel is safe. He and Achor will not take time to brawl. They are both striving for the prize." She passed a waterskin to Mara and left.

Mara walked through a forest of wheat. The tassels tickled her arms and sweat dribbled down her back. Beneath the low amber sun, rising and falling sickles glinted and the swaying wheat heads took on gilded edges.

Taking care to avoid the swinging blades, Mara offered water to the workers.

Ruth emerged from another path. "Come, rest and drink." She led Mara to a nearby stook, sat down, and leaned her back against the sheaves. "I have very little water left."

Mara lifted her waterskin. "I have plenty. We will not need to return to the well tonight. Have some of mine."

Ruth raised her cup. Mara poured for her and drank the cool water, too, soothing her parched throat. "Do you ever wonder how it would be to never thirst? To never have a need to draw water?" Mara could not keep the sad weariness from her voice.

"I have wondered many things." Ruth's eyes sparked with a hint of laughter. "But, in truth, never that."

Mara shut her eyes and listened to the swish of the sickle blades claiming their due. She settled against the stook. After a time, she dozed.

The blare of a ram's horn, a signal for the laborers to stop work and gather, roused her.

Both women jumped up and brushed the straw from their tunics.

The high priest rode his donkey to a spot between the largest two groups of stooks. He waved to his two scribes. "The sun is setting soon. Only the sheaves of Samuel and Achor need be counted."

The scribes each chose a row and reckoned.

Some of the harvesters whispered wagers.

Mara spoke into Ruth's ear. "If I were a man—a man of means—I would wager everything I owned on Samuel."

"In that, we are agreed."

The scribes returned. Each lifted his clay tablet toward the High Priest and shared his final count.

The high priest raised his hands for silence. "Samuel ben Abram has won the harvest prize. By merely three sheaves."

Villagers rushed Samuel, clapping him on the back. Some even lifted him onto their shoulders. Others secretly collected the winnings of their own side wagers.

As was the custom, when he was set back on the ground, Samuel carved his mark into the handle of his winning sickle. Mara smiled, certain despite the waning light, he could see pride in her eyes.

The high priest signaled, and the ram's horn blasted. "Though the contest is complete, the harvest is not. We must return to work until last light."

Achor stepped forward, his dark eyes flashing. He pounded the long handle of his sickle on the ground. "I demand a second reckoning. The counts were so close."

Something flickered across the face of the high priest. Mara once before saw the same furious face when someone had dared question his authority.

The high priest crossed his arms. "My scribes are accurate. There is no need of a further accounting."

Several villagers grumbled. Some had lost wagers. They slipped coins into open hands.

Mara gasped her outrage. Men were being bribed to clamor for a second count to challenge Samuel's hard-earned victory.

She ran to Ozri. "See those men. They are passing coins into hidden palms."

Ozri watched the men. "I do not see anything amiss."

"I saw what I saw." Mara hated the childlike whine in her voice.

Ozri crossed his arms. "A second count matters not. The first count was correct. Samuel won."

The villagers pressed forward and demands for a new reckoning increased.

The high priest got down from his donkey and waved Jareb and Enosh before him. "My sons, you are my right and left hands. Go now with the scribes and certify the stook counts. Men, continue to work your rows until my sons have completed the new count. We are wasting the last light needed for harvesting."

The people returned to work, but a thread of discord twisted through the crowd.

Mara's stomach knotted. Tempers were ready to erupt. The men were weary and hungry. The women were anxious to set out supper. And all were past ready to take to their sleeping mats, for this night would be short and the next day long.

Jareb, Enosh, and the scribes returned. The villagers stopped work and rushed close. The scribes handed their tablets to the high priest who studied the counts. He did not speak but walked over to his sons who stood together. "Jareb, this count of Achor's stooks was conducted before your eyes and is true?"

Jareb nodded.

"You must speak so all will hear."

"Yes."

"Enosh, do you certify the count of Samuel's stooks?"

"Yes."

"Do you both swear you know nothing of the other man's count?"

The brothers shot each other the same evil look they had before they beat Samuel. "We swear."

The high priest turned to the harvesters. His face changed as if he suddenly had a thought. "Achor, come before me."

Achor moved close and knelt before his father.

"Do you know of any cause why this count would be different than the first?"

"I—"

"Beware the penalty for false witness. HaShem knows all, even if Man does not."

Achor stood and smiled a sly, cunning smile." Father, you forget. I do not know the new numbers."

Murmurs of suspicion grew to shouts for answers. After all, money was in the balance.

Samuel lifted his sickle over his head. A victor's stance. A call for silence. "Priest, tell us the certified count."

"Samuel has harvested one less sheaf than Achor."

Samuel lowered his sickle. Disappointment and disgust flooded his face. He returned to the field to finish his row.

Mara's stomach plunged. The count could not be valid. One sheaf. One cursed sheaf. A fount of anger boiled through her veins. She must not speak. Nothing she could say would comfort Samuel.

Achor carved his victor's mark on the long-handled sickle and celebrated with his brothers around an open wineskin.

The high priest rode by. "The day is done. All save Achor go home for supper. Achor, you return to the fields. Finish your portion. Later, there will be time to celebrate your *victory*."

The way he said the word victory sounded like he had tasted a pomegranate gone rotten.

Mara watched Ozri. A look of suspicious disbelief settled on his face. He ran to the back one of Achor's stooks.

Ozri inspected several sheaves, then pulled four away from the others.

"What is it?"

"These four were tied by me. I never worked with Achor today. They do not belong in his stook."

"How can you know that?"

"I am left-handed. See how the first tie is crossed left over right. Achor and his brothers stole stooks from Samuel."

Mara followed. "Do not do anything rash. Acting in anger will not help Samuel and can only bring trouble for you. Go home for supper with the others."

Ozri shook his head. "Nothing good will come from ill-gotten gains."

7

Mara

The light was fast failing. The harvesters left. All save Samuel. His disappointment must only be outweighed by his temper. Mara lingered hoping to console him. To warn him to guard his tongue when Ozri told him the truth.

A grunt of effort, then a gasp of surprise drew Mara's attention. A sickle blade flew and dropped like a vulture into the field of wheat. A thud. The crunching of someone plunging through the wall of wheat.

"No ... No ... No ..."

Mara ran toward the anguished cry and came upon a scene so unexpected, so horrific, she knew the sight would haunt her all the days of her life.

Samuel was kneeling, Achor propped in his lap. His slashed neck gurgled with each breath, his lifeblood seeping into the black earth.

Samuel pressed his hands to Achor's mortal wound as if he could stem the spurting flow.

Achor clutched at Samuel, mouthed something, and stared toward her. He mouthed something more. The light in his eyes dimmed.

Samuel's eyes widened. A look of terror, as if he had been cursed, crossed his face.

Achor gasped his last breath.

Mara ran to Samuel. "What did Achor say?"

"*Run.* Then he pulled me closer. His utterance was only a rasp, but his lips sneered around the words, *Nowhere safe to run.*"

Samuel's tone was unearthly, his stare empty. "My sickle blade flew free from the handle."

Samuel needed her. His mind was muddled. She must stay strong for him. She must think for him.

"Achor's death was never planned." Samuel seemed snared in a nightmare.

"I know this was not murder, but none will believe you. The enmity between you and Achor was no secret. And not even an hour has passed since he stole the harvest prize. The gossips could spin many tales that would end with a fight to the death. You must run. Run for refuge."

Samuel eased Achor to the ground and stood. "I could run to the altar on Mount Gerizim and hold fast to its horns. But High Priest Johakim would be my judge." He wiped his bloody hands on his tunic.

"Even if the high priest declared you innocent at trial, Jareb the rightful Avenger would find a way to kill you."

Mara went to Samuel and placed her palm gently over his heart.

He roused and seemed to muster a will for survival. "Achor

spoke true. Anywhere I go I will always look back, always wait for a fatal ambush."

"Head for Jerusalem. You can blend with the crowds of Jews coming down from the feast at their temple."

Samuel looked down and shuddered. "We must pray Achor's body is not found right away."

"You must hide Achor's body behind a stook where the harvesters will not soon return." Mara looked down at Achor. Regret shivered through her veins. She pressed back all sympathy and girded her heart for battle. The battle for Samuel's survival. "Meet me at the well. I will bring food."

"I need my savings. I will tell you where my money is hidden."

"If I am seen, there would be questions." Mara reached into her tunic and withdrew the bag that contained the Magi coin. "I have something more precious." She looped the leather cord over Samuel's neck. "This may buy your life."

"What does this hold?"

"A rare gold coin." *My only inheritance from my mother.* Mara pushed back the pang of loss that stabbed her heart.

Surprise flickered across Samuel's face.

"The coin is mine and I give my gold to you freely."

"But someday you may have need of it."

"Do not worry, my bride-price is in safekeeping. My only worry is you. If I am not at Jacob's well by full dark, then I could not break free to bring food. You must fight to survive and trust that we will one day be together. Make haste."

Samuel moved close and searched her eyes as if in them he could read his fate. After several breaths, he seemed to come to a decision. "I will wait behind the Tree of Moreh, amidst the terebinth branches."

"Kiss me." Mara reached around Samuel's neck and drew him close.

Love lit his eyes, but his lips tensed. "Mara, my heart is yours, but we are not betrothed."

"I have no bridegroom and we must seize this moment. My first kiss belongs only to you. HaShem willing, may this kiss not be the only one we ever share."

"Would you kiss a manslayer?"

She looked into his eyes, assuaging the doubt she saw there.

"I would kiss Samuel, in whose heart lives no murder."

His lips met hers softly.

She responded with a passion she had never known, and he pulled her into an embrace that felt safe. She lay her head against his chest. They stayed entwined for several heartbeats.

A twig snapped, and their peace dissolved like a vapor.

They crouched, barely breathing.

Harvesters passed by, their voices carrying from a few rows away.

Samuel released her and looked down, a flicker of dazed disbelief clouding his face once again.

Mara shook Samuel by the shoulders. "At the well, make sure you are alone, then rinse your hands and tunic."

She rushed to the House of the High Priest, entered by the back gate, and went straight to the kitchen where she assembled a food sack and filled a waterskin.

HaShem, help me. Do not allow the spilling of Samuel's innocent blood.

How could she conceal the food bundle under her cloak?

She needed something to bind the bundle into the small of her back. She checked the hall. Finding no one about, she rushed to her chamber, lifted the lid of the cedar chest. At the bottom lay hidden the white linen *kitel* she wove for her bridegroom. Mara had dreamt of Samuel wearing this kitel one day at their wedding feast.

Mara nestled the food bundle in the kitel and tied it into

the small of her back winding the ends around her waist. She shrugged into her outer cloak.

Slipping out the door, Mara stooped and lifted a large water jar onto her hip.

"There is no need to draw water this evening."

At Naomi's voice, a startled cry escaped Mara's throat.

"I did not intend to unsettle you, child."

"Oh. I craved extra water to wash away the dust of the day and the heat of the harvest. I would gladly share with you."

"Wait for me, my girl."

"You are weary and need not come."

Naomi sighed and put on her cloak "You cannot walk alone this late."

"As you will, my lady." She must free herself from Naomi at the well. And pray Samuel would stay hidden.

They walked through the small circle of huts at the edge of the village. Ruth stood in her doorway, peering out. She waved to them.

"Come join us for the walk to Jacob's well." Naomi called out with a newfound energy.

No. No. No. More eyes at the well.

"Samuel has not returned." Worry thickened Ruth's tone.

"He may want to be alone and cool his anger. The loss of the harvest prize was quite a blow." Mara tried to sound calm and steady.

"I pray there is nothing more." Ruth wiped her hands on the towel at her waist. "A walk would do me good. Help me contain my own anger." She hoisted a water jar onto her hip.

Naomi and Ruth strolled toward the well. Mara lagged to keep the bundle for Samuel hidden.

At the well, Mara's mind scrambled for a way to distract them. "Here. Sit." Mara gestured to low boulders, a favorite gathering place of the village women. "Leave me to draw the water."

"We can help." Ruth's breathing was too swift, too shallow.

Naomi looked at Ruth. Concern flickered across her face. "My friend, we are no longer young." She sat, patting a nearby spot.

Mara looked up. "The windows of heaven are opening." Mara edged toward the well. "Tonight, I would be alone with the stars and my prayers."

The women began to chat, trading their aches and joys.

Mara walked to the far side of the well, set down her water jar, and turned away from the women. "Naomi and your ima are near." Her whisper faltered. She could not see Samuel's face. "I will leave a bundle and a waterskin on this side of the well. Wait until we depart and our voices fade."

Samuel rustled the branches to signal he heard.

"Do not dare speak, but know that my love for you endures forever." She unwound the bundle from her waist and left the linen kitel folded on top. The seamless robe reserved for all the holy days in the life of a husband. The robe she wove with her homespun yarn and heartstrings.

Samuel

Samuel treasured his last look at Mara drawing water at dusk. He would carry the image in his heart forever. He waited, picked up the bundle, and hugged it to his chest.

Fueled by the fear that flooded his heart, Samuel ran, feet pounding the road. His ears throbbed with Achor's last mocking words.

Run Samuel. But you have nowhere to flee.

A Certain Man

He sprinted off along the Way of the Patriarchs. He must keep moving. Achor's body could be discovered at any moment.

As a boy, he often watched the royal runners from atop the remnant of the old city wall. Messengers would run, walk, run.

Proper pacing was the secret of the swift.

The ancient road markers would serve him. He took up a running rhythm—two markers at a sprint, the third at a stride.

Samuel ran, his mind void of all thought, his heart void of all joy, his soul void of all hope.

The stars filled the firmament, a host of silent witnesses to his flight. He stopped, peered into the darkness behind, and strained to sift the night noises for any sound of pursuit. Hearing nothing, he sipped some water and took up the pace once again. The tip of the sickle moon was buried in the neck of Mount Ebal. An ever-present accuser.

Samuel ran hours of miles until dawn.

At first light, he found a cave, took the kitel from his waist, and pillowed his head. Every bone and every muscle screamed for rest. The sun rose and Samuel surrendered to a deep, dreamless sleep.

8

Caravan near Ramah

Samuel

Three nights Samuel ran by moonlight. Each dawn, he found a hiding place and slept until sunset. Last night, he could no longer run through the night. His food and strength were gone. By the time he reached the rocks jutting from the brush on the hillside, his back and chest were slicked with sweat. He fell asleep and dreamt of Mara.

The smoke of campfires. The smell of stew. Samuel's heart jolted. He bolted up, shaking off sleep and found himself in a nest of boulders. The first light of the third day silvered the horizon. He crouched and crept up the wall of boulders toward the bellows of camels and the neighing of horses.

He peered over the edge. A caravan camp. When he stopped last night, the crossroads below had been deserted. But now strings of hitched camels, tethered horses, and yoked oxen surrounded the camp. The central tent was splendid, constructed of heavy leather and iron poles with bronze fittings that gleamed in the sun. Fine rugs were spread before the entrance.

This caravan master was no ordinary pilgrim. Servants and slaves from far and near, all well-fed, tended to their tasks.

Samuel had never seen such opulence.

In the distance, beyond the cluster of tents, the city of Ramah was edged by a purple dawn.

If he could get work, the swarming caravan would be a good place to melt into the bustle, like butter melts into bread. His mouth watered and belly rumbled.

Samuel brushed off his clothes, washed his face with water from his waterskin, and girded his waist. He took up his cloak and bundle and scrambled down the rocks into the camp.

A wealthy man left the center tent and met Samuel's eyes. His silk turban and long silvered beard were styled in the way of the Jews, but his other garments were exotic, those of a far-traveled merchant.

Samuel knelt at his feet.

The man's face was not arrogant, not suspicious, but full of surprise. "Why do you, a Samaritan, kneel to me, a Jew?"

"I am in need of work." Just then, Samuel's stomach growled as loud as a donkey's bray.

The Jew smiled kindly. "You are in need of food, even if I have no work to offer."

"I am willing to do any work."

"Have you experience with camels?"

"I am a carpenter and could do repairs."

"That would be useful, but I am in urgent need of a *jamaal*. My best camel driver has broken a leg and will be unable to work for weeks."

Samuel met the master's eyes. "I have a willing heart." Now

was not the time to confess he was afraid of the spitting, smelly, stubborn beasts.

"The duties of a cameleer are not light."

"Do not pay me, but only feed me, until I am the equal of any of them." Samuel could not keep the desperation from his voice.

The merchant tugged his beard, looked as if he would ask a question, then seemed to dismiss it. "You begin now." He whistled through his teeth, three short blasts.

A wiry young man, clean shaven and dressed as an Egyptian, ran up and knelt before the man.

"Pil-i, this is our new camel driver—" The man turned to Samuel. "Forgive me—how are you called?"

Samuel considered giving a false name, but his name meant *God has heard*. Since he fled, he had asked much and been granted more from HaShem. He would not lie. "I am called Samuel. And for whom do I now labor?"

The caravan master pressed his hands together and dipped his head. "I am Yosef."

He turned to the Egyptian slave. "Pil-i, this man must take your brother's place. I will pay you extra to train him quickly." Yosef's lips twitched from a held-back laugh. "Samuel here knows nothing."

"Nothing about camels." Samuel met the Egyptian's eyes. "I am a carpenter."

Pil-i's face mirrored Yosef's mirth. "I am not a sorcerer. I cannot change a donkey into a stallion."

"I only ask that you turn a carpenter into a fine cameleer."

Worry flashed across Pil-i's face. "And my twin brother?"

"Have no doubt. as soon as your brother is healed, he will take up his place."

Yosef waved them toward the cookfires. "Both of you take

some stew and join me. We have a long day before us and there will not be another meal until after the sun sets."

"This way." Pil-i led Samuel to a cookpot. "At all costs, avoid the stewpot nearest Master Yosef." Pil-i fanned his hand in front of his mouth. "Master prefers the spices that burn the tongue and water the eyes."

Samuel grinned and his heart lightened. Already Pil-i was warming to the role of teacher.

They joined Master Yosef where a circle of camel saddles served as seats and devoured the savory stew.

Suddenly, Yosef rose and opened his arms.

Samuel looked toward the cries of welcome and rejoicing. A woman entered the camp, rushed past Samuel, and flung herself into Yosef's arms. "Kinsman."

"Miriam." He looked toward a young man dressed in simple garments who approached with the bearing of a king. "Shalom, kinsman."

"You were expected at the Feast in Jerusalem." The young man's voice was deep and compelling.

Yosef shrugged and his face showed little concern. "My tin shipment arrived in Arimathea three days late."

"HaShem knows of your predicament and awaits your offerings at the Temple."

Yosef drew his kinsman into an embrace and clapped him on the back. "My *Aryeh ben Judah*. You have grown in stature, and I trust also in wisdom."

What a noble name. *Lion of Judah*. Who is this young man that speaks with such authority? And who Yosef treats with such deference?

Pil-i jabbed Samuel's arm. "Come, the camels will not wait."

Samuel's entire day was spent with the camels. He slowly gained the trust of his red camel, Al Haml. She knelt and stood and allowed him to lead her on command. But he could not conquer his distaste for her bellowing or champion spitting. Praise HaShem, when Samuel was left alone with her, she never kicked or bit.

Pil-i returned lugging a camel saddle.

Another Egyptian, the image of Pil-i, limped up to them, leaning on a crude crutch. "I am Okpara. Al Haml is my camel."

Samuel patted her. "We will come to understand one another." She snorted and stepped back, barely missing Samuel's sandaled foot.

"My presence will calm her." Okpara's smile held no malice.

"Many thanks." Samuel gestured toward the crutch. "Tonight, I will fashion a new crutch. One better suited to your stature."

"A thousand blessings be upon you."

"Bring your camel to a kneel." Pil-i's tone was severe, but he could not hide his amusement with Samuel's clumsiness.

Samuel raised the lead rope. "Hoosh."

Al Haml knelt without prodding or protest.

Pil-i helped Samuel saddle the camel, all the while giving directions.

"Steady now, girl." Samuel walked to the camel's side trying to cover any fear in his gait. As warned, he did not look the beast in the eye. She would surely see his ignorance. He threw his leg over the saddle and perched on the hump. In a flash, before Samuel was well seated, the camel lifted her rump. He slid forward and grabbed the front pommel, sure he would fall. The camel's front legs unfolded, and Samuel was thrust backward, but managed to cling to the beast's back.

Okpara shushed and coaxed the quivering camel. Her lips

pulled tight, and her ears went back. "Remember. She is very timid."

Samuel released his death grip on the reins. He wiped his palms on the saddle blanket and nodded, afraid his voice would break like a boy on the cusp of manhood.

Pil-i took the lead rope and moved forward. "Al Haml must learn to trust you."

Samuel swayed with the camel's awkward lurch. After walking one circuit of the camp, Pil-i threw the lead rope up to Samuel. Al Haml continued her slow, comfortable pace.

Samuel's chest expanded with pride. He was a camel driver.

"Tomorrow, you will be a proper *jamaal* and ride legs up and crossed on the saddle. Take this next circuit by yourself."

Samuel settled into the camel's sway and let his mind roam. He was alive. He had food. He had work. Smelly work. Work that left his backside sore, but he must count his blessings. Finally, he could breathe easy.

The camel was calm, and her sway lulled Samuel. Soon his lids drooped and his shoulders slumped. He jerked, warding off sleep. Camel drivers must doze. Did they lash themselves to the saddle so they would not fall?

Without warning, the camel stomped, pummeling her front hoofs against the ground. Samuel was thrown side to side, his heels flailed, slamming the camel's flanks. The beast bolted. Samuel was thrown backward. Only a strong yank on the reins kept him seated. Shrieking at the cruel pull on her mouth, Al Haml swung her head, tried to bite Samuel's leg, then broke into a run as if pursued by a lion.

Samuel echoed her shriek. His heart galloped, winning the race against the camel's galloping feet.

"HaShem." Samuel's plea was the only word his mouth would form. "HaShem."

Out of nowhere, Aryeh appeared on the path a short distance in front of Samuel, arms stretched wide.

Al Haml galloped onward, did not pull up.

"Be still." Aryeh's clear, calm command could have been meant for Samuel or the camel. Or both.

Aryeh stood his ground, arms outstretched.

Two paces from running him down, Al Haml veered, stopped, and snorted.

Aryeh patted her neck and took hold of the lead rope. "Ride her in a tight circle until you both are at peace."

After several circles, Samuel's heart and breathing slowed. The beast stopped and stared back at him with innocent eyes. She batted her long lashes, curled her lips, and offered what Samuel could only hope was a camel smile.

He was still shaking. Baal's blood, the beast could have killed him. "Hoosh." Samuel barely managed to croak.

The camel knelt.

"Move slowly." Aryeh's calm command stilled Samuel's shaking.

Pil-i quietly came to Aryeh's side.

Samuel swung his leg across the saddle and slid to the ground. He locked his knees to stop the trembling.

Pil-i took the lead rope, and whispering honeyed words to Al Haml, led her away.

Samuel moved toward Aryeh. "You saved me. That camel must be possessed by a demon."

"Come." Aryeh led Samuel to the spot where the camel had spooked. Stretched across the rocky dirt lay a trampled Palestine viper. "Al Haml was defending herself and you. This would not be the first time a snake has brought death to a good man."

"You call me good, even though I am a Samaritan and you are a Jew."

"And are you not a good man? Are you not an *innocent* man?" Aryeh asked as if he knew the truth but wanted Samuel to examine his own heart.

The memory of Achor on the ground flashed before Samuel's mind's eye. A knot, equal parts fear and regret, twisted in his throat. "I am humbled that you think me good."

"Many in Jerusalem hate Samaritans. Perhaps you should trade your cloak for another. The pattern gives you away."

Miriam approached. "*Talyah*, we must leave. Our neighbors are waiting, anxious to return home to Nazareth."

Samuel smiled inwardly, watching her walk toward the road. Talyah, *child or lamb*. A name only a doting mother would use for a grown son. Caught unawares, the clot in Samuel's throat tightened and thickened at the thought of his own grieving mother. He swallowed hard. At best, Ima would be known as the woman who bore the manslayer, not the murderer.

Yosef joined them carrying a satchel. "*Aryeh*, here are some delicacies for you to share." They embraced. "I call you Lion, your Ima calls you Lamb, it is enough to perplex my new camel driver."

Aryeh stepped back and stared into Yosef's face seeming to consider his next words carefully. "Kinsman, when you are in Jerusalem, there is a plot of land you may want to purchase."

"Oh? What is so special about this plot?"

"It is a pleasant garden, just outside the city walls complete with an orchard, an olive grove, and a vineyard. Off to one side there is an olive press and ..."

Yosef's young kinsman hesitated, his expression unreadable. Perhaps a look of some secret sadness.

"Well ..." Yosef motioned for him to continue. "What more?"

"A tomb."

Yosef's eyes widened as if his eminent death had been foretold.

Aryeh did not seem flustered. "A new tomb. Never used."

"Do I seem so old that I am in need of a tomb?" Yosef's voice seemed edged with the belief that Aryeh knew his fate.

"Every one of us are in need of a tomb one day."

Aryeh's hushed tone seemed to pierce Samuel's side. If the Avenger ran Samuel down, he would soon have need of a tomb.

Yosef's eyes lit with a spark of curiosity. Then he shook his finger, the gesture of a rabbi raising a fine point of the law. "The Psalmist writes that the Holy One, the Messiah, will not see decay. Even he needs a tomb?"

"Especially the Messiah."

"I do not understand." He tugged at his beard.

"One day you will."

"Enough talk of death." Yosef raised his mantle over his head, ready to pray. "Each of us must go on with the lives HaShem has set before us."

A farewell sprang to Samuel's lips. "Aryeh, may all your comings-in and goings-out be blessed."

Aryeh waved and headed after his mother.

Yosef sighed deeply. "Aryeh ben Judah is not how he is called by others. It is only my fond name for him."

Samuel stared at the back of his savior, unable to turn away. Aryeh's form got smaller and smaller until he became a speck swallowed by the multitudes traveling home. Away from Jerusalem. Away from Samuel.

9

Shechem

Mara

Unable to sleep, Mara headed for the kitchen at first light. No one thought much of Achor's absence. He often sought the company of loose women. But on the third day, his brothers raised an alarm and the men left to search for Achor.

Four sunrises and Mara was still the only soul in Shechem who knew she was a widow. Kneading the day's bread, she pressed her distress into each folding of the dough.

Betrothed.

Widowed.

Un-bedded.

Worry leapt in her chest like a grasshopper prodded with a stick. The wait until Achor's bloody body was found was gut-wrenching agony. Agony she would gladly suffer longer, so Samuel could flee further.

"Good morning." Naomi's cheerful singsong pricked at Mara's heart.

She nodded, not trusting her voice. This kind woman had no inkling her youngest grandson was dead.

Naomi moved to the kitchen shelves. "Cheese and barley bread are missing." Her brows drew together with what seemed to be concern, not anger. "I hope no servant felt the need to steal."

Mara must take care not to lie. HaShem hated liars. "No, my lady. I gave those things and some olives and figs to a needy traveler."

Naomi turned toward Mara. She looked down, unwilling to meet Naomi's eyes. "You would have done the same." Mara thrust her hands deep into the heap of dough to hide their shaking.

"Yes, but we could have offered the traveler a meal and work storing the grain. The House of the High Priest Johakim should be known as a place of plenty and kindness and refuge."

From afar, a lone voice droned. The chant grew closer. The prayer for the dead.

The mourners were climbing the hill. Achor's body had been found.

Naomi's palm went to her heart as if she could shield it from bad tidings. She ran into the courtyard all the way to the gate.

Mara followed close behind.

This morning the pagan mountain was surrounded by a bloody sunrise and slashed by a crimson cloud across its neck. A tight lump formed in her throat.

Naomi waited, the hand over her heart rising and falling with each ragged breath. As the small procession snaked up the hill it became clear the chant was for a member of the high priest's household. Three men and the high priest escorted an oxcart. The dark clouds of an oncoming storm gathered behind them.

Naomi's eyes searched Mara's. "Have you seen my grandsons?" Her soft question sounded a prayer.

"I am sorry." Mara's voice broke.

"Sorry?"

Mara gasped at Naomi's sharp tone. "Sorry that I have not seen any of your grandsons this morning."

The dirge for the dead drummed in Mara's ears—liar, liar, liar.

"Lord , not one of our own House ..." Naomi gripped the iron-spiked gate. "The mountain of a man driving the cart can only be Ozri. And I know Enosh's walk." She squinted and pointed. "And there, Jareb is the tall one." Naomi reached for Mara's hand. "They went to search for Achor, but I do not see him."

"Come, you must sit." Mara steadied Naomi and moved her to the stone bench.

"The corpse could be some other man." Naomi stared at the nearing procession. "My son's face is streaked with tears." A soft groan seeped from deep inside her. "The prayer must be for Achor."

Mara must pretend to mourn Achor even though she did not grieve the loss of his taunts, or the loss of her wedding week under the huppa. She mourned that Samuel had to flee for his life. She mourned that her Beloved had to flee from a life with her.

She sat beside Naomi and laid a hand on her back.

Jareb walked ahead of the High Priest and pushed through the gate. A servant opened the other side allowing Ozri to drive the cart into the courtyard.

Jareb rushed at Mara, his face full of rancor and rage. He grabbed her arm and yanked her to her feet. "What do you know about this?" He waved a towel under her nose. "Well?"

With each heartbeat, the lump in her chest swelled until it was a boulder pressing against her breastbone. "That towel is mine." She kept her voice as flat as it was fearless. "The way the edges are finished is my handwork." She did not know where she left it.

"Your towel was found next to my brother's body." Jareb gripped her arm more tightly.

Ozri met her eyes and barely shook his head.

Jareb was lying.

"I must have dropped the towel when offering water." Mara wrenched away. "I had no part in the death of your brother."

"Enough bickering." The high priest's shout cut short all strife.

Naomi rose and took the high priest's hands. "Johakim, my son. Tell me. What has happened?"

The high priest looked down at Naomi with the pinched face of a grief-stricken father. "Achor's neck was slashed by a sickle blade. The blade alone lay next to him in death."

"Just the blade? How can this be?" Confusion quivered in Naomi's tone.

Jareb held up the sickle handle. "This belongs to Samuel. Here is the mark he carved when he thought he won the harvest challenge. I found the handle in the field a pace away from Achor's body."

The high priest looked to the sky. "But why?" His anguished cry seemed to question HaShem.

Jareb, eyes flashing, shook the handle. "This sickle was the outworking of a curse." He pointed the handle like a divining staff toward Mara. "Proof of the practice of dark arts." Behind him lightning slashed the sky, thunder shook the ground.

Mara's stomach twisted and began to twitch. Jareb had named her a witch.

Mara bit her lips. Any word spoken now could prove to be a snare.

Enosh turned his back to Mara. "Grandmother, we have wrapped Achor in layers of burial spices. Where would you have us take him?"

Naomi left the high priest and put her arm around Mara. "Achor's widow will show you where she wishes him laid."

The men lifted Achor's body from the cart and Mara led them into his bedchamber. A bedchamber she had thus far escaped. She gasped then coughed to cover her surprise. How lavish and wasteful. Fine silk linens, fresh flowers, exotic perfumes. Trappings meant to entertain women. Mara would never have been first in Achor's heart. Merely the first target of his cruelty.

"Place him on the pallet." Mara went to her knees, leaned her face close to the floor, acting the grieving widow.

Naomi ripped the neck of her tunic and knelt beside Mara. At the sound she sat back, still on her knees. Naomi rocked and moaned her mourning, singing a lullaby for Achor's unending sleep.

Enosh brought a handful of ashes over his head.

Johakim began to tremble and stood beside his mother. The Law forbid the high priest from mourning as other men.

Mara wept but not for Achor. She wept from fear she might one day face the pain of Samuel's death.

Enosh and Ozri lowered Achor onto the pallet and stepped away.

Ozri looked toward Johakim. "You have known Samuel

since he was a boy. His parents raised him in the knowledge of the Law and the Lord. He is a righteous man."

Enosh grabbed Ozri's sleeve. "Then tell me what a righteous man would do."

The high priest seemed to rouse from his sorrow. "At best, Samuel is a manslayer, at worst a murderer. Either way, he would run for refuge."

No one would consider Jerusalem a City of Refuge for a Samaritan. Mara prayed Samuel would be safe there.

Jareb pointed at his father. "You are High Priest of Samaria."

"Yes, and I will judge Samuel. But before a trial is held, Samuel must beg for sanctuary."

Jareb unsheathed his sword. "I claim the right of the Avenger of Blood." Jareb could not keep the lust for violence from his voice. "I am your oldest and strongest son."

At the word *son*, a flicker of something passed between the high priest and Naomi. A look heavy with a mystery Mara still could not fathom.

Jareb clutched the sickle handle in his other hand—a battle axe. "Who will go with me to track down this killer?"

The high priest held up a hand. "Before you have leave to go, a *minion* must read the Law at Achor's side and then, the ten men will place him in the family tomb."

Jareb cast down the sickle handle and waved his fist. "Samuel will reach refuge if I delay my chase."

Johakim crossed his arms. "Think. Where will Samuel run?"

"To the stone altar on Mount Gerizim."

Jareb's face contorted into the look of an angry pagan god. A brutal Baal, on whose altar rivers of innocent blood were shed.

"Samuel must already be clinging for life to the horns of the altar. You may not execute Samuel without a trial." The high priest's voice faded to a hoarse whisper.

Mara's legs cramped. She wanted to run to Jerusalem and look for Samuel, but she could not risk leading the Avenger to Samuel even if she must return to Tobiah. She shifted but remained kneeling. The ever-dutiful wife. Praise HaShem. Samuel had fled far from the altar.

Jareb leaned close to his father's face. "Only if that murderer is found clutching the altar with both hands must I stay my execution."

Johakim's face changed from mourning father to high priest rendering judgment. "Our Maker will not be mocked. Take great care to stay within the bounds of the Law."

Naomi stood. "Leave us. Mara and I must prepare the body.

Johakim pointed to Jareb and Enosh. "Gather the minion."

Mara and Naomi washed Achor's cold, gray body in silence. The smell of death was not completely covered by the burial spices. Mara broke open ampules of scented oils for burial. The room was filled with the musky scent of myrrh and the sweet, lavender-aroma of spikenard.

HaShem, I beg you. Do not let this be Samuel's fate.

They robed Achor with the high priest's new *kitel*. A robe never worn. Woven by Naomi for her son's priestly duties.

HaShem, grant my Beloved Samuel many years of feast days. May the kitel I wove for him serve as a mantel of protection under your wings. I beg you, send him someone to show him the way he should go. The way of escape.

Mara looked up at Naomi. "We need more burial spices." Anything to prolong the preparation of the body and allow Samuel more time to run, to hide, to plan.

Naomi moved toward the door. "I will go. I have the key to the spice chest."

Mara was left alone with Achor's body, the groom she had wished dead.

May HaShem forgive her wicked wish. May He not require as punishment, the life of Samuel, the bridegroom of her heart.

She heard footsteps outside the chamber and listened at the door.

"You are not Samaritans or under our Law."

Jareb's voice.

Mara pressed her ear to the door.

"Go to Mount Gerizim."

Jareb was plotting some evil.

"There you will find a man clutching the altar stones. When he falls asleep, his hands will let go. Move him away from the altar."

"Yes, Master Jareb." A deep voice.

"And then?" A young man's voice.

Mara did not know either of these voices.

"Block the path back to the altar and his escape. Reserve the kill stroke for me. He will wish he had been crucified."

Every word curdled Mara's stomach. Jareb was plotting to murder Samuel. Mara's hands covered her mouth. She must not retch or make any sound. Jareb must not know she heard every word.

Praise HaShem, Samuel fled Shechem. When Achor died in the field, and Mara told Samuel to run, she considered the hearts of the high priest and his sons. She had judged them rightly. The high priest would have set aside the heartbreak of a father for justice. Enosh would have wanted Mara set aside, left her destitute, and called that justice. And Jareb would have set aside any semblance of justice. He craved vengeance. His soul was evil. Seven-fold more evil than Achor.

A Certain Man

Mara

Mara stood at the courtyard gate. She bore no ill will against the villagers, who stole suspicious glances in her direction. The recent scandals in Shechem all centered on her.

Some time ago, Enosh and Jareb raced ahead to the altar on Mount Gerizim.

The high priest emerged from his house wearing the robes of priestly authority and judgment. Johakim's dark, silvered hair was damp from the ritual bath and slicked down under the priestly turban. Soon he would travel to the altar of sanctuary.

Achor was entombed. The Avenger was loosed. Mara was terrified.

Morbid murmurs ran rampant, swirling around Mara.

"Samuel hated Achor."

"He should be executed."

"I cannot sleep with a murderer in our midst."

Jareb and Enosh came galloping back, holding the reins of three horses with foreigners bound across their saddles. They dragged the men down and thrust them to the ground.

Gasps of alarm shot through the crowd.

One foreigner sprawled on his stomach, Jareb's foot on his neck, the tip of his sword at the man's throat. "You let the killer escape."

The man's eyes went wide. "No, we swear, there was no sign the murderer was ever there." The man slowly squirmed away from the sword. "I swear on the life of my firstborn. From the moment we arrived, no man or woman or child was ever there."

Jareb sheathed his sword, but his face remained an angry mask.

The high priest's look was tight, his face red with wrath. "Release them."

Jareb used his dagger and cut the foreigners' bonds. "These men are my hirelings."

The crowd became silent. Still as death.

Jareb pointed with his blade. "You three ride north, east, and west. Find the murderer."

"Jareb, you must follow the Law. You may not pay for Samuel's capture and no one may hinder his flight."

"Father, my men will merely bring me word of his whereabouts."

Enosh swung up onto his horse. "Brother, we will take the Road of the Patriarchs south to Jerusalem and beyond."

Jareb mounted. His high-strung warhorse neighed, trumpeted, and pawed the ground.

Tobiah rushed to the stallion's flank and motioned for Jareb to lean down. Cupping his hands around his mouth, he glanced at Mara then spoke into Jareb's ear.

Tobiah appeared to haggle over something.

A wicked look of amusement crossed the Avenger's face.

What cauldron of trouble had Tobiah stirred now?

"Ride with Enosh." Jareb's tone was fierce.

Enosh swung Tobiah up behind him.

A chill ran up Mara's spine then coiled around her heart. She shivered and hugged herself. *HaShem, protector of the innocent, save my Samuel.*

Jareb nudged his horse with a knee and his mount came around to face the high priest and the crowd.

"Achor's widow, come forth."

Mara looked toward the high priest who, despite the perplexed look on his face, waved her forward.

She moved to the front of the crowd. Her face and words must give nothing away.

Jareb pointed to her. "The pattern on Mara's robe is unique. The robe of the man you seek will be woven in this manner." He nosed his stallion through the crowd to Abram and Ruth who hovered, heads covered, swaying in prayer. *Swsshh.* Jareb's sword flashed before them.

Ruth and Abram stopped swaying and stood tall. Fearless.

Using the point of his long blade, Jareb lifted the hem of Abram's cloak. "These singular green threads will be woven into the murderer's garments, as well."

Jareb swung back and faced Mara. "As nearest kinsman, I claim the right of Levirate marriage. Woman, after your time of mourning, you will be a widow no more, but my wife. Your first-born will be accounted to the line of Achor."

Waves of horror and fear rushed through Mara. Her legs quaked and she locked her knees so they would not give way and betray her terror. A bone-deep moan escaped the high priest's lips and he locked eyes with Naomi. Had anyone else noticed the furtive look that passed between the high priest and his mother?

Tobiah, mounted behind Enosh, leaned down and met Mara's eyes. "Daughter, you are now set apart for Jareb. Your future is protected. Jareb and I have agreed, and the contract will be drawn."

"And your allowance is secure." Mara's tone boiled with bitterness.

The high priest took the reins of Jareb's horse. "All safeguards for Mara must remain in place."

"Understood." Jareb held his sword upright before his chest in the manner of a solemn Roman oath. "I, Jareb ben Johakim, The Avenger of Blood, do swear, until justice is accomplished, I will not shave my beard or cut one hair on my head. And I will take no wife into my bed."

Jareb sounded arrogant and sure and vicious. He reined his stallion hard.

It trumpeted its complaint, reared, and galloped away at a

breakneck pace. Enosh followed at a fast trot. Tobiah, his face frozen with terror, shared Enosh's saddle, clutching him around the middle.

Fear lanced through Mara's heart.

HaShem, Samuel's only refuge is in You.

She was the evening sacrifice. Her greedy father had once again secured a lifetime of ease. And once again, she had been sold to a bridegroom with a warped, wicked soul.

10

Caravan near Ramah

Samuel

Samuel leaned his head against Al Haml's side and braced himself for the ride to Jerusalem. Sheltered within the circle of tethered camels, Samuel traced the green pattern his ima so lovingly wove into his cloak.

Not far away, Pil-i made a nest of blankets in the bed of an oxcart for Okpara.

"Pil-i, please come check that I have not lashed this camel saddle too tightly."

Pil-i settled Okpara in the oxcart, approached and pulled on the leather camel straps. "You have done well."

Samuel removed his cloak. "Trade me your cloak for mine."

"But mine is not nearly so fine."

"In Jerusalem, Samaritans are hated."

Pil-i grinned "I will never be mistaken for a Samaritan." He pulled on Samuel's cloak and returned to the oxcart. Samuel watched as Pil-i bragged to his brother. His face changed and he came scurrying back.

"Okpara wants to trade his tunic for the fine linen one he saw in your pack."

"I mean no offense, but I will not trade my kitel. Not even for my life."

Pil-i left and delivered the message. Okpara glared at Samuel.

A dust cloud stained the blue sky above the Road of the Patriarchs. Samuel heard the thunder of galloping horses, and shrieks of fear.

Pil-i waved for Samuel to join him. "Bandits may be coming to attack the caravan."

In the distance, two horsemen reined in mounts that reared.

Samuel squinted. Jareb. And Enosh sharing a mount with Tobiah.

Samuel's heartbeat raced as it had when he was astride his runaway camel. He slipped away and hid amongst the tethered beasts.

Jareb and Enosh with Tobiah rode slowly up the hill.

They scanned the camp—a wake of vultures ready to swoop down and kill.

Jareb pointed to Pil-i. He and Enosh corralled him between their mounts. "Where did you get that cloak?"

"Traded it for my own."

Samuel peered through the forest of camel legs. He pulled his head covering across his face in the manner of the nomadic Bedouins.

Jareb reached down and grabbed the neck of Pil-i's cloak. "The man who wore this cloak killed my brother."

Samuel could see the handle of his sickle sticking out from Jareb's saddle pack. The victor-of-the-harvest mark seemed to mock him.

"Where is he?" Jareb pulled the sickle handle free.

Pil-i hesitated, then directed a fearful glance away from Samuel. "I do not know."

Praise HaShem, Pil-i was protecting him.

Jareb raised the handle and clubbed Pil-i, bringing him to his knees. "I am the Avenger of Blood. Tell me where this man ran."

Pil-i grunted and staggered to his feet. Jareb struck again.

Samuel wanted to cry out, but his tongue would not obey.

Be still. Watch. And wait.

Something seemed to whisper into the ears of his soul.

Yosef of Arimathea pushed through the caravanners. "Halt." His long, rich robes billowed about him. "Do not strike my slave again."

Yosef circled a finger toward the heavens and every man drew his sword.

Jareb's face contorted into an ugly sneer. "This Egyptian is a heathen to both Samaritans and Jews. If I beat him to death, I will pay you double the slave price."

With speed that belied his age, Yosef shielded Pil-i. "This man is priceless to me. If you attack him again, you will be brought before your own Samaritan authorities. Then no man can say I dealt unjustly with you."

Jareb made his stallion rear, his hooves striking out near Yosef's face. "Old fool, our only authority is our high priest."

Enosh urged his horse closer to Jareb's and smirked. "And the high priest is our father."

"Your father could never dispense blind justice." Disgust darkened Yosef's tone.

Jareb spat on the ground. "Samaritans will never recognize your Sanhedrin."

Gasps of outrage echoed through the camp.

Jareb had insulted not only Yosef of Arimathea, but also

their highest Jewish court. Yosef's men closed in on the horsemen.

"You are the one who is a witless young fool." Yosef yanked the sickle handle from Jareb's hand. "Harm my slave and you will be dragged before Pontius Pilate."

"What have you to do with Rome?" Jareb sounded unsure.

Yosef swept his arm across the surrounding camp. "As you can see, I am a wealthy man. Rumors run rampant in Rome." A cunning smile curled Yosef's mouth. "The emperor may soon appoint me Minister of Mines."

Tobiah leaned from behind Enosh and put out his hand to Yosef. "Sir, the sickle handle. Evidence for the trial."

Yosef put the handle in Tobiah's hand.

Jareb stood in his saddle. He pointed to Pil-i. "I will pay the price of seven slaves to any man, woman, or child who leads me to the killer who traded cloaks with him. This cloak belonged to the man who murdered my youngest brother."

No one moved. No one spoke. Even the children were still.

The accusing silence stretched.

It was not the peaceful silence of Sabbath rest. Not the dead silence of a sepulcher.

This silence teemed with temptation. The temptation of great wealth and great greed.

Men looked to their wives, their brothers, their mothers. Samuel studied their faces, their stances.

He could almost hear the gold coins clink as they counted the reward in their heads.

Yosef now knew Samuel was a fugitive. Would he disavow him?

Yosef raised his arms and the crowd gathered around him, turning their backs on the mounted intruders.

"According to the Law of Moses, the fate of a fugitive must be left in the hands of HaShem." Yosef settled on a boulder.

"None but the Avenger may give chase. These men are violent. Lawless."

Jareb glanced toward the camels.

Samuel looked down, saw his leather sandals. Too fine for a camel driver.

He wanted to step back, but any move might draw notice. He forced himself to remain still.

Samuel's mind swirled with worries. Yosef and Pil-i and Okpara had not spoken. Had anyone else noticed him wearing the Samaritan cloak before he traded it?

Maybe he was still safe.

Samuel eased near his camel's rump for a better view of the crowd. No one looked toward the circle of camels.

Jareb turned his horse north.

Praise HaShem. Jareb was leaving.

Suddenly, Jareb spurred his horse back to the crowd. "My reward still stands. If anyone would collect it, send word to Shechem, to Jareb at the House of the High Priest." He rode off at breakneck speed as if the battering of his horse's hooves would vent his fury.

Enosh and Tobiah followed, unable to keep pace.

The crowd stood staring at the churning dust.

Samuel's heart raced, his chest tightened, and fear clogged his throat. Surely someone would betray him.

Yosef looked around the camp and circled his arm overhead, the age-old signal to the caravanners to take their places in the procession. Travelers, camels, carts, and chattel moved in an orderly dance around Yosef.

Samuel signaled his camel to kneel, mounted, and brought her to a stand. He must blend with the other drivers. He forced himself to ride cross-legged.

The caravan traveled for long, dusty, boring hours. A hint of excitement rippled through the flock of weary travelers.

Jerusalem was near.

Samuel

At the crest of the hill, the golden roof of the Jewish temple flashed against the purple sunset.

Pil-i walked his camel past Samuel, seeming to ignore him. "Master's tent... when the camp sleeps." Pil-i spoke softly from the side of his mouth.

Master Yosef directed the caravan to a clearing west of Jerusalem. The people set up camp and lit cookfires.

Yosef joined Samuel and looked east. "Tomorrow when the sun rises over the Mount of Olives, we will watch the daybreak. The sun will light the path the Promised One will take to the Eastern gate and up to the Temple."

Age-old prejudices flared, and a primal hate boiled the bile in Samuel's belly. He glared at the temple. The Jews had rejected Samaritan offers to help build this temple and later destroyed the one Samaritans built on Mount Gerizim.

Samuel turned to Yosef. The stately Jew pushed back his head covering.

A slight breeze cooled Samuel's face and his anger blew away like chaff on a threshing floor. This Jew, a Pharisee even, had not betrayed him to the Avenger. Samuel and Yosef were not so different. HaShem made them both from the clay of the ground.

Samuel gestured to the tombs scattered across the Mount of Olives. "We both believe in the resurrection of the dead."

"The resurrection will begin there." Yosef's silver-streaked hair was crowned by the soft light of the sinking sun. "We both await the Promised One who will bring justice on the day mankind faces a final judgment."

Samuel's soul cried out to his Creator. "I run from Shechem in search of sanctuary and a just judge in this lifetime."

"*The Messiah.*" Yosef's smile glowed with pride and excitement. "Mine eyes have seen a great star that heralded his birth. Now a man, He walks the earth. But until His kingdom is come, do we not both need sanctuary from the wrath of the Lord?"

"Yes." Samuel followed Yosef's gesture toward a cookfire. "My ima told tales of a big, bright star and Magi who passed through Shechem. Perhaps there is more that unites than divides us."

A bowl of lentil stew was filled for Samuel. The people gathered and ate in groups.

Yosef motioned toward the next cookfire. "When Messiah comes, perhaps Jew and Samaritan will finally live in peace."

A woman ladled Yosef a full bowl. "Master, this is strongly spiced to your liking."

After the meal, pilgrim and slave alike withdrew to tents, carts, or bedrolls. The women moved throughout the camp spreading the fires to hurry the burn down to embers. Soon the entire gathering seemed to breathe as one, trading drowsy sighs for deep yawns and snores.

Samuel spread his cloak on the ground near the cookfire and closed his eyes. He would rest until everyone fell asleep, then go to Master Yosef's tent.

Even though Yosef was a righteous man, would he believe Samuel's story? His story seemed beyond belief.

11

Shechem

One week since Samuel fled

Mara

Hoofbeats, a shrill whinny, and the racket of a rider at the gate dragged Mara from her uneasy sleep.

Jareb's angry curses carried above the commotion of servants scrambling in the dark.

Mara pulled on her cloak and ran outside. She hid behind the wall on the stair to the roof. Jareb dismounted and his warhorse dropped dead.

A stable boy ran into the courtyard with a pail of water. He stopped at the downed horse.

Jareb grabbed the boy. "You halfwit. Tell the stable master to send someone other than an ignorant boy to buy new mounts."

Praise HaShem. Samuel must still be free to flee.

Mara held her breath and pressed against the stair. If Jareb did not catch sight of her, he would not have a chance to browbeat her.

He strutted toward his quarters at the far end of the mansion.

Mara sighed her relief.

The stable boy circled the fallen beast, muttering to himself.

The Bedouin stable master approached and put a hand on the boy's shoulder.

The boy looked up at him. "When Master Jareb left, this stallion was quite magnificent."

"Our people have been nomads and horse breeders for generations. You chose well, just as I taught you." The man knelt on one knee by the horse. "Come."

The stable boy crouched down beside him.

"See the stallion's death grimace—gums dry, eyes sunken." The stable master ran his hand along the flank. "And even at a full gallop he was not lathered in sweat. This poor creature was desert dry. Never watered." The Bedouin took a blanket from the saddle pack and covered the fallen stallion. "The horse did not fail the rider, the rider failed the horse."

Mara

Hours later Jareb slunk into the kitchen, bleary-eyed, stinking of barley beer and sweat from his late-night reckless ride.

Mara ground her loathing into the kernels of wheat in the large clay bowl in front of her.

Naomi waved to Jareb. "There is a fresh-filled water jar outside the door. Use the washbasin next to it."

Jareb's fist hammered the table. "I am hungry now."

"And filthy." Naomi's hand went to her hips.

Mara retrieved the bread from the courtyard oven and cut a generous piece.

Jareb dropped into a chair at the table. "Beloved, bring a water basin. Wash my hands, my face, my feet."

Mara cringed at the word *Beloved*. She tucked the bread knife into her waistband and wiped her hands on her apron.

Naomi blocked Mara's way. "She is neither slave nor servant."

"She is my future wife."

"Mara remains the widow of my youngest grandson. Are you a child who needs someone to wash you?"

Mara had never heard such a strident tone from this gentle, patient woman.

Jareb glared at them both, leapt up, and stormed into the courtyard.

Mara returned to grinding wheat with a vengeance.

Tobiah swaggered into the kitchen. "Woman, bring your wedding contract with Achor."

Enosh and Jareb followed Tobiah inside.

Mara did not move or speak or dare hope he would release her from the Levirate marriage.

"Go." The look on Tobiah's face was one she knew well. The same look he gave her before he beat her.

"Enosh, call father to be the second witness of my wedding contract. We will meet you in the study."

Mara went to her chamber. Her nightmare betrothal to Achor seemed from a past lifetime. Taking great care to keep her face an emotionless mask, she brought the gilded document Achor had replaced and started to hand it to Tobiah, but Jareb ripped it from her hand.

"Tobiah, make your mark here and I will make mine." Jareb picked up a nearby quill.

Tobiah screwed up his face and dipped the quill in ink.

The high priest entered adjusting his turban and frowning. "You vowed not to take a wife before justice was complete. You have executed Samuel?"

Mara gulped back a gasp and held her breath.

"No. But Samuel's death will come to pass."

Mara blew out her relief.

A wicked smile warped Jareb's mouth. "My vow was not to *know* a wife under the huppa. I can still bind her with betrothal."

Naomi put an arm around Mara's waist. "The *child* is still in mourning."

"Everyone in Shechem knows Mara does not mourn for Achor."

"Then why pursue an unwilling bride?" Naomi's tone dripped disgust and disapproval.

"I would snare the rabbit before she dares run to the arms of the murderer."

Johakim sighed as if shouldering the weight of Mount Ebal. "You will yoke yourself in an ill-fated union."

Jareb took a step toward Mara. "I will secure the right to sow an heir for my brother in his widow's womb."

Mara fled to her chamber and threw herself across the raised sleeping pallet. Jareb wanted to humiliate her, not honor Achor. She wept softly. She would not watch the men seal her future once again.

A loud knocking echoed throughout the house. She rose and peered around the lintel.

Enosh answered the knock at the main door of the mansion.

"I am Okpara." A small Egyptian man, leaning on a crutch, bowed awkwardly. He studied the richly appointed room, eyes glinting with unmistakable greed. "And I have left my master to bring word of the fugitive to the Avenger."

Mara leaned forward, straining to hear. The pagan claimed Samuel was a camel driver with a caravan on the way to Jerusalem.

"I would claim the reward, but I cannot return to my master."

"I am the Avenger. You will have a better place with me. If you serve me well." Jareb's proud tone cracked with bloodlust.

Mara eased her chamber door shut and collapsed against it. Samuel must have thought a busy caravan would be a safe haven, but now it was a trap. She returned to her sleeping pallet and knelt.

HaShem, please warn Samuel he has been betrayed and the Avenger knows his hiding place.

Caravan near Ramah

Samuel

A twig snapped, startling Samuel from his light sleep. Taking care not to wake anyone, Samuel hurried to Master Yosef's tent. The leather door flap was closed. He coughed, waited, then coughed again a little louder.

Yosef appeared and ushered him inside. Rugs from faraway lands were pieced together in exotic patterns. Sheer silks draped across the ceiling. On either side of the central room, curtains partitioned off a sleeping chamber and a work area with a table, chairs, and an open trunk of scrolls.

Samuel wanted to condemn Jareb and blurt out a defense. But he chose to weigh his words.

"Master Yosef, how may I serve you?" He realized with some astonishment he sought this Jew's approval, not because he was rich or religious, but because he strove to be righteous before the Lord of Abraham, Isaac, and Jacob.

Yosef sat on a high-backed chair near a small brazier. A tendril of smoke rose from the orange embers. The aroma of cedar chips and incense brought the altar on Mount Gerizim to mind.

Yosef gestured for Samuel to take a nearby stool. "Your predicament confounds me. My young kinsman Aryeh named you a good man, confirming my own judgment. You are no killer."

"Achor's death was never planned." Samuel's words rushed out as fast as a flash flood in a dry wadi. "But he swindled my beloved from me. Her greedy father forced her into a betrothal she abhorred. The whole town knew of our quarrel."

"And this high priest?"

"Johakim is a good man, but he has raised evil sons. Regardless of his judgment, if I stayed in Shechem, his sons would one day find me alone and my life would be forfeit."

Yosef stroked his long beard. "Let us reason together." He studied the fire, seeming to search for an answer in the flames.

Samuel's heartbeat sped, but time seemed to slow.

"Jareb and the people of Shechem would not recognize the ruling of the High Court in Jerusalem."

Samuel kept his tone flat, his voice low. "Never."

"Hmm." Yosef stood and paced between the curtains that flanked the center room. "To live in safety, you must first be found innocent by an authority all parties are *compelled* to recognize."

The older man continued to pace and ponder.

"Samaritans and Jews are subject to Rome. But the Romans have little respect for the Law of Moses or the differences that divide us." Yosef lifted his prayer shawl over his head, gently swaying.

Samuel felt a twinge near his heart. He had first sought the answers from his own mind rather than from his Maker. He joined Yosef's swaying. *HaShem, please give this man the wisdom to guide me.*

Yosef looked up at him, his face lit with inspiration. "You must plead to Rome, but you must beg sanctuary at the foot of the most strategic choice. You must run to Herod Antipas."

A shudder surged through Samuel. "Herod is a cruel man."

"The Romans call him King of the Jews." Yosef's tone was sly and scornful. "And we can use that to our gain."

"Why would Herod hear the case of a man outside the boundaries of his Roman rule?"

"Appeal to Herod's pride. Present your case as a dilemma worthy of King Solomon. You cannot trust the High Priest of Samaria and the Samaritans will not trust the High Court in Jerusalem. Herod had a Samaritan mother. He is the only man in all the world whose judgment can satisfy Samaritans, Jews, and Romans."

Hope stirred in Samuel's chest. "You have offered me the path to salvation. Only HaShem could have revealed this truth to you."

Yosef clasped Samuel's forearm. "HaShem speaks to those who have lips to pray and ears to hear."

Samuel took Yosef's other forearm. "And He blesses those who have the wisdom to listen. Master, if you are willing, I will stay with the caravan until we learn Herod's whereabouts."

"You must leave tonight."

Samuel's budding hope shriveled. "Have I given offense?"

"No. I beckoned you at the peak of darkness to give warning. Pil-i and Okpara are two sides of the same coin."

"I do not understand. Pil-i took a beating in my place."

"Both twins are excellent slaves, but Pil-i serves from his love for his master, while Okpara serves from love for his master's money. He will be unable to resist the bounty placed on your head."

"Master, master." Pil-i's frantic voice, cut into the tent.

"Enter."

Pil-i rushed in. "Okpara is gone. The first time I glanced at his blanket, all seemed well, but when I woke a few moments ago, he had not moved. And Okpara always fights epic battles in his sleep." Pil-i looked down, shamefaced. "My brother stuffed his cloak with camel blankets. He has gone to the Avenger."

Samuel stood, took a step toward the tent opening. "He cannot travel quickly on that broken leg."

Pil-i clutched his tunic. "There is no time. He is in league with his oxcart driver. The oxen, the cart, and both men are missing."

Yosef's eyes flashed. "Why would they steal from me? I have given them places all these years."

Pil-i looked down. "I know my twin. Okpara intended to betray Samuel and hoped to return before he was missed."

Yosef turned to Samuel and raised his hands in blessing. "Go now to Jerusalem. Run to Herod. Herod is your only hope."

12

Shechem

Mara

Mara's chamber door squeaked. She finished cutting the thread, looked up from her sewing, and tucked the small knife into her waist sash. Jareb entered and closed the door. The look on his face was full of lust and cruelty. Even more frightening than the look on Achor's face when he dragged her toward the huppa.

Mara's heart skittered and plunged into her stomach. *HaShem, hear me, save me. I never thought to bolt the door during the day.*

Jareb came toward her.

Mara wanted to clutch her robe, but she stood and smoothed it instead. He must not see her fear. Jareb's cruelty fed on fear. Straightening her head covering, she reached for the corner to veil her face.

"Stop. I have every right to gaze upon your face." Jareb's eyes flashed with savage lust.

She let her veil fall, fisting her hands so he would not see her fingers quivering.

Jareb's lewd leer crept from her toes to her bosom and defiled this chamber, her peaceful sanctuary.

Dread pebbled her skin, but she stood tall. Calling for courage in the face of her fear.

"Undress."

"No." She knew the dim light would not hide the heated flush of her shame and anger.

"Your father bargained for more gold. A second bride-price paid directly to him. I demand to see what my added coins have purchased." Jareb's vicious laugh sent a dread shudder around her heart.

"By the terms of my wedding contract, you are not free to take me under the huppa."

"Remove your robes."

"I will not play the harlot for you or any man." Her strong tones hid her terror. Her hand gripped the knife tucked at her waist.

"Do not defy me." Jareb rushed her and tugged at her neckline.

She twisted away, raised the knife above her head, and flashed him a look that left no doubt she would use the blade.

Jareb grabbed her wrist and tried to wrest the knife from her. Her hand went numb. She was losing her hold. Only one chance to escape. She mustered all her strength and thrust a knee into his loins.

He doubled over, let go of her wrist, and the blade sliced his palm.

Mara sidled away.

Jareb was an enraged bull, an enraged two-horned Baal. He charged her.

She swung the knife, and the tip slashed a long, deep track across his left cheek.

Pain and shock were stamped on Jareb's face. "One day, you will pay for this seven-fold." He touched a hand to his cheek, brought it down, and stared at the blood dribbling through his fingers. "These wounds will leave scars."

"Let your scars serve as a reminder that your wife is not your harlot."

"You fool. You have ruined me. You knew a scar would bar me from following my father as High Priest of Samaria." He lunged for her.

Mara screamed. A scream so desperate, it would bring the household running. A scream so piercing, Ruth and Abram would hear it in the village. A scream so heart-rending it would send a chill across Samuel's soul.

Jareb pinned her against the wall and leaned down, his angry breath on her face.

Mara's chamber seemed to close in around her. Suddenly, she had a vision of being shut up in a tomb. She struggled to catch her next breath. Then, Jareb struck her in the face.

Raising an arm to block his next blow, she slid down the wall.

Johakim and Naomi plunged into the room and dragged Jareb away from her.

"Cease from this sin." Johakim shoved his son to the front room, leaving the chamber door half-open.

Mara trembled in Naomi's arms and watched through her doorway.

"You tried to defile your child-bride." Johakim grabbed Jareb and shook him.

"She is mine to do with as I please." Jareb sounded murderous.

"Your wounds are a judgment. The Lord has set you aside. You will never be high priest." Johakim's voice brimmed with righteous fury. He shoved his son far from him.

Jareb's eyes sparked with a wicked light.

"If you ever again pursue such evil, then you are not blood of my blood." Johakim curled his lips under, shook his head, and walked back to Jareb. He tended his son's wounds in silence. The angry, anguished silence of a broken trust, a frayed bond.

As soon as Jareb's slashes were dressed, he rushed from the house.

Mara had maimed Jareb, salting his thirst for blood.

HaShem, hide my Beloved under the wings of your angel.

Naomi washed Mara's split lip and bruised face. "My poor girl."

"He tried to make me undress." The cool cloth stung and soothed.

Naomi's eyes glistened with tears of sympathy and sadness, just as they did every year when the Passover lamb was taken from the house for slaughter. "I must get some balm for your lip." Naomi left the room.

Mara rushed to her chamber door and threw the bolt. Her chamber might as well be a prison cell. A cell of her own making.

Mara carefully laid her cheek against the door, caressing the cool center plank. Samuel, so proud to work for the high priest, crafted this door only last year.

Low voices floated from the front room.

"... cursed field ... should have sold ..."

Naomi.

Mara pressed her ear to the door.

"... my beloved's shame"

Johakim.

Mara held her breath. Was this the secret Naomi and Johakim shared?

"Violated ... Law ..." Johakim's agonized voice rose. "Jareb ... Bad branch grafted into the House of Johakim."

"Shhh ... neither ... wanted ..." Naomi's tone offered comfort.

"HaShem knows ... sins of father ... my sins ... fourth generation." The sounds of the tight, tortured voice of the high priest mingled with the weeping of his mother.

Mara sifted the snatches of the story she overheard, separating the grains of truth from the chaff of deception.

A jolt of insight made her heartbeat hammer in her ears and her stomach swirl around a twinge of hope.

Did they suspect Jareb was not Johakim's son?

Mara's legs turned to soggy wool, and she slid down the door, hugged her knees. Perhaps Jareb held no right of Levirate marriage. Perhaps she could be freed from this unholy betrothal.

Mara stood, unbolted the door, and eased it open. Peering through the blurry slit of her swollen eye.

"At your wife's first childbed, I shuddered at the workings of her mind. What woman would name her firstborn *avenger?*" Naomi sounded appalled. "Now the black meaning of his name has been fulfilled."

"Jareb was circumcised into my House and is my son under the Law. He is the rightful Avenger."

"HaShem knows the full wages of your marriage lie, even if you do not. And one of your *undoubted* sons has been taken from you." Naomi sounded spent. Beyond hope.

Mara lay face down and pounded her anguish into the

floor. "Lord, I strive to keep Your Law. But where is Your justice? Jareb will be a cruel, merciless husband."

HaShem gave no answer, no comfort. He offered no relief from her smothering grief. Her prayers seemed to hover in the rafters and never reach heaven.

Jerusalem

Samuel

Samuel sat with his knees up and his back to the wall, under the arch of the city gate. Worry won the battle over his weariness. Sleep would not come. Wind whistled through the cracks in the wide stone gate and sounded like the scream of a desperate woman. Evil forebodings snaked up Samuel's spine.

Mara. May the Lord keep you safe.

The Herodian palace built by King Herod's tyrannical father was nearby. When the gate opened at first light, he would search for Herod.

Two beggars slept across the archway curled close together for warmth. One snored. The jarring snore echoing under the high stone arch. The other, a younger man, had a bandage wound around his head across his eyes.

Samuel shivered in the chill. His cloak was not as long or thick as the one he traded away. He pulled it closer around his shoulders.

The beggars stirred. The older beggar eyed him with suspicion and pushed up. "Stranger, you were not here when we bedded down."

"True. I hoped to arrive well before the gate was closed."

The bandaged beggar sat and leaned against the stone wall. "Why?"

Samuel stood, rubbed his arms, and stamped his feet, fending off the chill. "I have heard the Temple is a sight to behold. Have you been here long?"

"Each night we sleep here at the Golden Gate. Each morning we rush into the city." The bandaged beggar gestured with his hands. "We brave the jostling crowds through the gate called Beautiful into the Temple courts. There we stake out the best spots to beg from the Pharisees who make a show of their generosity."

Perhaps Samuel would find Herod there. "Where do the rich men pass?"

The older, thickset beggar crossed the gate and loomed over Samuel.

"Do not think to steal our places."

"Peace. Perhaps I could bring an offering."

The older beggar reached into his waist sack and drew forth a small clay bowl. "Then give your offering to us where it will save lives, not fatten greedy priests."

The bandaged beggar wrung his hands. "Forgive my brother's blasphemy."

Samuel took out a small sack with packets of dates and nuts and olives and handed it to the older brother. "The Lord will bless my gift to the needy."

He pulled his cloak close, hiding the kitel bound at his waist and the Magi coin pouch hanging from a leather strap around his neck.

The older beggar grabbed the sack and pawed through it.

He stared at Samuel, his brow plowed with deep ruts. "No offerings here ..." His face and tone were harsh. "Are you a zealot or one of the rabble who destroy the peace and safety of our temple mount?"

Samuel's chest tightened as if banded with iron. The beggars might sound an alarm. Samuel's answer must ring of truth. "No. I am a desperate man who seeks the cover of the Lord of Abraham, Isaac, and Jacob."

The bandaged man's cackle exposed a toothless grin. "In these hard times, me and my brother take cover under the gates of Jerusalem."

Pity pricked Samuel's heart. To be toothless at such a young age.

"Go then." An edge of distrust still colored the older beggar's tone. "You have no need to enter the city."

"I must find King Herod."

Something sad and sinister flickered across the older beggar's face. "If you have more food, my brother will tell you exactly where to find King Herod."

The bandaged beggar trembled, his face the color of a dead man.

Samuel pulled forth his larger satchel.

The older beggar grabbed it, but Samuel did not loosen his grip. "I will give you all of my food, but I must keep my watered wine and oil and lamp."

The bandaged man nodded. "I heard Herod's voice. He gave orders to a few guards when they rode out from this gate last night."

"Many powerful men issue commands at city gates. Why should I trust you would know Herod by his voice alone?"

The bandaged man's lips curled under, like a tightly sealed royal scroll. He was quiet for so long that Samuel thought he might never answer. The man's lips worked as if mustering the means to loosen his tongue.

"I once startled Herod's horse and it almost threw him. I will never forget the voice that ordered my teeth knocked out and my eyes gouged."

Samuel's voice almost failed him. "Tell me what you heard."

"Last night Herod said he would stay the night at the Inn on Jericho Road and buy horses at the Roman outpost today."

The blind man achieved a remarkable mimicry of royal speech. Without eyes, his ears were finely tuned.

Samuel handed the beggar his food. "Tell me the way to Jericho."

The older brother pointed. "That way. A half-day's walk. But the road is treacherous and favored by thieves."

Samuel, chest pounding, lifted his cloak over his head and hurried away. He fled in search of mercy from a cruel king, along an unforgiving road plagued by bandits. He stopped at the Gihon spring for water. The mouth of his waterskin bubbled as the cold water rushed in. He drank his fill then slung it over his shoulder. Not yet daring to run, Samuel moved quickly past the Mount of Olives.

The road skirted past Bethany. He picked up his pace, grateful the day was still cool. Three ancient fig trees arched over the path. Their roots were fingers spreading downward from gnarled trunks.

Samuel climbed the roots of one and plucked as many figs as his small sack would hold. The purple fig skins were already warmed by the sun. He bit into the sweet, red flesh. Though he wanted to linger, he pressed on toward Jericho.

13

Road to Jericho

Samuel

S amuel ran, where the ground would allow, along the rocky, steep road down to Jericho.

Tall trees gave way to leafy shrubs. Leafy shrubs yielded to low-lying desert thorns.

After hours, the path narrowed and pitched even more steeply. He was forced to slow to a wary walk. He dare not chance a fall. Especially since it had been some time since he met any other travelers.

A few moments later, the wary quiet was pierced by the bray of a donkey. Samuel slowly sidled around a bend. The pitiful creature, reins caught in a thorn bush, no master in sight, *whuffled* her distress. Large tears rolled from under the donkey's long lashes, carving wet streaks down her cheeks. Her dry lips trembled from thirst. Samuel poured water into his bowl and the donkey slurped thankfully.

Praise Hashem, the donkey was more sure-footed than he. Samuel led the donkey to a nearby boulder and climbed on. The donkey did not balk but moved forward seeming to understand they needed one other.

Samuel came upon a spot where the road slashed the landscape like a deep-ridged battle scar. The serpentine road pinched to a narrow path of heaped up red rocks, where only one man could pass. The donkey slowed, Samuel's heart sped. He could not ride here. Even at midday, this was an ideal spot for an ambush.

Samuel dismounted and led the donkey, scanning the cliffs above and behind him. The rocky road widened again, and Samuel edged around a blind curve, barely stopping in time to avoid a dead man crumpled on the road. "HaShem, be with me in this valley of death."

Burning bile flooded Samuel's throat. He swallowed hard. The last dead man he had seen was Achor. He would not retch. This hapless traveler had been robbed of everything, even his clothes.

Samuel's breaths came fast and shallow. The bandits could still be nearby. The magi coin hung heavy around his neck. Perhaps he should swallow it. No. He may have need of it soon.

He drew his knife. Samuel's heartbeat flooded his ears and he strained to hear.

He led the donkey around the body. Just as he was clear of it, the dead man moaned. Samuel scuttled several paces forward. He turned and stared, sick with fear.

The man was alive. Barely. Judging by his hair and beard he was a Jew. A mortal enemy.

Samuel took another step away. Jews called Samaritans dogs—the mongrels of Abraham. This Jew had surely been bypassed by his own.

There was no time. Samuel must make haste. His life

depended upon an audience with Herod. Surely this Jew was a dead dog, no matter what Samuel did. He hastened with care toward the next curve.

You know the agony of a brutal beating. You were once left for dead.

He could not ignore the still, small voice or the bristling hairs marching up his spine.

Samuel's mind flashed back to Achor and his brothers surrounding him. He winced, remembering the pain of their kicks and blows.

Perhaps you were rescued for such a time as this.

Compassion surged through Samuel's veins. He rushed back to the Jew's side and knelt. *Lord, forgive my heartlessness.* A hot surge of shame rushed through him. *That I would stop to save a donkey and not a man.*

The Jew was so still. Maybe now he was dead. Samuel put his palm near the man's nose and mouth. The breath of life blew softly against his hand.

"I will help you." Samuel took stock of the man's injuries. His right leg was bent at an unnatural angle and must be straightened and bound. Blood oozed from a deep head wound.

"HaShem, you are this poor man's Creator as well as mine. Neither of us are dogs. Show me what is needed."

Bandages. Without hesitation, Samuel unwound the kitel from his waist. He cut and tore Mara's fine linen handwork into long strips. Working quickly, he cleaned the man's wounds with wine and oil and bound them. His kitel, by tradition a bridegroom's garment and in due time his death shroud, had become this man's life-saving poultice.

The sun at its zenith bore down between the cliff walls. Samuel coaxed the man to take water. He sipped with great effort and fainted.

An inn should be nearby. The distant hills were sparsely

dotted with goats and sheep and the occasional herder. No one near enough to help him.

Thankfully, the Jew was short and slight. Samuel draped the senseless man across his donkey and used his cloak to secure him. The heat and exertion and exhaustion were taking their toll.

Samuel emerged from the blind curve feeling faint. The path dropped off on the side into a deep ravine, so Samuel let the sure-footed donkey pick her way ahead of him.

After some short twists in the road, the Roman outpost suddenly came into view, high at his left hand. And, at his right hand, just a hundred paces away, stood a large stone inn that seemed abandoned.

Sweat streamed down Samuel's face "Help." His legs gave way. Rocks stabbed his knees. His sight dimmed. Dark closed in. He could barely hear his own cry. "Help."

The inn door flung open, and a giant of a man rushed out. "Saw you through the window." He crossed his arms over his broad chest and stared at the Jew slung over the donkey. "You have brought me a dead man to bury. And a half-dead donkey. It will cost you."

"It has cost me ... perhaps my life." Samuel pressed back tears and collapsed onto his belly. "He was alive ..."

The man groaned.

"By all the gods, he lives." The innkeeper swiftly unlashed the Jew. Samuel turned onto his back, arms stretched out and watched as the innkeeper lifted the man and headed for the door. The sun caught the giant's innkeeper's blond hair. This man looked neither Greek nor Jew nor Roman. He was a pagan.

By now, Okpara would have reached Shechem. Jareb would be in pursuit. Samuel must run. But he could not. He could not even stand. He was spent and felt pulled into a fast-flowing stream of senselessness.

Whoever the innkeeper was, he was surely sent by the Lord.

Perhaps he was an angel.

Samuel

Samuel left his chamber and entered the front room.

The innkeeper turned from stirring the large iron pot hanging over the courtyard cookfire. "My name is Barid." His deep voice seemed befitting his big frame. "Hours of sleep seem to have revived you."

"Hours? But I must go on to Jericho tonight."

"Has the sun stolen your wits? It is dusk. You have seen how dangerous the way can be at night. And what of your brother in the next room? He lives, but drifts in and out of senselessness."

"He is not my brother. He is not even my friend. He is a Jew."

"And?" Barid took the lid off the pot and stirred. A meat stew judging by the aroma.

"I am Samuel, a Samaritan."

Barid moved inside and locked eyes with him. "The hatred between Samaritans and Jews is well known even to pagans." He tilted his head and frowned. A frown that demanded an explanation.

"He is a stranger I could not step over and leave to die."

"Lady Fortune was with that Jew when the man who found him was you."

"I will pay for his care, but I must hasten to King Herod. My life depends upon it."

A flicker of worry crossed the innkeeper's face but was quickly masked. "You do not look to be a wealthy man."

Samuel withdrew the Magi coin from his pouch and placed it on the table. The image of the dove glinted in the setting sunlight and seemed to wink at him.

"Your Persian coin is too precious."

"It is all I have."

"Be at peace." Barid crossed to the counter and withdrew a small wooden chest from behind a clay jar. He brought the chest to the table. "This is an inn. I will give you lesser coins in return."

This pagan was more righteous than many of the men in Shechem. Gratitude welled up and lightened Samuel's chest. "You must reckon the cost. The Jew's healing will take time and I cannot stay. If he dies, his burial will have a price."

"Even so, you must take these denarii and I will credit that you have given me two." Barid selected three coins from the chest and placed them on the table. "I will not leave you without your due, without even a lowly quadrans. You must stay the night, or you may not live to see Jericho."

"I cannot chance missing Herod Antipas."

"Herod and his bodyguards slept here last night. Today he travels to his winter palace to oversee repairs that will take weeks." The innkeeper pushed the coins toward Samuel.

Samuel dropped them into his leather pouch. "Wisdom whispers in my ear to stay the night." He tipped his head toward the back of the inn. "With your care, the Jew may claw himself up from the grave. When I return, I will settle any other bills."

Barid went out to the pot and ladled two portions of stew.

"Venison. Leavings from Herod." He set the bowls on the table. "Let me check on the Jew." He headed to the back.

Closing his eyes, Samuel thought of home and his beloved Mara. He bowed his head and lifted his palms. "HaShem, Maker of the Universe, thank you for this food, this shelter, this pagan."

After a moment, he opened his eyes and found Barid studying him.

Barid jerked a thumb over his shoulder. "The Jew barely roused but muttered about a priest and a Levite."

"Perhaps they will come here seeking him."

"Some common Jews may enter here, but a priest or Levite? Never. They would not soil themselves by mingling with unclean, unholy pagans like me. Or you." Barid attacked his stew with vigor. "Eat while our supper is warm."

Samuel considered Barid's features, wondering about the man's bloodline. "Your name. I have never heard it."

"My mother was Persian." He laid a hand over his heart. "May she be at peace in the Shadowlands."

"The few Persians I have seen are dark. Was your father fair?"

Barid's blue eyes blazed, and emotion flooded his face. "I am a child of war." There was unmistakable pain in the innkeeper's tone.

Samuel waited with an open face and an open heart.

"Captive women are ravaged by many conquerors. I am the child of many fathers and no father. My mother was smart and strong of heart. She survived."

Low moans from the back of the inn broke off their talk.

"The Jew sounds weak." Samuel stood and pushed away from the table.

Barid went out to the fire and returned with the stewpot and two lit oil lamps. "I would not wager the Jew will live through the night." The moans grew stronger. "On the other hand, I would not wager against him either."

"I will tend to him." Samuel went to check on the Jew.

The beaten man lay unmoving, now making no sounds. Samuel watched for the rise and fall of his chest. The man's breathing was shallow—barely there—but he was breathing. Samuel straightened the blanket and returned to the table. "The Jew's life hangs in the balance."

"May the gods of fortune be with him." Barid lifted the ladle. "More?"

"Gladly." Samuel held out his bowl.

"Before I was an innkeeper, I was a Roman soldier at the outpost on the hill. Men with head wounds must be watched carefully. I will keep vigil with you." He lifted a pitcher. "Barley beer?"

Samuel's mouth was full, he nodded.

Over the course of the long night, Barid shared his triumphs as well as his trials, and listened to Samuel's plight and tale of forced flight.

Samuel looked in on the Jew and returned to Barid. "Our Jew seems more awake, though he does not remember his name, his family, his home."

"*Our* Jew? *We* have become quite devoted."

Samuel laughed at Barid's teasing. "It is hard to hate a man whose wounds you have tended. Also, I have been in his place. Once I was badly beaten, but praise HaShem, my memory was restored."

"During battle, many of my soldiers suffered brutal blows to the head. Tomorrow, *our* Jew may remember some or none of his former life. His past, his place, his people may remain blotted out forever."

14

Inn on the Road to Jericho

Samuel

Samuel woke to the sweet smells of cinnamon and cooked apples. The sky beyond his backroom window was the slate blue of daybreak. He rose, strapped his satchel to his waist and followed his nose into the front room. A breeze from the open door refreshed the stagnant air.

"You must shore up your strength." Barid waved Samuel to the table and served him a two-fold portion of hot porridge.

"May you be blessed for your kindnesses to me."

"Take heart." Barid clapped him on the back. "Remember, God has heard."

A shiver of something Samuel could not name ran up his spine. "You know the meaning of my given name."

"I have the gift of foreign tongues." Barid's low belly laugh filled the room. "It is a great boon for an innkeeper."

"And the meaning of the name your mother gave you?"

This man's mother loved her son deeply, but what would a captive mother call a child of war?

The innkeeper's gaze softened. "In Aramaic, Barid means *malak*—messenger or angel."

An unseen soothing touch seemed to rest on Samuel's shoulder. He shivered. The hand of HaShem. He *had* sent an angel.

Barid turned toward the door, his stance tense, his eyes wary. "Riders on the road."

Samuel jumped up and looked through the front window. "No one."

"Ears often hear before eyes see." Barid moved to the open door. "I know every whisper of this road. Trust me. Someone is coming."

Samuel grabbed his cloak. "I must run."

"No." The big innkeeper blocked him. "No time. Hide with the wounded man." Barik prodded him into the back room. "Think. The Avenger seeks one man, not two. He hunts a Samaritan, not a Jew." A moment later Barid tossed in Samuel's blankets from last night and shut the door.

One high window. No way out. His fate had been sealed.

The Jew was unmoving and looked gray in the early morning shadows. Hinges squeaked. Barid must be closing the outside door giving Samuel more time to hide.

"Do not moan." Samuel whispered. A plan came to him. He spoke softly to the Jew, not at all certain he could hear. "Pretend you are dead." He draped a linen towel over the man's face, retrieved two coins from the pouch around his neck, and pressed them over the man's eyes, praying he would remain silent and still.

Samuel crawled onto the sleeping pallet between the Jew and the wall, dragging his things with him. He burrowed into the straw and covered himself with his cloak and blankets. He hoped the heap of his belongings would hide his form and appear to be the things of a dead man.

Heavy hammering on the inn door seemed to shake Samuel to the bone. His heartbeat raced past his sharp, shallow breaths.

The Jew next to him did not move.

"Wait." Barid shouted.

An eerie silence loomed for the space of several ragged breaths.

"Open. Now." The pounding resumed.

Jareb.

The inn went quiet. A seeping stillness before the squall.

"I come. Break my door and you will be neither fed nor watered."

"We have no need of either." Jareb again. Pride and disdain in his tone.

"You speak true. For, if you damage my door, you will be dead."

The heavy door creaked open. "I was clearing the chamber pots and took time to wash my hands." Barid's tone was laden with contempt. "You will forgive the wait."

"A Goliath of a man."

Tobiah's trembling, slurred voice. Jareb must have offered him blood money. The slothful drunk would do anything for gold. Sell his daughter. Betray her beloved.

"It is unwise to open a door uninvited. Did you not learn this at your mother's knee?" Sarcasm and rage colored Barid's tone.

"A thousand pardons." Jareb's tone was oiled with a hollow apology.

"And what has this commotion to do with me?" Barid's tone carried all the innocence of a dove and the cunning of a snake.

"Friend, when the door was not opened right away, I feared

the cutthroat who murdered my brother had killed the master here."

"We know the killer was hired onto the caravan of Yosef of Arimathea." Tobiah was pandering to Jareb again.

"Ah ... Master Yosef. He has not passed this way in months."

Scrapes. Thuds. The sounds of men searching the front room.

"What do the four of you—" Barid coughed and cleared his throat. "—expect to find under my counters and in the corner larder?

Four men. Samuel's brow beaded with sweat. Would the innkeeper help fight Jareb and his men?

"As Avenger of Blood, I claim the right to search the back rooms."

"I am ruled only by the laws of Rome." Now Barid's voice was flat, giving nothing away.

"Even so, we will search. Resist and we will draw our swords." Uncertainty hovered in Jareb's voice. Perhaps he judged that four men might not be sufficient to subdue an enraged Barid.

"Avenger or no. If you dare draw your sword on me, in my inn, you will not live to see sunset."

"We have no fight with you if you have nothing to hide." Jareb's oily tone had returned.

Taking care to keep covered, Samuel palmed the knife at his waist and slid it to rest along his thigh.

The men ransacked the room where Samuel had slept. Angry grunts were followed by the crashes of an overturned table and chair.

The door to the Jew's room creaked open. Samuel peered out from his hiding place.

The black outline of Jareb, sword still sheathed, loomed in the doorway.

Samuel's heartbeat was a racing chariot with the thunder of a thousand galloping horses pounding in his ears.

Jareb threw an arm across his face and turned away. "A corpse. You did not warn me there was a corpse."

"Did I not warn you it was unwise to open a door uninvited?"

Jareb stepped back.

"Who is the dead man?" Tobiah's whine was filled with suspicion and revulsion.

"The Jew was brought to me late last night and left for burial." Barid's taunting laugh baited Jareb. "Do you wish to see the body?"

"No."

Jareb sounded farther away.

"None of us may enter the room. The corpse would make us unclean. Did anyone else pass by?"

"Only the man who brought him." Barid yawned, loudly sighing out his boredom. "He must be half-way back to Jerusalem."

Jareb swore vows of violence and vengeance that curdled Samuel's blood.

"Do you need provisions?" Barid was playing the part of a merchant anxious to make a sale.

"We are well supplied." Tobiah's tone was still laced with fear.

"Where will you go now that your hunt has been fruitless?"

"We will join my men who continued south from Jerusalem." Jareb sounded as if he was moving to the door.

Bless Barid. Now Samuel knew Jareb would not go to Jericho. If Samuel could stay alive and reach Herod, he might still win sanctuary.

HaShem, let this Jew live, but I beg you keep him silent and still as the dead.

At long last, Jareb tromped outside. Horses whinnied. Whips cracked. Hooves slapped the rocky ground.

Samuel commanded each muscle, taut as a bowstring, to slacken. He waited for his heartbeat to slow. Barid would signal when Samuel was safe. His full bladder begged for relief.

The Jew jerked, blew out a deep breath, and moaned.

Samuel was so startled he nearly passed his water.

Then, the Jew tossed the linen away from his face and rolled onto his side. The denarii pressed over his eyes clinked against the stone floor.

Footsteps. Barid entered the room. "The Jew lives."

Samuel threw off the heaped blankets and sat up.

"And so do you." Barid grinned, a lopsided grin. "Your enemy is deceived."

"My death has been delayed. For today."

Samuel

Samuel rode Barid's mule to the forge just inside the main Jericho gate.

"*Quo vadis?*" A man called from the stable behind the forge.

Latin. Samuel's stomach lurched. He had not expected a Roman. "Barid told me to board his mule with you." Samuel answered in Aramaic, the language of trade.

A brawny man came out from the stable. "If Barid trusts you with his most precious mule, then you are welcome."

He moved like a soldier, of an age to be Barid's younger brother, but leaner—built more for speed and cunning. His well-muscled arms and legs bore scars the size of small coins. Slag burns.

Samuel studied his face. A thin white scar ran from the corner of his lower lip and slashed his jaw.

"I am Dex."

His crooked smile was not distressing but disarming.

"Bring the mule. It is time for her supper and yours."

"I am called Samuel. I can pay." He reached for his money pouch.

"Tonight, you are a guest."

"I must find work and shelter."

"As long as you have need, stay in the stable and pay me with chores."

"Many thanks. I will help you settle my neighbors for the night."

A flicker of confusion crossed Dex's face, then vanished.

"Neighbors." Dex laughed long and loud. "We have all known worse neighbors than these beasts."

They fed the mule and six other mounts and cleaned the stalls.

Samuel's stomach growled.

Dex flashed his crooked smile. "Come."

Samuel followed Dex into the stone house. A covered iron pot and a basket of freshly baked bread had been placed on the low table. The aroma of pungent spices was foreign, but still made Samuel's mouth water.

He studied the room. No sewing. No loom. Nothing womanly. "Someone has gone to great trouble."

Dex's eyes clouded and his lips tightened. "Last summer my wife was taken by a fever."

Samuel's heart hitched. "I understand the pain of losing ..." His voice twitched.

Dex clapped Samuel on the back. "Do not be trapped in

my sinking sands of sadness." Dex gestured to floor mats. "Please, sit. Young ladies leave me delicious dishes every day. Most made by mothers eager for their daughters to wed a prosperous widower."

What Samuel would give to enjoy a meal prepared by Mara, no matter how bland or burnt. "An enviable problem."

"A problem I savor each evening." Dex lifted the cover and ladled the meal into bowls.

"How did you come to be a blacksmith in Jericho?"

"We will trade stories."

Samuel lifted his hands. "May I offer a blessing over the food?"

"Mithras has preserved my life, but one can never be too blessed."

Ah. Just as Samuel thought. Roman soldiers worshiped Mithras. Samuel murmured a prayer.

Dex took some bread. "Your prayer was familiar, but ..."

"I am Samaritan."

"Beware. In Jericho, Jewish priests hold much land and wield much power."

Dex sprang up, hurried to the rough beam shelf, and returned with a stone jar. "This strong drink will loosen our tongues and strengthen our stomachs to tell the things which rend our hearts and kill our hope." He poured two generous cups. "A draught of daring."

"How did you come to be here?" Samuel lifted his drink.

"Like my father before me, I was an armorer for Rome. My pension and rewards financed the forge and stable. Soldiers, travelers, and townsfolk stop here but I remain alone. Without my cherished wife." Dex drank deeply then leaned back. "And you?"

"My Beloved lives but is lost to me." Samuel squelched his fears and shared his plan to beg Herod for sanctuary.

Dex rubbed his smooth chin. "The thorn in your side will be plotting how to capture Herod's ear. He sometimes lives at the Winter Palace in Jericho but does not hear petitions. A throne room might offend the ruling Roman tetrarch."

"What am I to do?"

Dex downed his drink. "Herod is your best chance for mercy, but you cannot approach him without invitation."

Dex's face took on the sly look of a seasoned soldier forming a battle plan.

"Contrive to be hired to work on Herod's palace renovations. Distinguish yourself with Herod's overseer. Then, if the Avenger comes to Jericho, fling yourself at Herod's feet. His overseer may vouch for you."

"Who hires the laborers?"

"Herod's chief overseer, who owes me a debt." Dex took an amulet strung on a cord from around his neck. "Show this to the man hiring the day-laborers at the palace gate. Leave before first light. The hiring will be completed by dawn."

Before the first cock's crow, Dex awakened Samuel. They shared a light meal. Dex headed for the forge, fire already blazing. Samuel headed for the Winter Palace.

As he walked away, the ring of the hammer striking the anvil seemed to stamp sadness onto Samuel's heart. His home was forfeit. His parents were forfeit. His bride was forfeit. Everything his beloved Mara had given him was gone. The kitel she fashioned with loving hands. Gone. Mara's precious Magi coin. Gone. And the right to kiss Mara's lips and feel her loving touch. Gone.

Why, Lord, why? I am not a perfect man, but you know I am an innocent one.

The rays of the sunrise stuck the palace gate, bathing it in a golden light. Warmth settled on Samuel's shoulders and sparked the dying embers of his hope.

All was not lost. He and Mara both still drew breath. Their hearts still longed for one another. The gate swung open. Samuel entered the courtyard in search of his destiny and Herod's overseer.

Shechem

Mara

Mara rushed to Jacob's well, one water jar balanced on her head, the other cradled in her arm perched on a hip. The sickle moon sank its blade into the crimson clouds of dawn.

She must hurry before another woman arrived to witness her deception.

The night watchmen who guarded the crossroads passed by.

Several flashed her sympathetic looks. Samuel had been much admired. And Achor much despised.

One guard stopped. "You are alone. Samuel would want one of us to see no harm comes to you. I will wait while you draw water."

A lump thickened in Mara's throat. "You are most kind, but you need only light a torch for me. Fire will protect me from man or beast. The other women will soon be here. Go, break your fast."

The guard walked to a dying watchfire, lit a torch, and planted it in pile of nearby rocks.

"Many thanks." Mara put down the water jars.

As soon as he was out of sight, Mara reached inside the smaller jar and pulled out the linen towel she slept on every night since her betrothal to Jareb. The towel bore a secret red stain. Her first moonblood. Taking up the torch, Mara moved near the ancient terebinth tree where she parted with Samuel. She laid the towel on a boulder, set it ablaze, and stared into the flickering flames.

Mara cringed. The blood-stained linen burning on the boulder looked like a bloody pagan sacrifice on a stone altar. The cloth quickly turned to ashes that she buried under nearby stones.

When she placed the last stone, she remembered one of Ruth's stories. Long ago, Jacob buried foreign idols beneath this tree. Now the ashes of her bloody linen laid mingled with the ashes of ancient idols. But she would not foreswear her falsehood. She would live with her lie rather than go to Jareb's bed—even if her spirit never felt clean again.

Mara looked up at the light-streaked sky. The rising sun formed a sickle behind a distant hill. Since Achor's death, Mara saw sickles everywhere.

At night, her sleep was tormented by the memory of Samuel's blade aloft in the sky, and Achor's life severed from this world. By day, her thoughts were tortured by the memory of Samuel's blade turning end over end, and Samuel's life severed from Shechem. Severed from her.

The voices of the village women carried from behind the rise. The younger women arrived first, and several gathered around Mara.

"How were Jareb's face and hand slashed? Was Jareb truly ambushed on the road to Jericho as he claims?"

Mara was thrust back to the moment of Jareb's attack. Cold dread ran through her veins. She could not quell her shuddering or her runaway heart. Or the memory of Jareb looming over her.

"Be still you clucking chickens."

Ruth.

Mara's heart slowed.

"See how your pecking has troubled her." Ruth put a hand on Mara's shoulder. "Jareb can never be high priest no matter how he came to be scarred."

"Bless you." Mara reached up and squeezed Ruth's hand.

One of the young women, Delilah, lifted the water jar where Mara hid her stained linen cloth. "Here, I will draw this for you while you draw the other."

Mara's throat and chest tightened. She could not let a water jar that had held blood pollute the well water. "No." Her tone was sharper than she intended.

Delilah grabbed the crossbar rope. "What troubles you?"

"It leaks."

Delilah peered into the jar. "It is dry inside and out. But—"

"It leaks." Mara grabbed the jar and threw it against the nearest boulder. Clay shattered. Shards sprayed. One lie fed another before an hour lapsed.

"You are not yourself." Delilah drew Mara aside and turned to the others. "Draw your water, do not wait for us."

Something flickered across Delilah's face. She withdrew a packet from her waistband. "I brought this for you. Make a tea of these herbs while the moon is young and drink it every day for a week. Your moonblood will never flow or will cease. Afterward, drink the tea every new moon you wish to remain untouched by that fiend, Jareb."

Delilah took Mara's hand and placed the packet of herbs into her open palm. "Quick, hide the packet away from prying eyes."

Delilah's bloodlines were rooted in Assyria. Surely this was a forbidden pagan practice.

"I have no more use for these herbs." There was triumph in Delilah's tone. "The man my father preferred tired of waiting for my womanhood. He took another woman to wife and I am betrothed to my Beloved." She drew her water and headed home.

Mara was now of two minds. She slid the herb packet into her tunic next to her heart.

Naomi arrived carrying a small jar. "You left so early this morning." Naomi's voice was weak and breathy.

Mara drew the water and they made their way back to the House of the High Priest.

Naomi touched her arm.

Mara slowed.

"Tonight, do not let Jareb's eyes rest upon you. He rants and raves each time his spies return without news of Samuel."

Mara stopped at the iron gate with Naomi. "You watch over me as you would a daughter."

"At each turn, HaShem has shown me, He would have you safe."

"But Naomi, I also fear for you."

"When Jareb is in a black temper, even Johakim has no sway. So, I laden the table with rich food, water the wine, and send only male slaves to serve."

A knot of sadness settled in Mara's throat. Naomi was as trapped as she in the web of evil that had a stranglehold on the House of Johakim.

They passed through the gate into their palatial prison. Mara hurried away to brew her first draught of the herbal tea. Anything to delay the marriage bed.

15

Jericho

Summer, nigh on three years since Samuel fled Shechem

Samuel

During the last three years, not a sunrise passed that Samuel did not pray for Mara. And not a sunset passed during those years that Samuel did not pray they would one day be together. At midday work break, he sat in the shade of a large terebinth tree in Herod's palace garden. Carving a small game piece, Samuel watched the wood curl. The rhythm of his whittling helped him sift his memories.

Surely by now Mara had become a woman and been taken to Jareb's bed. And by now, she may well be a mother.

Samuel considered his long stay in Jericho. For his first three days, he had presented the amulet at the palace gate. The one Dex gave him to gain favor for hire by the overseer. Finally, on the third day, he was sent to work in the palace gardens. After three weeks, the overseer's shadow fell on him. Samuel's stomach wrenched whenever he remembered the man said he would no longer be hired each day.

But Samuel misunderstood. The overseer handed him a pass-stone given to the workers needed for the entire project.

Samuel worked harder than all the other men. Many made no secret they hated him for striving to stand apart. But he was desperate to draw the favor of Herod so he could someday plead for sanctuary.

Then, three more months passed and Samuel was handed a stone imprinted with a foreman's mark. Every man Samuel chose for his crew was an outcast in a city where Jews, priests, and Levites held such sway.

Now, after years, his men were no longer outcasts, but a family who shared not only a barracks but also one another's disappointments and dreams.

Yet not once in those three years had he caught a glimpse of Herod.

The cymbal rang. Samuel put down his whittling and returned to the garden. He drank deeply from his waterskin, wiped his dripping brow, and removed his tunic. Like the rest of his men, he worked in a loincloth in the heat of the day. All afternoon Samuel dug the fertile black earth. He looked back over the row of small trees he had planted.

Every day he toiled in Herod's expansive gardens and pressed back his fear. Not the niggling fear of a bite from a hidden viper, but the hounding fear of a blind-sided deathblow from Jareb.

Samuel hoped to attract the king's notice with his elaborate plans for the palace gardens. At the end of each wheat harvest, the overseer delivered Herod's praise and extra coin to Samuel and his crew. But not once had Herod asked to see the men who transformed his gardens into a paradise that was now the talk of Jericho.

The overseer approached. "Herod plans to bring his new paramour here when he returns from Jerusalem. He wants a private garden for her with a secret entrance from his chambers. Render several drawings."

Samuel would contrive a chance to meet Herod. "When the king sees the plans, there will be question heaped upon question."

"King Herod will require your wisdom. I will suggest he meet with us both."

Samuel's heart skipped like a stone across a smooth lake. He laughed his first unbridled laugh since he fled Shechem. Finally, he would see Herod face to face.

Samuel

Samuel sat with the overseer on a fountain wall in Herod's newest palace garden. The overseer unrolled the scrolls and studied Samuel's latest designs.

"I suspect Herod will choose the fanciful hanging garden, in the style that made Babylon a wonder in all the world."

"When will the king see us?"

"Not until his lady arrives." The overseer took the scrolls and walked away.

For days Samuel practiced possible dialogues with Herod. Samuel's chance came none too soon. Last night, one of garden crew spoke of strangers seeking a murderer.

Since, he had slept with one eye half-open and one foot on the floor, ready to run. His gut simmered sour at the thought of his besmirched honor.

The signal for afternoon break sounded. Samuel retired under a nearby terebinth tree that reminded him of home. His men knew when he retreated there, he craved solitude. Samuel's mind was a jumble of horrifying, hopeful, and even impossibly happy consequences of his meeting with Herod.

He removed a square of olive wood and a knife from his pack. Carving settled his soul. The sign was to be a gift for Dex with whom he always ate the Sabbath meal. He could not abide the Jews on the Sabbath. Better to sup with a man who made no claim on the Law. Shavings curled as he cut away all that was not part of the emerging scene—a horse beside a stable and a forge with a horseshoe resting in the fire.

Dex would be pleased. He had remarked on the sign of a cluster of grapes and a sheaf of wheat that Samuel carved for Barid.

Samuel considered his next cut. A shadow fell across his work.

His glanced up into the accusing glare and ugly snarl of a Jewish priest.

"The Law forbids the creation of any graven image."

Samuel's breath caught and onrushing alarm sent a shudder through his heart.

"But—"

"Silence." The priest waved his Levite servant close. "Or I will have you scourged before you are dragged to the feet of Herod."

Samuel's lips clamped—a vise, choking off his defense. He may have escaped Jareb, but few could escape the reach of the pervasive Levites. Moments ago, he dreamed of the king's praise. Now he would be hauled before him in disgrace.

"Pick up your idol."

Samuel stood and tucked the sign under his arm.

The priest and Levite led Samuel from the gardens.

The overseer jumped into their path. "He is not a Jew, and he is my best gardener."

"Unless he is a Roman, Levites are charged with enforcing the Law in Jericho." The Levite prodded Samuel with a walking stick as if he were a beast of burden.

The overseer followed. "Fear not, I will not forsake you."

Samuel looked heavenward. This was madness. He would never dare carve an image to be worshiped. The penalty for such an offense was death by stoning.

The priest and Levite brought Samuel to the House of the Chief Priest of Jericho. Expansive fields surrounded a house that was much larger than Johakim's house in Shechem. The overseer did not speak, but he never left Samuel's side. Two guards opened the iron gate that led to the mansion.

At the priest's signal, one bound Samuel's hands behind his back. "Take him to the prison cells below."

The priest's command sent a rush of boiling anger through Samuel's veins.

The overseer advanced on the priest, stepping much closer than seemly. "Herod will hear of this outrage."

"In this city of priests, Herod does not rule." Disdain seeped from the Levite's tone. "Touch me and you will join your gardener."

The second guard moved closer, hand on the hilt of his sword.

The overseer folded his arms across his chest. "Beware the wrath of Herod. I have seen his temper rage when a man unwittingly touched one of his women. And you have snatched Herod's gardener from Herod's palace. You will rue your trespass."

The priest gestured again to the guards.

They grabbed Samuel, but he planted his feet and resisted. Prison. No one knew what awaited him there.

The guards pulled Samuel toward the chief priest's

mansion. He went limp, forcing them to drag him on his back, the heels of his sandals plowing furrows in the dirt.

The overseer called out. "Herod will be told that you waylaid his gardener. Do not dare to question or flog him."

Neither the priest nor Levite answered.

The overseer's expression hardened, his teeth bared like a street dog guarding a bone. "Priest, your fields are dry this year. An untimely fire would be unfortunate." His tone held no emotion which made his threat even more ominous.

The priest said nothing, but blocked the overseer's path. The guards lugged Samuel into a hall and down three stone stairs. At a Roman arch, one guard lit a torch from a nearby brazier.

Samuel was hauled into a cluster of windowless cells hewn out of a cave beneath the chief priest's house. They stopped at the first one. Samuel was shackled hand and foot to chains fed through iron rings on the wall. The guards closed the cell door, leaving him in the dark. A dark more black than pitch. A dank, foul smell enveloped him. His heart thrashed against his ribs. He could not take a full breath.

HaShem, what has provoked Your anger? Show me my sin that I may repent.

Samuel sat against the wall, hugging his knees. He had wished Achor dead for months before that fateful day in the field. Now he suffered because his wish had come to pass. "HaShem, shield me from my enemies just as You did at the Jericho Inn." Hearing the echo of his words seemed to lend them power. His nose went blind to the foul odor and his breathing slowed. He would pray for his friends, his family, and his Beloved until exhaustion overwhelmed him.

———

Shechem

Mara

Mara stood over the cookpot in the kitchen courtyard staring into the steam. Three Passovers since Samuel fled. No news of him. No news Jareb had killed Samuel. No news he had even been sighted.

Was her beloved Samuel well? Was he safe? Was his heart still entirely hers?

The pot bubbled—the rumbling bringing to mind her brews of forbidden tea. The pagan tea that safeguarded her from Jareb's lust. For three years, she had staved off any return of her first moonblood by portioning the herbs into a weaker and weaker tea. Each new moon, Naomi looked at her with questioning eyes. And each new week, Jareb had her chambers searched for any signs of sorcery. But he would never find the herbs she had hidden under a loose stone in Naomi's chambers.

Mara stirred the pot of stew, calming the roiling boil.

Okpara rushed into the kitchen and waved to Mara to come inside. "Master Jareb sends word. There will be eight men at supper tonight. He ordered a lamb slaughtered."

Naomi tied an apron around her waist. "Okpara, put the lamb on the spit for roasting in the men's courtyard."

Okpara nodded and hurried away, his broken leg entirely mended.

"Mara, stay in the kitchen this evening, where I can shield you from Jareb's mistreatment."

Mara grabbed the smallest knife and slipped it into her waistband, making no attempt to hide her actions from Naomi. "I will defend myself."

"As would I." Sympathy softened Naomi's face. "I wish Johakim were here."

"When does Johakim return from the burial rites of his cousin?"

"Eight more days."

Mara walked outside to the cookfire and moved her hand over the pot, wafting the aroma of the simmering stew under her nose. Her mouth watered at the sweet smells of mint and apricot mixed with cumin.

Naomi stepped into the doorway. "Mara, please take some sauce to the spit."

"But Jareb might be in the men's courtyard." Mara clutched the knife at her waist.

"Do not worry child. Jareb and Enosh are not back. They return at sunset with the guests."

Mara took the bowl of basting sauce and walked the long length of the house of the High Priest. Some proud Samaritans boasted that the mansion rivaled the House of Caiaphas, High Priest of Jerusalem. At the far corner arch, she shuddered, and passed into the men's courtyard—the site of her betrothal to Achor more than three years past. The spitted lamb hung over the fire. Okpara sat on the fountain wall drawing on papyrus.

"Here is the basting sauce." She waved at his sketch. "Come, watch me baste. Turn the spit slowly and baste often. Do not become distracted with idle pastimes and neglect the lamb."

Okpara set his drawing aside and joined her.

Mara swiped the lamb with sauce then handed Okpara the hyssop brush. He did the same. Satisfied he would not ruin the lamb, Mara turned to leave.

"My Lady. I would show you my drawing." Okpara picked up the papyrus. "The demon who murdered Achor will soon be caught."

His sinister tone sent a rush of panic bristling up her arms.

"You seem sure." Perhaps Okpara practiced the dark arts of Egypt.

"Yes. I never forget a face." He turned the papyrus toward her.

Okpara had captured an exact likeness of Samuel—so true that Mara walked forward and reached out to touch Samuel's cheek. She caught herself and pulled her hand back. "It is forbidden for Samaritans to make such drawings." If she still had her Magi coin, she would have been sorely tempted to buy the forbidden drawing of her Beloved.

"Yes, Master Jareb told me."

That fiend. "What else did your master say?" Mara's stomach turned like the lamb on the roasting spit.

"The Law forbids him to pay me for these likenesses."

"Likenesses?" The earth seemed to move beneath Mara's feet, and she leaned against the fountain wall. "There is more than one?"

"This is the sixth."

"But why?" She cringed at the panicked screech that invaded her voice.

"Eyes everywhere will see these drawings. And the murderer will be found."

Samuel.

How could he hope to hide with so many eyes watching for him?

"One day I will be mistress here." The threat of power in her tone.

Doubt flickered across Okpara's face. "I never should have boasted of my skill with the quill or my ready recall of faces."

She must tread carefully. "Bring me first report when the murderer has been sighted and I will treat you with favor."

HaShem, I beg you ... keep Samuel from the talons of the circling vulture, from the clutches of the Avenger of Blood.

A Certain Man

Mara

Mara sat on her raised sleeping pallet and folded the empty pouch of forbidden herbs.

A week ago, Naomi saw the blooming bloodstain on the back of Mara's tunic. Now, she was honor-bound as witness to the truth. At sixteen, Mara's body finally betrayed her.

Jareb's beard was overgrown and wild, his hair long, bound back with a leather cord. He had not taken a wife despite his father's pleas for him to set Mara aside and give him a grandson. Strangely, Enosh also had not taken a wife, claiming Jareb should wed first.

Still, part of Jareb's vow was unfulfilled. He had not slain Samuel.

A gentle knock interrupted her musings. "Come."

Naomi entered the room wringing her hands. "Jareb has called the villagers as witness and ordered you to the center of Shechem."

"Why?"

"His eyes glint with a dark light and I fear the twisted workings of his mind."

Mara girded her heart, her mind, her soul for battle. Samuel would want her to keep her wits and courage. No matter what befell her, she would not be broken.

Mara arranged her veil and followed Naomi to the clustered huts. Ruth and Abram came out from their home, her former safe haven. They stood at her right and left hand. A quiet comfort. Mara's heart wept for them. They had lost not only Samuel, but also her, whom they counted as their only daughter.

She glanced over to the hut beside them where Tobiah lay

in drunken oblivion. At least today he would not seed further trouble.

Jareb, Enosh, and the high priest entered the clearing. The villagers slowly gathered. When they saw her, some looked heartless, others looked worried.

Jareb stared at her, his evil countenance giving away nothing.

Mara's legs trembled, and she took Abram's arm. A horrific thought invaded her mind. Had Jareb killed Samuel?

Ruth slid an arm around Mara's waist and squeezed. "Help me sit on this boulder, for I suddenly feel faint in the evening sun."

"Gladly." Ruth's quick thinking covered Mara's weakness, and her touch imparted a new strength. Mara straightened.

Jareb stepped close. "Woman, widow of the murdered man, all have heard me vow that I would not take you under the huppa until justice was done."

Mara did not move. But her heart raced, her stomach roiled, her soul wept. *HaShem, do not let my wicked tormentor's next words be that Samuel is dead. I can bear all else.*

"Despite my unflagging search, Achor's killer has not been found." Jareb turned, appealing to the crowd. "I pray HaShem has executed justice by some other means."

Mara took a slow, deep breath. She must tread with great care. "Under the Law, without a body, Samuel cannot be deemed dead." If she held Jareb to his vow, she was safe.

Ruth's soft weeping behind Mara threatened to wring telltale tears from her eyes. She clenched her jaw. She would not show fear or sorrow or weakness. She shrouded herself in silence.

"My brothers, my father, and my father's father have no heir." Jareb pointed at Mara. "At long last, my betrothed has attained womanhood."

Silence was Mara's best weapon.

"We must fulfill the purpose of a Levirate marriage, the provision of an heir for Achor. Release me from my vow to kill Samuel before our marriage is consummated."

Mara resisted the angry retort at her lips. Her heart thrummed with hope. If she sacrificed her own safety, she could save Samuel. "Surrender your vow to kill Samuel. And I will void your vow. Samuel never plotted murder."

Mutterings of shock, approval, and speculation ran through the gathering.

"May HaShem bless you and keep you." Abram's soft prayer floated to Mara's ears.

The high priest raised his arms for silence. "Jareb, this is a righteous solution. A vow for a vow."

Jareb stomped and spit. "I will never relinquish my right as Avenger. Achor would curse me from the grave."

The high priest stepped close to Jareb. "If Samuel came to trial and was found guilty of unintentional murder, what would his punishment be?"

Jareb looked pained to speak. "Banishment in a place of sanctuary until the death of the high priest."

"Until my death." The high priest's face carried the sorrow of a disappointed father. "Give up this thirst for Samuel's blood. I desire an heir born soon. An heir I can come to know."

"Never." Jareb's shout cut through Mara's heart.

Naomi stepped forward. "Jareb, I beg you. Relinquish the right to search for and execute Samuel."

"Never. Not as long as I draw breath."

"Then you will never warm my bed until Samuel lies cold in his." Mara would not break before these hair-splitters of the Law. She stood tall and walked toward the House of the High Priest.

"Wait."

She halted at Jareb's angry shout. Perhaps she had saved Samuel. She turned. "Do you agree to my terms?"

"No."

"Then I have no other words for you."

"Woman, I have words for you." Jareb waved her back to the clearing. "Kneel before your husband and hear my command."

She knelt, fulfilling the Law.

"If you will not welcome me to your bed, and deny me any other wife, you may not tempt me with your beauty." Jareb walked behind her and yanked off her head covering and veil. "See the temptation I face every day."

"May you reap every kernel of evil you sow." Ruth rushed between Jareb and Mara. Her protest started the villagers grumbling.

"Abram, remove your wife and leave me to deal with mine."

Abram moved Ruth to the side and put his arm around her waist—whether to hold her up or hold her back Mara could not say. She knew one day Jareb would exact revenge for his scars.

Jareb loosed her hair from the braid that ran down to her waist. "Women, shear her. Leave her hair close-cropped as a newborn lamb."

Not one woman moved.

Naomi shook her finger under Jareb's nose. "If you do this evil, may I never have an heir from *your* bloodline." She flashed a look at Johakim that carried a rebuke.

Jareb shot a confused look at Naomi and Johakim. After a moment, he seemed to shake off his confusion. He grabbed Mara's hair and pulled a dagger from his waist. "I will cut her hair myself."

The high priest moved to Jareb's side and uncurled his son's tight grasp on the dagger. "This is your right. But leave the cutting of her hair to those who care for her." He handed the dagger to his mother.

Ruth joined Naomi and together they carefully lifted a small section of hair at the back of Mara's head. The gritty sound of the knife sawing through her taut lock of hair turned her stomach, but she set a peaceful expression on her face. An expression as unmoving as the Holy Mountain.

Jareb retrieved the curl from the ground and dangled the glistening copper strand in front of her eyes. "I will keep this next to my heart until I come to warm your bed."

"Why? Since you can no longer serve as a priest, have you become a secret sorcerer? Will you use my hair for divination?"

Jareb dropped the curl as if it were a viper.

"You accuse me, yet your moonblood tarried these many years. That is *unnatural*." He glared at Mara with the searing eyes of a demon. "Perhaps *you* are a sorceress."

16

Jericho
Summer, Day after Shavuot
Three years to the day since Samuel fled

Samuel

Samuel languished in his cell, judging day from night only by the strength-sapping heat and the teeth-chattering chill. By his reckoning, he had been imprisoned more than one day, but less than two. He swallowed. Tongue thick, throat parched. Treated worse than a beast of burden, he had not been fed or watered. But neither had he been flogged or tortured. He was entombed in a cave. Forgotten.

HaShem, remember your lowly servant.

Samuel felt along the stone wall searching for a damp spot. He licked the stone sweat, tasting the grit and sulfur and age.

Suddenly the cell door screeched open. His heart flipped

and he flung his arms across his eyes against the blinding torchlight.

"Herod has called for you." The overseer helped Samuel to his feet.

"May HaShem reward you." Samuel climbed the stairs, stretching his stiff legs. The late morning sun warmed his chilled bones, but the white light watered his eyes and blurred his sight.

The priest, the Levite, and the Chief Priest of Jericho waited near one of the many mikvahs scattered across the city. Their hair and beards were still wet from the purifying bath.

Samuel and the overseer approached the holy men who sniffed and covered their noses with their hands.

The chief priest pointed down a nearby hill. "Show him to the wadi to wash away the stench of the dungeon."

The overseer lifted Samuel's shackled hands. "You dare bring him before Herod in chains? The king is in high temper today."

"Release him." Worry crept into the chief priest's voice.

The guards unlocked his hands and feet.

Samuel rubbed his chaffed wrists.

The overseer led Samuel down to the stream. "Hurry. Wash. The king is waiting."

Samuel waded into the fast-running stream, his skin tingling under the icy flow. He dunked under, let his clothes billow, and stood, shaking the water from his body.

He returned in time to see the high priest hand his carving to the overseer who stared with dismay. "You are dripping wet."

"Let us go, I will dry quickly in this heat."

At the palace gate, the overseer produced his amulet, and the group was led across a large courtyard, through a stone arch to a banquet hall. A richly dressed man sat in a highbacked chair in the center of a dais at the head table. His short, cropped hair and trimmed beard were worn in the style of the Romans.

This must be Herod. The man he had prayed to meet. The man who could grant him sanctuary, restore his family name, wipe away his shame. But now, given the grave charges against him, he could not ask Herod for anything.

Samuel's accusers did not cross the threshold.

Herod's eyes flashed something sinister, something terrifying. "Now, most esteemed holy men, tell me why my gardener was arrested."

The chief priest waved to Herod from the doorway. "We have priestly duties and cannot enter your house."

Herod rose and pointed. "You breached my fields and abducted my gardener." Herod spoke through gritted teeth. "I ... will not ... come out."

Samuel looked back. The three men seemed to come to some agreement.

Both priests remained outside, while the Levite scuttled to Herod.

"Justify your trespass upon my land." Herod's tone simmered with barely contained fury.

The priest took a step back. "We spotted this man carving a graven image. Blatantly defying the Law."

"What say you, gardener?"

"The Law forbids fashioning an idol *for worship*."

"You have twisted the clear meaning of the Law."

Herod's glare halted the Levite's protest. "On many matters three rabbis will hold steadfastly to four opinions." Herod's smile was laced with scorn. "Chief Priest speak." Herod's booming voice echoed through the hall.

"This Samaritan *dog* flaunts his warped interpretation of the Law." The chief priest of Jericho matched Herod's thunderous tone.

Herod's face went dark and dangerous. "Tell me, priest, is the son of a Jewish mother a Jew?"

"Yes. Since the time of Moses."

Samuel's chest lightened. The chief priest was about to learn how badly he had mis-stepped.

"It follows, then, the son of a Samaritan woman is a Samaritan. And a *dog*." Herod's face was a death mask. "It is well known that my mother was a Samaritan."

The faces of Samuel's accusers went ashen.

"Pontius Pilate is Prefect here, but *I* have the Prefect's ear." Herod rose. "The accusation was made on my land, against my gardener." He strode across the dais. "Judgment should be left to me. Do you not agree?"

Each accuser barely dipped his head, resentment flickering on their faces.

"Speak. While you still have tongues to answer."

"Your judgment will stand." The chief priest sounded as if he had been chewing sand.

Herod returned to his chair. A look of curiosity crossed his face. "Show me the carving that has caused such strife."

The overseer handed the wooden square to Herod. The king traced the outline of the forge with a finger and seemed to study the emerging horse's head. "Gardener, why carve this?"

"My Lord." Samuel bowed. "It is a sign for the forge and stable."

The Levite pointed at Samuel. "Why not write the sign?"

Samuel looked only at Herod. "This close to Jerusalem, which language should I use? Hebrew, Latin, Greek, Aramaic? Some cannot read. All can decipher a picture."

Herod held up the unfinished carving. "Chief Priest, tell me what you see."

"A lit forge. The head of a horse."

"No images are lawful?" Herod stroked his beard.

"That is the Law."

Samuel's temper flared at the simpering tone of the high priest.

"Priest. What are those bells attached to the hem of your robes?"

"Pomegranates crafted in silver."

"So, your very garments feature a graven image."

"These bells remind the people that the hundreds of aspects of the Law are like the many-seeded pomegranate."

The king's eyes flashed with the hunter's thrill of a kill. "Then staring at the pomegranate could encourage worship of the Law rather than the Lord. In fact, the Sadducees make such charges against the Pharisees."

The chief priest's face flushed crimson and he entered the room. "Unlike the horse, the pomegranate has no breath of life, so it is an unlikely object of worship."

"Gardener, have you anything more to say in your defense?"

"Though horses may serve the gods, neither Romans nor Greeks worship horses. The Canaanites and Egyptians have no horse god. And no one in Samaria has ever worshiped a horse."

Herod turned the carving toward the high priest. "The horse in this scene depends upon man for food, shelter, and care—hardly a god-like creature." Herod lifted the carving high. "This sign is meant for trade—not worship."

The chief priest's displeasure rumbled in his throat. "At least command this man to cease from such work." The chief priest straightened. His stance proud, unyielding.

"You push me too far." Herod jumped up and spat at the feet of the holy men. "Did not Solomon's throne have a lion carved at each arm? Did not each tribe of Israel have a banner and a symbol? Do not try my patience with such drivel. Or you may find that the fields you rent from me are twice the price." Herod sneered. "Or not available at all. Now leave me."

Samuel's accusers hurried away.

Herod leaned forward to return the sign to Samuel, but abruptly pulled it back and stared. "You carved the sign of wheat and grapes at the Jericho Inn."

"Yes. A gift of thanks for the innkeeper."

The king handed the sign to Samuel and lifted his hand in dismissal. "Enough of this foolish sea-battle in a wash basin."

Samuel and the overseer backed with respect toward the door. No sane man ever turned his back on Herod.

Samuel studied his feet. His spirit seemed to sink to his toes. He did not dare ask for sanctuary. And he might never see Herod again.

"Gardener ..."

Samuel looked up. A look of inspiration lit Herod's face. "I have a commission for you."

Shechem

Mara

Naomi and Mara stood at Jacob's Well at first light. It had been two weeks since Mara's hair had been shorn. She turned away from a lone woman approaching, unwilling to confront either the judgment or pity in her eyes.

"Tamara." Ruth's voice reached out. Mara turned and ran into the arms of the only mother she had ever known. The stone wall around her heart crumbled and her tears flowed freely. The burden of woe knotted in her stomach began to unravel.

For a long moment, Ruth hugged her tighter, then stepped back.

Mara looked away. "I cannot bear for anyone to see my shame."

"No need to shrink from me." Ruth gently eased Mara's head-covering down. "It is barely dawn and already sweltering."

Even though Mara could hear the love in Ruth's voice, she could not meet her eyes.

Ruth stroked Mara's scalp and laughed softly. "The soft down of a chick. You could not possibly recall, but you had no hair until you had seen two Passovers, so I remember this look quite fondly."

An amused twitch flickered at the corner of Naomi's lips. "There was once a baby boy who had no hair and his ears stuck out."

Ruth wagged a finger at Naomi. "My Samuel grew into those ears and the village girls thought him quite the catch."

Mara remembered and laughed. *May Samuel, too, find some laughter amidst our sorrows.*

The murmur of the women walking to the well floated on the morning breeze. Ruth arranged Mara's headcover. The three women finished drawing water and left.

They passed a cluster of young girls who glanced at Mara with wariness. Some crossed the road, as if her ill fortune might be catching. And Jareb had seeded suspicions that Mara practiced the dark arts.

A low rumble at Mara's back grew to the thunder of galloping horses. Three riders sped past them. One reined hard, his mount rearing.

Okpara. Mara pressed a palm to her galloping heart. Once his stallion settled, he motioned for her to come close, well away from Naomi and Ruth.

"My drawings have borne fruit. The murderer has been sighted."

"Where?" Mara kept her face and voice calm.

"Both Hebron and Golan."

Ancient cities of refuge. But she had sent Samuel to Jerusalem.

"The servants were loose-lipped." Okpara rubbed his thumb against two fingers. "I paid good coin."

"When did they see him?"

"Six months and three months past." He lifted his reins. "Now to Master Jareb."

"My husband ..." Mara gritted her teeth at the word. "... is hunting with his brother."

"When he returns, tell him I have news." He turned and rode toward the House of the High Priest.

She would never tell Jareb.

Naomi and Ruth joined Mara.

"What has that slimy snake to do with you?" Naomi asked, curling her upper lip.

Naomi's disgust pricked at Mara's shame. She felt slimy too. "He bid me tell Jareb of his return."

"He spoke many more words than these." A war of emotions played across Ruth's face. Hope for word Samuel was alive. Fear for word he was dead.

Mara laughed. A sound that seemed false to her ears. "Okpara always begins with an elaborate tale highlighting his clever ways."

"Any news of Samuel?" Ruth wrung the front of her robe.

Mara took Ruth's hand. "Okpara's word is not trustworthy."

"Come." Naomi took a few steps. "Our households need this fresh water."

They walked up the hill. Mara's refusal to release Jareb

from his vows meant she was heading back to a prison without shackles, without locks. A prison of her own making.

17

Herod's Palace, Jericho
Late Fall

Samuel

Samuel sanded the olivewood bench he fashioned for Herod's new woman. A carved garden bench with a peacock pair forming the back had been Herod's idea. For five new moons Samuel had met with him often— to plan the private garden, choose the wood for the bench, and hone the design. Never once had Samuel dared to ask for sanctuary. Each time he had been tempted, a small voice spoke to his soul. *Be still and know that I am Lord.*

Samuel knelt and ran his fingers over the peacock's tail fanning out behind his mate, the peahen's head resting against his breast. The king wanted to inlay the tail with jewels. But Samuel convinced him the unadorned flow of the wood grain was more suited to the garden escape.

He prayed the king's paramour would be so pleased with the bench, he would be granted a favor.

The palace buzzed with rumors of the king's lust match. Samuel gathered hints during the time he spent with Herod. She lived in this palace as a child. Herod met her on the shores of Caesarea while awaiting a ship to Rome. Samuel kept his own counsel, but he suspected the king's paramour was Herodias. His niece. And his brother's wife.

Someone came up behind him.

"My lady arrives within the week." Herod's tense tone shattered the serenity of the garden. "This bench must be finished."

Samuel remained on his knee and turned. "All that is needed is an anointing with oil and buffing to a warm glow."

Herod drew near and caressed the neck of the peahen. "You will unveil this masterpiece for my queen."

"I would be honored."

The king had *married* the mystery woman.

"It is not every man I allow near her." Herod laughed, but his tone was barbed with warning. He grabbed the corner of his cloak, flung it over his shoulder, and strode away.

Samuel finished and gathered his tools. He glanced at the low sun and rushed toward the forge. The market of Jericho was crowded with farmers closing their stalls and shopkeepers shuttering their doors. Both the young and old hurried home before sunset ushered in Sabbath rest.

Dex also ceased work at sunset out of respect for Samuel's faith. But today Samuel arrived early, and the forge fire was already doused. Something was amiss.

Dex waved him into the stable and slid the door shut. "A messenger from Barid arrived for you an hour ago. We must go to the inn at once."

"Why would Barid send for me? And on the Sabbath?"

"It must be a matter of life and death ... probably yours." Dex's words were clipped and dripped with impatience. He yoked an ox to a large cart. "I will drive you under a pile of straw with barrels of barley beer tucked close around you."

Samuel climbed in the back and Dex spread a thick layer of straw over him. Dex grunted and the barrels scraped as they were lugged into place.

Samuel pulled his robe over his nose and mouth and fought the urge to cough on straw dust. The stable door creaked open, and the cart lurched forward. Samuel settled on his side.

The rocking of the cart should have lulled him to sleep, but the churning of his gut kept him on edge. He had never left the boundary of Jericho where he could run for refuge or vanish into the crowds.

After several miles, the oxcart stopped. Dex whistled softly.

Livestock bleating, lowing, braying. The tramping of a crowd. They must be stopping for a caravan. Camels bellowed, their drivers shouted.

Samuel closed his fingers around the dagger at his waist. He had been betrayed by a camel driver once. And, on the road to Jericho one never knew if a stranger was friend or foe.

"Blessings on your House." Dex called, not a shred of anxiety in his voice.

Samuel peered through the straw. The sky was deep scarlet. The sun and his heart sank into the oncoming dark.

"Stay down." Dex whispered to Samuel and started up again.

When the ground levelled out, the oxcart slowed. "Barid. Is there room at the inn?"

"You are my only guest. Theo will tend the ox. Drive around the back."

The stable door creaked open. And shut. Samuel sat up and stretched.

A man with a crutch stumbled back against the feed trough. "You gave me a fright."

Samuel startled. Theo was the Jew he had rescued. "No more than you did long ago." Samuel climbed down, laughing. "I hid by your bed. Then you sat up. Risen from the dead."

"You must be Samuel. My deliverer from bandits and burial." Theo grinned, a gap between his front teeth.

Dex handed Theo the reins. "Join us when the ox is settled."

He leaned heavily on his crutch and led the ox away.

Samuel's mind flooded with the memory of the beaten Jew. "Poor man."

"Come." Dex clapped Samuel on the shoulder. "He does not seek your pity." They headed for the stable door. "Theo will not leave this place."

"Is he not entirely right in the head?" Samuel kept his voice low.

"Most of his memory is as lame as his leg." Dex tilted his head. "Theo is the name Barid gave him. He does not remember his birth name, his family, his home. But he searches the face of every traveller, seeking the pitiless priest and Levite who left him to die. Their faces haunt his dreams and his days. Barid fears what he may do if he ever comes eye-to-eye with those heartless men."

Glancing back, Samuel watched Theo shift, hobbling on his too-short crutch. After Sabbath he would make a longer one. Samuel's stomach soured. Once before, he fashioned a crutch, and the ungrateful wretch betrayed him.

Okpara. A dread chill crept across Samuel's neck. Within the space of an hour, he had thought of the evil Egyptian twice.

Dex opened the stable door. "Pull up your mantle."

Samuel covered his head, pulling his chin back into a tunnel of folds and followed Dex to the inn.

Barid flung open the door, pulled Samuel into the room, and flashed a tight smile, his brow cinched into a frown. "May all the gods be with you. Your god. My gods."

Dex stepped in and closed the door. "And any unknown god." He held up a fist, thumb wedged between his mid-two fingers.

Barid made the same sign. "Do you think the Roman fig fist will ward off evil for a Samaritan?"

Dex shrugged. "It cannot harm."

"Why did you send for me?"

"The Avenger sent new spies throughout all of Judea." Barid gestured for them to sit at the table.

"The land is filled with Samaritans and gardeners—many resemble me. Why are you so distraught?"

Barid reached into his robe and passed Samuel a small parchment. "Jareb's spies carry this."

Samuel was confronted with his own likeness. His stomach churned and his thoughts rippled in befuddled circles. "No Samaritan or Jew would draw this." The parchment began to slip from his shaking hand.

Barid took it. "Jareb has an Egyptian servant with a peculiar memory for faces and a particular talent for rendering them."

"Okpara." Samuel winced with revulsion. The man had betrayed him twice.

Theo came in from the stable.

"Samuel has seen his likeness."

Theo took the parchment from Barid, crossed out into the courtyard, and tossed the drawing in the fire. "Now that forbidden image will not bring judgment on this house."

"The Egyptian has drawn many more." Dex frowned as he did when the molten metal would not mold perfectly beneath his mallet.

Theo served bread and barley beer. He hobbled toward Samuel, his face contorting with pain.

Samuel's palms slicked, remembering the agony of his own beating by the high priest's sons.

"You have a choice." Barid lifted his beer and drank deeply. "Run from Jericho. Or throw yourself at Herod's feet."

Samuel chewed a bite of bread, buying a moment to consider. A lump of dread clumped around the bread dropping down his throat.

The look on Dex's face went from friend to soldier. "Do not delay. Delay is a death-trap."

Samuel looked around the table at the faces of Dex, Barid, and Theo. "Herod has been pleased with my work. My best chance is at Herod's feet."

Dex propped his chin on his fist. "His moods are mercurial but—"

A woman's scream startled them all.

A clang of swords. Grunts of a fight.

"We must save her." Samuel unsheathed his short sword. Dex and Barid followed his lead.

Theo stood, dagger drawn, leaning on his crutch.

Barid glanced at him. "You best serve here. Prepare for the wounded."

Samuel charged out the door, Barid and Dex at his heels. They slowed at the road and crept around a blind curve.

A curtained litter was under attack. The liveried guards were slain. Three of the four bearers had fallen. The last bearer was run through before Samuel's eyes. The litter tipped and hung precariously over the steep cliff.

Barid slew two of the bandits and left Dex to finish the last one.

"The litter." Samuel ran toward it.

Barid grabbed a corner of the litter booth.

Samuel parted the curtains. A woman sprawled against the far wall.

"Do not move. Give me your hands. Slowly. One at a time." Taking care not to shift the litter, Samuel reached both arms deep into the booth.

"Do not touch me, I am Royalty." The woman's face was in shadow, but the conceit in her tone was on full display.

"Any men here who bear remnants of royalty are dead. And they were your attackers." Samuel could not keep his tone free from scorn.

The litter shifted. Barid groaned.

"Powerful men have plotted against me before." Her words were strong as iron but there was a tell-tale quiver in her voice.

Dex rushed in and grabbed the other end of the litter. His shoulders shook under the strain.

Samuel's fear flared to white-hot fury. "Take hold. Your litter is a hairsbreadth from toppling over a cliff.

"Haul my litter back onto sure ground."

"Grab hold or I will withdraw my arms. Why should we plunge to our deaths at the whim of a spoiled woman?"

Samuel's words struck their mark. The lady latched onto his arms, her nails digging deep into his flesh.

"Hurry." Barid moaned.

Samuel dragged her toward him. The litter shifted. Neither Dex nor Barid could keep hold. Samuel yanked her violently against his chest.

The litter crashed over the cliff.

The royal woman stepped back, adjusted her head covering and robes. "Bring torches."

His friends, winded and spent, stared at the demanding woman.

She drew herself up and crossed her arms.

Barid ran to fetch torches.

Samuel sucked in air and scowled at the woman of obvious privilege.

She regarded him with the cold golden eyes of an owl. No sigh of relief. No tears. No words of thanks.

Dex shot a challenging look toward the lady. "Be alert for a new attack. These rich men were no ordinary bandits."

"An extraordinary woman has extraordinary enemies." She lifted her chin and stepped close to the first corpse. "I will inspect the dead."

Barid returned with the torches. "It is fortunate my inn was quiet tonight, or we would not have heard your scream."

"I do not scream." The woman's glare was as sharp as an obsidian blade. "Ever."

Had the horror of the last moments left her addled?

She gestured toward a body. "Show me his face."

Dex rolled the dead man.

She looked and moved on. "Search each corpse for papers or scars."

Samuel lifted his torch above the next victim. A young woman. The screamer. He looked to the royal woman.

"My favorite handmaid." Her eyes flicked over the lifeless girl. "I suppose we must cart her to Jericho for burial."

The woman strolled through the carnage as if she were in her private garden. "A bodyguard is missing. He was either coward or spy. Either way, he will rue the day he was born."

Dex beat a fist against his chest, the traditional salute. "The justice of Rome will be served."

"When the missing guard is captured, only I will determine the manner of his death." She turned her raptor-like eyes toward Samuel. "An offense to me or mine is never forgotten."

Samuel left this royal woman no choice but to touch him. And she had taken offense. His heart slammed against his breastbone with the force of a battering ram. This woman, whoever she may be, was merciless, heartless, soulless. But above all, she was ruinous.

"What of these other bodies?" Dex lapsed into the role of loyal soldier.

"Strip the attackers of their weapons and armor. They may reveal their patron." The royal woman pulled her mantle closer. "My servants and guards ..." She pointed. "... here, here, and here. Collect their worldly goods for their kinsmen but cast all bodies into the ravine."

Dex glared outrage. "My lady, with respect, your guards felled in battle have earned burial rites."

She straightened, a warning flare in her glare. "I will not enter the Winter Palace and greet my new husband escorted by a troop of rotting corpses."

Samuel had enraged the new queen. His stomach seized as if he had been impaled by a carpenter's gouge. Herod may be an old fox, but Herodias was a she-wolf.

18

Shechem

Late Fall

Mara

"Mara, come quickly."

Abram's choked call came from the front gate.

In the kitchen, Mara stopped rinsing a clay plate and looked up at Naomi. "Something terrible has happened."

"We come." Naomi arranged her head coverings. "Remember your veil."

Mara ran outside.

Abram looked haggard, bone-weary. "Ruth wants to bid you final farewell."

"How can this be? We visited two days past." Shock and sadness set Mara's heart sprinting.

"A sudden fever. Last night she seemed better, but at first light ..." Abram's voice stumbled into a soft sob.

Naomi handed Mara her veil. "Go. I will follow."

Mara rushed toward Ruth's house. Her racing heart snagged on a bitter root. "A sudden fever should smite Jareb, not Ruth." She entered the dimly lit room and removed her veil. Soft amber light from nearby oil lamps crowned Ruth's face. Mara took Ruth's hand, timeworn by labors of love.

She opened her eyes. "Come close." Her whisper was soft but steady.

Mara sat on the raised sleeping pallet and dabbed a damp towel gently across Ruth's brow.

She brushed her knuckles against Mara's cheek. For as long as Mara could remember, this touch had offered her safety, comfort, love.

"My girl, my life has been filled with blessings." She cradled Mara's cheek in her palm and met her eyes. "*Tamara, my sweetness, do not mourn me.*"

Mara could not keep back one lone tear. "Samuel should be here." An ember of bitterness flared.

"Shh." Ruth drew small circles on Mara's hand with her thumb. Mara was a little girl again, Ruth drawing circles to soothe her to sleep. "Though HaShem has not reunited me with Samuel in this life, we will be together in the next one."

Cold dread made Mara shiver. Was this a sign Samuel was dead?

"HaShem will keep my son safe in the palm of His hand." Ruth patted Mara's arm and took slow small breaths. "Shalom. I have no fear of death."

Mara coveted Ruth's calm, but capturing her peace was like trying to collect sand in a sieve. "It eases my sorrow that you are at peace, without fear or regrets."

Ruth gazed away. "Oh, I do have one regret."

"Do you wish to share?" Mara leaned closer.

"The Promised One is now a man who walks amongst us. I

will not live to see him with my own eyes." Ruth's voice was hushed, but earnest.

Bright rays of sun shone through the high window and swathed Ruth in golden light.

"May HaShem grant me the wisdom to know him when he comes." Mara squeezed Ruth's hand.

Abram and Naomi entered and went straight to Ruth's side. She reached up and brushed the cheeks of each one like a mother caressing her precious newborn.

Ruth turned back to Mara. "You are the keeper of the Persian coin your mother left for you. Proof the Magi passed this way. They believed the new-born King of the Jews might also be the Promised One of Samaria."

Mara felt as if a heavy mantle yoked her shoulders. She looked down.

"You are trembling. What troubles you?" Ruth lifted Mara's chin.

Mara wanted to lie but if she did, she would live with the shame that she held back the truth from Ruth.

"The coin is gone."

Ruth shuddered.

"Was it stolen or lost?" Ruth's voice now so small, Mara strained to hear her.

"I gave the coin to Samuel. He had need of it when he fled for his life."

"My girl, do not fret." She gazed toward the door seeming to search for the future there. "The Magi foretold any who owned the coin would come to know the Taheb."

Ruth smiled and sighed. "Samuel has the coin. May he meet the Promised One face to face. And even though I will not, I know the Redeemer lives."

"Bless you, Mara." Abram's voice cracked under the weight

of his sorrows. "Because of your sacrifice, our son had the means to escape."

"Husband."

Abram took Ruth's hand. "Yes, my Beloved." He kissed her cheek.

"One day Mara will bear Samuel a son. Our line will live on." Now Ruth's voice was as weak as the chirp of a wounded bird. Her life-light faded as the sun set over Shechem and her last breath.

In that moment, something sacred seemed to rustle through the room. And Mara's soul.

"All is well." Abram kissed Ruth's hand. "Blessed be the name of the Lord."

Jericho

Nearly three years six months since Samuel fled

Samuel

Samuel paced outside the gate to the Queen's Garden. A month had passed since he had completed the peacock bench. A month since the fateful attack on Herodias. The next day, the queen had summoned Dex and Barid into Herod's presence. Both men had been richly rewarded. Samuel had been richly ignored.

Samuel prayed Herodias clung more to gratitude for deliverance from death than to offense over his unwanted touch and reckless words.

"Enter." Herodias sat running her palm along the edge of the wooden peacock's tail. Herod stood behind the bench gazing down at his queen.

The pebbled walkway crunched beneath Samuel's steps.

Herod looked up. "My queen desired to meet the man whose creation has so pleased her."

Samuel stole a quick look at her face.

Herodias snuffed her flicker of recognition.

Samuel lowered his eyes and knelt.

"Rise." She extended her hand.

Samuel kissed her ring, taking care not to touch her hand.

"I would reward your work. In your art there is subtlety. A subtlety that may not mark other aspects of your life."

Samuel waited in disciplined silence, determined not to visibly bristle at the queen's jibe.

"My love, how will you reward this man? "Herod kissed the top of her head.

"You must help me choose." She rose and moved where the golden sunlight shimmered on her cheeks and neck.

This woman even used the sun to her advantage.

"His weight in gold." Herod gave Samuel a look as if they were soldiers in league with one another.

Samuel's jaw tightened. He needed sanctuary. Gold would do him no good in the grave.

"Something unique." The queen's eyes glinted in a way he could not read. "Commission something monumental that will establish your name and his for generations."

Samuel's gut twisted around the suspicion Herodias might be setting a trap.

"Yes. For my new city, Tiberius." Herod clapped his hands. "Samuel, what say you?"

"Nothing would please me more."

A fragment of a frown creased the queen's brow. "I hear a hesitation. There is something more?"

HaShem, put wise words in my mouth. "Perhaps my Lady would use her sway with the king on my behalf."

"Someone has taught you the safety of a tame tongue."

Humiliation singed Samuel's cheeks.

The queen looked fondly toward Herod. "Continue."

"Yosef of Arimathea advised me to beg the king for sanctuary."

"I am not the Tetrarch or High Priest here." Herod moved to sit on the bench and patted a place at his side.

Herodias joined him.

The king turned away, caressed his wife's knee, and traced a finger upward, as if they were alone.

She placed her hand over his. "You forget this man's reward."

The king turned back to Samuel. "Why do you need sanctuary?"

Samuel recounted the fateful day when his sickle blade flung free.

"And why did Yosef send you to me?"

"I could not flee to any city in Samaria. But you are called King of the Jews. Rome has appointed you Tetrarch of Galilee, and your mother was queen of Judea, but born a Samaritan. You are the only man in all the world whose judgment all three factions would accept."

Herod looked uncertain. "My lady?"

"My Fox. I am certain your quick mind has already devised a way to avoid offense to the Prefect Pontius Pilate and the High Priest Caiaphas."

"Indeed. They are expected here tonight." Herod's cackle sent a dread shiver down Samuel's spine.

The queen caressed the long neck of the peacock. "This woodwork is exquisite. I would mourn the loss of such artistry."

"My queen. No man can resist your requests." Herod stroked his beard. "You shall present this man's case."

"As you wish." The queen appeared astonished but pleased.

Herod bent, kissed his queen on the lips, and waved Samuel away. "Report to the palace gate at sunset."

Samuel rushed to the forge to seek counsel from Dex.

"First you must thoroughly wash. All priests are obsessed with the clean and the unclean, but Caiaphas is reported to be particularly offput by any earthy odor. His use of incense and perfumes borders on the effete." Dex spat the last word.

"And Pilate?"

"Pontius Pilate wants to be known as a just man. With him, stress your innocence."

Dex threw Samuel a linen towel. "Make haste. The woman who cooked my supper tonight will groom you."

"How much longer will the fathers of Jericho let their daughters vie for your favor?"

"In truth, the woman you meet tonight has won my heart, though her cooking yet needs some motherly nurture."

Samuel smiled to himself. Mara's meals had often needed Ima's ministrations. He hurried down to the stream behind the forge and splashed in the icy water.

When he returned to the house a tall, raven-haired Roman beauty trimmed his hair and beard. Dex handed him a cup of wine and set a plate of cheese, olives, and flatbread before him. "It would not help your cause to faint from hunger before powerful men."

Samuel partook but tasted nothing. After more than three long-suffering years, his fate would be sealed in less than the span of the next watch.

The young woman cleared the table.

"I must leave, the sun is low." Samuel lifted his chin toward her. "You have chosen well."

Dex lifted his cup. "May your unseen god go before you, go with you, and go behind you."

"From your lips to the Lord's ears." Samuel finished his wine.

"And may my gods give you favor with Rome, Judea, and Samaria."

A shudder of revulsion ran through Samuel. He would never seek the favor of any powerless pagan god.

Samuel headed for the palace gate. The sun set behind the city wall. A servant met Samuel and brought him to wait behind one of the portico pillars in the palace courtyard.

From his vantage, he watched a large retinue reclining at supper. Caiaphas at a separate table at Herod's right was served separate food. Herodias reclined on Herod's left, dressed in crimson in the style of Rome. At times, she rested her head on the king's chest and spoke so only he could hear.

Pontius Pilate dined at the left hand of the queen. He seemed to relish the proximity and more than once reached out as if he would caress her. Each time, she artfully avoided his touch. Each time, Herod's eyes blazed with possessive fury.

Pilate reached for a curl nestled at Herodias' bosom, but she rose from her couch, leaving his fingers pinching air.

Caiaphas leapt up. "Among our people, no man may touch another man's wife." The high priest's tone was well-honeyed, but undertones of vinegar bit through.

Pilate's eyes narrowed, face flushed blood-red. "Your queen dresses as a ravishing Roman lady. For a moment, I was home in the Eternal City where no such provincial prohibitions are the custom." His words seemed part prideful excuse and part sincere apology.

Herod's expression remained thunderous. "Even so, there is no place under the sun where any man who touches my wife will live."

173

Samuel had touched Herodias. His knees turned to sludge. He leaned back and slid down the pillar. In truth, she had grabbed him when her litter plunged over the cliff. Perhaps she was shielding him. More likely, the she-wolf was protecting herself from Herod's jealous rage.

Pontius Pilate shot a murderous look at Herod.

Herodias rose between the two men, swirling her layered diaphanous tunic. "Bring my harp. If it would please my lords, I would calm two prowling lions with song."

A stool was placed where all could see, and Herodias arranged her tunic to drape beautifully. She cradled a harp in her lap. Her long, graceful fingers slowly plucked a melody. A well-known shepherd's love song in the ancient tongue. A song of love for the land and for the shepherdess.

A single tear trickled down Herod's cheek. He captured it in an alabaster ampule. The last haunting note hung suspended in the air. The guests, in awe-struck silence, waited for the tone to die.

They erupted with enthusiastic applause.

Pontius Pilate stood clapping. "The song seems to have great meaning."

Herodias nodded to him. "A song sung since our people were ruled by Shepherd Kings." She plucked a strong chord that commanded attention. "Now, an offering in honor of Rome's beginnings."

She strummed the harp in lively fashion and sang an ode to the wolf that nurtured Romulus and Remus, twins who founded Rome. Between the sung verses, her fingers flew like butterflies showing her absolute command of the instrument.

At the last jubilant chord, Pontius Pilate jumped to his feet, and flung a kiss into the air. "Magnificent. Will you teach my harpist? For this song would be much admired at the court of Emperor Tiberius in Rome."

"Gladly." Herodias turned to the nearby scribe. "You did record all the words?"

He nodded.

Pilate laughed. "Do you alter the words with your audience?"

"No, my lord. The tune and the text were composed now as you heard them."

A bolt of fear burned through Samuel's veins. This brilliant, cunning queen could no more be trusted than a wolf in a sheepfold.

Pilate swept an arm across the room claiming the banquet hall was now under his authority. "What favor would Herod's queen request of Rome?"

"A woodworker has placed a dilemma before my husband." She waved Samuel forward. "I seek the wisdom of both you and High Priest Caiaphas. I would assure he continues to create carvings for me."

Pontius Pilate turned to Herod. "Tell me the dilemma."

Herod recounted Samuel's predicament with uncharacteristic empathy.

Caiaphas rose. "The Samaritan High priest has authority. However, as father of the victim, his judgment would be tainted."

"Both Samaritans and Jews seek to serve the God of Abraham, Isaac, and Jacob." Herod's speech seemed a mixture of prejudice and pride.

Pontius Pilate sat on his couch and looked from Herod to Caiaphas. "Since Herod Antipas rules over Jews and is the son of a Samaritan woman, the suggestion that he hear the plea for sanctuary seems a clever compromise. A compromise Rome would welcome and endorse."

Samuel held his breath and his chest tightened around his rising hope.

"Send a message to High Priest Johakim at Shechem." Pilate signaled a nearby scribe. "By order of Rome, all concerned must appear at the bema in Jericho one week hence. Herod, Caiaphas, and I will preside at the judgment seat."

The High Priest of Jerusalem reined in a rebellious look "As Rome ... umm ..." He cleared his throat as if he had swallowed a gnat. "Requests."

Samuel might be granted sanctuary. He freed his captive breath.

"The new Prefect Pontius Pilate has confirmed his reputation as a just man." Herod's tone was oiled with flattery. "Peace in Judea is fragile. May your trust in my rule grow."

The scribe presented the parchment.

Pilate signed it with a flourish.

Herod turned to Herodias. "Warn your woodworker to stay within the walls of the Winter Palace where my protection is clad with iron."

Herodias offered Herod a small smile of approval.

In one week, Samuel's fate would be sealed. His stomach churned a slurry of knee-weakening worry and chest-lifting hope.

19

Shechem

Mara

Mara poured freshly drawn well water into large standing stone jars just outside the kitchen door at the Palace of the High Priest. In the nearby tree, a pair of doves cooed a quiet evensong, lulling the setting sun and Shechem to sleep.

For three days, Ruth slept with her ancestors in the family burial cave. For three days, Abram did not sleep or eat or weep. Finally, when Mara visited this morning, he took a morsel of bread. For three days, Mara had carried Abram's grief and cast hers away.

A Roman runner rushed into the courtyard. Mara's pulse throbbed in her neck and her swallow was tight.

Johakim and Jareb came out to meet him.

Mara gathered her courage and slipped behind a tree.

Jareb sneered at the runner clutching his knees, gasping for breath.

Johakim looked worried, whether for the man near collapse or the content of his message, she could not say.

The runner took out a small parchment scroll wrapped in leather.

Jareb lunged for it and the runner moved the message behind his back. Jareb's hand went to his sword.

Johakim blocked Jareb. "Be still. The runner must follow orders."

The messenger straightened, chest lifted. "To Johakim, High Priest of Samaria, and Jareb, the Avenger of Blood. By order of Pontius Pilate, you must appear in Jericho at the seat of judgment four days hence. Samuel ben Abram has been granted refuge in Jericho until his trial."

Mara's heart bumped like a rock rolling down a steep cliff. Praise HaShem, Samuel was alive. She hugged herself and strained to hear over the drumming in her ears.

"Bring all witnesses and evidence. Herod, Caiaphas, and Pontius Pilate will render judgment." The runner placed the scroll in the High Priest's hand.

"I will compose my response."

"Only your presence is required."

A flicker of shock hardened into a look of anger on Johakim's face. "Rome and the Jews usurp my authority."

"Make ready for the trip." Jareb motioned for Okpara, standing near a column.

Mara stepped into view. "I will feed the runner."

"Of course." Johakim nodded absently.

Mara led the runner to the kitchen and served bread, honeycomb, and wine. "Tell me, is Samuel well?" Though her eyes were dry, she could not banish the tears from her tone.

The runner crammed a piece of honeycomb into his mouth

and seemed to study her eyes. His look softened. "He is as safe as any man who has caught the particular attention of the queen."

A vulture of jealousy thrust a talon into Mara's chest and plucked out her heart. "What is Samuel to the queen?" Her mind raced and she braced to hear the reply.

"A man greatly favored."

Darkness crowded the edges of Mara's sight.

"Sit before you swoon. He is merely her chosen worker of wood." The runner broke another piece of bread. "Even Herodias would not dare inflame the passionate possessiveness of the king."

His words were a balm. Her wounded heart nestled back into her chest. "Though I cannot pay, please tell Samuel ..."

"Another honeycomb will be payment enough. I will tell him your heart is true."

Jareb invaded the kitchen and grabbed Mara by the arm. His grip shot needles of pain down to her fingers. "Go. Make ready for Jericho."

Mara bit her cheek so she would not cry out. Fear and pain seemed to arouse Jareb's wanton lust for cruelty. And for her.

"You will watch Samuel's name be ruined, watch him be judged guilty. And watch me kill him."

Mara pressed back a scream of outrage, but the smallest scrap of sound whimpered from her lips.

Jareb shoved her toward the door. "I will stake Samuel to the ground." His bloodlust seemed to set the scar on his cheek aflame. "An agony not unlike crucifixion."

Mara ran to the nearest bush and retched. She wiped her mouth and turned toward the sound of someone approaching.

Ozri led a fully laden donkey into the courtyard. Tobiah staggered behind him.

"Why are you here?" Mara searched Ozri's face.

"Jareb has compelled our testimony."

"What witness can you possibly offer?"

Tobiah sneered and Ozri looked at his feet. "Tobiah will not say, and I do not know. But it pains me my words might cause Samuel harm."

"Where is Abram?"

"He mourns Ruth. He will not come."

Anger simmered in Mara's stomach and sorrow clutched at her heart. Abram had left Samuel to face his enemies alone.

Jericho

Mara

On the appointed day, the men dismounted, and the women climbed down from the oxcart. Johakim pounded his priestly staff on the floor of the stone arch into Jericho. He looked imposing in his black turban and robes. "To the bema, the judgment seat."

Jareb fell into stride next to his father. Tobiah followed.

Mara and Naomi adjusted their head-coverings and trailed behind the men.

They passed through the gate into the market and Ozri tethered the mounts and ox. Roman guards were posted every few paces. To the west, under a white canopy, three judgment seats stood on a marble dais. In the center, the iron throne of Rome. A spread-winged eagle formed the back, splayed talons formed the arms.

Mara shook off a cold shiver that made her heart stutter.

To the left, the cedar chair for Caiaphas was carved with pomegranates, the symbol of the Law.

The third chair, bejeweled with malachite, was draped with banners of the tribes of Samaria.

High Priest Johakim walked forward. "We will wait here before the dais."

Naomi put her arm around Mara and pulled her close. "The malachite throne must have belonged to Malthace, the Samaritan mother of Herod Antipas."

"So much pageantry, so many thrones." Mara's voice faltered and faded. "So many judges may not bode well for Samuel."

Mara looked about the square. Sellers arranged their wares, but the market was deadly quiet. No banter between merchants and buyers, no shouts from children at play, no barking from dogs begging for scraps.

A crowd gathered and fragments of talk from a family nearby drifted to Mara's ears.

"Three thrones." An old woman sounded excited.

"The accused must be important." Her grown son looked awestruck.

"This man matters to Herod's harlot." The father spoke too loudly, as if he did not care who heard his insult.

The strapping son punched his father in the jaw, dropping him with one blow. "Barely sunrise and already loose-lipped from wine." He shared a look of disgust with his mother.

"Take your father home before he gets his tongue cut out."

The son slung his senseless father over his shoulder and left.

Mara sent the old woman a sympathetic look. She knew well the destruction a drunkard could wreak.

Jareb stood next to Tobiah. This morning his gait was steady. His eyes were red, but not rheumy. Jareb must have made sure Tobiah was sober. But before midday, the wine cravings would craze his mind and torment his tongue. Then what evil would the man who sired her provoke?

A shofar sounded. The sight of a ram's horn upturned against a daybreak sky never ceased to pebble the skin of Mara's arms.

A charioteer drove Pontius Pilate through the Eastern gate, his standard flying from the rear of his black chariot. The Prefect wore elaborate armor, his helmet topped with a red crista of feathers more suited to a triumphal entry than a trial.

Herod rode into the marketplace astride an alabaster warhorse. His priceless Tyrian purple cloak billowed behind him.

Caiaphas, in richly appointed robes and flowing black turban, entered the marketplace on a well fed, docile donkey. The priest's spidery legs dangled almost to the ground. He looked ridiculous rather than regal. Mara could not suppress a snigger despite the grave situation.

The three judges sat on their thrones. Secular and religious scribes cordoned off separate areas. Servants offered the judges wine. The crowd jostled for position.

Pontius Pilate raised his hand. Silence sliced through the square. "Where is the accused?"

An elaborate litter hung with curtains bearing a gold-threaded pair of peacocks was carried to a prominent place facing the dais. Following the litter, a phalanx of guards surrounded Samuel.

He was guided to a place before the triumvirate, all the while searching the crowd. He finally found Mara's eyes and flashed her a look of longing.

The curtains of the litter were drawn open. Mara leaned forward. A woman lounged in shadowed profile.

Herod smiled. "Ah, my queen, I did not expect you this early for you are more owl than lark."

"My King, I would never miss the meeting of three great minds who seek truth and justice in this perplexing matter."

The queen's melodious voice carried clearly as if she were a born orator. "Before you begin, if I may my lords, I would address the High Priest of Samaria."

A flush, the same scarlet as the dawn behind him, streaked across High Priest Johakim's neck.

Pontius Pilate glanced toward the litter. "If the queen does not speak, we will be left wondering if her words would have altered our course."

Caiaphas frowned but dropped his chin, signaling reluctant consent.

Herodias descended from her litter and turned to High Priest Johakim. "The sudden loss of your youngest son ... I cannot imagine your sorrow. There is nothing in all the known world I would not do to protect my daughter, Salome." Herodias' glistening un-spilt tears only enhanced her charm. "If Samuel is proven a murderer, I would never harbor him." Her hand fluttered to her throat and her voice broke beautifully over a hint of humility.

High Priest Johakim's face softened. "I strive to be a just man."

"Will your heart truly submit to the verdict rendered here today?" The queen's tone was sweet, soothing.

"Why concern yourself with my heart?" Johakim's voice held surprise.

Herodias glanced toward the judges then back to Johakim. "Where your heart goes, there follows the submission of Samaria."

High Priest Johakim placed both hands over his heart. "As a man, I am moved by the queen's compassion. As High Priest of Samaria, I am appalled my authority would be usurped." He sighed deeply. "But, as a father, I am relieved I need not wrestle with judgment of the man who took my son's life."

"Johakim, High Priest of Samaria, will you cede your rule in this matter to me?" Caiaphas almost sounded sympathetic.

"I will. If you will accept a prayer for wisdom from me. For we are both children of Abraham who must serve two masters. Rome and the Lord."

Caiaphas rose, went to Johakim, and lowered his head.

Herod leapt to his feet and joined Caiaphas in front of High Priest Johakim. "Bless me as son of a Samaritan mother."

Pontius Pilate tossed the look of a smitten youth toward Herodias and joined the other before Johakim. "Rome, too, covets the prayers and blessings of all of her subjects."

Johakim raised his hands and blessed all three judges.

A trickle of hope warmed Mara's veins. May the Lord's mercy endure forever.

20

Jericho

Mara

Herod raised his head and stepped back. "Bring the accused, Samuel of Shechem, to stand next to his accuser."

The judges returned to their thrones.

Jareb eyed Samuel and gripped his short sword.

Two guards moved in.

Herod jutted his chin toward Jareb. "Release the sword or lose the hand."

Jareb jerked his hand from the hilt.

Herod pointed at Jareb. "Avenger. Speak."

"At the wheat harvest, three years past, this man murdered my brother."

"Why?"

"He coveted my brother's betrothed. The woman who stands here with us."

"Who are the others with you?"

"The woman's father and the apprentice in the woodworker's shop."

Ozri squirmed and shuffled his feet.

Herod squinted into the early morning sunlight. "The Avenger's father is here. The woman's father is here. Where is the father of the accused?"

Ozri stepped forward. "It grieves me for Samuel to learn this way, but his father mourns the passing of his mother."

Samuel looked like he had been struck by lightning. His hands clutched the neck of his tunic ready to rend it.

"Now is not the time for grief or strife." The queen's sharp tone cut deep. "Woodworker, your mother would want you to keep your wits and speak for your life."

"Let us hear the evidence." Herod sounded as if he was already tiring of the trial.

"Samuel is guilty. I demand my right as Avenger."

Worry wound around Mara's hammering heart.

"Your demands mean nothing." Pontius Pilate flicked his hand toward Jareb. "I say Roman judgment, Roman punishment."

Mara wanted to throw herself at the judges' feet, but kept still. All had witnessed those condemned by Rome lining the roads—ghastly skeletons guarding the gates. The crucified.

Mara gnashed her teeth at the vision of Samuel condemned.

"Proceed." Pontius Pilate shifted on his throne and yawned.

Jareb elbowed Tobiah to step forward.

He drew himself up, clearly relishing the hushed attention

of the crowd. "On the road to Mara's betrothal, Samuel cursed Achor and wished him dead."

Samuel stared, his face stone.

"This man worked in the woodshop with the murderer." Jareb shoved Ozri forward.

"This was the sickle Samuel wielded that day?" Jareb raised the blade in one hand, the handle in the other.

Ozri nodded and slid a sympathetic look toward Samuel.

"How can you be sure?" Jareb's taunt sent a swell of bitter gall into Mara's throat.

Ozri touched the handle. "Samuel carved this mark as victor of the harvest challenge."

Jareb jabbed his knuckle into Ozri's chest. "This blade was found beside my dead brother."

"Yes." Ozri looked like he wanted to drop Jareb into a pit of vipers.

Jareb waved the bloodstained blade and the long handle at Herodias. "You have taken the side of a liar."

She motioned for a servant to take the blade and handle to the judges.

Jareb turned back to the dais. "This murderer tried to hide his sin. The blade was taken from its slot and the leather lashing was cut."

"No!" Mara's mouth betrayed her. "The blade flew through the air and swooped down into the field."

Jareb grabbed her shoulders. "You harlot, you lie to save your lover." He shook her and threw her to the ground.

Dazed, Mara hauled herself to her feet.

Jareb raised his hand to strike.

Caiaphas pounded his staff. "Later, you may do with your wife as you will. Now, you will uphold the dignity of the court."

Jareb lowered his fist. "She bears false witness."

Mara's anger stewed in her stomach, then spewed from her lips. "I saw the blade take flight."

Wide-eyed confusion flickered across Johakim's face. "You saw the death of my son?"

Jareb blocked Mara from the view of his father and the judges. "Under the Law, a woman cannot bear witness."

"Enough. Let us hear from the accused." Herod turned to Samuel.

"Mara speaks true. The blade broke at the peak of my swing and flew over many rows of barley. A man cried out. I ran to the spot where the blade dropped. Achor lay on the ground, the point of the blade buried in his neck. Blood bubbled from the wound ..."

Samuel's voice faltered.

"Mara rushed up a moment later. The wound was clearly mortal. I pillowed Achor's head on my lap and we eased his journey to the afterlife."

Caiaphas rose. "Then, Achor's death was murder without malice."

Jareb stomped. "Lies heaped upon lies."

Pontius Pilate pounded his fist against the arm of his throne. "Romans teach it is better to let ten guilty men go free than to condemn one innocent man to death. I seek the truth. For Rome."

"A lying harlot cannot lead you to truth." Jareb's face purpled and he spat at Mara's feet. "Samuel and Mara plotted together to ambush Achor where no one would see."

The fickle crowd turned hostile, thirsty for blood.

Rotten vegetables and clods of dirt rained around Mara and Samuel's heads.

"They made a fool of him."

Some picked up stones.

"They should die together."

Pontius Pilate signaled the guards at the walls to move in. "Silence."

An uneasy quiet descended on the crowd. They were in close quarters, surrounded by Roman soldiers.

"This woman may be neither harlot nor liar." Pontius Pilate's roar rang across the marketplace. "Let her speak."

Mara chose her words carefully. "I was an unwilling bride. But as the Almighty is my witness, my desperate hope was for divorce, not death." Mara's voice hovered in the slowly stretching silence.

"My Lords." The call of Herodias. If her tone were not so sultry, her low pitch could be taken for that of a man. "You surely have discerned the word of this woman is not needed."

Mara's heart seemed to stop.

Pontius Pilate raised a curious brow.

Caiaphas looked away as if the queen had not spoken.

But the shrewd timbre in Herodias' tone seemed to spark something in Herod's mind.

The king stood, a cunning smile curled his mouth. "My clever queen will enlighten the crowd."

Jareb snarled like a dog that has lost its bone to a stronger cur.

Herod extended his hand and helped Herodias up the stairs onto the dais.

What hubris. Mara was quite certain Herod had no notion what Herodias would say. But he would lay claim to her wisdom. Mara's heart quickened with new hope.

The queen addressed the mob. "The blade bears bloodstains, yet not one drop of blood has soaked the handle. The handle was not attached to the blade when it struck the victim's neck."

Jareb shook both fists. "Then Samuel cut the blade free to

... to make Achor's death seem merely fatal fortune." Jareb stuttered.

Even he did not believe his accusation.

Herodias ignored Jareb. "My Lords, I am sure you have noticed the leather lashing was not cut clean but worn slowly and finally gave way."

The judges inspected the lashing.

Jareb pointed at Mara. "Then my brother's death was not fate, but sorcery." His face contorted and the jagged scar on his cheek looked like a side-winding viper. "I presume the queen knows nothing of witchery."

The crowd murmured like a flock of disgruntled geese.

Herod leapt to his feet, eyes flashing.

Mara glared at Jareb.

"Peace." Herodias lifted her chin and scanned the crowd seeming to dare another to accuse her. "I know nothing of sorcery." She cast an amused smile toward Jareb, a cruel cat torturing a cornered mouse. "And this young woman also knows nothing of sorcery. I would stake my life upon it."

Herod's brows drew together. "How can you be so certain my love?"

Herodias gestured toward Mara. "See how she glares at the avenger. If she possessed a snake's whisper of dark power, this man would already be dead."

The King laughed heartily. "Well spoken." He rose. "We will retire and take refreshment. At the ninth hour our judgment will be announced."

The merchants opened their stalls. Villagers bartered for food and wares. And dogs ran amongst the children.

The people of Jericho were at peace. But Mara and Samuel had been thrown into a tempest that might tear them apart forever.

"We will safeguard the accused in the sanctuary of the

Winter Palace." Herod stood. "Guards. Re-form the queen's escort." The guards surrounded Samuel.

Herodias called out to the last guard in line. "And bring the Avenger's unwilling wife. I would not have harm befall her before judgment."

Jareb shot a glare loaded with poisoned arrows at Mara.

She ran from the dais and squeezed between guards to Samuel's side but did not dare touch him.

Naomi pushed through to Mara. "Where you go, I must go."

Herodias turned to Naomi. "What right do you have to intrude?"

"I am Naomi, the mother of the High Priest of Samaria. Since Mara's betrothal, it has been my honor to protect this virtuous woman."

"Protect her from—"

"The Avenger. And herself."

"Continue. Do not leave us standing in the square awaiting enlightenment."

"Jareb vowed not to know his betrothed until Samuel was dead. But Jareb attempted to disrobe her, and Mara slashed his hand and face."

"So, the sacrificial dove has talons." Herodias looked at Mara with unabashed admiration. "My guards are protection enough."

"My lady, if Mara is left alone with Samuel, it will be considered adultery."

Herodias waved Naomi away. "Your provincial morals are tiresome. Shechem must trust that I, Herodias, will safeguard Mara's purity."

Mara's heart plunged as if she had been thrown into a dungeon. The people of Shechem would never trust Herod's harlot. Again, her honor was besmirched.

Samuel

Samuel and Mara were led into a small dining alcove. He peered around the columns and saw the royals reclined, eating at the head table.

The servant left, and Mara's eyes flashed with panic. "We are not to be alone."

"By letter of the Law, we are not alone. No wall separates us from the royals. But we are tucked away from the eyes and ears of those in the main banquet hall."

Samuel wanted to see Mara's face, yet a veil was draped beneath her eyes. He wanted to touch her, but she was wife to another, a man devoid of honor.

The smells of the savory feast turned his stomach. His fate would be decided by sunset. Life or death. Sanctuary or crucifixion.

Mara met his love-filled gaze with tears in her eyes. "I feared you were dead."

"I feared you lived a widow in Tobiah's house, little more than an abused servant. Never, even in my darkest night, did I suspect your father would sell you again."

Mara looked away.

Samuel cursed his careless words. He had shamed her. "Forgive me. We have so little time." He reached for her hand. She did not move away. He stopped himself within a hairsbreadth of touching her. Love and longing rushed through his veins, set his skin on fire, and leapt across the space between them.

Mara's eyes widened. Did she feel the same fire?

"Let us speak of other things."

He withdrew his hand. "Ima is gone."

"She was at peace." Mara pulled her cloak close. "Her deathbed blessing was a whispered promise that we would one day be wed, and I would be delivered of a son."

Samuel's heart caressed every nuance in Mara's voice. He dared not speak of his love for her.

"I brought a linen towel your ima wove. A token of remembrance." Mara slipped it to him. "Your Abba so misses his beloved Ruth."

"Even in the face of his sorrow, why has Abba not come to the final judgment of his only son?" Samuel could not keep the tight hurt from curdling his stomach or coloring his tone."

"Before we left, Abram beckoned me remind you that spoken words can be overheard and truth twisted." Mara lapsed into a strong Samaritan accent, difficult for the Jews to follow.

A wave of understanding settled Samuel's stomach. Abba knew, in Jericho, he could have been called as the second witness who heard Samuel wish Achor be stricken dead.

They both picked at the simple food before them.

A servant girl came to the column. "Make ready to return for judgment."

Samuel rose, tucked the towel at his waist, and stretched out his hands to bless Mara. "May the Lord be with you and keep you."

Mara stood at a seemly distance. "May the Lord open the eyes and hearts of the judges."

They were led back to their places at the bema.

Samuel

Once again on the dais, Herod lifted his hands.

The crowd stilled.

"Before we render judgment, need anything further be voiced?"

Jareb slammed his fist on the edge of the dais. "These lovers had the chance, the blade, and the reason to kill my brother. Achor's blood cries out for justice."

Herodias stepped down from her litter. "At the banquet hall, I set my spies upon this couple. They did not touch. They did not speak of love or lust. The woman wore a face veil she never removed—even to eat."

"You cannot know every word spoken between them." Disrespect dripped from Jareb's tongue.

"Oh, but I do." Herodias pulled a scroll from her long sleeve. "My little bees hovered nearby. Never noticed. Here is a perfect record." She passed the scroll to Herod. "For my lords. As the avenger claims, Samuel had both the will and the weapon to kill Achor. But I would wager my crown neither he, nor this woman, have the mind or heart to commit murder."

Herod took the scroll. "Come, let us reason together."

The judges formed a tight circle. After some moments, they returned to their thrones.

Herod raised his hand. "Samuel of Shechem has been found innocent of malicious murder. All vows made by Jareb as the avenger of blood are void."

Samuel's heart danced, but he kept his feet firmly planted, waiting to hear the bounds of his sanctuary.

Caiaphas rose and walked to the edge of the dais. "The Law of Moses states a man who has committed murder without malice must be confined to his sanctuary city until the death of the high priest."

Herod stood by Caiaphas. "In this unusual circumstance we have appointed Jericho as the sanctuary city and the boundary line two hundred cubits from the city wall."

Pontius Pilate remained on his throne. "Both Achor and Samuel are Samaritan, therefore the death of the High Priest of Samaria will mark the end of Samuel's exile in Jericho."

Johakim was not old, and Mara was wed to Jareb. What hope could Samuel hold for Ima's prophecy?

Naomi knelt before Pontius Pilate.

He offered an open palm. "Speak."

"Under the ancient traditions of refuge, it was customary for the mother of the high priest to bring food and provisions to the claimant of sanctuary. I request permission to do so with each season."

"What an unfathomable custom." Pontius Pilate shook his head. "Why?"

"If Samuel accepts my gifts, he has promised not to pray for the death of my son, the high priest."

"Rise. You have my permission to return to Jericho, but Jareb or the High Priest of Samaria are banned. Another must escort you."

Mara stepped beside Naomi and addressed Pontius Pilate. "Let Samuel's father accompany Naomi."

Pontius Pilate gestured for the scribe to record his permission.

May Mara be blessed. Samuel would see Abba again.

Without warning, Jareb dragged Mara toward his horse.

Samuel lunged for them, but Ozri snagged Samuel's cloak and his strong arms banded Samuel's chest. "Be still. She is not your wife."

Jareb shoved Mara onto his mount, climbed up behind her and clutched her tightly. He rode close to Samuel. "All my vows are canceled. Straight to the marriage bed."

Jareb's words were a lance that pierced Samuel's side. He was rescued from death, but Mara's torment was just beginning.

21

Jericho

200 cubits from the wall

Mara

Mara jounced astride the racing horse. Jareb's arm pressed under her ribs. His chest pushed against her back. Too close.

"You clutch me too tightly." Her voice hitched, hungry for air.

"My bride would rather fall from a galloping horse than be held close."

For the first time Jareb's tone held more loathing than lust. A shudder slammed through her. Soon Jareb would take her as his spoils of war.

HaShem, protect me from this demon whose wickedness is without end.

Jareb halted and faced toward Jericho.

Mara watched the gate close on the forbidden city and her forbidden love.

Jareb stroked her shoulder.

Mara held herself rigid and watched the traveling party join them.

Okpara sidled his horse beside Johakim on his donkey.

"Okpara, take Tobiah and measure exactly 200 cubits from the city gate."

"Yes, master Jareb. And ...?"

"There raise the huppa." Jareb's breath blew hot on Mara's neck.

Okpara and Tobiah rode away.

Mara's shaking grew so violent it seemed the ground was quaking, sharing her outrage and terror.

"A huppa? Here?" Johakim's mouth turned down with disgust. "This is not a seemly place."

"A huppa planted on the boundary which neither Samuel nor I can cross is most seemly. Samuel can watch his beloved enter the tent a virgin and come forth a consummated wife."

Mara flinched at another stab of fear.

Naomi descended from her covered oxcart and approached.

Jareb handed Mara down from the stallion. "Woman, prepare my bride without delay or I will take her to my bed straight away."

The men quickly raised and readied the women's tent. Naomi put her arm around Mara and led her into its shade.

The servants brought light refreshment. Naomi poured a cup of blood red wine. She lowered Mara's veil and handed her the cup. "Drink. This will help you bear tonight's burden."

Mara snatched the cup and downed it without taking a breath. She held the empty cup forward. "Another." She craved oblivion.

Naomi poured.

Mara pushed the cup closer. "To the brim."

Naomi sighed but complied.

Mara upended the cup and wiped the dribble from her chin. Just as Tobiah did when he was deep in his cups.

Naomi removed Mara's head covering. "Come, I will help you wash, then dry your short hair."

"No."

Naomi reached for an alabaster ampule. "At least let me apply some perfume."

"I will go to Jareb unwilling, unwashed, stinking of Jewish Jericho."

"His temper will burn as hot as a brick kiln."

"Then HaShem will preserve me in the fiery furnace. If He does not, use the perfume for my burial." Mara rummaged through her bundle.

"What do you seek?"

"Here." Mara held up a folded linen cloth, the unique green thread ran along the finished edge. "My virgin show cloth. Tomorrow I will have proof no man has ever known me. Proof Samuel and I were never lovers. Proof I have spoken the truth."

Naomi opened her arms.

Mara rushed into her embrace, summoned the strength to submit and the courage to endure. She had vowed to survive.

Okpara called out. "Jareb summons his wife."

Mara lifted the tent flap. She crossed the short space to the wedding tent. No sooner had her foot fallen at the threshold than she was yanked into a crushing embrace.

Jareb's eyes burned with desire. His fingers raked her hair and his mouth smothered hers.

After what seemed a lifetime, he broke the revolting kiss.

Jareb could take her body. But her mind, heart, and soul would always be set apart, waiting for Samuel.

Jareb dragged her toward the pallet.

"Vengeance is mine."

Jericho

The Forge

Samuel

Samuel and Dex climbed the outside stair to the roof of the house at the forge that joined the Jericho wall. "Let us drink to the redemption of your good name."

The canopy that covered half the roof flapped. Samuel placed his hands on the waist-high wall and stared at the road.

Dex passed him a large cup of barley beer. "Mara will be long gone from view."

Something caught Samuel's gaze. "Tents. Just outside the city."

Dex drank some beer and shook his head. "A foolish place to set up camp. Too far from the wall. Too exposed."

Samuel strained to see in the failing light. One tent was white. What felt like the soft scurry of a death-walker scorpion raced across his heart and he braced for the sting.

"By the horns of Baal, that beast has set up a huppa. Jareb will make Mara pay for my escape from his sword."

Dex placed a hand on Samuel's shoulder. "Jareb is taunting you to break the bounds of sanctuary."

"I must protect Mara."

"If you allow that snake to draw you out, he will kill you.

Then, Mara's humiliation will count for naught. Stay here. I will fetch more beer."

Samuel paced along the wall, his eyes never leaving the wedding tent.

Dex hastened back up the stairs with a large pitcher.

"I must go to the boundary and call to Mara so she will know I am near."

Dex held up a palm that urged restraint. "Would you add to her shame?"

The question was a nine-inch nail driven into Samuel's heart. He tipped his cup and drank his fill.

"Mara has borne enough shame. Since birth." Samuel looked up at the brightening polestar. Like HaShem, the star never wavered.

"This battle has been lost, but you and Mara live to wage the next one." Dex matched him drink for drink, but unlike Samuel, his tongue did not slur, and his hand did not shake.

Samuel threw his clay cup down onto the street. The shatter of shards against the rocky road was meant to be a vent for his pent-up rage. But it was not near enough.

He watched the wedding tent. The oil lamp was snuffed. Samuel pushed away from the rooftop wall and staggered toward the outside stair. Mara was defenseless, trapped in the dark with a brutal beast.

Dex blocked his way. "Stay here. Do not chase trouble."

"My head knows that is true, but my heart screams. I cannot desert Mara."

Dex studied Samuel's face. "You are not fit to ride, to fight, or to hide."

Samuel pulled away. "Baal's blood. I will go anyway." He tried to pass Dex.

"I feared you would."

From nowhere, a fist crashed into Samuel's jaw, and he

sank to the ground, trapped in a thickening fog. "You ... struck me."

Dex's face blurred and Samuel fell into the onrushing black.

Mara

Blinding sunlight knifed through the open tent flap onto the sleeping pallet. Mara's head pounded. Waves of pain wracked her battered body, visions of last night wracked her harried mind.

Do not cry out.

The deep-seated ache in Mara's back and chest sharpened and stabbed with every breath. Last night, though she had been the scapegoat for all Jareb's fury, her face and belly were spared.

A shadow moved near the brazier. Jareb lurked nearby.

Do not cry out.

Mara slitted her lids and held her breath.

She would feign sleep and fend off the next beating. A beating that—as sure as sunset—would come again.

Do not cry out.

Samuel had survived the past day. Mara had survived the past night. She would live 'til the morrow. And until the next morrow. And the next. And the next. Until the dawn of a morrow when she and Samuel were both free.

Mara sniffed. Smoke. The stench of burning cloth. Without thinking, she opened her eyes. Her virgin show-cloth hung from a stick in Jareb's hand. An edge of the smoking linen flared, ablaze over the brazier.

"No, no, no." Mara leapt up, ran, and reached for the fiery remnant.

Jareb, a cup of wine in one hand and her blood-stained show-cloth in the other, dropped it onto red-hot coals. A *whoofff* of fire consumed it.

"Why?" Mara's stomach snaked around a leaden lump of hate.

Jareb's scarred face pulled into the smile of a torturer who takes pleasure in his work. "You slashed my hand and my face. Those scars banished me from the priesthood. Without your show-cloth, you will be shunned in Shechem."

Do not cry out.

Do not let Jareb see your pain, your fear, your hate. Let him believe he is powerless to move you.

"Woman, bring me wine."

She brought a pitcher and a cup and retreated out of his reach.

Rage roiled in Mara's heart. Jareb was drunk. But she wanted him drunk to oblivion. And when he was senseless, she wanted to uproot a tent peg, pick up a mallet, and drive that iron peg into his skull.

Long ago a heroine drove a tent peg into the skull of a sleeping enemy.

But Mara was no heroine.

She simply wanted to survive. And she desperately wanted Jareb to die.

"Pour for me, woman."

She filled his cup.

Jareb did not know she had cheated him when she took the pagan draught that delayed her oncoming womanhood. He did not know she had cheated him when she burned her first moonblood cloth. The vision of that fire brought her sins to mind and Mara to her knees.

As you sow, so shall you reap.

HaShem.

An eye for an eye. A tooth for a tooth. A fire for a fire. Moonblood cloth for virgin show-cloth. She had not trusted HaShem's provision. His protection. His providence.

How much regret could one heart hold?

HaShem, forgive my sins against you. For you hate liars and love those who chase after the truth.

Jareb clutched Mara's robe.

Do not cry out.

He pulled her back to the pallet, the wine pungent on his breath.

"Hashem, free me from this fiend."

A sudden wind blew long and strong through the tent, killing the fire and uprooting an iron tent peg.

Jareb glared at her as if she had summoned the sudden blast of wind.

She stared at the tent peg. Was it a sign?

Jareb picked up a mallet and moved to reset the peg. He bent, his hands and legs unsteady.

"The wine has left you besotted." As much as she wanted Jareb dead, she would not kill him.

He lifted the mallet to set the peg and another great wind made his hand falter. He pounded the peg through his foot, staking himself to the ground.

He screamed and cursed the wind, the peg, and Mara.

Blood seeped around the peg jutting from Jareb's foot.

"You made me do this."

"Let me cleanse that wound before it festers."

Jareb's jaw clenched. "Do. Not. Touch. Me." He sat, yanked the peg from his foot, and muffled a scream of pain. "Your sorceries will not stave off my getting an heir on you." His words were raspy groans.

Mara stared at Jareb's pooling blood.

Do not cry out.

"Woman. Staunch my bleeding, bind my foot."

Mara grabbed a towel, muttering to calm herself as she ripped the towel into strips.

Pain plowed deep wrinkles across Jareb's brow. As soon as the bandage was tied, he pushed to his feet and hobbled back two paces.

His dark eyes shuttered with suspicion. She had never seen that look.

"You are afraid." Mara took a step toward him. "Of me."

Jareb flinched. "You have been muttering. What spells did you whisper?" He grabbed her by the throat. "What curse did you call down upon me?"

He flung her away.

She fell onto her hands and knees. "Your wounded foot was not a curse from my lips, but misfortune from your own clumsy hand." Mara rose.

"Misfortune." Jareb ran a knuckle across Mara's neck. "Samuel's sickle slashed my brother's neck." His voice mocked her. "That was misfortune, not murder." He grabbed her waist and pulled her close.

Too close. She could barely breathe.

"Perhaps you are a witch. Speak disaster or death upon me and I will have you stoned. Heir or no heir." Jareb brushed his knuckle along her collarbone.

Do not cry out.

"I am ... no witch." A surge of white-hot loathing coursed through Mara's veins. "Were I a witch, you would be dead. Or unmanned."

Jareb yanked his hand back as if he had touched a branding iron.

A Certain Man

Shechem

Mara

Two weeks had passed since Mara returned to Shechem, but Jareb had not come to her since his foot was impaled. Only Ruth's prophesy of a reunion with Samuel kept Mara from climbing Mount Ebal and throwing herself from a cliff.

She followed the aroma of fresh honey-cakes to the kitchen.

Worry lines, like the cracks in a dry riverbed cut deep around Naomi's mouth. "Jareb's jaw is locked. For three days he has not taken food or water. He swears you have cursed him."

"And what do you believe?"

"That they are the ravings of a man doomed to die. I have seen this sickness. After a stab wound that festered."

"If he dies—"

Naomi touched Mara's shoulder. "When he dies—before the week is out—you will be twice-widowed."

"What must I do?"

"Come. The family keeps watch in Jareb's chamber."

Mara followed Naomi down the dim hall and entered the darkened room.

Jareb lay on the pallet. Johakim sat by his son's side. Jareb's glassy eyes suddenly seemed to see her. He pointed.

"Witch." His hand dropped and he looked at Johakim. "Condemn her."

"Liar. Would you bear false witness on your deathbed?" Mara's cry seemed to strike a blow.

Jareb's legs and back spasmed.

Naomi whispered in Mara's ear. "Loud noise triggers the agony."

Through the day and the next night, Jareb suffered bone-wrenching spasms. He cursed Samuel. He cursed Mara. And he cursed HaShem.

At daybreak, Mara left the chamber, craving fresh air.

After a few moments, the door opened, and Enosh ushered her back inside. One great spasm and Jareb arched. His body was a bridge. Only his head and his heels touched the pallet. A shriek gurgled in his throat, his mouth pulled wide and tight, baring his clenched teeth.

"HaShem, let him depart." The words no sooner escaped Mara's lips than her hated husband breathed his last. Mara gasped. Would the others think this was not sympathy but sorcery?

"Mara, I would speak with you." The high priest's sad eyes lightened with relief.

Mara knelt. Jareb had accused her of witchcraft. Her life was in Johakim's hands. "Priest, I throw myself on your mercy."

Johakim looked from Enosh to Naomi. "No one beyond this room has heard Jareb's last mad accusations. I will not shame the family with his lies."

Naomi helped Mara to her feet.

Johakim turned to Mara. "I have no doubt Tobiah would contract the next levirate marriage, but if you will agree to marry Enosh and bear one son, when that heir is born, I will pay three times the bride-price directly to you, not to your father."

Mara had no choice, either way she would be married to Enosh. But with Johakim's help, she would have her own means.

Enosh eyed her warily then turned to his father. "What if she is a sorceress?" His voice was weak and wheedling.

Johakim's face hardened. "Jareb was bad seed. Rotted to the core."

What an odd thing for Johakim to speak over his own bloodline.

"But I do not wish to marry." Enosh's whine seemed to infuriate his father.

Johakim gripped the robe of his only remaining son. "If you shrink from the duty to carry on my line, then you are not my son. Not my heir."

"You would disinherit me?"

"If Mara or marriage does not please you, after the heir is born, you may divorce her."

"Will you agree, my dear?" Naomi's eyes brightened. She could not keep her hope for an heir from flickering across her face.

Mara turned toward Naomi and looked down. "Samuel." A soft whisper escaped her lips. A secret prayer.

"Rome has confined Samuel to Jericho." Naomi's voice was gentle, but carried the hard truth Mara wanted to deny. "Ruth would wish you to be safe and secure."

Mara could not keep the bitter glare from her eyes. "Ruth would not wish me to share a bed with a man who beat her son and left him to die."

The high priest blanched.

Naomi looked away.

Enosh wiped his eyes, his chin quivering. "You saw me strike Samuel once to prove I took Achor's side. When you ran, I pled with Achor and Jareb to stop beating Samuel. I threatened to witness against them if he died." A strangled sob cut off Enosh's words. "We left Samuel in the field, but I returned with a servant."

"You coward. You half-buried him. You left him for dead." Mara pummeled Enosh's chest.

"Only when we heard Samuel was carried home did I stop my search." Enosh gently caught and captured Mara's fists. "Please forgive my sin against you and Samuel. Father, forgive me." Enosh knelt.

Tears streamed into Johakim's beard. "Enosh, how you have eased my guilt for raising such cruel sons. I will make a sin offering for you in the morning."

Mara crossed her arms. "Enosh must vow to never hurt or shame me."

Samuel was alive. And she had promised to survive.

Enosh extended a hand. "I will treat you with great respect."

Mara's heart lightened with hope. After an heir was born, she would be free. *HaShem has spared me a lifetime with Jareb and provided me a way back to Samuel. One day.*

Mara placed her hand in Enosh's. "Let it be so."

22

Jericho

Spring, Fours months after Samuel's trial

Samuel

S amuel left the forge, grateful for the light of the full
moon, and headed toward the gardeners' quarters. This
was the fourth Passover meal Samuel spurned sharing
amidst the Jews of Jericho. As always, he supped with his
pagan friend Dex.

Samuel considered the four months since his trial and the
years of exile that loomed before him. During the light of day,
he carved expansive panels for Herodias. Yet he could not push
Mara entirely from of his mind. During the dark of night, he
was afflicted by thoughts of Jareb brutalizing her. And at the
break of dawn, he was plagued by his own needs, for love, for
comfort, for touch.

He turned into the dark alley. Had he committed some

unpardonable sin? Why did the Lord not move to save his Mara?

His sandals slapped the deserted street. Dread tightened his chest and prickled across his neck. This next narrow bend was a perfect place for ambush. And Jews did not venture from their homes on this night. He quickened his pace, peered ahead, and spotted one of his garden crew at the barracks door. He sighed his relief and slowed.

A swift blow to Samuel's back stole his breath and knocked him to his knees. Pain pierced his side. A blade was pulled from his flesh. Bloody foam filled his mouth. He could not call out.

HaShem, have mercy. Do not let my life be taken by a poisoned blade.

Mara

Mara sat with Naomi in the women's courtyard where there was a bright patch of natural light. Their skilled fingers spun fine threads from the oily wool that would be woven into blankets. The clatter of hoofbeats broke their companionable quiet.

Okpara appeared at the archway. "Master Enosh has returned."

"Thank you. Go attend to his horse." Naomi's voice was pleasant. "Soon we may have a little one to spoil." Naomi hummed a happy little tune.

What would Naomi say if she knew her grandson only once managed to consummate the marriage in all these months? Since that night, Enosh made a great outward show of coming to Mara's chambers each week, but once there, he did not touch her. Perhaps he worried that she practiced the dark arts.

"Enosh leaves for weeks. I know not where." Mara was double-minded. She did not know how to ease his apathy but was in part also relieved. Perhaps his reluctance not only to marry but also to lie with her spoke of a secret love.

"Mara, take refreshments to Enosh's quarters. Perhaps over these last ten days, your husband has missed you." Naomi's eyes twinkled with a lightheartedness Mara had not seen for some time.

"It may be some time before I am with child." She went to the kitchen and prepared a tray of honey-cakes and fruit. In truth, when Mara watched young women cradle babies, she did long for a child to hold and to love. A thread of hope tugged at Mara's heart then tangled like a spider's web that snared its unsuspecting prey.

Naomi joined her. "Go quickly. I will follow with fine wine."

Mara made her way down the long portico to the men's wing where Enosh's bedchamber had been since childhood. He steadfastly refused to move into more opulent quarters closer to the heart of the house.

Enosh's door was slightly ajar.

"I hate it here." A petulant voice carried to Mara's ears. "You neglect me whenever we are in this house."

"My neglect is caution for both our sakes."

Enosh loved another woman. A wave of humiliation caught Mara unawares. Enosh's indifference left her wondering if her woes had stolen every shred of her allure.

"Show me you love me." The voice was low and sultry.

Mara crept to the door and looked around the doorframe. The lovers were entwined in a shadowed kiss. Who was her rival?

Enosh shifted, revealing the face of his lover. His manservant.

Mara locked her knees and clutched the tray that threatened to topple. Like bricks added to the top of a half-built wall, so many ignored inklings piled into place. She looked back and motioned Naomi to join her. Mara hated to confront Naomi with another ugly truth, but moved aside so the two lovers were in view.

Naomi dropped her tray and the cups shattered.

They jumped apart and covered themselves with their cloaks.

"This levirate marriage has been a sham." Mara's tone was furious, laden with threat.

"My son, Johakim, will die of shame if Enosh's desires come to light. Enosh and the manservant will be stoned."

"Both deaths will serve me." Mara's stomach twisted at the rancor in her voice. "With Enosh's death, I will be freed from marriage. With Johakim's death, Samuel will be freed from exile." Saddened and shamed, bile crawled up from Mara's sour stomach and burned her throat. Her soul had turned rancid.

Naomi, eyes wide with shock, looked stricken. "I beg you. Whom among us is free from secret sins?"

Did Naomi know of Mara's sin? Her moonblood lie?

"I cannot live with more shame, more bloodshed, more death." Naomi glanced at both men now wrapped in their cloaks, looking at the floor. She faced Mara. "One day, when you are a mother, you will learn that nothing can separate you from the love of a child or his children."

"Women cannot bear witness against us." Enosh, eyes glinting, had gathered some grit.

Mara would not relinquish her power over him. "At my mere suggestion of your sin, the rumor ravens' suspicious eyes will track you everywhere you go."

Naomi took both of Mara's hands. "Please, set aside your ill will."

"I have no desire for revenge or bloodshed. Or Enosh. I want my freedom."

Something cunning flickered across Enosh's face. "I will grant you freedom for your silence—and take you safely to Samuel in Jericho."

Mara's heart raced as if she was already running toward Samuel. "Let it be so."

Enosh's lover fell weeping at Mara's feet. "Bless you for your mercy on us."

Mara helped him stand. "May HaShem forgive my many sins. You must face Him with yours."

The manservant scurried from the room.

Naomi gathered the fragments of the clay cups. "Enosh, call the scribe and witnesses. Give Mara a *get* of divorce. You must leave this very night."

Desperation claimed Enosh's face. "Where can I go? What can I do?"

"Escort Abram, Mara, and me to Jericho." Naomi lifted her tray.

Mara turned back to Enosh. "You must swear to never return to Shechem, or follow your father as high priest."

"Neither my manservant, nor I, will ever set foot in Shechem again."

Naomi took Enosh by the arm. "Come. We will compose a loving farewell letter to your father. You will not be disinherited."

Mara's heart danced, and her soul sang. She was finally free to run to Samuel. Free to live and love and wed.

Jericho

Samuel

Samuel looked up at the bright, clear sky. Praise HaShem, he still drew breath. For weeks, he hovered at the door of his tomb, but today at last he sat on a stool in a sculptor's outdoor workspace. He rubbed his throbbing side and looked up at Pyrce, the Greek sculptor, beside him. "When will this pain leave me?"

"Patience."

Samuel studied the massive marble statues in various stages of completion and undress that surrounded him. "Your wife has tended me for more than a month."

The sculptor shrugged. "Woodcarver, you barely survived the stabbing. But one day you will be fully restored." Pyrce looked toward the gate. A hint of fear darkened his eyes and weighted his voice. "The queen will accept nothing less."

Herodias swept through the open iron gate into the courtyard. "Pyrce, you have served me well." She turned to Samuel. "Can you describe your assailant?" Her tone was hard, edged with fury, but her raptor eyes were softened with concern.

"No. He struck from behind, but he whispered in my ear, *For Jareb.*"

"So, he was not a bandit but a hired assassin. He will try again."

The queen looked at Pyrce. "You will hide my woodcarver among you Greeks. He must disappear as quickly as an early morning mist. With good fortune, the assassin will assume his target crawled into some hovel and died."

Herodias stepped toward Pyrce. Using a closed hand-fan she lifted his chin and turned his head side-to-side. "Make this man look like you, a blond Greek. Disguise him so well even his mother would not know him. He will be your apprentice and finish my wood panels in secret."

Herodias looked over her shoulder at Samuel. "You will remain a free man, but if you want my protection, you must hide as a slave." She headed for her litter at the gate.

Pyrce took out a small knife and lifted a fist of Samuel's shoulder-length hair.

Samuel studied the stone frieze leaning against the far wall, ignoring the clumps of hair dropping around him.

Pyrce patted Samuel's shoulder. "Your shearing is complete."

He reached up. His head was covered with curls as tightly wound as lamb's wool.

"If only your eyes and hair were light like mine. For I am a handsome man. No?" Pyrce clapped Samuel on the back and laughed at his own jest.

Samuel tensed and stood. Some Greeks were known to be lovers of other men. "I prefer beautiful women."

Pyrce moved in front of Samuel and studied his face with such intensity that a flush flared on his neck and singed his cheeks.

"It is true, I desire to sculpt you." Pyrce pressed Samuel's shoulders signaling him to sit down. "But all my other desires are for women."

Samuel sat. "What more must be done to disguise me?"

"Tomorrow, we lighten your hair. Now we shave." The Greek retrieved his leather satchel and whetted a blade. In silence, he removed Samuel's beard with slow strokes.

Samuel ran his fingers across his face. "I have not felt the cleft in my chin since I could grow a beard."

"I will bring a short tunic and cloak. We will burn what you now wear. No one must ever uncover a scrap of your past."

"Thank you. I am Sa—"

Pyrce's hand covered Samuel's mouth. "Never speak your name, then it cannot be tortured from me." He lifted his hand. "I will give you a new name. You have been born again." Pyrce grinned, amused by his own banter. "Didymus, I think."

"That means 'twin'?"

"Or double. And are you not a new twin of your old self?" Pyrce clapped his hands. "Am I not clever? The queen thinks 'tis true. That is why she entrusted me with you."

"Without doubt, you are humble."

"That also 'tis true." Pyrce bowed deeply, grinning like a king's fool. "Didymus will live with my family in the Greek quarter. Never reach out to anyone from your past life and risk alerting the assassin."

"I understand." Samuel would not risk putting his family or friends in danger.

"You will carve inside. Never work wood in public." Pyrce walked toward the gate. "For show, a part of each day we will open the gate and you will learn to cut stone in the courtyard."

Pyrce leaned close. "Before I go, we must create a past that explains how Didymus came to Jericho."

Samuel matched Pyrce's dramatic whisper. "My father was a merchant who lost his fortune in a shipwreck. I was sold into slavery to cover the debt. If I learn to sculpt stone, then I will have a skill that will buy my freedom."

"Yes." Pyrce slapped the stone dust from his hands. "And your Greek is not fluent, because your father was not Greek." He picked up his smallest awl and hammer. "We must mark you as a slave."

Samuel put the shaving satchel strap between his teeth and pressed his back against the stone wall.

Pyrce stretched out Samuel's ear and with one swift blow

drove the point of the awl through his earlobe and threaded an earring through the hole.

Samuel winced and pressed a linen scrap against his bleeding ear.

"You will sleep here at the workshop until your ear heals, your hair lightens, and your Greek improves. There are blankets in the corner. Do not light a fire in the courtyard. It would attract notice."

"And tomorrow?"

"Before sunrise, I tend to your hair."

23

Jericho

Samuel

S amuel shivered and shifted where he lay on the packed dirt floor of the sculpture studio. The embers in the firepit outside had turned to ash long ago. Even death could not be this cold.

HaShem, why have you forsaken me?

He rose, the blanket draped across his shoulders and peered through the doorway. The haunting sickle moon taunted him.

Fear not.

The voice Samuel thought had abandoned him.

As the sun banishes the moon, light defeats darkness.

He swallowed hard against the tight knot in his throat, unable to look away.

At first light, Pyrce came through the gate. "Didymus, we must go to the Jordan river."

"But the river is beyond the bounds of my sanctuary."

"I sent word to Herodias. Her spies will protect you."

HaShem, not Herodias, be my bulwark of protection and power.

The prayer hummed through Samuel's veins, soothing the drumming of his anxious heart. He followed Pyrce eastward to the Jordan and they picked their way down the bank.

Pyrce removed jars and a bowl from his pack. He filled the bowl with wet silt and opened the jars. "One part potash with an equal part vinegar." Using a wide brush, he stirred the paste then, nose wrinkled, eyes watering, brush dripping with the foul-smelling potion Pyrce headed toward Samuel.

"At the first hint of burning, the paste must be washed away. Our aim is blond, not bald." Pyrce sniggered and moved closer.

"I will never pass as a blond Greek." Samuel backed away. "Must we do this?"

"Even your mother must not know you."

Samuel started to protest that his ima was gone, but he must banish any mention of his Samaritan life.

"You no longer run your hand across your head or cheeks in search of your shorn hair and beard." Pyrce lifted the brush. "You no longer wince every time the wind lifts your short tunic. You wear a slave earring. Why balk at this?"

"I fear neither blond nor bald. I cannot bear the stink."

"With time the nose goes blind to even the most putrid smell."

Samuel wrinkled his nose. "Not mine. This stinks like something a misguided Magi would concoct from donkey droppings and myrrh."

Pyrce slathered Samuel's scalp with the bubbling paste.

Samuel swallowed hard. "Smells both delight and offend me."

Pyrce wore his race on his face. Greeks were curious reasoners. "What stench last tormented you?" He massaged Samuel's scalp.

"Camel's breath. Last night ... I dreamt of camel's breath." Samuel shuddered. "Worse than any Roman privy."

"A camel? Up close?"

"I can still see her soulful eyes, her droopy, swollen lips, and bared, jagged teeth. I was never certain if she meant to bite or to kiss."

"I have known such lovely, unpredictable women." Pyrce laughed. The sound of a man who laughed with his whole body and whole heart.

Samuel sat on a boulder. "Will the stench linger?"

The Greek dropped his brush in the bowl. "It cannot. Or what woman would ever apply it?"

"A woman who wishes to never be bedded." Samuel pinched his nose. "For the rest of her life."

Samuel looked upstream. The dark form of a man standing in the river was gilded by the dawn mist. The daybreak slashed the sky and river blood red. The stranger wore a camel's hair garment cinched with a leather girdle and his wild twisted locks tracked down to his waist. He lifted his arms and face to the sky.

"I am a voice crying in the wilderness."

The booming voice rumbled like thunder across the rippling river. Samuel glanced back to Pyrce. "Who is that?"

Pyrce stared upstream. "The nearby fishermen say he is a prophet."

Samuel's heart quickened. Ima had believed the Promised One would be a man now.

"Others say he is a madman, possessed by a demon."

"And who do you say he is?"

220

"I say there is no need to make a choice." Pyrce shrugged. "Are not all Judean prophets madmen?"

"Prepare ye the way of the Lord." Sunrise haloed the holy man with hues of amber, red, and purple.

Samuel closed his eyes against the blinding light. He lifted his hand to his brow and looked again. The mist and the man had departed.

The paste on Samuel's hair began to burn. "Quick. Rinse this away." He scratched the angry skin on his neck.

Pyrce poured water over his head, but Samuel's scalp still burned. He ran into the river and fell backward into the cool water. He emerged and looked upstream. The river was free flowing. A mikvah. Suddenly Samuel understood. The prophet had been purifying himself. But for what purpose?

Pyrce pointed to a large flat rock. "Let your hair dry in the strong sun."

Samuel stretched across the warm rock. "Ah. After the bone-cold night the heat soothes my aching limbs."

"Rest. I will keep watch."

Samuel drifted off, lulled by the ripples of living water.

Someone touched his head. Samuel jerked awake.

"Time to check your hair." Pyrce lifted a short curl. "A start. Two more treatments should suffice. Come back to the studio and begin training as my apprentice."

Samuel

Pyrce and Samuel walked into the studio courtyard. The stonecutter pointed to a man-sized block of marble. "Take the largest chisel and chip away chunks from the edges. Anything beyond this line of chalk goes."

Samuel worked quickly. The feel of the chisel gouging the stone was familiar, but stone needed a much heavier touch.

Samuel set down his tools and rubbed his upper arm.

"I will send a warm supper and more blankets." Pyrce put down his chisel and hammer. "Tonight promises to be colder than last night."

Samuel's shoulders rounded, shivering at the memory of the cold last night. "Please send some cloth to wrap my hands and fend off cold blisters."

"Yes. Chilblains will not serve either of us well." Pyrce slung his satchel over his shoulder and left.

The large low studio windows allowed a flood of natural light. Samuel climbed onto the deep window ledge, leaned his back against the wall, and hugged his knees.

The sun set, the moon rose.

Prepare ye the way of the Lord.

One day would he be called to serve the Promised One? Samuel's stomach lurched. HaShem did not call his prophets to a safe portion or path.

Light footfalls. Just outside the studio. Samuel crept into the shadows of the far-most corner.

"Didymus." He studied a slender young woman in the doorway. Her long, dark hair glistened in the moonlight. She held a basket piled with blankets and linen cloth. "Pyrce sent me."

"Blessed be Ha—" He swallowed the praise that would betray his past. "Many thanks." He stood.

She arranged the blankets into an inviting nest on the floor. Every few moments her wary eyes shifted his way. Then her uneasiness changed to a shy, yet seductive, smile.

"Go before the streets are not safe."

She touched her earring. "No one would molest the favorite slave of Herodias."

Her earring matched his. He was marked as a slave of the queen. "But the queen will have need of you."

"I am not leaving. I am the comfort woman sent to warm your nights."

"Go back to the queen. I have no use for you."

The young woman fell to her knees. "If I fail to please you, I will be given to the entire Roman regiment on the hill." Fear filled her face and voice.

Samuel remembered Herodias standing over the corpse of her devoted handmaid. The servant's death meant nothing to the queen. The hard-hearted, cunning queen. She now not only offered him a woman he dare not refuse but also planted a spy in his bed.

The young woman stepped toward Samuel and encircled his waist with her arms. "I am to serve you this night and all nights to come."

Samuel's heart raced away from temptation, but his legs were leaden, planted in place.

24

Jericho

Mara

Mara looked up at the Jericho gate. The last time she had gazed upon it, Jareb's foot was impaled, and she was at the mercy of his vengeance. The hasty trip with Enosh and Abram had been tiring but Mara's weariness waned, and her heart fluttered with hope.

"May you and Samuel find happiness." Enosh handed her the *get*. "Now we are divorced."

Mara held the *get* close to her heart. "May you find peace."

Even though she had forced Enosh to divorce, she would never have revealed his forbidden tryst. For she, too, was without excuse. Her own secret sins would merit a sentence of death under the Law.

"Shalom." Enosh rode away.

"Let us ask after Samuel." Abram hurried through the stone archway.

Once before, she entered Jericho through this gate. Then, she was Jareb's caged bird. Today she would fly free. Straight into the arms of her beloved Samuel.

A blacksmith's hammer rang at the nearby forge. The smithy paused, waved them to his tall water jars.

Mara drew a cup for Abram, then herself. "Bless you, sir."

The smithy headed toward Mara and met her eyes with an intensity that stole her breath. "You are called Mara, the beloved of my friend Samuel." His face was full of sympathy and sadness. "I am Dex."

"Where is Samuel? I must see him."

"You are the wife of the Blood Avenger." Dex checked over his shoulder. "Jareb and those of his House are banned from Jericho."

Mara handed her *get* to the smithy. "I am no longer of Jareb's house."

Abram stepped forward. "I am Samuel's father and have leave to be here."

Dex opened the *get* and read it. "You are divorced from Enosh not Jareb?"

"It is a long tale. And I have vowed to never speak the reason."

Abram put his palms together. "Enosh has sworn never to return to Shechem or harm my son."

"Where is Samuel?" Mara's stomach squirmed.

Dex would not meet her eyes.

"What news do you withhold?"

"Come inside." Dex led Mara and Abram to the low table. He looked at a young woman bustling behind the kitchen table. "Mara and Abram seek Samuel."

"I am Sophia, Dex's wife." She poured watered wine. "Months ago, Samuel did not report to Herod's garden."

"And he never returned to his woodshop." Dex sounded defeated.

Mara's chest seemed shackled by iron bands that crushed her every breath. Her mouth went dry. She reached for her cup as a drowning man reaches for an outstretched hand and drank. "Go on."

"Have you heard from my son?"

"Nothing. But I was a Roman commander nearby." Dex crossed his arms over his broad chest. "In time, I will learn Samuel's fate from one of my men."

Mara searched the worry lines etched around his eyes and mouth. "There is more ..."

Dex looked toward Sophia.

She put her hands on her hips. "I would want to know."

Mara leaned toward Dex. "Tell me."

"Herod's men found a trail of blood and a poisoned knife in an alley near where Samuel slept."

Ice rushed through Mara's veins, and she slumped back. Numb—beyond words, beyond tears, beyond hope.

Abram clutched at Dex's sleeve. "But Samuel's body has not been found."

"True." Dex's tone held no comfort.

"Unless I see his body with my own eyes and touch it with my own hands, I will not believe he is dead." Abram grabbed Mara's hand. "Ruth's foretelling promised you a son of my son."

Could she hold fast to Ruth's deathbed promise? Mara dragged in ragged breaths. Her hope quickened. Once before she had found Samuel buried alive. She would find him again.

Mara ran out into the streets of Jericho screaming Samuel's name. She raced through serpentine alleys without heed to the looming darkness.

A Certain Man

Samuel

Samuel stared into the starlight streaming through the studio window. The comfort woman lifted one of his curls. "Your hair is much lighter. Soon we will live with Pyrce."

A close look at the achingly beautiful woman would invite lust. Samuel turned away.

The woman stepped around him, eyes flashing. "You may no longer pretend I am not here." She touched his pierced ear. Her glistening eyes narrowed, fending off tears. "Though you have never asked, my name is Zosime."

"A pleasant name."

"A strong name. The Greeks have called me *survivor*."

"There must be a tale behind such a name."

"One day I may trust you enough to tell it."

For the first time Samuel studied her green eyes. Almond shaped eyes that clouded to a gray storm.

Zosime no longer looked hurt. She looked angry. Good. Anger would hone her craftiness and keep her alive. Compassion took hold of Samuel's heart. "I will call you Zosi."

She knelt and joined the separate sleeping blankets into one nest.

"Even if we crawl under shared blankets, I will not couple with you."

She clutched his robe. "One day Herodias will call for me and I must report we have shared the same bed."

"She will assume that we have, since you have stayed."

"The queen assumes nothing. My lips may lie, but my blush will betray me." She pushed away from him. "Pray the queen does not ask how many times you have known me."

A jolt of revulsion sliced across Samuel's heart. "Herodias would ask such a thing?"

"Without hesitation."

Samuel's stomach twisted like a sodden rag wringing out bitter bile. "What will you answer?"

"I will tell Herodias you have known me every night." She locked eyes with him. "Only such a falsehood is not fatal." Zosi turned from him and her bold-faced lie.

Now the bile crawled up his throat.

"Your face was persuasive." Samuel's tongue faltered on the falsehood.

Zosi turned back. "Each morning, I will take a flower offering to Aphrodite and plead with the goddess of Comfort Women that the queen does not have me inspected."

"Inspected?"

"Herodias sent you a virgin." Zosi traced Samuel's lips. "The queen will simply send other women, until there is one you cannot resist." A tear slipped down her cheek. "Or you tire of sending comfort women to their defilement and death."

Zosi's touch sent terror through his veins and shook him to the core.

"Would that you were unable to resist me."

Samuel lay down in the blanket nest.

Zosi joined him, curling her back into his chest.

Nearby an innkeeper shouted. Harlots called out enticements. A panicked woman screamed. The frenzy in her voice clutched at Samuel's soul. Poor woman. *HaShem, grant her peace.*

For the blink of an eye, the disembodied voice sounded like Mara calling his name, but it faded.

Samuel's heart hitched.

Screee. Screee. Screee.

Zosi startled and reached for a talisman strung around her neck. "An owl foretells my death." Leaping to her feet, she faced each of the four winds, waved the charm, and muttered.

"What is this?" Samuel rose.

228

"A spell of protection." Zosi sat on the low window ledge. *Screee.*

An owl landed on the closest olive branch and a sickle moon rose over its head.

Samuel swung a blanket around Zosi's shaking shoulders.

The hairs on his neck bristled. He could not throw off the niggling feeling that death had swooped into his world.

Shechem

Mara

Mara's screams for Samuel in Jericho had been fruitless. She lost her voice and her will to survive. After three days, Abram brought her back to Shechem. Now Mara wandered through the dim halls of the House of the High Priest and into the kitchen.

Naomi eyed her with unmasked concern.

"For months you have walked among the living as one who is dead." Naomi handed Mara a warm flatbread. "Eat."

She broke the bread into small pieces, scattering them on a plate. A picture of her life.

Johakim walked in from the courtyard. The poor man still held out a shred of hope that by some miracle she was with child and Mara could not dissuade him. "Your flesh withers. Your bones jut out. If you do not eat, you will die."

She stared at her plate, her limbs leaden. "Would that be such a great loss?" Her lifeless croak was the first sound she had uttered in days.

Naomi's mouth tightened, and her eyes glinted. "Would Samuel have you give up hope and die?"

"Samuel is dead. Only in the sleep of death will we be together."

Naomi picked up Mara's plate and hurled it at the wall. Mara flinched at the sound of shattering clay and the fury on Naomi's face. "If you were dead, would you want Samuel to surrender his life so heedlessly?"

Mara looked away.

Naomi crossed to Mara and lifted her chin. "Answer me."

"I would want Samuel to live and be blessed, but I no longer have the strength to battle my woes."

"Despite your melancholy, you can choose victory." Johakim's tone was so kind, yet so cutting.

Mara flinched and glanced into Johakim's eyes. "I do not understand."

"Remember Joshua, the great commander of old. The battle is not yours, but the Lord's." Johakim lifted a hand, blessing her. "Take your mind from your own sorrows."

Naomi came close and patted Mara's back. "Ease the sorrows of another. Then, your own soul will begin to mend."

A demanding knock thudded at the doorpost. Mara looked through the open kitchen door and into the face of a stranger. His black eyes glinted like an obsidian blade. With guile or greed or guilt she could not say. But surely nothing good. She looked away but could not bring herself to leave.

"I must speak with Jareb ben Johakim."

The man was a foreigner. Unclean. Johakim rose and went out into the courtyard.

Mara and Naomi crowded the doorway.

"Jareb is dead. I am the head of this house."

The foreigner's face did not change. "Even so, you must pay the remainder of the dead man's debt."

Johakim tugged at his beard. "Before I honor Jareb's debt, I must know the amount and the reason."

"I know nothing of the reason, but my master sent me to collect."

The stranger, too well dressed to be a servant, was lying.

He reached into his cloak and withdrew a signet ring. "This was my master's surety."

"It is Jareb's." Johakim sighed. A sigh mourning a new source of shame.

Okpara, who had been working outside, sidled up beside Johakim. "My master kept a meticulous ledger. The debt will be listed there."

"Bring it." Johakim's voice shook.

Mara clutched the sides of her robe.

Okpara rushed inside toward Jareb's vacant chambers and brought a leather-bound scroll outside. He unrolled it. "Here." He pointed to a line.

Johakim peered over his shoulder.

Okpara had found the entry too quickly. He knew about the debt.

"The first payment was made the very day Samuel was granted sanctuary in Jericho." Johakim gasped. "A small fortune. Enough to purchase seven bond servants for life."

"How much is a life worth?" The stranger's tone bit with sharp challenge.

"A life is priceless." Johakim's tone was sure and pure.

"Some lives are priceless." The stranger sneered. "You just told me some can be purchased."

Okpara ran his finger along the scroll. "The debt is to be paid to the bearer of Jareb's signet ring."

"Did you know of this matter?" Johakim loomed over the treacherous slave.

"During his final days, Jareb spoke of his ring and this man." Okpara held out a hand to the stranger. "But my master required proof the deed was accomplished."

231

The stranger reached into his satchel and pulled out a scrap of folded linen.

"Common linen is no proof." Johakim crossed his arms.

"But this cloth is not common." The stranger opened the bloody scrap.

Mara's heartbeat rammed against her ribs. Ruth's green thread tracked across the scrap.

"Jareb paid you to murder my Beloved." She lunged at the assassin, raked her nails across his face.

He shoved Mara away. "The dead man's debt must be paid."

Mara ripped the neck of her tunic, scooped up ashes from the cookfire, and spilled them onto her head.

Samuel's death was a bitter drought. Mara's life was a bitter fate.

A new seed of bitterness took root in Mara's heart and sprouted into a thorned thicket that strangled her soul. She could barely breathe. "From birth, Tobiah has called me Mara. *Bitter.* I was well and truly named."

25

Jericho

Samuel

Samuel crossed the sculptor's studio and retrieved his foreman amulet for Herod's garden. He returned to Zosi and looped it over her neck. "Wear this when you report to the queen this morning. Tell her I asked you to wear it always."

"Will she know what this means?"

"Perhaps not. But the amulet bears the seal of Herod. I would entrust such a treasure only to a woman who pleased me."

Zosi studied the amulet then flung her arms around Samuel's neck. "May all the gods bless you. You have spared my life."

For years of mornings, Samuel awakened, yearning with needs of both heart and body. He gently pried Zosi away and set her at a safe distance.

"What more should I say?" She looked up at him with trusting adoration.

"Tell Herodias my heart belongs to my Beloved, but with time, my body will belong to you." As soon as the words left his lips, Samuel's soul shrank from the ugly truth of his utter loneliness laid bare.

One unspoken thought hovered between them. Samuel's body did not belong to Zosi.

Yet.

Samuel

Samuel looked from the window of the chamber he and Zosi shared into the courtyard of Pyrce's home. Less than one cycle of the moon and desire had vanquished his resolve. He felt he had betrayed Mara with Zosi, even though Mara was wed and warmed another bed.

Zosi slid her arm about Samuel's waist, rested her cheek on his chest, and gazed at him with adoring eyes.

He untangled from her. "Our touching is a thing of the dark, never the light."

Her hand covered a strangled sob. She lifted her chin, but her lip quivered. "Am I such a source of shame I must be banished to the dark?"

A pang of pity stabbed Samuel's heart. Zosi was grasping at some shred of dignity. "Forgive me. Though you will never have my heart, you will have my respect, my protection, my comfort."

"I must go help with the cooking." Her voice hitched.

"Wait. What if you should bear a child?"

"Though you are a sham slave, I am a true one. Any child of mine would belong to Herodias."

"One more snare the queen would wield over me." A mantle of cold worry weighted Samuel's shoulders. Both he and Zosi followed a trail of loathsome choices. Both were survivors.

Shechem

Mara

Mara and Naomi hurried to the audience hall in the House of the High Priest. Johakim sat in his highbacked chair.

Tobiah stood before him. "Mara's good name is fodder in the yapping jaws of the village gossips." His voice dripped feigned dignity. "They chew the cud of scandal."

"Leave." Naomi's tone was unyielding. "Two more months before we know with certainty that Mara is not with child."

Tobiah left grumbling.

Mara followed Naomi back to her chambers. Sorrow welled up in Mara's soul. "I never considered I might be barren forever."

Naomi glanced at Mara. "You have wasted away. Eat some meat. Drink some wine. Your courses will return."

Naomi sat on her pallet, seemingly unaware of her soft wheeze.

"You rest. I will go to the well."

Mara walked down the hill to Jacob's well, one waterpot on her hip, another on her head. She spoke Naomi's wisdom into the wind. "Forget self. Serve others."

As soon as Mara arrived, the village women departed,

pretending they had not seen her. The scandal that Jareb had hired an assassin blazed through Shechem.

She filled the large waterpot, removed the cup from inside the smaller vessel. She drew more water and filled the smaller waterpot. Dipping her cup, she drank greedily.

Suddenly, she felt eyes upon her. A foreigner sat under the terebinth tree of Shechem. His horse and two fully laden donkeys were tethered close by. The poor, thirsty creatures pawed the ground, likely smelling the fresh ground water that fed the well.

Mara spilled her large waterpot into the nearby trough. "Your beasts need water." She dipped her cup and held it out to the man. "As do you."

He took the cup. "Woman, a thousand blessings on you and your house."

His deep resonant voice was compelling. For the briefest moment, she glanced at his face. Eyes the brown of lush fertile earth. Full lips hidden in a short curly beard. Pearl-like teeth.

Mara's cheeks warmed. She had shared a cup with this man as a bride shares a cup with her groom. Though perhaps ten years older than she, the man was vital and devastatingly handsome. He seemed blind to his allure which heightened his charm.

She refilled the large waterpot and topped off the trough. The beasts slurped greedily.

"Your husband is a most fortunate man. A lovely wife with a kind heart."

"I have ... no husband." Mara's voice tripped over the confession.

"Oh."

Mara kept silent. What could she say that would not tarnish her further in the stranger's eyes.

"May the Lord send you comfort."

A jolt ran through Mara's veins. She had never looked at any man other than Samuel with any womanly regard. Was her attraction a sign that Samuel was dead? Or had her utter loneliness made her an easy mark for sin?

"A gift for your kindness." The man reached into his satchel and withdrew a thin gold bangle.

Mara, entranced, allowed him to slip the circlet onto her wrist. He took care not to touch her skin.

"And I would ask of you one more favor." His voice was smooth as marble.

Mara tensed, ready to run. She was alone, without protection. Had the stranger taken her acceptance of the gift as a promise of more intimacy?

His face took on a gentleness. "I mean you no dishonor but humbly ask you to direct me to the House of the High Priest."

"Come. I am of that household." Mara started up the hill.

The stranger led his horse and donkeys at a proper distance behind her.

Jericho

Samuel

Samuel ran his fingertips along the rough surface of the giant stone in the studio courtyard. Wood was soft and warm and spoke to him. Stone was sharp and cold and mute.

"I barely speak Greek and do not speak the language of stone."

"It is your good fortune. I am fluent in both." Pyrce took the tools from Samuel. "Go home. I will follow. The light of the sinking sun is perfect for my next cuts." Pyrce moved to a statue he had just begun.

Samuel wiped the stone dust from his hands and watched Pyrce. A few deft chisel cuts and the face of a goddess began to emerge from the marble. The ethereal light waned to lily pink. Samuel could almost imagine a blush coloring her cheek. Though he would never worship a goddess, something in the sculptor's work evoked a sense of the sacred.

Pyrce put his tools down. "Ahh, you are still here." His stomach growled. "Time to fill our bellies" He patted his middle. "Thanks to you, my household eats from the queen's table."

They hurried home. Samuel crossed the threshold and sniffed. "Something smells wonderful." Suddenly hungry, his mouth watered. Unexpectedly weary, his shoulders slumped.

"Venison simmered in a sweet and savory sauce." Zosi sprinkled a pinch of salt into the large pot and stirred.

Four generations of Pyrce's loud and loving household gathered. This family both eased and sharpened Samuel's loneliness. He should have been in Shechem, married to Mara, at his own family table.

After the meal, Samuel retreated into the torchlit inner courtyard, surrounded by squeals of happy children. He took a whittling knife from his waist sack and sat on the low fountain wall. A tiny whistle slowly took shape. His heart and soul longed for Shechem—a lifetime away from this pagan place.

A woman wailed. Samuel tensed, his knife stilled.

Inside the house, Zosi murmured comfort. The woman's weeping faded to whimpers. Then silence. He returned to his whittling.

Light footsteps. Coming near. He looked up. Zosi's eyes were uncertain. Her lips pinched.

Trailing Zosi was a Cushite woman. Skin the color of

burnished bronze, hair like the blackest of wool. The cat-like kohl around her eyes was tear-streaked but did not diminish her beauty. She knelt at Samuel's feet, cradling a wooden harp.

"I am Prima, first player in the queen's kinnor choir. I fell. The long arm of my harp cracked, and its voice was strangled."

Zosi handed the harp to Samuel. "Can you mend it? If the queen discovers the harp is ruined when a dark mood is upon her, Prima may also be strangled."

Samuel examined the broken arm. "The crack is not through-and-through. When must you play?"

"Tomorrow evening." Prima looked up at him with pleading eyes.

"Good. I will seal the crack."

Prima clutched Samuel's ankles and kissed his feet as if he was the embodiment of a Greek god.

The touch of her lips made his stomach curdle. He wanted to shake off her touch but studied the harp to hide his revulsion at the woman's worship. "Come inside." Samuel set up a makeshift worktable and Zosi gathered tools.

Prima sat on a nearby bench, Zosi at her side.

Samuel mixed a paste of wood dust and resin. He slathered the crack and handed the harp to the Prima. "Play, but do not touch the wet paste."

Prima strummed then switched to a bone plevum to pick the strings. "The tone is restored, but the mend is glaring." She bit her quivering lip. "The queen will surely notice."

"Wait. The paste must dry." Samuel took the harp and laid it on his workbench. "This harp's voice is different from the one the queen plays."

Samuel remembered the power of the harp-song when Herodias soothed Herod and Pontius Pilate. Though he had never carved an instrument of any kind, his fingers burned to fashion a harp with a new voice.

At first light, Samuel sanded the restored arm to a seamless finish. "Return in two days, and I will replace the entire arm of the kinnor."

Prima took the harp and kissed Samuel's feet again. "May the gods grant your every desire." He wanted to stop her worship, but a Greek would welcome it.

Prima rose and hugged Zosi. "I owe you my life."

"As I owe you mine."

Prima headed toward the palace, the harp cradled on her hip.

"Prima saved your life? When?"

"After I was first sent to you. The queen doubted we had coupled."

Zosi laid her hand over her heart. "Prima distracted Herodias with a flurry of false song requests for the evening banquet. The queen rushed away to practice. If Herodias discovered Prima lied, she and I both would have died."

Samuel pulled Zosi into his arms.

Shofars sounded across Jericho as the sun splintered the horizon. The Feast of Trumpets. The New Year. Would HaShem once again write Samuel's name in the Book of Life?

Shechem

Mara

Mara sat with Naomi in the sunny courtyard. Naomi pulled a needle through her fine stitchery. "You would not be the first woman to meet her future husband at a well."

Mara wished she had not confided her attraction to the

stranger. She was uncertain if he shared her feelings or would ever return.

"Tell me about this stranger."

"There was something familiar about his look, the way he formed his words."

"Did he appear to have a Samaritan bloodline?" A calculating look crossed Naomi's face and settled into a smile. The satisfied smile she flashed when she arranged a fortuitous match. A smile that reminded Mara that Naomi was the longstanding matchmaker of Shechem.

A servant girl stepped into the courtyard. "The high priest requests you both join him in the audience hall. He is with a stranger."

Mara put on a head covering, chest fluttering, cheeks burning.

The servant girl's sandals rapped against the marble floor. They followed her through the colonnade and entered the audience chamber.

At Johakim's right hand, her stranger waited. The sparkle in his eyes eclipsed the smile on his face.

Mara looked away, sure her hot blush crept onto her neck.

"My son, you called for us." Naomi bowed her head.

"Yes, mother." He gestured toward the stranger. "I would ask you to hear an offer."

He turned to Mara. "This man, a cousin from the line of my mother, is urgently in search of a second wife." Excitement colored Johakim's tone.

Naomi stepped close to the stranger, seemed to study his face, and addressed her son. "Is this Seth? The youngest son of my oldest sister's son?" A frown buckled Naomi's brow. "A second wife? When was he widowed? How many children has his first wife left behind?"

Thankfully, Naomi voiced Mara's most urgent questions.

"His first wife lives, pleases him, and has produced three healthy heirs." Johakim grabbed the edges of his outer cloak.

Mara's hands turned to ice, her heart turned to stone. *Second wife.* Why would a good man, with a wife who pleases him, and healthy heirs, seek another? She would not let her longings for love direct her destiny. She headed for the door.

Naomi touched her arm. "Stay. Listen. My son must have gleaned some merit from this man's proposal." She leaned close and whispered. "This branch of my family is righteous, rich, and refined."

Johakim coughed. Mara glanced his way. "Seth can well provide for more than one wife."

"So, I am to be sold again." A quiver invaded her voice.

Listen with an open heart.

She chose a softer tone. "Can this man also quench my father's greed?"

"Seth will fulfill the promises of all previous contracts. We will all be freed from Tobiah's demands."

"A kinsman redeemer." Mara spoke softly under her breath. "I never expected to be a second wife. Ever."

"And I never expected to beg to wed a woman who has had three husbands. But the unexpected can be the spice in our lives."

Though, Seth's tone was light-hearted and disarming. Mara flinched at the unvarnished truth of his words. No one would beg for a thrice-wed woman. Was Seth mocking her?

"Forgive me, your misfortunes are no light matter." Seth's face became serious. "I never suspected my father's Roman citizenship would see me conscripted into the army."

Johakim put his fingertips together. "Put precisely, Seth needs a *new* wife. If an adequate gift is placed into the palm of Seth's assigned commander, Rome will allow Seth to follow our tradition. The Law of Moses exempts a man from war for one year after taking a *new* bride."

"Mara, I would never force marriage upon you. Please consider. Tobiah's demands would be satisfied. Any son of ours would continue the House of Johakim." Seth moved close. "And I would have a year of grace and peace."

Mara placed her hands on her hips. "Are you a coward, then?" Her tone was playful, not petulant. Her benign barb was rewarded with Seth's soft smile.

"I am more singer than soldier. More poet than politician. More wordsmith than warrior."

Perhaps marriage to this winsome man could serve them both. "How would you win me?" Mara's tone held a note of hope that caught her unawares. Hope she thought dead.

"I vow to be gentle. I vow to provide for and protect you and any children. For I am not a coward, but a hater of bloodshed and a lover of peace." Seth took her hand. At his touch, a spark seemed to sear them together.

Mara studied Seth's solemn face. "When must you have your answer?"

"Within the hour."

"So soon?" Mara's stomach knotted around strands of dread and desire.

Seth folded his arms. "Yes, I must pay the commander in time to stay my conscription."

Johakim turned a nearby sandglass. The sands of time sifted.

"You will have my answer before the sandglass is empty." Mara left the house. She walked past the house of Abram who still watched for the return of a son whose assassins had been paid.

She walked past Tobiah's hut. As ever, he lay sprawled in the yard.

Moments later, Mara found herself thirsty and alone at Jacob's well without a vessel to draw water. How fitting. The well. The place of her parting from Samuel and the place of her meeting with Seth.

The sand was sinking in the sandglass. What if Samuel was alive? What if Johakim died and Samuel could return? Not caring who may see, Mara stretched face down in abject submission.

Lord, show me Your wisdom, Your will, Your way.

The sun beat down and sweat beaded her brow. A soft breeze offered comfort and a small voice spoke to her soul.

Trust Me to order your path.

Mara returned to the House of the High Priest and entered the audience hall. The final few grains dropped in the sandglass. The timing of HaShem was never early, never late. Always perfect.

Naomi and Johakim waited at the table. Seth paced behind them. His look bore the same mix of dread and hope she had seen on Samuel's face when he awaited his sentence in Jericho. Mara pressed her hand to her chest hoping to stem the stabbing pain of that memory.

She held out her hands to Seth. "I would humbly add three requests."

"Speak them." Seth's tone was part curiosity, part hope.

"Will you denounce any claim as an Avenger of Blood? Never require me to leave Shechem? And set me free after the year of your military leave, if that becomes my wish?"

"So it shall be."

A slurry of fear, excitement, and desire stirred in her stomach. "Then I will marry you this hour."

Johakim rose. "Mother, please call two witnesses. I will amend the contract." He reached for the parchment and dipped his quill.

The scratching of the quill seemed to scrape Mara's heart. Her life was captive for one year. Afterward, if by some miracle Samuel was found, they could be married and live safely in Shechem.

If Samuel would have her. A woman who was barren, berated, and beleaguered.

Tired before her time.

Naomi returned with two witnesses and poured wine into the wedding cup.

Seth lifted the cup and drank, then handed it to Mara. She drank. Peering over the brim, she met his brown eyes flecked with gold. His face filled with joy and hope and peace. She could not help being drawn to him. "A new year. A new beginning."

There is a time for every season under heaven.

A voice spoke to her soul. An echo of the voice at the well.

A time to weep. A time to laugh.

A time for war. A time for peace.

A time to withdraw. And a time to embrace.

26

Jericho

Samuel

At Pyrce's house, Samuel bent over his workbench, absorbed with the repair of a harp. He often worked late into the night on his quest to fashion the harp that hummed in his head and strummed in his soul.

Zosi rushed in close, shattering his reverie.

Samuel rose. "You were to attend the queen all night."

"The queen has returned from Jerusalem in a rage."

Samuel took her hands. "What has happened?"

"A wild man, the one called the Baptizer, blocked the royal litter. He condemned the queen and her marriage."

A picture of the prophet standing in the river haloed by a fiery sunrise flashed across Samuel's mind. He pulled Zosi into his arms. *HaShem, help us.* "Where is the Baptizer now?"

"Like a specter, he vanished into the crowd."

"The Baptizer humiliated Herodias in the crowded streets."

Samuel wiped his palms against his short tunic. "She will be a threat to anyone nearby until she exacts her revenge."

Zosi glanced around. "Shh. Never forget. The walls have eyes and ears even in the Greek quarter."

"Let the queen's temper cool. Stay here until morning."

"I must protect my slave sisters in the kinnor choir." Zosi's voice was steady. "I came to beg you to pray to your unseen god who is above all others." She left as quickly as she had come.

Samuel draped a cloak over his head as a makeshift prayer shawl and looked out the window toward Mount Gerizim. He lifted his hands and swayed.

HaShem, protect these innocent women who serve an angry queen.

Since donning his pagan disguise, Samuel had abandoned all prayer rituals. Even when alone.

Now, despite his worry, his spirit swelled with a reborn joy. Suddenly, the cry he heard in the wilderness came to him.

Prepare ye the way of the Lord.

Could the Baptizer be the Taheb? Ima claimed the Magi coin was proof the Promised One was born nearly thirty years past. Mara's Magi coin. The coin he forfeited to pay for the care of a wounded Jew. An ethnic enemy.

Oddly, he had no regrets. The gold coin bought the breath of life for one hapless man.

HaShem, I beg you. Protect the prophet.

Now he prayed for the Baptizer. Another innocent man defying death. Another hapless Jew.

Samuel

247

Samuel sat at his bench surrounded by a bevy of harps in all stages of completion. He could hardly believe so many months had passed.

Heavy footsteps approached at a trot. Litter bearers. Samuel went to the door and helped Zosi down from the royal litter. "We are ordered to Machaerus." Her breathless voice quivered. "The queen has gone ahead."

"But I am confined to Jericho."

"The queen has spread word abroad that you were murdered. Maintain your disguise as a Greek slave and you will be safe."

"Why are we ordered to Machaerus?"

"Unrest boils throughout Judea. Machaerus is impregnable."

"And my harps?"

"You are to pack your entire workshop. When Herodias is troubled, she plays the harp, finding abandon in her artistry and solace in the supremacy of her skill."

"What could possibly trouble the most powerful woman in all Judea?" Samuel could not keep the resentment from his voice.

Zosi looked over her shoulder and leaned close. "A man with more sway than she. A prophet."

Samuel mirrored her whisper. "The Baptizer? "

"Since the day the prophet railed against the queen in the street, Herod has not visited her bedchamber. And the lustful eyes of the king wander to a new Favorite."

Samuel

248

The journey to Machaerus was slow. Samuel trudged beside the litter. He could best protect Zosi on foot. The final ascent to the Black Fort was plagued with steep drop-offs. On three sides, the terrain was so forbidding, no army could scale the cliffs. Three towers perched, like hungry vultures, over each ravine. Samuel and Zosi arrived in the lower town mid-morning of the third day. The memory of the queen's plunging litter invaded Samuel's thoughts.

At his signal, the bearers set Zosi's litter down. He parted the curtains. "Rest inside."

Samuel waved to the lead bearer. "Send word to Herodias. Your men cannot safely bear this large litter up the steep, winding road to the palace peak."

The man nodded and ran up the path.

At midday he returned leading a donkey. "This beast is gentle, sure-of-foot."

"Many thanks," Samuel said.

Zosi left the litter, yawning and stretching away sleep. "The queen will be waiting."

Samuel lifted Zosi onto the donkey's back, took the rein, and trudged up the treacherous path to the palace. The soldier at the gate brought them to a garden surrounded with colonnades and a portico leading into the palace.

There the queen reclined on a banquet couch and picked at the sumptuous meal set before her. She offered Zosi a bite of roasted quail from her hand. A token of great favor from queen to slave.

"Didymusssss ..." The queen leaned toward him.

Samuel hated the way Herodias stretched his Greek name into a hiss.

"Craft for me a singular harp. A harp sure to recapture Herod's heart."

Samuel clasped his trembling hands behind his back. The

queen's desperate demand seemed headstrong and hopeless. Was not Herod's heart his own?

Shechem

Mara

Mara hummed at her loom under the roof canopy. Seth played his kinnor, matching her soft sound. For months, his melodies had echoed their contentment throughout the House of the High Priest. Seth had spoken truly. Her fourth husband was more singer than soldier.

"Before you travel to Megiddo, sing my favorite song. The one you wrote."

Seth smiled. The faraway smile of an artist in communion with his Creator. Mara wove cloth, Seth wove words.

"You must promise not to weep at my tale of the lost dove that returns to his love."

Mara nodded, her throat clotted with emotion. Seth did not suspect that she wept for Samuel when she heard the dove song. Or perhaps he did. She had found Seth to be discerning and compassionate. With his patience, Mara learned the marriage bed could be a place of pleasure and harmony.

She had come to love Seth. Not in the way of first loves. Not in the manner that she loved Samuel. HaShem had created Samuel for her from the beginning of all time. But Samuel was dead. Seth was alive. And he was a blessing from the Lord. A husband for this season of her life.

While Seth sang, she packed supplies for his journey.

He strummed the last chord.

She waited until his music trailed away. "When will you return?"

"Is there any certain day you would have particular need of me?" His voice carried a smile.

"No." They could try for an heir any time. Her moonblood had never returned. She swallowed against her dry tongue. She feared her womb would be unfruitful, not merely for a season, but barren forever.

"Come." Seth walked outside.

Mara shook off her sadness. She wanted Seth to remember her at peace. "I will walk with you to the well and draw water for Sarah so she can stay with her husband."

"Sarah, the good friend of Naomi and Ruth?"

"Yes, and midwife at my birth. Her husband Daveed had a spell yesterday morning."

"What kind of spell?"

"For a few moments, he could not speak. Now he seems weary." Mara arranged her veil, hoisted a waterpot onto her head and another onto her hip.

They strolled through the village. At the well, the women nodded, drew water, and left. Her marriage to Seth had eased the vicious shunning, but she was still kept at arm's length.

Seth touched her cheek. "Just as you looked when we first met. May the Lord bless you and keep you."

Mara checked they were alone, then offered her lips. "May the Lord speed your safe return."

Seth kissed her lightly. "You know I must visit my first wife and family." He traced her lips with his thumb.

"It is only right." She gritted her teeth against a rebellious tear.

At this well, she was always left empty.

Waiting.

Thirsting.

For something or someone to mend her broken soul. For something just beyond the horizon. For someone just out of sight.

Mara

Mara leaned against the well and stared toward the bruised horizon. Reds bled to purples and purples to ambers. Soon the golden light would surrender to the looming dark.

Nights without Seth were long, lonely, loveless.

He had been absent for months, but faithful to write. At first, Naomi read Seth's letters to her. Then she taught Mara how to decipher them. Seth was such a scholar. He would be pleased with her fledgling attempts to read.

Mara spotted a lone figure riding a horse toward Shechem.

She squinted, unable to make out his face or clothing, but there was something familiar about the way he carried himself.

The black stallion raised its head, pounded a hoof, and whinnied.

The rider waved to her and spurred his horse to a gallop. Mara's heart and feet raced, robes flying. She knew that neigh, that white blaze on the stallion's muzzle, that rider.

Finally. Seth was home.

He came close and reined his mount.

Mara opened her arms and ran to him.

Seth reached down, caught her, and swept her up behind him.

"How I have missed you." Seth turned to kiss her properly.

She leaned toward him and matched his passion.

"Wife, it seems you also missed me."

Heat simmered on her neck and steamed onto her cheeks.

"Perhaps more than I realized." She hoped he would not think her a wanton woman.

The horse resumed a trot, and she clung tightly to Seth's middle.

Something in the leather satchel slung over Seth's shoulder jabbed Mara's side. "Let me move this to my shoulder so nothing comes between us."

"Nothing should come between us." Seth leaned back nestling closer. "Especially tonight." He handed her the satchel. "Take care. It cradles a new harp. One with such a wistful voice."

"But the sound of your first harp was so pure."

"Wait until you hear this one sing before you mourn the other." Seth prodded his mount forward.

She laid her ear against Seth's back and listened to the steady thrum of his heart. "We have days for me to hear what draws you to this new harp."

Seth tensed, sat straighter.

She could not fathom what was wrong,

At the House of the High Priest, Seth dismounted and lifted her to the ground. A pained expression flickered across his face.

"Husband, what troubles you?"

His hand, gentle on her chin, lifted her eyes to his. "We have only this one night, Mara, before I must report to the Roman legion at Megiddo."

A tight ball of worry tightened her stomach. "Your year of leave has seemed so short."

Johakim and Naomi hastened to greet Seth.

Seth stroked her cheek and leaned close to her ear. "Do not fret. There is good news. I will share when we are alone."

His whisper tickled Mara's face and she laughed. A light,

easy laugh. "I fret because I forgot. My waterpots wait at the well."

The evening meal with Naomi and Johakim was peaceful, but unending. Mara's cool calm was at war with the heat of her desire. When they retired, she welcomed Seth into her bed with a newfound urgency. Later, they settled into a nest of pillows.

"Husband, you promised good news."

Seth rolled onto his side and propped his head on his hand. "I am to be scribe to the commander at Megiddo, a boon for a man with no taste for war."

"So, you will not fight?"

"I will never be placed near the front lines." Seth's laugh rang with happy relief. "After all, the historian must live to tell the tale, sing the song of the hero."

"We must celebrate. Play the new harp." Mara lounged on the pillows.

Seth strummed her favorite ballad of lost love.

Mara closed her eyes and let the music seep into her heart. A vision of Samuel came to her. A vision so intense she could almost believe he truly stood before her.

Seth plucked the last notes letting the melody drift away. "My sweet wife."

Mara's eyes watered. Samuel had called her sweet. A lifetime ago.

Her husband kissed her tears, staving off her sadness. And pulled her to his chest. "You pine for a son. Lord willing, this night I have planted the seed of an heir within your womb."

The arm of the kinnor pressed painfully against her side. She moved back.

Seth saw that the harp jabbed her. "Forgive me." He put the harp away, returned and pillowed his head on her breast. Within three shared breaths he was asleep.

A Certain Man

Mara

Daylight pierced Mara's chamber window. Seth bolted awake and sprang from bed. "Late arrival at a military outpost will not be tolerated."

Mara and Seth headed for the kitchen where servants had left parcels of food for Seth's journey. Naomi and Johakim were not there. She and Seth would have a few more moments alone. "I will pack the food."

He handed his satchel to her. "And I will see to my mount."

Seth brought his stallion to the courtyard. Mara fed the horse an apple and patted his white blaze. The stallion nickered his thanks. She handed Seth his harpsack, a wineskin, and the satchel. "I will walk with you to the well."

"My sweet wife." Seth kissed her, pulled back, and let his gaze linger. "I dare not tarry, but I would seal your beauty in my mind's eye."

Seth mounted the stallion and galloped away—racing from the caresses of his wife into the clutches of war.

27

Machaerus Palace, Judea
Two Years Later

Samuel

S amuel sat with Zosi and Prima at his worktable. Queen
Herodias had created a curtained space for him in a side
enclave of the throne room at Machaerus. For more
than two years, he had honed his harp-making skills.

Zosi rubbed her rounded belly as if trying to calm the child
within.

Without warning, the heavy tapestry across from Samuel
lifted and Herodias entered.

An exquisite beauty on the cusp of womanhood followed
the queen and let the tapestry fall. Her dove eyes sparked
silver.

Samuel looked down, not daring to study the young woman
closely.

"Mother, is the harp completed?" Worry was woven through the young woman's tone.

"This is my daughter, Salome." The queen's owl eyes glinted gold. "Show me the harps."

Samuel's heartbeat throbbed in his ears. How much longer would the queen indulge him?

Samuel selected a kinnor and brought it to the queen.

Herodias sat next to Prima and played. "This is a fine harp, but nothing extraordinary." She turned it. "There is no makers-mark."

"It is not my work," said Samuel. "Now try this one."

The queen caressed the harp and strummed. "The back is rounded like a bowl. Like my rounded slave, Zosi." She bent her ear to the strings, testing the limits of the highs and lows. The room seemed to hold its breath awaiting her verdict.

The queen handed the kinnor to Samuel "Be sure to carve a makers-mark on this one."

"I mark each of my harps."

Queen Herodias would be furious if she knew he could not bring himself to give up the mark he used in Shechem.

"Then add a number to separate the queen's choices." Salome moved closer.

The scent of fresh-gathered roses clung to her. Samuel nodded.

"Now." There was iron in the queen's command.

Samuel carved a numeral one.

"Numbered harps will remain at court. All others you may sell." The queen moved to the workbench and traced the number. "Healer of Harps, make me a harp that sings to the angels."

Samuel looked away, his breath bound by an emotion as unexpected as it was unexplained. "There is a harp-song in my head and heart. That the sound remains unheard and unshared haunts my soul."

"Before Herod's birthday, hand me *that* harp. A harp to work a miracle for me with the king."

Samuel battled to keep his face from showing his doubts. "The harp will be complete when Zosi is ripe for birthing."

The queen patted Zosi's rounded middle. "If both my new harp and my new baby slave are birthed in the same week, it will portend good fortune." Her eyes glinted with undisguised cunning. "If your harp helps me win back Herod's heart, I must consider a just reward."

Salome took the harp from Samuel's hand and touched the fresh slash, the number he cut into his creation. She looked to Herodias. "Let the harp-maker marry Zosi. Then she would be free."

Samuel slid a look of apology to Zosi, his stomach devouring itself like a trapped rabbit gnawing its own limb.

Zosi turned to the queen. "We share the same bed but can never be wed. Samuel's heart waits for another."

Samuel's thoughts scrambled for a way to help Zosi. "But perhaps I could work to purchase Zosi's freedom."

"First conjure a harp without equal." Herodias lifted the tapestry curtain. "Salome. Prima. Leave us."

They hurried out.

The queen let the tapestry curtain fall and smirked. "Herod was intrigued with my gift for the audience hall and boasts that this tapestry once hung in a harem in Persia." Herodias strolled the length of the curtain, her finger tracing the scene of a wealthy man surrounded by courtesans in a paradise garden. She aligned her gaze with the eyes of a tapestry figure. "Make sure the king never learns that each set of eyes are loosely woven as windows for spying."

"Zosi looks and listens at the curtain only when we are alone."

"What have you learned?"

"The king sees the usual ambassadors, advisors, and supplicants." Zosi glanced at her sandals.

The queen's gaze flicked between Samuel and Zosi. "Do not dither, girl. Tell me of the unusual."

"Herod's new Favorite is always at his side."

"Does he give her grand gifts? Ask her thoughts?" The queen's voice grated like a blade scraping stone.

"She shares Herod's preoccupation with the Baptizer and often asks for him to be brought before them."

"Why?" The queen's voice turned to iron. Her face turned to stone.

"Herod asks how he can secure the favor of the Lord. The Baptizer calls for the king to repent of his incest and set you aside." Zosi's voice faltered to a croak.

"The king's harlot seeks to take my throne." Queen Herodias' words pelted the air, spewing a poisonous potion. She grabbed a goblet and flung it toward the wall.

It glanced against Zosi's temple, drew blood, and clattered against the stone.

Zosi wobbled, her face ashen. "My queen. Permission to sit."

Herodias nodded, her eyes distant, distracted.

Outrage fueled Samuel's pounding heart. He helped Zosi to the workbench and pressed a cloth to her brow.

Behind the peevish queen, the curtain lifted, and Salome slipped in—fear on her face, a finger to her lips. "Mother, I was waiting for you. The king is coming."

The queen glared at Salome. "You were spying." Her face softened. "Good girl. Lie and spy. And you may survive to thrive."

The queen's whisper was cut off by sounds of the king and his attendants entering the throne room.

"Put down all rebellion." King Herod's bellow was fearsome even behind the tapestry curtain.

Samuel had never heard the king so enraged.

"The traitors have been captured and crucified."

A new voice.

Samuel peered through the eyes of the tapestry. A messenger.

"The bronze eagle standard was swiftly recovered."

The king stomped. "Did the sun set with the eagle of Rome in enemy hands?"

"Yes, my king."

Herod sat on his throne. "Order the commander to decimate his legion, then fall on his sword." Herod pulled his new Favorite onto his lap.

She stroked Herod's beard." My king, what means this word 'decimate'?"

"The legion is counted, and every tenth man is executed." The king's now-measured voice was more terrifying than his rage.

The scrape of chains near the enclave bristled the hairs on Samuel's arms. He well remembered the chafe of shackles.

"My king. The Baptizer."

Samuel started at the closeness of the jailor's voice.

The Baptizer still wore a camelhair garment, but his hair had gone gray, and he was wasted and weak.

Queen Herodias joined Samuel at the tapestry.

The Baptizer was forced to kneel, then dragged to his feet.

"Are you the Promised King? "The king pointed at the prophet. "The Messiah?"

Samuel held his breath. From the moment he saw the

Baptizer in the river Jordan, that same question had burned in Samuel's soul.

"My answer remains the same. I am ... not ... He." The Baptizer spoke with calm control.

The new Favorite leaned forward. "Then, who are you?"

"I make straight the path for the One whose sandal I am not fit to tie."

The Favorite touched Herod's arm.

He waved permission for her to continue.

She rose. "Where were you born?"

The Baptizer flung back his long ropes of twisted hair. "Not in Bethlehem."

The Favorite tipped her head, her brows drawn down. "The One of whom you speak. Where was he born?"

"Bethlehem in the shadow of Migdal Eder, the tower where the sacrificial lambs are birthed."

Herod stood. "When?"

"When the wondrous star shone over Judea." The Baptizer's voice rang out across the large hall.

"When Magi from the East came to my father's court." Herod rubbed his chin. "How can you be certain you have baptized the Messiah?"

The Baptizer looked heavenward. "When certainty fails and doubt tortures the soul, the righteous cling to faith."

The Favorite's eyes widened, and her mouth formed the smallest of cryptic smiles. "If the Baptizer speaks the truth, the baby born King of the Jews escaped the sword of your father, the Butcher of Bethlehem."

The Baptizer pointed a gnarled finger at Herod. "Repent. The will of the Lord will not be thwarted."

Herod rose. "Take this man back to the dungeon." His tone betrayed his fear of judgment. He offered his arm to his Favorite. "Come my lovely, let us walk in the gardens."

Herodias turned from the tapestry and drew in a ragged breath. "The Baptizer will never banish me from my throne."

Samuel checked Zosi. Her head wound had stopped bleeding.

The queen approached them. "Why is the king's harlot concerned with the birth of the Promised One?"

Zosi took the rag from Samuel. "Her mother's firstborn was one of the slaughtered baby boys of Bethlehem. Now she searches for the one baby who escaped. No one knows if she seeks to adore or annihilate him."

"Either way, Herod's new Favorite keeps the Baptizer's demands to divorce me in the king's ears."

The queen seemed to suddenly remember her silent daughter and turned to Salome. "We must devise your dance for the King's birthday banquet." Herodias lifted one of Salome's dark curls. "I have designed your garment with seven veils, each one a color of the rainbow."

"I have no desire to excite the king's lust." Salome lifted a proud chin.

Herodias backhanded Salome across the face. "Trusting fool."

Salome pressed a hand to her crimson cheek.

"Herod decimates decorated legions. He plotted to kill his first wife. He may decide to rid himself of me."

Such violence. Such evil. Samuel wanted to walk away, but no one walked away from a queen or a princess. Nor could he leave Zosi when Herodias was so volatile.

Queen Herodias shook Salome by the shoulders. "If my music does not bring the king back to my bed, we have nowhere to run. No one to protect us."

Salome's chin quivered. "Forgive me, mother. I did not know."

A Certain Man

The queen pulled Salome close and stroked her hair. "If I fail with my music, you must dance for your life. And mine."

Jericho

Mara

Mara carried water to Sarah's house. Since the recent passing of Naomi, her friend Sarah and Mara were both grieving. She filled a cup, went to Sarah's pallet, and guided the cup to Sarah's cracked lips. Mara braced for another cruel loss.

Mara pulled a chair close so she could make out Sarah's breathy, weak speech.

"I miss her." Sarah's wheeze became a cough.

Mara patted her hand. "So do I."

Sarah appeared to gather her strength. "Such sadness. For you to enter Naomi's chamber and find her ... gone."

"The very day I sent Seth off to war." Mara's heart thrummed a silent lament. "Naomi gone. Without warning. Without goodbyes." Mara's voice faltered over her mountain of losses.

"We have the blessing of farewells." Sarah held Mara's hand. "And must not leave them unspoken."

Their farewells would speak in their quiet touch as much as in their words.

Tears spilled onto Sarah's cheeks. "I wish I could spare Daveed the pain of loneliness after I am gone."

Mara held Sarah's hand and stroked with her thumb. "You have sons. He will not be alone.

"Sons will not warm his bed." Sarah's voice was suddenly

strong, but she slumped under the weight of her grief. "At night, without my warmth, Daveed will be cold as a corpse."

A tear spilled onto Mara's hand.

HaShem, speak to my heart. What am I to see?

An Anointing.

"Until the morrow." She kissed Sarah's brow and left.

Mara walked toward the House of the High Priest and pondered the still, small voice. Anointings herald new beginnings. New beginnings follow endings. Sarah's end was near, but how was that a beginning for Mara?

Watch and wait.

The voice. Again.

Dread ambushed her. Mara lifted her skirts and ran. Her breath and heartbeat raced through her fog of fear. She sped to the spot where she bid farewell to Seth.

Hashem, help me. I am so alone.

You are never alone.

Her breathing quieted and her heart slowed. An eerie sense of calm flowed through her. like the calm of a sky before a tempest.

A mounted messenger trotted up to the gate. "Johakim, High Priest of Shechem."

Okpara came running and opened the gate.

Mara nodded toward him. "Fetch your master." She took a dipper, drew water from a tall stone jar, and handed it to the messenger.

He smiled his thanks and drank his fill.

Johakim hurried toward them.

The messenger pulled a small scroll from his robes.

The seal of Herod. Mara laid a hand over her skittering heart.

Johakim opened the scroll and sagged. Okpara barely caught him. He and Mara helped Johakim to a nearby bench.

Johakim stared, his eyes dim. The scroll slid from his lap onto the ground.

Mara picked up the scroll and spotted the word *Seth* but could not decipher much else. Her heart hammered nails into her tight chest. She turned to the messenger and waved the parchment. "What does this say?"

"My lady, I do not know."

"You must tell me." Her pitch rose, riding the wave of her panic.

"Even in the face of torture, I could not say. I cannot read."

Johakim muttered prayers, his gaze fixed on Mount Gerizim.

Mara swallowed forcing down the fright tightening her throat.

"Seth is named here. I am his wife." She pushed the scroll back into Johakim's hand. "Speak."

His gaze took on a deep tenderness more terrifying than the gaping jaw of a lion. "You are no longer a wife, but once more a widow."

"Seth was a scribe, not a soldier." Mara's whisper sounded like a voice from the grave.

The high priest wrung his hands. "Seth's legion let their bronze eagle standard fall into rebel hands. The legion was decimated."

Mara looked to the messenger. "I do not understand."

"Every tenth man was bludgeoned to death by the other nine." The messenger took a sack from his mount. "Seth's first wife sent this to you."

The harp. Mara clutched it to her heart. "His first family buried him in Megiddo?"

"No. He lies in a mass grave."

Mara tore at her hair. "HaShem, what more must I endure?"

Johakim studied the scroll, his face unreadable. "Okpara, feed this messenger." Johakim waited until they withdrew.

"There is more." His tone was as gentle and sad as Seth's dove song.

Mara hugged the harp and held her breath.

"Rome has confiscated Seth's lands and legacy. The first wife and sons sold themselves into slavery."

Mara's thoughts tumbled over each other like a rockslide that begins with pebbles and ends with boulders that strike and crush and bury whatever lies below. "Seth made provision for me in the contract." A disembodied voice seemed to speak her disembodied thoughts.

Johakim's voice shook as much as his trembling hands. "The bride-price paid to Tobiah is untouchable. The gold Seth set aside for you is forfeit to Rome."

A burning like lye bored into Mara's stomach and clawed up into her throat. "Yet again, I am left to the mercy of the greedy, ever-besotted Tobiah."

The High Priest wobbled to a stand. "As long as I draw breath, you will never be a slave to Rome or Tobiah."

"Johakim, you owe me nothing. You have been kind and forgiving of a withered woman who has given you no heir."

Johakim removed his priestly turban and crumpled to his knees. "You do not know of my sin against you. Shechem does not know of my sin against them."

Johakim's ramblings were gibberish. Had grief addled his mind?

He shook his turban at the heavens. "But over the last seven years, HaShem has meted out his judgment. My House has been cut off. My line ends with me."

28

Machaerus Palace, Judea
Near Passover

Samuel

Prima led Samuel and Zosi into the throne room to places at a low table. "When needed, you must tune and tend the harp."

Herodias sat before the dais, harp in her lap, poised to play. Samuel helped Zosi onto a bench.

Her hand went to her belly. "She kicks."

Samuel smiled. Zosi insisted the child was a girl. Aromas of fresh rich food wafted to him. Aromas that mingled with the stale leavings thrown to the dogs that lay in wait beneath the table.

Herod's new Favorite dozed in a chair next to the king. Drowsy, drugged, or drunk, Samuel could not say. Nobles and guests gorged themselves or sprawled across the tables and floor.

Zosi gasped and spread both hands across her stomach as if to hide the eyes of the babe within. "Pray to your god that our daughter will never see such debauchery."

The king reached for a silver pipe joined to a fog-filled bowl. Bleary-eyed, he took a puff and held it in his cheeks. Persian pleasure smoke. The drone of deep-voiced flutes filled the room. Herod raised a hand, and a drumroll silenced the gathering. The king lurched to his feet. "For the final night of my birthday feast, I give you the music of my woman."

The queen rewarded the king with a brilliant, seductive smile, but clutched the harp in a white-knuckled grip.

Zosi spoke in Samuel's ear. "Herodias is in grave danger. The king called her his woman, not his queen."

Herodias played, her harp-song caressing the kinnor and the king. The melody melted into a sultry show of her mastery of the music and the men who had succumbed to her touch. Her fingernails were talons plucking Herod's heart from his chest, swooping his sinful desires back to her breast. Her fingertips were raindrops dancing on thirsty earth.

The king licked his lips. Parched.

The queen's last lusty chord woke her rival.

The new Favorite smiled, gloating down from the dais, placed her hand on Herod's cheek, and turned his face and heart back to her.

The queen guarded her brilliant smile. A loss would never cross her face. But her carefully woven spell was dashed, crashing against the marble floor at her bejeweled feet.

"Zosi, fetch Salome." Herodias whispered through smiling lips. "Her dance must drag victory from the flames of defeat."

Zosi waddled off, rubbing her back.

The banqueters returned to their plates and their perversions.

Zosi waved a hand from a break in the tapestry draped behind the throne.

Herodias picked up her harp and nodded to the drummers. A thunderous drumroll ended with a jolt.

Herod bolted away from his Favorite.

The hall went still.

The tapestry draped behind the throne parted.

Salome, veiled from her gold-banded brow to her ruby-ringed toes, struck a serpentine pose. She slithered between the Favorite and the king. The harp melody enhanced every undulation of the mystery woman. Her diaphanous draping hinted at an exquisite form, but left all else to fantasy.

Every eye was fixed on the willowy dancer—even the women could not look away.

Strong arms from behind the chair clutched the Favorite, covered her mouth, and hauled her away.

The queen's last, desperate gambit was in play.

Salome shed the red and orange veils. Her shoulders glistened from the powdered gold brushed on her oiled skin. Tiny anklet bells tinkled in rhythm with her subtle swaying.

Samuel met Salome's inviting gray eyes peering over her veil. She threaded her dance past him. A rush of desire flooded his veins. He forced his thoughts from the forbidden. *HaShem, deliver me from evil.*

Zosi slipped back by his side. "Watch for any threat to Herodias or Salome."

Samuel studied every cranny, every shadow. In Herod's court, treachery could breed in any corner.

Salome flitted just out of reach of the king. She slowly shed the yellow and green veils that covered a scant jeweled top.

Herod began to stand, but Salome playfully pushed him back onto his throne and twirled away from his grasping fingers.

The king reached for his pipe and dragged in another deep breath.

Herodias increased the speed and fervor of her music.

The king blew out the smoke, his head crowned with a coiled vapor of milk of the poppy.

"Salome must win the king before he is overtaken by the fog of fools." Zosi's tone was laced with worry.

Salome freed the blue and indigo veils from the sparkling girdle that wrapped her tiny waist. She swirled in and out of the king's reach, veils fluttering like butterfly wings. Salome's dark curls, now uncovered and unbound, had been entwined with long blond and red tresses. Tresses that flared as she whirled—tickling and taunting the king's cheeks. She could be every woman. She could be any woman.

The last veil hid Salome's lower face, highlighting her kohl-lined eyes and lapis-dusted lids.

Samuel strained to hear snippets of chatter. A drunken crowd could turn nasty in a gnat's breath.

"Is she Greek?"

"I wager from beyond the seas of Tarshish."

"My coin is on Persia. See how she moves."

Salome brandished one veil like a whip.

Zosi gasped. "The virgin does not know she invites violence." She leaned close to Samuel. "Some women have never returned from the king's chamber."

Salome danced on.

A lewd laugh was choked off by a cough.

"Who is she?"

"Wait ..."

Salome dropped to her knees.

Herodias plucked strong climactic chords.

The final violet veil slipped from Salome's face.

"The princess."

"The king's niece."

"The queen's daughter."

Herod's face blanched. His lips trembled. His mouth dropped open. And he could not seem to close it.

Salome went to the queen's side, but kept her eyes locked on the king.

He flushed and his face changed. He seemed to shake off all caution. "Name your prize."

The queen exhaled a triumphant sigh.

Salome shot a sidelong look at her mother, approached the dais, and knelt.

The king rose. "Come girl, name your prize."

"I want John the Baptizer."

Herod's face was the death mask of a vanquished gladiator frozen in horror.

Samuel's stomach twisted around a blade of fear and guilt and shame. Salome must not press her wicked request.

"Give me only his head."

"Name some other thing, though it be half my kingdom." The lingering lust on the king's face was replaced by a darkening storm of anger and fear.

Salome lifted the king's platter, dumped the food, and thrust it into his hand. "The Baptizer's head. On this golden platter." Salome stepped back and pouted prettily. "It is my only desire."

The guests murmured.

Herod raised both hands. "My word must be kept."

The Captain of the Guard hurried away.

Samuel's palms slicked. His harp had helped cast the seductive spell.

Salome sat on the step several paces from the king's feet.

"Smart girl. Stay there." The queen seemed compelled to

whisper her thoughts to Samuel. "Let Herod believe this was Salome's choice. Her choice, alone."

The banqueters returned to their lusts and their gluttony.

Samuel shuddered and tried to shake off his disgust. The Lord despised the spilling of innocent blood. He looked to Zosi. "It shames me that we have helped the queen snare an innocent man. And for this we will suffer."

Zosi looked pale, spent. "The Baptizer will not be the last innocent man condemned by King Herod."

The torch-light sconces burned low. Lengthening fire-shadows danced on the walls. "Your harp should sing lullabies for our daughter." Zosi's sleepy voice trailed off, her head on her arms at the table.

Samuel stared at the soothing shadows. After a time, his heavy heart and heavy lids drooped, and he dozed.

A scream pierced the darkness. Samuel and Zosi startled awake. One of the banquet slaves pointed to the dais. The Captain of the Guard carried a bloody platter with the Baptizer's head—eyes and mouth open—still calling men to repentance.

Salome, sitting on the stair, turned her face away from the sickening display.

Herod tore at his hair. His lips twisted into a snarl, and he pointed at Salome. "This was not my wish, but yours."

Salome looked back to Herod's furious face and seemed to shrink like a wounded waif.

"Rise and receive your prize."

She rose, quivering and unsteady.

The Captain of the Guard thrust the platter at her.

A look of sheer fear flickered in Salome's wide eyes. She turned and gazed up at King Herod with the look of a trapped doe. She blinked and for the span of a heartbeat looked likely to flee.

"Salome." The queen's face was as still as the sea after a tempest, but her eyes were as sharp and hard as a slashing sword. Sharp as her will. Hard as her heart. "Take the platter. You must obey your king."

Salome turned toward the queen's unwavering voice. Bolstered by the strength in her mother's command, as if in a trance, she slowly lifted her arms and stared at The Baptist's severed head.

The Captain of the Guard waited until she turned her palms up and placed the platter into her hands.

The platter wobbled and blood splattered onto her palms. She placed the platter at the king's feet, picked up one of her veils from the floor, and scrubbed her skin with a vengeance.

"The Baptizer's blood will stain your hands. Forever." The king stood and strode from the room.

"Zosi, help." Salome pressed her sheer skirt to her mouth. "I am going to be sick."

Zosi hurried to Salome, wiped her brow and palms.

Suddenly, Zosi's grim, pinched face was overtaken with surprise. She looked at Samuel, her eyes wide. "My birth-waters." A puddle spread on the floor. "Your daughter is coming." The puddle turned red. Blood red.

Samuel ran to her. Zosi swooned into his arms.

A rush of blood. A river of blood. His Zosi. He could feel her life slipping away.

Queen Herodias stood and pointed to a guard. "Bring a physician. Perhaps he can save the babe in Zosi's womb. Though I will miss the mother, she will soon lie in a cold, dark tomb."

A surge of horror slammed through Samuel's veins. He could not speak. He could not breathe. He could not even pray. His daughter would be born into a sea of blood.

Shechem

Mara

Mara set the waterpot on Sarah's threshold. Her small service of drawing water for Sarah gave her a reason to visit daily. Before she could call out a greeting, Misha-el, Sarah's oldest son, threw open the door. "She is asking for you."

Her friend lay still and small and fading. Daveed sat in a nearby chair holding her hand to his lips. The younger son, Dan, stood vigil in the corner.

Mara went to Sarah and stroked her damp brow. The old woman's unbound hair was a mass of tangles splayed around her head like a twisted fisherman's net. "I am here." Mara filled a washbasin adding lemon slices and rose petals.

Daveed shivered, his hands violently trembling.

"My sons, take your father into the sunlight. He needs warmth." A small sob escaped Sarah's lips. "Warmth I can no longer give."

The sons helped their father to his feet and went outside.

Mara prepared her heart for another leave-taking and washed Sarah's face. She could barely lift her head. Three deaths in as many months. First Naomi, then Seth—both under a sickle moon. Now Sarah would follow before the next full moon.

Mara put a fresh linen tunic on her.

"Of all the children I have ushered into this world, you are the one I would have chosen to prepare me for the next."

"Shh. Rest." Mara combed the tangles from Sarah's hair.

The comb caught on a knot. Sarah winced.

"Forgive me."

She brushed away Mara's apology. "Without me, Daveed will be cold. Cold as death while he still has life."

"Shh."

Sarah suddenly took Mara's hand. "Promise me you will never let Daveed be cold." Sarah's tone was so forlorn. "Promise me."

"I promise." Mara kissed Sarah's brow. "I will call your menfolk."

Sarah lay back down, her face calm.

Mara slipped toward the door. She would stoke the fire all night. Cover Daveed with warmed blankets. But this was such an impossible promise.

"Tamara."

Mara turned back.

Sarah raised a hand in blessing. "Fear Not. Nothing is impossible with the Lord."

Mara

Three days later, Mara arranged her veil, entered the High Priest's study, and stood at his right hand.

Sarah's sons Misha-el and Dani-el waited before the heavy oak table. A sea of scrolls and quills separated her from them.

"Before our mother lapsed into a deep sleep, this woman made a promise." Dan's tone was tense and demanding.

The High Priest glanced at Mara.

"This woman promised that at the passing of our ima, she would make sure our father was always warm." Misha's voice was kind and confident.

"A vow born from her love of your parents. A vow this woman will keep." Johakim shrugged. "Why should I need to intercede?"

"All night, my father shakes violently even with the fire fully stoked. The moment our mother passes from this life, Mara must marry him. The only way she can honor her vow is by warming his bed. Abba is so frail, he must not spend even one night alone." Misha's voice broke.

Mara's panicked chest clamped around her runaway heart.

The high priest met her eyes, a flicker of fear in his own. "Come, sit."

Mara's heart seemed to rupture. She took a half-step and stumbled.

The high priest helped her to a chair.

"I promised to watch over Daveed, stoke the fire, cover him with blankets. Not blanket him with my body."

"The sons of King David made such an arrangement." Misha looked toward Mara, his eyes pleading. "It would be a blessing for my father and our family."

"She may choose to bless your family, but you must in turn provide for her." The high priest crossed his arms. "There is the matter of the bride-price."

"Our mother made us swear on the lives of our firstborn that we would provide generously for Mara." Misha's face took on a new look of authority. "Upon my father's death, she will inherit the shepherd cottage and field just outside the town."

"If Mara marries again, her husband will provide for her and the cottage will revert to me." Dan's tone was cold and angry. The cottage must have been part of his inheritance.

"Why are you here now?" Mara looked from one son to the other.

"We want the contract drawn and signed so our father will not spend one night alone." Misha's voice broke.

A twinge of sadness tightened Mara's throat. Misha was already mourning his mother.

"Wait in the courtyard. I would speak with this woman." The high priest lifted a hand, dismissing Sarah's sons.

They retreated, whispering prayers.

"What say you?" The high priest poured her a cup of water.

Mara wrung her hands—hands now suddenly cold as snow. She sipped the water. Fear darkened her divided mind. "I vowed to keep him warm, but I never ..." Her voice fell away, trailing into the chasm between yes and no, right and wrong, sure and unsure.

She studied Johakim's eyes.

He drew in a slow breath, seeming to search his stores of wisdom. "Promise-keeping often demands more than we ever expected." He sat next to her. "Your future would be secure, free of Tobiah. I will not live forever. Could this be a provision from HaShem?

"What is your wise and righteous counsel?" Mara's heart thrummed like one of Seth's harp strings.

The high priest looked up, seeming to seek word from heaven. "For seven years, your will has been ignored. Consult only the Creator."

How tender Johakim's heart had grown. How different from the man who upheld the letter of the Law at her first betrothal.

"Tell the sons of Sarah, I will give them my answer at this hour, three days hence."

Johakim's eyes flashed approval. "Let it be so." He headed toward the courtyard.

"Wait."

Johakim turned.

"This is such an unexpected, unsought, unusual request."

Mara barely dared to think her question. "Could it be I am somehow chosen?"

High Priest crossed his hands over his heart. "You may have been anointed for such a time as this."

29

Machaerus Palace, Judea

Samuel

Samuel sat at his workbench in the throne room enclave, tucked behind the tapestry curtain where he felt safe to grieve his loss of Zosi. Samuel's newborn daughter whimpered, and the wet nurse put her to the breast. He looked at the tiny babe with wonder, grateful for some remnant of Zosi to love.

Here, he was also safe to mourn the beheading of the Baptizer who promised the coming of the Taheb, the prophet who would be greater than Moses.

The curtain lifted and Prima entered.

Samuel handed Prima the harp he just finished making. "I am anxious to hear this one."

Prima sat beside him and strummed a soft, sweet song. His daughter fell asleep, her lips opening and closing as if singing along.

"My baby seems to know that melody, though I have never heard it."

"Zosi sang it when she was with child. A winsome soldier bought one of your harps and taught us his song of lost love." Prima glanced at the baby and giggled. "Her lids are heavy, her mouth a circle. She is milk drunk."

The wet nurse brought the baby to Samuel and left. He cradled her in one arm.

Prima stopped strumming. "Zosi told me of your first love." *Mara.*

His lost love. *Mara.* The missing half of his soul.

"I loved Zosi too. She loved me first and bore my precious child. Zosi's last sigh was traded for our babe's first breath, as if she willed her daughter to live in her stead." He would never be like Mara's father and blame the babe for the loss of the mother.

"She has Zosi's green eyes and sweet small mouth." Prima touched the baby's cheek.

She plucked a lullaby that brought to Samuel's mind the murmur of light rain on a tile roof. "One day, this must be your daughter's harp. I will teach her to play."

Samuel nodded. "This kinnor sings the sound my soul has been seeking, but the queen may choose to keep this one."

Prima leaned close. "Place a scrap of linen in the soundbox and tune the harp lower. The sound will lose its luster. Your daughter's legacy will be secure."

The tapestry lifted. Salome stepped in, eyes distant, hair disheveled. She crossed to the wash basin and scrubbed her red, raw hands in rhythm with her singsong mutterings.

The princess dropped onto the pile of pillows and hugged her knees.

The quiet stretched to a smothering stillness.

Samuel's stomach tightened around a clump of pity and revulsion. "What has happened?"

The tapestry lifted again. Herodias entered. "Since the night Salome was called to the king's chamber, her mind has been undone."

Salome's serene smile seemed to lock on something beyond the workshop. "Terrible kings do terrible things."

Her smile was at war with her words. Something terrifying flickered in her eyes. A hint of cruelty coiled at the corner of her mouth. "Things can happen to kings." Salome's eyes were empty—those of a woman gone mad.

Herodias turned to Prima. "Take the princess. Give her a calming brew. Play your harp lively and loud so no one will hear her damning chants."

Salome hugged her knees tighter and rocked. "Terrible, terrible things happen to terrible, terrible kings."

Prima took Salome's hand and shot a worried glance toward the queen. "Each day the brew takes longer to calm her."

Herodias' face was stone-steady, but she could not cover the spreading red splotch on her neck.

The queen moved to the tapestry and peered through the eye holes. "The throne room is empty." She placed her ear to the opening. Her stony mask cracked, eyes widened with alarm. "The king comes. Go before the princess hears his voice."

"My queen, your cloak." Prima swung the queen's cloak around Salome, hiding her dry handwashing.

Speaking in soothing tones, Prima began an amusing story and guided Salome from the workshop.

Herodias stepped toward Samuel and looked at the baby in his arms.

He wanted to turn away from this evil woman and shield his daughter from her talons. Instead, he loosened the swaddling around her face, and hoped that the queen would not touch her.

Herodias extended a ringed finger and stroked his sleeping daughter's cheek. "My newest slave resembles her mother. She will grow to be quite a beauty."

Samuel's hand crushed the edge of the swaddling cloth. He would die before he would leave his daughter in the clutches of this debauched king and depraved queen.

"You wince when I touch the babe?" Her voice brimmed with offense.

Samuel's palms slicked, his mind raced. He whispered. "I worried you might wake her." He flashed her his most sheepish smile. "She has just fallen asleep."

"It is time she is named. All births in Herod's household must be recorded." The baby opened her eyes, and the queen took her from him.

Samuel swallowed hard and ate his anger. "What will you name her?"

Please, Lord, not a pagan name that invokes an idol.

His nameless baby blew contented lip bubbles.

"If you would claim her as yours, *you* must name her."

Samuel drew in a steadying breath. "I would not only claim her, but also buy her out of slavery."

The queen's expression clouded to something he could not read. Something sure to be dangerous, devious.

"Redemption of a full-grown female is seven years of labor."

Samuel's heart hitched. His knees turned to wax.

HaShem.

Be still.

"For an infant whose father has a trade, I will be generous. Serve me as bond servant for half the seven years."

"Agreed." One day his daughter would be free.

"What will you call her?"

Zosi should have named their child. What would please

her? What would please the Lord? A sweet name. A joyful name. He would not yoke his girl-child with a bitter name, as Tobiah had done.

"I will call her Zimrah. My song, my joy."

The queen's eyes narrowed. "You are no longer a son of Abraham, but a Greek called Didymus." The queen glared at Samuel. "Name her now or I will."

"She will be called ... Lyra."

The queen clapped with delight.

"How clever. The Greek harp-maker's daughter named *Harp.*" Herodias favored Samuel with a smug look of approval. "Herod will be amused. His name means song of the hero."

The wet nurse returned.

"Woman, hurry. Ready the babe to present to the king."

The nurse swaddled Lyra in a fresh blanket.

Samuel lifted the tapestry curtain.

"Lyra provides me an excuse to speak with the king. To bring me back into his head. And bring him back into my bed." The queen glanced at Samuel. "Stay back. Do not speak. Herod believes you are dead."

The king entered and dropped onto his throne looking bored, besotted, and lonely. The Favorite had not been seen since Salome's dance. Herod glanced at the empty throne that trumpeted his rejection of Herodias.

The queen curtseyed.

"My lord, the newest addition to our household may amuse you." Herodias lifted Lyra from the nurse's arms, stepped onto the dais, and turned her to face the king.

"Ha." Herod slapped his knee, laughing. "She smiled at me."

At the crack of the slap, Lyra whimpered.

The queen put the baby over her shoulder and patted her

back. "Since Herod means song of the hero, the Greek harp-maker named her Lyra—something musical in your honor."

"The babe and I have made one another laugh." Herod took Lyra into his arms. "My lady, such a clever gift."

Samuel gasped. No air. His chest was granite. He could not and must not speak.

"My lord, forgive me." Herodias knelt at the king's feet. "I am not so clever and did not think of it. The father and I have already signed the contract for her redemption."

Lies fall from this queen's lips as easily as the morning dew falls from heaven.

"The word of a queen must be as trustworthy as the word of her king." The king handed his baby back to Herodias. "Live long, Lyra."

The queen stepped off the dais. The wet nurse scurried to take Lyra and brought her back to Samuel.

Careful to keep his face down, he cradled Lyra and moved behind a pillar where he could see, but not be seen.

"Come my queen, you have been absent from my side far too long." The king extended his hand.

The queen took the king's hand and her place on the throne, disavowing she had ever been set aside.

"We will hear the day's petitioners."

The king rendered judgments, often leaning an ear to Herodias, who whispered her counsel. The affairs of court finally concluded, Herod rose and offered his arm to the queen.

The queen slipped her hand into the crook of Herod's arm. "My lord, if it please you, I will follow in a few moments. I have directions for the harp-maker."

"Must you tend to that now?" The king whined like a spoiled child.

"Yes. It is a surprise for you."

"What is it?"

The queen shook her finger at Herod. "If I were to tell you, the surprise would be ruined."

"Do not tarry." The king smiled suggestively and swept from the room.

Lyra nuzzled at Samuel's chest, seeking a breast. He put his little finger in her mouth.

Herodias approached Samuel. "Take the princess from Machaerus before her chants convict us all of treason."

"Where?"

"Take our daughters by an out-of-the-way route—by way of the Salt Sea." Something in the Queen's tone warned Samuel of danger. "There, a boat carrying bitumen waits on the shore. Bypass Jerusalem and go to Jericho. Lyra will be a darling of my court and the wet nurse will sequester Salome in the women's quarters."

"As you have commanded."

"Then, you may go to Shechem."

"But, Jareb—" Samuel could not keep the tremor from his voice.

"My spy found an Egyptian servant in Shechem who traded news for gold. Jareb died of lockjaw. Your brave beloved Mara is free to marry."

Mara. His heart pounded a fierce gallop back to her. But, his chest reared, reining in his heart. "I cannot leave Lyra."

"You cannot stay in Jericho. Even disguised as Didymus you might be recognized. You will serve me best from Shechem."

A lump clotted in Samuel's throat. "Am I not to see Lyra until her redemption?"

"You may see her when Herod goes up to Jerusalem for Feasts." Herodias planted her hands on her hips, her eyes narrow and hard. "Swear you will serve me well."

"I will."

"Go then. Marry your beloved."

A shiver raced through Samuel's soul. It was seven years since he had fled from Shechem.

Mara

Mara sat on a boulder under the looming terebinth tree facing Jacob's well. Jacob the Liar.

How fitting. Mara the liar. For years, her moonblood lie kept her from Jareb's bed. But HaShem had punished her and left her barren. Now she must decide whether to marry Daveed or one day risk poverty. This was her valley of decision.

Long ago, between these mountains, Joshua confronted the people. *Choose. The altars of HaShem or the altars of Baal. Serve good or serve evil.*

A group of young girls walked toward the well. They stole glances at her but turned away. News of Seth's death had slammed shut all gates of friendship save for Sarah, who mourned Seth with her. Mourned for the only husband whose death Mara counted a loss.

Ruth was gone, Naomi was gone. Soon Sarah would follow and Mara would be bereft of any womanly comfort.

She could not abandon Sarah. She had been the midwife at Mara's birth that caused her mother's death.

Mara's lip trembled. Could she bear waking one morning warming Daveed's corpse?

She buried her face in her hands. She had not offered prayers for so long. Afraid she would be met with sickening silence. More afraid of His answers.

HaShem, what is Your will?

Choose love.

She arranged her veil, her steps lightened by a surety of purpose.

As she passed through the village, the rumor ravens ran ahead and flocked at the open courtyard gate of the House of the High Priest. They parted as she walked through them and joined the high priest and Sarah's sons.

Misha met her eyes. Dan looked away.

The high priest held up his hand for silence. "Woman, what is your decision?"

"I choose to ease Sarah's heart. When the time comes, I will wed Daveed."

The high priest nodded to the scribes, his eyes shining. "The contract has been drawn."

Mara smiled behind her veil. Johakim had known her choice before she did. Murmurs of approval passed through the gathering. Sarah was much loved, even as Mara was not.

Relief flickered across Misha's face. "Come. Our mother asks for you."

Falling darkness smudged the gold sunset with streaks of gray. Sarah's sons waited silently outside their childhood home. Mara stepped inside.

Sarah lay on the raised pallet, eyes closed. Daveed sat on a stool holding her hand. "She is with us, then she is not." His voice hitched over his heartbreak.

Sarah's eyes fluttered open and a small smile flickered across her face.

Mara went to her and kissed her brow. "I have come."

"You have granted my last wish. May HaShem honor you above all the women of Shechem."

"Be at peace. I will heat some savory broth."

Sarah patted Mara's hand. "I have blessed my sons, their wives, and their children. Tell them to depart and pursue righteous lives." Bringing Daveed's hand to her lips, she gazed at him with such fondness. "I have all I need."

Mara delivered Sarah's message. The family whispered their final farewells toward heaven and left.

Mara returned and served the broth.

Daveed helped Sarah take sips and drank his bowl slowly, hands trembling—unsteady from age and cold and sorrow.

At full dark, Daveed joined his wife on the sleeping pallet.

Mara kept watch in the nearby chair, content with them and her choice. Throughout the night, she checked the devoted couple and the cookfire just outside the door. When she could no longer stay awake, she curled up near the warm embers of the dying fire.

Misha had been wrong. Sarah's parting was not so near. For three nights, Mara tended the pair as if they were her own parents. How different her life would have been if her mother had lived to love and be loved by Tobiah this way.

At daybreak, Daveed rose and kissed his wife. She sighed her last breath and slipped away.

Mara retreated outside and left Daveed to his last leave-taking.

Dan, the younger son, spotted her and approached.

"Your mother has left this world."

"My wife will come and prepare her body. Make ready to wed before the sun sets."

Misha joined them. "Father must be made ritually clean before he can wed." He turned to his younger brother. "Bring the high priest who will put all things in order."

Over the next hours, the villagers mourned and escorted Sarah's body to the family burial cave.

Mara walked to the House of the High Priest, packed her things, and returned to Daveed's house. She mourned Sarah alone. Apart. Always an outcast.

Propping open the door, Mara swept the stone floor, and hung the blankets out in the sun. She picked up a large wooden pot stirrer and beat the dust from the blankets and the hurt from her heart.

Perhaps Mara's sacrificial service to Sarah would lift the curse from her life. She struck the blankets harder and faster as if flogging herself.

When Mara was spent, she ran inside and sank to her knees, sweat and tears streaking down her face.

HaShem, I cannot carry this burden alone.

Something rustled behind her. She wiped her brow and calmly turned to face her fate.

Three village women waited at the open doorway, holding cooking pots. Two were old, one younger. The old one in the center took a step forward. "Let us serve as your wedding attendants."

"Why would you wish to do so?" Mara made no attempt to hide either the relief or the wariness she knew was warring on her face. She had hardened her heart against their slights. But she had told herself a great lie. The lie that she did not need a bond with other women.

The other old woman's eyes were red. "We loved Sarah and Sarah loved you. By fulfilling her dying wish, we see that you truly loved her."

The young woman lifted her cooking pot. "Your wedding supper."

The stone wall that encased Mara's heart cracked. She waved them in.

They washed, combed, and braided her hair, bathed her body, and clothed her with clean clothes.

The youngest woman went to the harp-sack propped against the wall. An eagerness seemed to shine in her eyes. "Perhaps I could play a song to bless your wedding?"

Mara gasped. "That was Seth's favorite harp."

The woman looked down. "Forgive me. I meant no offense."

Mara's heart was pricked by the young woman's kindness. "Please play. I should not kill the harp's song forever."

"I hear the bridegroom's procession." She took up the harp and slipped away.

30

Shechem

Mara

The joyful jingling of hand timbrels and soft singing sounded in the distance. The song grew in strength and speed. Soon the bright sound of Seth's harp joined the melody.

The music stopped.

The bridegroom had arrived.

Mara's remaining two attendants arranged her garments and veil and led her outside.

Servants helped Daveed down from the high priest's donkey.

The high priest conducted the simplest of ceremonies. Mara's mind wandered to dreams of the wedding stolen from her by the assassin who murdered Samuel.

"Here is the cup." The priest's voice brought her back.

Daveed sipped the wine, and she did the same.

Misha and Dan signed the wedding contract. The scribe sealed the scroll. The high priest handed it to Mara. "Your surety against poverty."

Tobiah was clear-eyed and seemed to stare curses at her. She shivered under the weight of his malignant look. The demon of drunkenness was familiar. This sober specter was bone-chilling.

The high priest helped Daveed to a chair. "Peace be with you both."

Johakim departed and Mara was left alone with her fifth husband. An ancient bridegroom who shivered even in the warm evening air. She placed a blanket over Daveed's lap and served a plate of the wedding supper.

"At my age, a man cherishes each sunset and each sunrise. One never knows which will be his last."

"Shh. Do not speak thus." Mara served herself, turning back in time to see the plate start to skid from his lap.

She caught it and set both plates on the bedside table.

"My hands shake more than ever before."

"Today you are overwrought. Tomorrow you will be stronger." Mara dipped bread in the stew and fed him, in turn taking bites from her own plate.

Daveed's eyes dimmed and he retreated to a place in the past. "The ways of HaShem are truly mysterious. Who was to know when Sarah chose to save the baby rather than the mother, that the same baby would be the one called to fulfill her final wish?"

Icy fingers clutched at Mara's heart, sending a chill through her veins. She touched his hand. "What are you saying?"

"Both Ruth and Sarah attended your birth. A long and difficult one. They told me the whole of it when they buried your mother. It is time you knew."

A knot of emotion swelled in Mara's throat. She nodded, gesturing for him to continue.

"A choice had to be made," Daveed said, lifting one hand then the other. "The mother, or the child."

Mara trembled. She wanted to put her hands over her ears, to block what she feared would come next. But her hands were occupied feeding the man who would feed her the truth.

"Tobiah demanded they save your mother." Daveed waved away the bread in her hand. "Sarah bade me take your father outside with a full jar of un-watered wine."

The sorrowful silence stretched until Mara thought her racing heart would rupture. She tapped his hand. "And ..."

"Your mother said every good mother will die for her child. Such love is the blessing and burden of motherhood." Daveed gazed tenderly at Mara. "She made Sarah and Ruth swear to save your life first and to never share her choice with Tobiah or you."

"My mother sacrificed her life for love." Mara's heart faltered. "What more do you know of my birth?"

"Your mother kissed you once and lifted you to her breast. When you had partaken of her milk, she surrendered you into the arms of my Sarah, and passed into the bosom of Abraham."

"And Tobiah?"

Daveed grimaced and shook his head.

"Tell me. I must know the whole of it."

"Your father was full of the venom of wine and woe. When you were brought to him, he said *Leave that mother-killer out on Mount Ebal.*"

"But I was not left out to die." Mara's whisper was full of fear. Could she bear to hear the unwashed truth?

"Never. We are not pagans. Ruth was newly delivered of a sickly daughter, so she became your wet-nurse."

Mara brought a warming stone from the edge of the

cookfire. Samuel once had a baby sister. A sister neither he, nor Ruth, nor Abram ever mentioned. She laid the stone under the blankets on the sleeping pallet.

"Ruth's daughter died two months later—two months longer than anyone expected her to live."

Mara returned to sit by Daveed. "How sad. Ruth lost her only daughter before she lost Samuel, her only son."

"Your mother named you Tamara after the sweet date palm. But your father chose to call you Mara. Ruth told Tobiah each time he called you *bitter* the memory of the woman he loved was besmirched."

"I thought Ruth called me Tamara as a way to soothe the bruises Tobiah's tongue left on my soul."

"Often I have wanted to beg your forgiveness." Daveed's eyes glistened and his feeble voice cracked.

"Why? You have always been kind."

"Though intended as a one-time balm, I was the first one to offer Tobiah a full wineskin of strong drink to dull his pain."

Mara squeezed his hand. "Do not trouble yourself any longer." Mara locked eyes with him. "The second wineskin and each one thereafter was Tobiah's choice."

Daveed braced his hands on the table and pushed to a stand. He shuffled toward the door.

She took his elbow. "The sleeping pallet is this way."

"Yes, but tonight I want to watch the first stars shine through the windows of heaven."

"A sight I would gladly share." Mara helped him outside.

The Evening Star appeared. "The first star this night—so big, beautiful, bright." Mara's chest lightened. The starlight seemed to rain down a mantle of peace that settled over her shoulders. This marriage was the will of HaShem.

Mara glanced down. The wedding harpist had left Seth's harp leaning against the doorpost. Sadness cracked Mara's heart like a shattered egg. Seth had been kind and gentle, and she had come to love him.

Daveed coughed and leaned against her.

"Come husband, I will help you get settled for sleep."

"My dear, a moment longer. I would savor every starry night remaining for me."

Mara picked up the harp and tucked it under her arm.

Daveed, shaking and unsteady, headed for the house. At the doorway, he glanced up as if bidding the stars *shalom*.

She propped the harp next to its sack against the wall and headed to the pallet where she settled Daveed under the blankets.

"Ahh. Warm." His face relaxed.

"I will warm more stones and set the room to rights before I join you."

"May the Lord bless you, Tamara."

Tonight, she would sleep with the assurance her mother had loved her.

Mara

Mara squinted against the gray dawn and slipped from the sleeping pallet she shared for the first time with her frail, wizened husband.

Daveed was warm and snoring. Mara was tired and dazed.

She moved to the basin and splashed water on her face. Perhaps that would clear the cloud that trapped her between truth and dream.

The harp sat on its sack leaning against the wall.

Mara swallowed hard against the burr of sorrow that snagged in her throat. How she missed Seth's songs, his laugh, his touch. She crossed the room and picked up the harp. The rounded back gleamed, struck by a sunbeam. A mark was carved into the wood.

Samuel's mark.

Mara's heart hammered so hard she thought it would break open her chest. She could not think. She held her breath to silence the sound of her loud, ragged breaths.

Samuel's mark. The maker-mark he placed on every tool he ever fashioned.

Mara blew her breath out slowly, trying to slow her speeding heart.

She sat, sifting her jumbled thoughts. Samuel was a woodworker, not a harp-smith. Samuel was murdered and the assassins paid. Seth bought the harp from a Greek in Machaerus, not a Samaritan in Jericho.

The footsteps of Mara's disbelief staggered in shaky circles.

She lovingly traced the makers-mark with one trembling finger. That this mark was carved by Samuel was undeniable. That this mark was etched on Seth's harp was unexplainable. But this mark made one other truth unassailable.

Samuel was alive.

Mara's hands and heart quaked. A hot wave of fury swamped her.

Death and divorce had left her abandoned by four husbands. Abandoned and cursed.

Samuel was alive and she did not know where to search for him.

Even if she found Samuel, she could not run to him. She was a one-day wife. A woman bound to another man.

Untouchable.

Mara's anger turned on her, like the pagan symbol of a serpent eating its own tail. Her anger burned cold in her chest.

A cold that froze her heart, her marrow, her soul. A cold that left her shivering with an all-consuming rage.

HaShem let her believe Samuel was dead. HaShem whispered that marriage to Daveed was His will.

Why Lord, why? She crumpled to her knees and tore at the neck of her robe.

Samuel was alive. An answer to her years of prayers.

Mara would never again dare to pray.

Never. Ever.

Answers to her prayers were like roses. There were always hidden thorns. Thorns that pricked and drew blood. Thorns that pierced her heart and poisoned her faith. She would never again pray to such a cruel Lord. She would never again seek His favor. Or His forgiveness.

The Lord had kept Samuel from her for seven years. If He would withhold His blessings, she would withhold her trust.

"I will never again seek Your ear. Nor will I give You mine." She raised a defiant fist to the heavens.

"Lord, I will not follow after You. If You would curse me or bless me, You must come to me. You must curse or bless me face to face."

31

On the Road to Jerusalem

Samuel

Aglint from the golden rooftop of the Temple of the Jews quickened Samuel's heartbeat and steps. Jerusalem. On to Jericho. And then, at long last, Shechem. To Mara.

The royal runner came alongside Samuel. "The litter bearers tire."

Samuel wiped his brow. "At that tallest fig tree, we will rest."

Once Salome and the wet nurse tending Lyra were settled, the bearers moved away and took their ease.

The nurse downed a cup of water and poured one for Salome.

Salome shook her head.

"Drink or be heat-sick and unable to help with the babe."

Salome took a long drink.

The wet nurse handed Lyra to Salome.

At first, Samuel cringed when the princess touched Lyra, but she was gentle, yet fiercely protective. He now welcomed the relief Salome offered the exhausted nurse.

He must remember to call the princess Yonah, meaning *The Dove*, the new name the queen gave her daughter.

Samuel sat beside the princess. "Will the queen trust me to keep Yonah's secrets?

"The queen trusts no one, but she has the power of life and death over your daughter. She knows you will never betray her."

Salome sang softly and rocked Lyra to sleep.

Travelers coming from Jerusalem, many looking over their shoulders, passed by. Terror marred their tear-streaked faces.

An old man hobbled close.

Samuel whispered. "What has happened?"

The old man drew in a deep breath and Samuel held his. "The Nazarene has baited the Pharisees. There will be trouble."

Salome stood. "Who is this Nazarene?"

"A prophet. Some say he is the Baptizer returned to life."

Salome handed Lyra to the wet nurse and dry scrubbed her hands. "Terrible things happen to terrible ..." Her loud voice carried, and pilgrims stared.

"Lyra needs you to be calm." The wet nurse guided Salome back into the litter and tugged the curtains shut. She rushed back to Samuel. "Yonah must be secreted away without delay."

The last pilgrims passed.

The royal runner joined Samuel. "We must make haste so the litter is not trapped by the crowd. Litter bearers and runners can sustain a trot. You cannot."

"Go. I will follow."

The litter bearers and runner left at a fast pace. He doubled back to Samuel. "Weave through the masses. Walk forty paces. Trot twenty."

Samuel walked, staring at the widening gap between him and his helpless daughter. He counted off the paces between him and his future and began to trot. Mara ... Mara ... Mara ... Your bridegroom is nigh.

Samuel

Samuel plodded along the Jericho Road beside the litter. The taxing pace yesterday left him sore and sullen.

Through the night, Lyra had squawked her hunger. Hours passed and her cries had grown more pitiful. Samuel reached for the litter curtain. One of the women sang a lullaby. Lyra's cries stopped. He would leave the women to their fragile peace.

The song was broken off by a stifled scream. Salome, holding Lyra, opened the curtains. Her eyes were clear, but flashed fear.

Samuel's throat tightened around a spike of dread. He called out for the bearers to stop and thrust his head past Salome. The nurse lay senseless against the pillows, her breast scarlet. A red streak tracked up her neck.

Salome placed a wet cloth across the nurse's brow. "Her blood is poisoned and her milk may be dried up."

Samuel looked at Salome, making no attempt to hide the horror on his face.

"It is the milk fever. The death trap of every wet nurse." Salome's tone sounded worried, but determined.

"What more can be done?" Samuel pressed down the panic that writhed in his stomach.

"Willow bark will break the fever." Salome rummaged through her things and pushed several slivers of bark between the nurse's lips. "We need to cool her."

"There is a stream at the bottom of the wadi."

Salome handed him towels. "Soak these."

Samuel picked his way down the steep cliff to the rushing water, soaked the towels, and rushed back to the litter.

Salome flung open the curtains, Lyra still in her arms. "The nurse is dead, the baby has not fed well for hours, and the litter is as hot as a brick kiln."

Lyra whimpered. Her next weak cry pierced Samuel's heart like a soldier's lance.

The runner moved to help. "I will run the baby to the inn. I am fastest." He reached for Lyra.

Salome twisted away, clutching Lyra close. "No. She is mine."

"Can you run on this ground? Do you know the way?" If the runner suspected Salome was a princess, he would not dare speak with such disrespect. "Give me the baby."

Salome surrendered Lyra to him.

He tied Lyra to his chest with a bearer's short tunic.

Salome touched Lyra's back. "She will be too hot wrapped that way."

"My hands must be free to break a fall." The runner hastened along the rocky road.

Salome clung to Samuel's arm and followed. He took care that she did not wrench an ankle.

Samuel had never wished for a child. But now, he could not picture a life without Lyra. With each footstep the weight of father-love pressed deep into his heart. "HaShem, forgive my sins and do not count them to Lyra."

My ways are not your ways.

He had heard that voice before. On this very road. And his choice to heed that voice had saved his life.

"Samuel, run ahead. They may have need of you." Salome let go of his arm and he rushed forward.

Finally, up ahead, the sign of wheat and grapes Samuel carved so long ago.

Barid ran out from the inn. "Welcome, Greek. Your runner handed the baby over and collapsed. Barley beer and water have revived him."

"Does the baby live?" Samuel braced for the worst.

"Yes, but she desperately needs milk. My servant Theo has gone to milk the goat." Barid waved him toward the door.

Samuel ran inside. Lyra lay on the table. Silent. Still. Barely breathing.

Theo, the Jew Samuel rescued, hobbled in carrying a bowl of goat's milk. "Maybe she will take this." He soaked a twisted rag and brushed it between her lips.

Barid looked from Samuel to Theo. "Why do you care so much for this young girl-child?"

Samuel wanted to scream *Because the child is mine.*

He suddenly realized neither Barid nor Theo knew him disguised as a Greek. He fought to keep his voice calm. "Because we are on a task commanded by Herodias."

"My baby." Salome burst across the threshold and ran to Lyra. She threw open Lyra's wrappings. "Cool water."

Barid brought a pitcher. "Fresh from the stream."

Salome doused Lyra and she seemed to rouse. Pulling Lyra's cheek out, Salome dribbled the milk. The baby swallowed. She dribbled more, but this time milk overflowed Lyra's lips.

HaShem, have mercy.

Salome massaged her throat and coaxed a swallow from his dying daughter.

Samuel drew in a deep breath of relief. "Where did you learn that?"

"Watching my mother's servant tend a poisoned spy."

Barid and Theo glanced up sharply, questions clouding both their faces.

"We must sponge my baby again with cold water."

Her baby. Samuel would let Salome live this delusion if it kept her treasonous tongue at bay, kept her tending his child, and kept Lyra alive.

Samuel sponged Lyra and Salome dribbled more milk. Lyra slowly began to swallow.

Samuel touched her cheek. "She is drinking."

Barid placed his hands on the table and leaned toward Samuel's face. Recognition flickered in the innkeeper's eyes. "I am reminded of another that coaxed life from death here."

Before Barid could call Samuel by name, he interrupted. "My name is Didymus."

Barid grinned at Samuel. "At least you do not bring me a corpse to bury."

The innkeeper had uttered similar words when Samuel brought him the dying Jew. He was signaling he would not give Samuel away.

Theo went to the door. "The litter bearers are here. I will bring water and barley beer out to them."

Salome rocked the sleeping baby. "Lyra must have a wet nurse soon."

Theo poured the milk into a jar and stoppered it. "I will take this down to the cold stream."

Barid waved a hand toward Theo. "Continue straight to Jericho and bring Dex's wife. She nurses a young infant."

Dex. His blacksmith friend from the forge.

Theo glared at Barid. "Are you crazed? The priest and the Levite who left me to die might pass by and I will miss my chance for revenge." He hobbled toward the door.

Barid moved swiftly and blocked Theo. He stooped eye-to-eye with the angry man. "Your life was redeemed seven years ago." Barid glanced at Samuel then back at Theo. "Now you are called to save a life."

Theo studied Samuel's eyes. His face changed. He recognized Samuel the Samaritan under his Greek trappings. "Forgive me. It is a mitzvah to save a life." Theo took his cloak from the wall hook and lifted the walking stick Samuel fashioned for him. "This has served me well."

"I can go more swiftly." Samuel went to the door.

Barid raised a hand. "Theo will take my ox and cart. Bandits would not dare attack the friend of Dex and servant of Barid, two retired centurions of Rome. He will bring Sophia."

Theo, his crutch in full swing, lumbered out the door.

A soft song called to Samuel from the far corner where Salome rocked his beloved daughter.

Barid moved with Samuel toward Lyra where they watched the baby for a few moments.

"She seems a little better, yes?" Samuel's voice faltered.

"Who is this baby to you?" Barid edged Samuel toward a private space behind the high kitchen serving counter.

"My daughter."

"You are on the queen's errand." Barid's head jerked up. "Is the baby also her daughter?"

"No. The mother was my comfort woman who died birthing Lyra."

"And the young woman holding Lyra? Is she a slave too?"

"She is a captive to her shame, guilt, and mad mind. More than that you do not want to know."

304

Barid served Samuel and Salome a hearty meal. She held Lyra in one arm, played with her food, but did not eat.

The golden light of sunset faded. Samuel's stomach soured and a wave of fear drove burning bile into his throat. "Theo should have returned by now."

Salome's eyes went wide, and she pulled Lyra closer. "Pray to your god. The powerful god of the Baptizer."

"HaShem, hear the plea of a desperate father for his helpless babe."

A thunder of hoofbeats galloped toward the inn.

"A traveling party." Barid readied the table and filled a pitcher with watered wine. He cupped his ear. "Coming from Jerusalem."

The door opened. Heavy footsteps and a greeting shout woke Lyra. Her weak cries were heart-rending.

Dex walked in. Sophia followed, cradling an infant.

"Thank the gods you have come." Barid motioned them to the table. "I sent to Jericho and here you are coming from Jerusalem."

Dex looked confused. "Why?"

Lyra mewled like a weak kitten.

Sophia approached Salome who stared vacantly. "Girl, feed your baby."

Samuel stepped close. "The mother is dead. The wet nurse died on the road. And I am the father." Samuel took Lyra into his arms.

Sophia studied Samuel's face and a soft smile blossomed at the corners of her mouth. "I know that voice. We feared you were—"

"Call me Didymus."

Sophia turned to Dex. "Take our sleeping son and place him in his basket." She sat and lifted her arms. Samuel placed Lyra in Sophia's lap. She coaxed Lyra to take her breast. The baby sucked slowly, then slept. Sophia gently shook Lyra awake and she suckled again. Sophia smiled and looked up. "Be at peace Didymus. Your baby will live."

"Come, Dex, sit at the table." Barid brought olives, cheese, flatbread, and honey.

Salome hovered over Sophia. The moment Lyra finished feeding, the princess scooped her up and signaled for Sophia to give up the chair.

"My baby will live. My baby will live." The princess rocked the baby in rhythm with her singsong chant.

Sophia raised a brow toward Salome but joined them at the table.

Dex stuffed a piece of flatbread into his mouth.

"The babies were not the only ones famished." Sophia laughed and took a large piece of cheese.

Barid wiped crumbs from his chin. "No errand for Herodias is ever without peril."

Dex looked up from his food. "Herodias?" Distaste colored his voice. "What errand?"

"The baby is Samuel's." The words spilled from Barid's mouth.

Sophia touched Barid's arm, a gentle caution.

"I mean Didymus."

Dex looked at Samuel. "There was something familiar about you, but ..." Questions swarmed in his eyes.

"I must take my baby and this young woman, Yonah, to Jericho."

"Why?" Sophia looked to the corner where Salome wrapped the sleeping baby in her cloak next to her heart.

"Why?" Dex's tone was demanding.

"The wet nurse was to keep them at the Winter Palace, hidden away from the sight and schemes of the king."

"A search for another wet nurse would draw attention."

Dex turned to his wife. "Sophia, if you are willing to nurse her, the queen will surely be grateful."

"I sense Didymus has not yet told us the whole of it." Barid took a deep drink and sighed. "At least the baby is not the queen's daughter."

"No ..." Suddenly, a sly smile crept onto the princess' lips. "But I am."

Barid and Dex and Sophia tensed and stared at Samuel.

"I am Salome."

Samuel rose and went to her. "Shh. Remember, we call you Yonah."

"Yes, my former name must be blotted out." Salome patted Lyra's back. "Terrible kings do terrible things. Terrible things happen to terrible kings." Salome suddenly thrust Lyra into Samuel's arms and viciously scrubbed her hands.

Sophia touched Dex's arm. "This troubled young woman has need of our shelter—perhaps more than the baby."

Dex covered Sophia's hand with his own. "Sheltering her is dangerous. She speaks treason against the king."

"Wicked kings ..."

Sophia went to Salome. "Shh. Be at peace. Let us walk with the babies before evening falls."

Salome quieted and took Lyra from Samuel.

Sophia's son wakened and blew baby bubbles in his basket. She picked him up and walked near Dex. "Husband. The baby and Yonah need us."

"Stay close." Dex opened the door. Sophia and Salome left, each with a babe in her arms.

Barid brought a fresh pitcher of barley beer and raised it to Samuel and Dex. "To help us plan."

Dex leaned back in his chair. "Why should the prin— Yonah dread and despise the king?"

"At Herod's birthday feast, she danced, drawing his notice." Samuel took a long drink.

"What kind of notice?" Baird refilled Samuel's cup.

"All the wrong kind. It is a long tale." Samuel shook his head trying to clear the awful memories. "Yonah must be hidden where only those loyal to the queen may see her lost reason or hear her chants of treason."

32

Shechem

Mara

The harp propped against the wall was a silent witness that Samuel still drew breath. A truth that took Mara's breath away. She lifted the harp and caressed the makers-mark. Samuel was alive.

She gently set the harp in its proper place. A place ever before her face.

"Daveed. Mara. A blessing on your house." Abram's call from the open door was spirited and strong.

"Shalom." Daveed's answer was faltering and feeble.

Would it be a kindness or a curse to show Samuel's father the makers-mark?

Abram carried a small parcel. "Here are some herbs Ruth gathered long ago. Some may provide warmth." He handed the parcel to Mara.

"How kind of you to think of me." Daveed motioned Abram to a chair. "Come. Sit for a while."

Mara unwrapped the parcel and sorted the smaller packets, sniffing each one. Cinnamon. Ginger. The last did not have a strong smell. She unfolded the packet to reveal a spice the color of the rising sun. She licked her finger, dipped it, and tasted. Turmeric.

"A tea of all three should help keep Daveed warm." She smiled but could not fully meet Abram's eyes.

"What tidings at the crossroads?" Daveed's body was feeble, but his mind was still sharp.

Abram leaned toward Daveed, lips curled with amusement. "The Pharisees in Jerusalem are in an uproar. Just before last Passover, a young rabbi overturned the moneychanger tables at their temple, calling the place a den of thieves."

Mara put a pot of water over the cookfire for the herbal brew. "Why would he do such a thing?"

"Some Jews whisper that he is Messiah." Abram shrugged. "But false messiahs wandered the land before this man was born. And there will be false messiahs after he is in the grave."

Hope lightened Mara's heart. "One day the true Promised One will come. All of Shechem saw the wandering star that was witness to the birth of a great king."

Daveed shook his head. "That was almost thirty years past."

"But do you not see? That baby is now a man who walks throughout the land." Mara's palms lifted as if of their own accord. "We must be found watching and waiting for him." She touched her neck where the Magi coin she gave to Samuel used to rest.

A look of fervent faith flared in Abram's eyes. "I will watch and wait for his coming as steadfastly as I wait for Samuel's return."

Mara slumped onto a nearby stool.

Daveed clapped his hands. "Perhaps he will declare Mount Gerizim the true holy place and rebuild our razed temple."

"We seek news from Jerusalem, but someone with means seeks news from Shechem." Abram looked at her, his eyes so like Samuel's.

Mara's glance slid to the harp, her breath fast and shallow. "Who would care about this village?"

Abram's voice was soft but compelling. "Someone seeks news of you, Mara."

She met his look. "Me?"

"Is my wife in danger?" Daveed's tone had taken on unexpected strength.

"Some weeks ago, the high priest caught his Egyptian slave selling information to a stranger."

"Okpara. That devious man." Mara's voice was so quiet, she could scarcely hear it over her runaway heartbeat. Samuel must be asking after her.

"Who sent the stranger?" Daveed pushed up straighter in his chair.

"The stranger knew nothing. Not who sent him. Not who paid. Not why the news was of import."

"What report did Okpara give?"

"Under threat of the lash, and the promise that he could keep the gold, Okpara admitted he told the stranger that Jareb was dead."

"Jareb's death was widely known, not worth the bribe of a spy." Mara sprinkled the herbs in the boiling water.

Mara did not know where Samuel was, but he knew where she was. She was right where he left her. Still in love with him. Still not free. No longer young, no longer innocent. Samuel would come for her. But when he found that HaShem had cursed her, he too would shun her and leave her alone, smothered by her sins and lies.

Samuel

Samuel hurried on foot, nearing the crossroads of Shechem. Before he left the inn, he sent the runner to Herodias with word that Yonah and Lyra were safe at the forge where no one would expect a princess living as a servant.

After seven years, Samuel's life had begun to right itself. Mara was free. He would marry her and work for Lyra's redemption. Every vestige of his pagan life as Didymus would be dead.

Ahead of him, three women, shadowed by the sinking sun, walked with water jars perched on their heads. The jars were the last burden they would carry before the oncoming Sabbath rest.

At the well, no one was drawing water. Somehow, he expected to find Mara alone. But for many years, nothing had been as he expected.

Where was Mara? Abba would know.

He continued, looking to the horizon. How he had missed this view of Shechem at sunset—the fiery copper light yielding to gold and purple. He came to the village center. Neighbors stared, looked away, and shut their doors to the stranger. The pagan. They did not know Samuel, clean-shaven, and dressed as a Greek.

A peace settled around his heart. At long last, he was home.

Tobiah glared at him from his cold cookfire just in front of his hut. Mara was not there.

Samuel placed his hand on the door of his childhood home,

then stopped. The villagers would fear a foreigner had breached Abba's home and would descend like a murder of crows. "Ab—" He started to call out *Abba,* but a pang of caution cut off his voice. He would play the Greek for now. "Abram."

The door opened. Abba glanced at him and waved him away. "I cannot mend anything on the Sabbath." He started to shut the door. But Samuel blocked it with his foot. Abram's angry eyes studied Samuel's face. Abba's eyes lit with recognition, he gasped and pulled Samuel through the doorway into his open arms.

Samuel kicked the door shut.

"My son." Abba touched Samuel's shaven chin and reached up to tousle his short hair. "My son." His voice broke. He began to tremble and reached for Samuel. "When Jareb died, Mara and I searched all of Jericho. Mara mourned. I refused to believe you were dead. Even when assassins came and collected their blood money."

"Why?"

"I clung to your ima's deathbed vision of your heir." Something dimmed the joy that shone in Abba's eyes. "You cannot see Mara now."

Samuel nodded. "Yes, I must wait until Sabbath ends. I have waited for years without hope. With hope, what is one more day of waiting?"

"Much has happened since your trial in Jericho." Abba went to the simmering pot in the courtyard, ladled out bowls of stew and brought them to the low table. "You must be hungry."

"Yes, the day has been long." Samuel brought bread from the kitchen and sat across from Abba. "But a traveler shared his oxcart most of the way."

Abba had aged. Time had etched deeper lines, slowed his gait, bent his spine. "For years after your ima died, I took my

Sabbath supper at the home of Sarah and Daveed. Sarah joined Ruth in the afterlife one week and one day past."

"May Sarah be at peace." Samuel broke and blessed the bread, tasted the stew. "You did not cook this. What thoughtful woman remembered you this Sabbath?"

"Shechem's newest bride." Abba paled and looked away.

Samuel placed his hand over Abba's trembling one. "You miss Ima."

"Yes. When you take a wife, may she outlive you. From the Beginning, HaShem knew that it was not good for man to be alone." Abba covered Samuel's hand with his other one. "My son. Why did you come here now? Why after so long?"

"Herodias told me Jareb was dead, and Mara was free. Herod has forbidden any other Avenger. Much has changed. I am not the same man who fled Shechem."

Abba crossed his arms across his chest. "And I would hear all of it. Every jot. Every tittle. Every heartbeat."

"That may take until dawn."

"Then best to begin. Why do you dress as a Greek?" Abba dipped his bread into the stew.

"I will come to that." Samuel drew in a bracing breath. "Let us begin with the assassin's attack."

Samuel told Abba his tale. All except any mention of Zosi or Lyra. Or Yonah.

Abba listened quietly. "You trust the queen to protect you?" He stood, stretched, and poured some watered wine.

Samuel thought back to the severed head of the Baptizer and shuddered. "As long as my life serves her purposes."

Abba handed him a full cup. "I can still read your face. You have kept something back. What hold does the queen have on you?"

Samuel's throat tightened. He swallowed his shame. "You are a grandfather."

"Ruth's vision has come to pass." Abba raised his hands to heaven, his arms quivering. "An heir." His smile gleamed like sunrise. "My bones sing. That I may live to see your son."

Samuel moved around the table and took Abba by the shoulders. "This baby is not the fulfillment of Ima's vision."

Abba's face brimmed with questions.

"You are a grandfather. Not to a son, but to a daughter. Not of our people, but born of a pagan. Not of a free woman, but from a slave of Herodias. The girl-child is also a slave."

Abba's smile trembled and wilted. His arms drifted down.

Samuel held his breath, praying that Abba's love would prevail over his prejudice against pagans.

A new light flickered across Abba's face. Once again, he raised his arms to heaven, his smile restored. "May HaShem bless her and keep her. She is blood of my blood and bone of my bone."

Samuel glanced in the direction of Tobiah's hut. "Some fathers would have put aside a pagan granddaughter."

"You have survived. And like our forefather Joseph in pagan Egypt, you remain a man of faith." Abba touched the sleeve of Samuel's short tunic. "Must you live and dress as a Greek?"

"No. I was told Shechem is now safe."

Abba clapped his hands. "Where is your daughter? I would hold her. Claim her as mine."

"To redeem my daughter, I am a bond servant to Herodias for the next three and a half years."

Abram grabbed Samuel's hands. "You will take me to my granddaughter."

"We must wait until the time appointed for my first visit. Please do not speak of my daughter until I find the words to tell Mara. Where is she? I will go to her when Sabbath ends."

Samuel wished from the depths of his soul that he could run to her now.

Grief darkened Abba's face. The same grief and the same tears he shed when he had told Samuel of Ima's death. Abba opened his mouth, but only a quiet croak came forth. He took a deep breath.

"My son. My son." He pulled Samuel into his arms. "For years Mara thought you were dead. For a week and a day, she has once again been wed."

Mara

On the porch, Mara's fingers plucked at the green threads stretched across her standing loom. Two weeks past, news of Samuel's return blazed through Shechem. She rolled her shoulders back and tilted her head side to side, releasing the cramps in her neck.

She had not seen Samuel, even from afar. Even so, her eyes constantly searched for him. Did his eyes not also crave hers?

At the well, she caught snatches of news. Even Abram had not known Samuel when he returned dressed as a Greek. Now, he dressed as a Samaritan. And his hair and beard were growing back.

Mara shook her shoulders, shaking off the dangerous thought. Samuel could not approach another man's wife. All eyes were upon him. Upon them. Watching. Waiting for their first glance. Their first words. The rumor ravens scanned with suspicious eyes, ever ready to accuse adultery.

Mara took up the shuttle again. This morning as she drew water, Mara overheard the young girls plotting ways to attract Samuel. The memory ignited a jealous flame around her heart.

She wove for hours, fingers flying, shuttle gathering speed. She wove without care, looking beyond the loom as if she could peer into the future.

Her shuttle caught and she ran her finger over a flaw in the intricate pattern. Her mindless rush had left a ragged knot. She began to rip out her mistake The reworking would take all afternoon and she would lose the best light. If only she could rip out and rework all her shameful sins.

"Wife."

Mara startled. She had forgotten Daveed was nearby at the cookfire.

"I would speak with you."

Mara went to him and lifted the fallen blanket back onto his shoulders.

He nodded. "Bless you. Please sit."

Mara sat on a nearby stool.

He covered her hand with his own. "You are an angel who warms not only my bones, but my heart and soul. I am feeble and old. But I am not blind. Or dead. And while I still draw breath, I would offer you a kindness."

Mara's stomach tightened. If she were honest with herself, a hidden corner of her heart wished herself free. Wished him dead. "Daveed, your hand is cold." She stoked the fire, unable to look at his face.

"You were pledged to an evil man. Then your Beloved was forced to run for his life."

Mara's lip trembled.

"My Sarah and I prayed throughout your many trials. Now, Samuel has returned, risen from the grave. I have not shared the joy of his return with Abram. And you have had no chance to speak with him. Or shed happy tears that you both still draw breath."

Mara wished she could blot out her evil wishes.

"It is not seemly for me to talk with him." She bowed her head so he would not see her brimming eyes. She pressed her head-cover to her face.

"Sarah and I were especially fond of you both."

"If I were to see Samuel, the gossips would pounce."

"Next Sabbath, my new wife will make supper for Abram just as Sarah often did. Of course, his son would also be invited."

Mara's heart quickened around the rising hope of sharing Sabbath bread with Samuel. She hugged herself. She would hold her hope close.

A sudden chill closed cold fingers around her heart. "The men may be satisfied with such a supper, but the women—"

"Will have no reproach if our guests include the high priest, as well as my son, Misha, and his wife. Do you agree?"

The cold fingers that clutched her heart melted. "If it is your wish."

"I could release you from this marriage."

Mara shivered. "But you cannot release me from my pledge to Sarah. A pledge I gave willingly, lovingly."

"A promise you would not have made one day later."

"Should a promise be broken when it becomes difficult to keep?"

"No." Daveed coughed, his shoulders shook.

Mara held a cup for him. He sipped and spluttered. "We are agreed. You will remain my wife. And this Sabbath, you will cook for Samuel."

Mara put a hand to her burning cheek. She was no longer the young woman Samuel had left. Surely her face had aged, ravaged by the troubles that seemed to cling to her. She glanced at Daveed.

"Do not worry. My Sarah and I grew old together, yet we always gazed at each other through the eyes of our youth."

He had read her thoughts and sought to ease her worry. How could even the most hidden room in her heart wish this kind man dead?

Would Samuel detect the bitter root that strangled her soul, and felled her faith? Mara shook off her misgivings.

"My last sunset is near. Please set my chair so I may watch this one." Daveed rose. "In sleep, Sarah calls to me."

Mara moved his chair.

"Only in sleep, am I reunited with my beloved Sarah. Each morning, I wake disappointed at the divide between us."

"I understand." For years she dreamt of Samuel only to be left bereft upon waking.

Daveed seemed held captive by the golden sky and setting sun. She glanced at him fondly, wrapped his blanket close.

You have chosen rightly.

She had turned from HaShem. Perhaps He had not turned from her.

33

Shechem

Samuel

Abba knocked. Samuel stepped up to the door of Daveed's home. Mara was within–just behind that door. He fought to settle his racing heart and steady his runaway mind.

The door was flung open by Misha's wife. She smiled a welcome. Samuel could not keep the surprise from his eyes.

"Come." Daveed, at the low table with Misha and the high priest, waved a tremorous hand.

The high priest rose. "At Daveed's request we will share the Sabbath table as family."

Abba and Samuel sat beside one another. He did not dare look for Mara.

"We must serve the meal before the sun sets." Mara stood by the courtyard cookfire and ladled the stew into bowls.

The warmth from the fire gilded Mara's form and tinged her cheeks pink.

Samuel knew his hot cheeks were as ruddy as hers were pink. But his cheeks were flushed from the weight of his secrets, not from the flames of a fire. They had been separated for a week-of-years, surely Mara had gathered some secrets of her own.

Mara and Misha's wife served the meal, then sat together at the foot of the table.

The high priest chanted the age-old prayer over the bread and the wine. He lifted his hands. "HaShem, bless this House."

Samuel searched his heart for hatred of the high priest who had placed the Law above love. Yet Samuel could not summon a featherweight of hate. Only sorrow. Sorrow for the sins of the priest's sons. And his secret sorrow. Over Zosi. His secret sin. His love of a pagan. *Lord, may Mara forgive me.*

Mara's eyes had not yet met his. When they did, his eyes must hold no hint of lover. No hint of pity. And above all, no hint of rejection.

He must tell her he admired her righteous choice to serve Daveed. But most important, he would vow he would not wed, but wait for her to be free.

Mara returned to the kitchen and brought a bowl of figs.

She handed it to Samuel. "I thought you were dead." Her glistening eyes locked with his.

A legion of unspoken words passed between them.

"I am grateful to be alive and honored to share this table." He took the bowl from her.

She moved to her place with Misha's wife.

The priest raised his cup to Samuel. "To life."

Samuel's mind flashed to the ripped kitel and Magi coin with which he had redeemed a Jew from death to life.

The priest broke a piece of bread. "Allow me to serve you." He placed it before Daveed, then took one for himself.

Daveed took small bites like a sickly sparrow.

Samuel would not have to wait long for Mara. His chest tightened as if trying to cage the evil wish that crouched in the darkest corner of his soul. The last time Samuel wished a man dead, Achor soon sprawled before him, his lifesblood flooding the ground.

HaShem, save me from my deceitful heart and the destruction it calls down on those I cherish.

A plate was passed to Samuel, the bread now in parts. Broken. Like his and Mara's hearts.

During the Sabbath meal, heaping servings of laughter and love were shared. Only Samuel did not speak. Only Mara did not look at him. Yet Daveed spoke with all and smiled fondly at them both.

Misha's wife began to clear the plates.

Mara stood.

"Wait." Daveed struggled to stand. Abba helped him rise. "I would speak the truth that nests silently in this room." His lips pursed around each shallow breath. "I have offered to release Mara from this marriage."

Samuel's heart clutched. If only Daveed would speak the words of divorce, Mara would be free.

"But my loyal new wife has chosen to keep her vow to Sarah."

Samuel's heart had been placed in an olive press and every drop of hope sluiced away.

"Abram and his son have always been men of honor." Daveed reached for the table and eased down onto his bench. "I grant Samuel permission to visit with Mara. All in Shechem recall seven years ago they wished to marry."

Daveed looked at every guest, meeting each eye.

"They have had no chance to share the sadness of Samuel's sudden flight or the joy of his safe return. Such a visit could not be counted as sin."

Abram took Daveed's hand. "Sarah and Ruth would both approve. But they would have been careful not to let Samuel and Mara visit alone. For it would only serve to feed the rumor ravens."

The high priest smiled softly at Mara. Samuel suddenly realized the priest had developed a deep fondness for her. "Let them speak across the room where none will hear, but all will see and bear witness to their righteousness."

Mara

In a corner, facing away from the table, Mara sat on a bench, an arm's length away from Samuel. He looked neither Greek nor Samaritan, but foreign —his hair shorn, his beard merely a shadow on his face. But the dimple that creased his chin was an endearing reminder of his boyhood.

She collected the courage to meet Samuel's eyes. Eyes, ever so familiar, full of love and longing. But eyes that were also foreign, shadowed by the years stolen from them both.

Samuel seemed to make a great effort to find his voice. "Praise HaShem, we both survived."

His first words confirmed his trust in the goodness of the Lord. A trust she no longer shared.

"When Enosh divorced me, I searched for you in Jericho." Hand trembling, she reached toward his face, then caught herself and placed her hand over her heart. "Even though you were lost to me, I prayed you were alive." Mara shuddered. "But an assassin was paid. I despaired."

"Abba told me." Samuel fisted his hands at his sides. "When Jareb dragged you into the wedding tent, I feared you would not survive the night. I decided to rescue you and run."

"Herod would have hunted us down."

"Yes. To stop my foolhardy plan, a friend struck me hard in the head rendering me senseless for two days."

Mara gasped and hugged herself tight.

"Then I feared you might not survive a childbirth."

"I am barren."

Something flitted across Samuel's face.

"Abba has told me of your woes." Samuel's voice hitched. "You live. All else matters not one jot." Samuel looked over his shoulder.

Her eyes followed his. No one was paying any heed.

"I will wait for you." His eyes seemed to light on something. He rose and picked up the harp. Seth's harp of *Samuel's* making.

"This—"

"Bears your makers-mark. The moment I saw it, I knew you were alive." Mara's voice faltered. She pressed back tears and steadied her trembling lips.

"While hiding, I became a harp-maker. This one was sold to a soldier."

"Seth. My late husband. He sang a haunting song of a dove and a lost love."

"The same song he taught to Prima ..." Samuel's face and voice were furrowed with sorrow. "And Zosi."

"Who is Zosi?" Mara's stomach curdled around the name he said with such fondness.

"The favorite slave of Herodias."

Mara's jealousy withered, but her stomach did not calm. Samuel had not told her all. But then, she had not told him all.

One day when she was free, they would lay bare their entire truths.

"I grow weary." Daveed's weak call brought Mara back to her shivering husband.

The high priest rose. "We must depart." He and Misha settled Daveed on the sleeping pallet.

Daveed looked across the room. "Abram, do you have more herbs? The tea Mara brews greatly relieves my chills."

"I will send the remainder to the well with Samuel tomorrow."

Mara glanced at Samuel and banished all longing from her voice. "Until daybreak. At the well."

Samuel

Samuel stood far off and watched Mara draw water with practiced ease.

Since his return, he saw the village with new eyes, grateful for the rhythms of daily life. Each morning, the women drew life-giving water and baked the bread that fed Shechem. Every season, they birthed the sons and daughters that sustained their people, the Samaritans. One day, his daughter would be one of them.

Mara. His woman at the well. Samuel wanted to run to her, hold her, never let her go.

From this distance, in this light, her face was just as he remembered. A sweet, innocent face full of love and laughter and hope.

At Sabbath supper, her eyes were dimmed by some hidden pain. Her smile was not so full or free. The light in her soul seemed snuffed by sorrow. One day, he would restore her joy.

Mara was alone. He would go to her. He took one step.

"Stop."

Samuel jumped at a woman's voice. A voice he knew but could not quite place. He turned and was confronted by a dark-eyed beauty, water jar on her hip. The potter's little girl, now a woman in full bloom.

"She is a married woman." The potter's daughter lifted a shoulder, her dark hair spilled from her veil. Samuel's mind flashed to Salome and her seductive dance of seven veils.

"I am not."

"Not?" Samuel's mind scrambled to glean the potter's daughter's meaning. Her puckered lips offered a kiss.

"I am ... not married." Her low, raspy voice suggested so much more than a kiss.

Samuel did not meet her eyes. At Herod's court, he had learned to hide his aversion to wanton women.

The potter's daughter sidled toward him and reached up as if she would stroke his short whiskers.

He squirmed at the thought of her touch and sidestepped her reach.

The young woman's eyes widened and her mouth tightened. Likely, her advances were never rebuffed.

"Why are you here?" She glared toward Mara then back to him, eyes flaring accusations.

Samuel fumbled through his waist pack and removed the herb packet. "I brought this for Daveed." Samuel hated the half-truth buried in his words. Above all, he wanted to see Mara.

"I will take it to her." The young woman reached for the packet, letting her cool fingertips linger on his wrist.

At her touch, the feel of wriggling vipers raced up his arm.

"No." Samuel pulled the herb packet close to his heart.

The young woman shrugged, walked to the well, and spoke to Mara.

Mara walked toward Samuel.

He met her halfway, holding out the herbs. She took the packet, not touching his hand or looking him full in the face.

More village women were gathering at the well.

"Daveed will be so grateful you found the herbs he requested." Mara spoke a little too loudly.

The back of Samuel's neck prickled. Mara wanted to be overheard. A hostile silence surrounded them. The rumor ravens were perched. Searching for a weakness to peck. A sordid story to caw.

Samuel dared not stay. He could never see Mara until Daveed was dead and buried and mourned.

34

Shechem
Six months later

Samuel

Daveed had been married and buried in the span of month. Samuel, his heartbeat and feet racing, ran toward the setting sun and the shepherd's cottage where Mara had lived since Daveed's death.

For six months, Samuel pleaded with the high priest to give him leave to court Mara. Since Daveed's death came so closely after his wedding, the high priest insisted Samuel must wait. After all, Mara was not a poor widow without means. This morning, after six months, the high priest finally relented.

Samuel raised his fist to rap on the door, his breath coming fast and shallow. But before his hand touched the wood, Mara flung open the door wide. "I did not think you would come so soon. I did not think ..." Her voice, watered by tears, seemed swept into a whirlpool of emotion.

Samuel opened his lips to speak, but words would not come, so he covered her lips with his own.

She responded with a passion that threatened any restraint he might have sworn. He gently pushed her away. "We must not." His voice and heart stuttered.

"We must." She removed his outer cloak. "You are free, and I am free. I will not wait another flit of a butterfly wing."

Mara walked to the sleeping pallet, glanced back, her eyes wide, lips parted. No trace of doubt or shame or shyness flickered across her face. "I am my Beloved's, and my Beloved is Mine. Let no man tear us asunder."

Samuel went to her and laid her gently on the pallet. "It is sunset, the beginning of a new day." Nothing would keep them from this joining, this paradise. They would be wed tomorrow.

Throughout the night, they shared the secret sorrows of their years apart. Mara told him of her desperate search for him in Jericho.

Samuel's stomach lurched. "One night outside the wall of the Greek quarter, I thought I heard you call my name. Now I am certain." They lay side by side, her cheek resting over his heart.

Mara wept into his shoulder. "You did not answer. I was so utterly alone."

Samuel pulled her closer and stroked her hair. "I am glad Seth eased your loneliness."

She moved back and stared into his eyes. "Something in your voice whispers that your loneliness was eased in the arms of other women."

"Mara ... you were many times wed." Samuel hated the accusations that crept into his voice, hated the visions that crept into his head, hated the thoughts of other husbands that crept into their bed.

For the blink of an eye, Mara winced. But then, her face

shifted from hurt to forgiveness. "Though our bodies have joined with others, our souls have always been set apart for one other. And tonight, you are entirely mine."

"You are my wife for life."

Later, Samuel watched Mara sleep. As he drifted off, two thoughts began to gnaw. He had yet to speak to Mara of Zosi and Lyra. He had yet to make Mara his wife under the Law.

At sunrise, Samuel sat across the table from Mara. "Beloved, you found comfort and love with Seth when you thought me dead." He kept his tone gentle.

"Did you think me dead when you sought comfort in the arms of other women?"

Mara's jealous tone set Samuel's teeth on edge. "No. The comfort woman sent to me by Herodias would have been defiled by an entire regiment if I did not accept her."

"She was merely a comfort woman?" Mara's voice lightened.

"In the beginning. Later ..." Samuel fought to keep the depth of his fond feelings from his face. "We must not begin our marriage with secrets or lies."

Mara came around the table, sat close, and placed her hand on his. "Tell me all."

"At first, there was a bond with Zosi. Later, there was something more."

"More?"

"She bore my child."

"Your child?" Mara's hands went to her belly. She slumped as if she had been kicked from within.

How could he have been so dimwitted? Mara was barren. She looked into the distance, her face stone.

The tears he expected to see in her eyes were in his alone.

His tears seemed to grieve her again. She ran toward the door.

A Certain Man

"Wait."

Mara did not slow.

Samuel's chest was a vise clamping his breath.

Mara

Mara ran down the rocky slope through thatches of knee-high grass, past the sheepfold. Samuel's son had been born. The son that had been promised to her on Ruth's deathbed. She stumbled and crumpled to the ground, panting like a woman in labor.

Last night, for the span of a few hours, she hoped HaShem had lifted the curse from her. Samuel was free. She was free. He was hers. She was his.

Now she knew. HaShem had not relented. Because of her moonblood lie, He had dried up her womb. His promise of a son for her was revoked. Forever.

Years of pent-up pain broke free, drowning her spirit. Everything she hoped for turned to sorrow. Everything she touched wilted away.

Mara pushed up to her knees, her sobs settling into a snarled knot in her throat. The distant hill was dotted with grazing sheep. She rose and ran into the far pasture.

Samuel no longer had the kitel she had so lovingly woven, or the Magi coin she had so willingly given. Her offerings had saved his life, but their loss was a sign. Without the kitel, Samuel was not meant to be her bridegroom. Without the coin, she was not meant to see the Promised One.

Mara stopped when she could run no further. And she could never run past herself. Never escape this pain. Last night, she let herself hope to be Samuel's bride. This morning, her hope had died. Not only was she cursed. She was the curse.

If she married Samuel, he would die. Mara was certain.

In the distance, Samuel ran toward her. She pulled her head-covering over her face, surrendering to the dark and her woe.

After some time, she sensed Samuel step close. He kept a patient silence. The undemanding silence of lovers. The silence that is broken in its own time.

Mara did not look up, did not speak.

"Beloved." Samuel's voice hitched. "I did not mean for word of my child to cause you pain."

She wanted to die.

Samuel removed her head covering.

She pulled away. "Your truth is unchanged. You have a son with a comfort woman. HaShem has given our promised son to a pagan."

"Beloved." He drew calming circles on her back. "My baby is a *daughter,* not a son."

"My husband is dead. The mother of your child lives."

Samuel's face flushed with some strong feeling she could not read.

He touched Mara's cheek. "Zosi sighed her last breath when our babe gasped her first."

Mara sat, took his hand, and pulled him down beside her. "To witness a last breath exchanged for a first ..."

Samuel's look of sorrow seemed to settle to one of quiet strength. "The Lord gives, and the Lord takes away. Blessed be the name of the Lord."

Samuel had clung tightly to his faith. Mara had flung her faith as far from her as the bright morning star rising over the hill.

Mara stood, hands clenched. "I no longer trust that

HaShem is good." Mara's voice slapped the air. She drew her robe around her and lifted a defiant chin. Her narrowed eyes flashed, daring the Lord to smite her. "I will not bless His Name."

Her words seemed to cleave Samuel's heart.

"HaShem has turned His face from me."

"Mara, such hardness of heart. Zosi, like you, was ill-used by people with power. Your hatred of HaShem terrifies me beyond all reason."

Samuel came to her and enfolded her in his arms. She stayed stiff. Unyielding.

The wind blew around them, whipping their robes.

Mara lifted her face to him. "Do you not see? I was mistaken. The curse is yet even worse."

The terrified look on Samuel's face sent cold-as-death shivers down her back. "Zosi did not bear a son. Perhaps HaShem has revoked the promise of a son from you, also."

The wind blew harder, plastering their robes to their bodies like burial shrouds.

Mara was half-crazed with fear and shame. And crazed with something else she could not name.

Samuel pulled her to his side and led her toward the cottage. "Come back to our bed, my beloved."

At that moment, an unkempt shepherd boy emerged from the tall grass. His face flushed red. His fist raised. "Beloved? Bed? And my grandfather not one year dead."

Mara tensed. Daveed's grandson. The youngest son of the youngest son, Dan.

Samuel glared at him. "You have been spying."

"I am not a spy. These are our pastures, our flocks." He brandished his shepherd's crook across his chest. "You are the one who trespasses."

Samuel stepped closer. "How long were you there?"

"Long enough to hear your harlot blaspheme HaShem." The boy spat at Mara's feet. "Would that I had a second witness to your wicked words." He bolted into the long grass.

Mara gasped and started to sink.

Samuel lifted her into his arms, hurried back to the cookfire at the cottage porch. He eased her to sit on a mat and stoked the fire.

Mara's shivers grew to violent shudders. She leaned forward, hands outstretched. Her shaking calmed. "Daveed's grandson will bring trouble back to my door."

"We will go to the high priest and marry. Weep no more. We will have the son that was promised to us."

Mara could not hide the anger and shame in her voice. "I thought I was cursed, but now I know it is even worse. I *am* the curse."

"I will never believe you are a curse."

"Death is my bedfellow. I swear by HaShem, whom you still believe to be good and just, I will never marry you."

"And I will never marry another."

"Then your House will surely end."

Samuel's breath seized. "After all we have endured, you would be the stumbling block to our marriage? Our joy?"

Mara rose and walked back into the cottage, softly shutting the door.

"Without you, I have been locked back in that dark, dank prison cell in Jericho." Samuel pounded on the door. "Your rebuke is beyond bearing."

Mara leaned against the cottage door and caressed it with her palm. After a few moments, Samuel rapped lightly. She opened the door and met his gaze. Samuel's clear brown eyes turned smokey like a snuffed candle. "Beloved. Would you deny our contentment last night?"

"I will hold the memory in my heart until the end of the age."

"What would you have me do then?"

Mara's heart galloped, running a chariot race in her chest.

Samuel waited for her answer in a silence. She dared not soften her resolve. Mara could not confess her qualms. If she married Samuel, he would die. Even speaking the words might cause Samuel's death. Pagans understood that words carried power.

"What have I done to deserve your silence?"

Mara heard the anger creep into his disbelief. Let him be angry. Anger would harden his heart.

"I am not your wife under the Law."

His lips parted, but he did not speak.

Every shred of Mara's being wanted to place her arms around his neck and draw him close. Offer comfort.

"After countless years, you cast me off?"

A sudden inspiration struck Mara. She knew how to protect his life. "I will share life's path with you, not as wife, but as your comfort woman."

Samuel flashed her a look full of fire. He turned and walked away. Slowly. Like he hoped she would yield. Call him back. Call him husband.

He was almost to the tall grasses. She must not yield to her wants. His life was in the balance.

Samuel spun and ran back. Grabbing her shoulders, he shook her gently as if trying to wake her from a night terror. "Why. Tell me why?"

She shook her head and bit her cheek.

"There must be a reason."

"You must trust me." She touched his lips. "I dare not speak the reason aloud."

"HaShem knows my deepest desires. I want a wife, not a comfort woman."

"Have these years apart not shown you HaShem rarely gives us all we want?"

35

Shechem

Samuel

Feeling like an overburdened ox, Samuel trudged to Abba's house and stepped through the door. He trusted HaShem, but his happiness was fast fading.

"My son, your face is a thundercloud." Abba rose, poured a cup of watered wine, set it on the table, and gestured for Samuel to sit. "Tell me."

Samuel picked up the clay cup and flung it at the wall.

Abba's eyes widened but he held a guarded quiet. A quiet that tempers chaos. A quiet that gives room for a heart to find its way.

"I will never understand that woman."

"You did not come home last night." Abba's tone cradled a careful question.

Mara. His lips tingled at the memory of her lips on his.

Abram pressed his fingertips together, likely unaware of his slight sway.

He was praying. Little did Abba know how much Samuel needed that prayer.

Samuel poured another cup, downed it, and wiped his mouth. He had come to the end of his hope.

Abba tugged his beard and frowned. "Is it really that dire?"

"Mara and I spent the night as man and wife." He clutched the cup, knuckles white. "And Daveed's youngest grandson knows."

"A timely wedding contract will keep Mara from shame."

Samuel's tongue was lifeless, unable to voice the depth of his pain.

Abba seemed to study his face.

"Mara says she will not marry me. Because she loves me." Samuel paced. "She will not explain." He paced. "And her stance is beyond reason."

Abram came alongside him. "Mara has suffered much. Perhaps her barrenness is an unbearable burden with which she would not yoke you."

"I vowed I would never marry another."

Abram raised his eyes to heaven. "Trust HaShem."

"There is a growing bitterness in Mara's heart." Samuel slapped the table. "She no longer trusts that HaShem is good or just."

Abba gasped and touched his brow, lips, and heart to ward off evil.

"Abba that is not the worst of it."

"What could be worse?"

"Daveed's grandson overheard Mara's blasphemy."

A Certain Man

Mara

Mara lay on her pallet gazing through the open door of her cottage. The moon was full and bright, mocking her dark mood.

For hours, sleep hovered just out of reach.

This evening, at the well, the potter's daughter had swept an arm toward Mara. "Behold, a new widow with a new man in her bed."

Daveed's grandson must have been flapping his jaw.

The young woman's face had then twisted around a mocking smile. "Is it true you will not marry Samuel?"

When Mara confirmed her refusal, the brazen potter's daughter boasted that Samuel would one day wed her. Mara had been distraught and distracted. She hurried back to the cottage, leaving her water pot at the well. Tomorrow she would reclaim her water pot and the fragments of her life she had left behind.

She wanted Samuel by her side, but she had stabbed a sword into his pride. Would he come to her bed if they were not wed? If he did, would he be safe from her curse?

A jealous chill coiled around her heart. The thought of Samuel with another woman was beyond bearing. At long last, Mara succumbed to a tormented sleep.

Something dragged Mara toward wakefulness. Light. Was it daybreak? Had she left a lamp lit? She slipped back toward sleep.

The smell of smoke jerked her awake. An eerie orange glow loomed at the window. She ran outside.

A burning bush.

Mara's heart raced and her chest tightened. The fire was growing.

A figure lurked in the shadows. She had been lured into the

339

open. What must she suffer now for her sins? She would not let him touch her—she would die first.

Mara scanned for anything she could use as a weapon. She picked up a shepherd's crook that lay on the ground nearby.

"Marry Samuel. Release all claim to this cottage."

Daveed's grandson.

"Or one night you will wake to the thatch above your head ablaze."

She brandished the crook and the boy fled.

Mara stared at the burning bush hoping somehow the flames would reveal her future. That boy could make trouble that threatened more than her cottage. Samuel must not know of the fire. And she could not rely on HaShem for rescue.

36

Shechem

Samuel

Abba wheezed, unable to match Samuel's pace toward the House of the High Priest.

"Johakim will help." Abba lagged and sank onto a boulder facing the road behind them. "Look, a royal runner."

Samuel returned and sat beside him.

There was something familiar about the runner. His stride. His size. Samuel squinted.

The royal runner approached and stopped. "Greetings Didymus. A fuller beard and I would not have known you."

"In Shechem, I am called Samuel. This is my father."

The runner bowed toward Abba. "A message by mouth for Samuel."

"You may speak freely before my father."

"Come to Jericho Inn. The lives of both daughters are in the balance."

Samuel jumped up. Lyra needed his protection. Herodias was never one to embellish.

Abba grabbed Samuel's arm. "First, we must see the high priest. Daveed's grandson will start trouble for Mara."

"My daughter, or my Beloved." Samuel looked to the heavens. "HaShem, would you make me choose?"

Abba stood. "Hurry ahead my son."

"I also carry a message for the high priest." The runner drank from his waterskin. "I will follow with your father."

Samuel ran up the hill, chasing his runaway thoughts. Daveed's grandson could not prove Mara's heresy. Surely, she would not be so foolhardy as to repeat her bitter blasphemy.

Samuel grabbed the gate, shook it, and shouted. "I must speak with the high priest. Now."

Okpara came running and unlocked the gate. The hairs on Samuel's arms bristled. This man betrayed him to Jareb for silver. Bits of knowledge snapped into place like an Egyptian puzzle ring. He was the spy who sold news for gold. But his report brought Samuel back to Shechem. The evil seed Okpara had sown, the Lord had harvested for good.

Okpara ushered Samuel inside. The high priest was seated at his table, a scroll before him. "I heard the urgency in your voice all the way from the gate. So, tell me the terms of the wedding contract."

"There will be no contract. Mara will not marry me."

The High Priest listened as Samuel confessed all. Their night together, the threats of Daveed's grandson. And lastly, Mara's struggle with faith. "What am I to do? I cannot leave her out there ... a lost lamb among a pack of wolves."

Dan charged into the room, his face twisted with fury. "Mara—"

Misha followed and dipped his head to the High Priest. "A thousand pardons for the breach of your peace."

"When is the wedding? Dan's shout slammed against the walls. "The shepherd's cottage should revert to me as my inheritance."

The high priest shot Samuel a temper-your-tongue look.

"Mara has not consented to marry."

Dan glared at Samuel.

"With time, Mara will relent and marry me."

Dan shook a fist at Samuel. "Mara refused to marry so she can keep the cottage."

Misha turned to his brother. "Silence. You shame our House. The woman has lost five husbands. Let her grieve and heal. One day she will accept Samuel's love."

"Generosity with what should have been mine is easy for you brother."

"I gave you an extra portion of silver." Misha took Dan's arm.

He pulled away. "Silver will be spent, land will provide a perpetual blessing."

Samuel stepped between the two brothers and handed Dan a silver coin. "Take this as a vow of good faith. If Mara will not marry me, I will convince her to become my concubine and sell you the land at an excellent price."

"Why should I buy back my own land?" The cords of Dan's neck were taut bowstrings.

"An urgent matter calls me to Jericho." Samuel kept his tone calm. "Upon my return we will come to an agreement."

Dan sneered. "The last time you left, you did not return for seven years."

Burning anger surged through Samuel's veins. His jaw and fists clenched.

"By the Feast of Succoth." Dan pounded his fist onto the table. "I will build my booth on the land of my father."

The high priest turned to Samuel. "What say you?"

"Agreed."

The High Priest cast a stern look at Dan. "If any ill should befall Mara or her possessions, remember your threats have been witnessed. Go now."

Misha and Dan passed by Okpara leading the royal runner in to see the high priest. "My Lord, a royal runner."

The runner stepped up to the table, struck a fist against his heart, and handed a sealed parchment to the high priest.

He unrolled the parchment and Samuel studied his face. His expression was a blank tablet.

What business could Herodias have with the High Priest of Samaria? A man she had only seen once at Samuel's trial. Samuel wiped his slick palms and held his breath, waiting for some inkling.

"It seems you are not the only one who has urgent dealings with Jericho. Okpara, saddle a horse for Samuel."

"Yes, my lord." The Egyptian eyed him with curiosity, then ran off.

Samuel sent the high priest a questioning look.

"When you have concluded your business, go to the forge near the Jericho gate."

"I know the place." Had Dex and his household been drawn into some intrigue. Was Lyra still with them? And Salome? "What would you have me do?"

"You are to bring me the money and plans for a dovecote." The high priest smiled. A smile lined with uncertainty.

There were messenger doves at the forge in Jericho. What plot was Herodias hatching?

Samuel hurried outside, took the reins from Okpara, and mounted.

"If the stallion favors his right front foot, let him rest." Okpara patted the horse's neck. "I removed a rock from his hoof last night."

"You are fond of him."

"Yes, he suffered much abuse at the hands of the Avenger. We are brothers in beating." Okpara let his tunic fall, baring his back—scarred from scourging.

Samuel gasped, unable to hide his sympathy.

Okpara replaced his tunic. "Go with your god."

Samuel rode toward the crossroads and spotted Mara drawing water. She saw him on horseback and her face changed to the look of an abandoned child. She dropped her waterpot and it shattered against the stone wall. For a moment she stared at the shards at her feet. Then she turned and ran.

"Beloved. Do not run from me." He urged the stallion forward and caught up with her. "Please, Mara. I must leave. My daughter is in danger. But I will hurry back to you. HaShem will be my shield."

Mara looked up and shuddered. "I fear Daveed's grandson."

"Ozri will move my worldly goods into your cottage. The villagers will assume we are to marry. Upon my return, if you will not be my wife, would you still accept a life with me?"

He paused. "But not as a comfort woman."

"What do you mean?"

Samuel dismounted. "You would be provided for as my concubine." His words seemed to punch into Mara's chest. Both her hands covered her heart, and she shrunk back.

Samuel pulled her into his arms, cradling her head against his shoulder.

Mara rose to her toes and kissed his cheek. "My life has been filled with leave-takings. I will not watch you ride away." Her only other answer was silent tears.

Mara

Mara picked up a broom and began to sweep her cottage. Surely Samuel would be safe from HaShem's curse if she were only his lowly concubine. She would begin her new, humbled life with every corner clean. She would never be a wife or a mother. She would always be a curse. But amidst her sorrow, she would clutch at one straw of happiness.

Mara spotted the harp against the wall and picked up the sack to cover it. Something small was wedged deep inside the sack. She fished it out, unwrapped a layer of linen, and found a scrap of parchment and a small leather pouch.

Seth's script.

My dear wife. May this coin please you by calling to mind your best-loved song.

Mara's fingers trembled. Her soul and her sanity were teetering on the edge of a precipice. And she was unsure if she would fall, right herself, or be rescued by another. Mara opened the pouch and poured the coin into her palm.

A golden dove winked up at her. A coin just like the Magi coin she gave Samuel so long ago. Mara's mouth went dry. Her breath rushed out.

She studied both sides. It was not the same coin. The image was sharper, and it shone like a new dawn.

Chills ran up Mara's arms just as they did each time she was told the story of the Magi visit and the birth of the Promised One.

Mara wandered outside and sat on a stool on the porch. Sheep and goats roamed the slopes. A flock without a shepherd.

"Shalom, Mara."

She startled at the shout.

Abram climbed the hill, leaning on his staff.

Mara stood. "Shalom."

Abram eased onto the stool.

She ran inside and brought a cup of water.

He nodded his thanks. "What else is in your hand?"

"A coin I found among Seth's things." She handed it to Abram. "Just like the one my mother left with Ruth."

Abram examined the coin. "Do you think it is also a sign that you will see the Taheb?" Excitement shivered in his voice.

"I dare not hope." Her voice faded to a hoarse whisper. "My hope has been dashed so often."

"Mara. Mara." Abram patted her hand. "Shattered hope is the work of the Evil One. HaShem restores hope." Abram handed the coin back to her.

"Would that I still had your faith. One moment, the coin seems warm in my hand. Comforting as sun on sand. And I feel the Promised One is near." She stared at the image of the dove. "The next moment, the coin seems cold, like a whipping wind that chills to the bone. And I fear I will never see Him."

Watch and wait.

Mara began to tremble. HaShem had heard her profane taunt to meet her face to face. She did not understand how or where or when, but she had no doubt HaShem was coming. Her meeting with the Lord would end—either with death and damnation—or with rebirth and forgiveness. Either her name or her sin would be forever blotted from the Book of Life.

Watch and wait.

Abram leaned on his staff and stood. "Any sign of trouble?"

"All has been quiet."

Relief flickered across Abram's face. "Good." An ember of wariness still smoldered in his voice.

"Tell me."

"Dan's wife, Delilah, whispers that Daveed's death came so close to Samuel's return, some would suspect poison or sorcery."

Fury flooded through Mara's veins. "That pagan half-breed knows her sorceries and poisons better than I." Delilah had given Mara the herbs that delayed her moonblood and started her along the path of her great lie.

"I will send Ozri to keep watch over you until Samuel returns." Abram stepped out from the porch. "And stay away from the women at the well. Then your life will be less in their minds and less on their tongues."

"I have enough water for two days. Then, when the sun is high and fierce. I will go to draw water. No one will be there."

37

On the Road to Jericho

Samuel

S amuel let the stallion set the pace on the road toward Jericho. The sun was sinking, and the stallion began to favor his right forefoot. Samuel stopped and tended the hoof. He would sleep under the stars. Rushing into a dark night was fraught with dangers. For Samuel, danger of an ambush. For the stallion, danger of a fall.

At first light he resumed his brisk ride, but nearing the forge he reined the stallion to a walk to fend off attention or alarm.

Dex was not in sight, but the forge fire was stoked and dancing. There was a flash of movement behind the workshop. Samuel dismounted and quietly made his way there.

A woman was humming the dove song. He moved closer and spotted Salome. She was sweeping the dovecote floor. She seemed calm, content, and of sound mind. Two messenger doves flew in and landed on a perch. She hand-fed each one and gently unlaced messages from their legs.

Since Yonah means dove, this picture of Salome tending the doves in his mind's eye would remind him to always call her Yonah. She returned with a dove readied to fly with a reply and tossed it into the bright morning sun. The dove took wing, cooing a farewell.

Babbles and burbles came from a basket on a boulder. A baby pushed up and peeked over the edge. Zosi's eyes.

Lyra. How she had grown. How he had missed her.

Samuel's throat thickened but a wave of joy overshadowed his sadness. Yonah smiled the smile of a young adoring mother and lifted Lyra over her head. Lyra giggled. A giggle of pure delight.

Samuel stifled a laugh.

"You slept well." Yonah kissed her brow. She turned Lyra and sniffed her bottom. "And you are wet and hungry. Which shall we tend to first?"

Just then, Yonah spotted Samuel. Her face changed and her eyes widened. Not with fear. Not with madness, but with a sort of bewilderment.

"I do not know you." She shook her head and seemed to clear a mist from her mind. "Yet, I do know you."

Of course. Yonah had never seen him with a beard, or in Samaritan garb. "I am Lyra's father, come for a visit."

"I care for her as would a mother who birthed her." She hugged Lyra tight. "We must never be parted."

Samuel tensed. When Lyra's redemption was complete, would Yonah refuse to return his daughter to him? He chose each word warily. "I am grateful for your constant care. May I hold her?"

"Let me clean her up first."

"Hello, old friend." Dex was at Samuel's shoulder.

"Even though you are the size of a horse, you never fail to sneak up on me."

The blacksmith shrugged and hugged him too tightly, unaware of his strength.

Sophia joined them. Her hug was gentle, warm, and welcoming. Samuel kissed her on the cheek. "I can never repay you. Without your mother's milk my Lyra would have died."

"She is like my own babe."

Samuel cast a glance around. Sophia's son was not there. His stomach tensed inside a fist of worry.

Sophia patted his hand. "Have no care. My strong son sleeps in the house."

The fist of worry opened, and Samuel's stomach relaxed.

"I will miss Lyra." Sophia's voice skittered across a sigh.

"It is not time for her redemption." Samuel shot a questioning look at Dex whose face was tense and pained.

Something was very much amiss. Samuel's palms slicked and his stomach soured.

Dex clapped him on the shoulder. "We will explain, but our loss is your gain." He turned toward the house. "Come." He spoke in Samuel's ear. "Herodias waits inside."

They entered the house Samuel remembered so well. After a moment, he found Herodias standing in the shadowy corner. She was plainly dressed beneath a hooded gray cloak. Not one piece of jewelry adorned her ears, her arms, her neck.

The queen stepped from the shadows. Her gaze was one he knew—part cunning, part concern. "The king has arranged a marriage for Princess Salome."

Samuel's heart pounded out a warning. If Salome wed, they were all dead. For surely the moment she saw Herod she would spew treason.

"Henceforth, the girl at the dovecote will be Yonah." The queen's voice dropped to a sorrowful whisper. "No longer a princess, but forever my daughter. My brave girl who danced for her life and saved mine. No one who knew the princess must ever catch sight of Yonah. That is why I sent for you."

"What must I do?" Samuel prayed her orders would not delay his return to Mara.

"Take Yonah to Shechem. No one would ever look for her there."

He wanted to grab Lyra and run, but she was a slave. Would Herodias take his baby to Herod's court as hostage to his loyalty? "And Lyra?" He waited, simmering in silence. The silence hovered until it burned white-hot like iron in the fiery forge.

"When Yonah tends Lyra, she is in her right mind. Samuel, you remain my bond-slave until Lyra's redemption day. Take both to Shechem. Yonah will serve as her nurse."

Dex took his cloak from the hook. "When Herod learns the princess he pledged as a political prize has run away, he will send out a search party. If he ever suspects Yonah was here ..."

"We must leave the forge." Sophia moved toward her son's basket.

"No. You must tend the dovecote." The queen's raptor eyes turned on Sophia. "Yonah has taught you?"

Sophia nodded, looked down, wrung her hands.

But Dex looked directly at the queen, his face set, his eyes challenging. "We risk our lives for a dovecote?"

"Do not defy me." The queen's shoulders shifted.

A warning chill crept across Samuel's neck. He must distract the queen from Dex's defiance. He stepped in front of his friend. "You have a plan in place. A plan even a fool could not ruin."

"Yes. But some things are dangerous to know." The queen's eyes were lowered as if safeguarding her plan.

Dex moved to Samuel's side. "And some things are more

dangerous to withhold. Only a foolish commander sends his centurions into battle blind to the plan. And, my queen, you are no man's fool." Dex's words were now weighted with reason, not rebellion. "I suspect your tactics would match Alexander the Great."

The queen laughed. An easy laugh that seemed to say flattery that amuses me may well be rewarded.

She lowered her hood, her posture regal. "There is a second Salome."

"Who is she?" Dex asked before Samuel could speak.

"A distant cousin without family, who wishes to live the life of a princess. A woman I have spent months training to mimic Salome—her look, her voice, her movements. When she is sent to be married, she will be fully veiled. If the king calls for Salome, after the cruel night he spent with her, he will not question that she avoids his gaze and trembles prettily."

Samuel wanted to shout with joy. A second Salome would protect the true princess and them.

"What of all those who dressed and trained this second Salome?"

Herodias had a way of looking down on a man even though he was a head taller. And that was how she looked at Dex now.

"Not one of them still draws breath."

Dex looked as appalled as he had when Herodias refused to bury the guards who defended her litter.

Sophia whimpered and the queen rounded on her. "It would serve you well to remember only the strong of spirit survive to serve me."

In the space of a single breath, Sophia put on a mantle of strength. Her son wailed. She picked him up and bounced him in her arms. "Yonah must remain a servant forever?" Sophia's voice carried a carefully veiled edge of disbelief.

"Better for my daughter to live safely as a servant of sound mind, than as a mad princess whose rants could ruin us all." A flash of sorrow shadowed Herodias's face. "Enough. Soon the second Salome will marry Philip the Tetrarch and live well away from the eyes of Herod, the Old Fox."

Herodias lifted her hood and headed for the door. "I must return to court. Dex, travel to Shechem with Samuel and help guard our daughters on the way. Sophia, stay and tend the doves."

Samuel nodded.

Dex put his arm around his wife. "I will not tarry."

"The High Priest of Shechem has tasked a servant with building the dovecote I commanded."

"Okpara," Samuel ground out the name, "will sell his soul for coin."

The queen's eyes flashed. "He is not to be trusted with secrets—or the safety of our daughters. But he is my spy. For now, Okpara has sold his soul to me."

"Nevertheless, I will watch him closely." Samuel fought to bridle his temper.

"Take some messenger doves. Yonah will train them. Then swift messages can be sent between us. Messages hidden from runners and rulers."

"I will bring Yonah from our dovecote for your leave-taking." Sophia laid her son back in his basket.

"No. Yonah must forget me. Forget she was ever a queen's daughter. Simply take me where I can watch her unseen."

"Come." Sophia opened the door. "To protect my son, I must lose Lyra. My heart weeps with yours. For even if our children are taken from us, a mother is forever a mother."

Sympathy welled in Samuel's chest and blurred his sight. He blew out a double-minded sigh. Sadly, his friends had lost Lyra. Gladly, he could now raise his own daughter, and raise her as a Samaritan.

38

Shechem

Mara

Mara looked ahead. At midday, the well was deserted. No women to shun, mock, or accuse. She wiped her brow, let her head-covering fall to her shoulders, and reached for the rope twined around the cross bar.

She began to draw water and let her mind wander. As a girl, she loved going to the well. Here, Joseph's bones, brought out of Egypt, were buried. Here, Ruth and Sarah helped her draw water and taught her the ways of her people and of women. Even though motherless, she had a place in Shechem. And here, she met Seth, the husband she learned to love.

But this crossroads was also witness to sadness and secrets. Here, Samuel fled for his life. Here, she had been shunned by the village women. Here, she burned her moonblood cloth and buried the ashes under the terebinth tree.

Mara looked toward the tree and gasped. She was not alone. A stranger sat on the boulder where Seth had rested the day they met. He was not boldly beautiful as Seth had been. The cut of his beard and the pattern of his fringed garment gave him away. He was tall for a Jew. Why would he risk travel through Samaria?

"Give me a drink." The stranger stood and moved toward the well.

Surely, he would consider all Samaritans unclean and all women unworthy. Even her own people would not speak with her. But the young man looked tired and thirsty.

"How is it that you, being a Jew, ask a drink from me, a Samaritan woman?"

The stranger waited patiently as if he knew she would never refuse anyone who needed her.

Mara filled the water jar on the wall. A strong thirst could make anyone break with tradition.

"Jews have no dealings with Samaritans."

He smiled the smile of a pleased rabbi ready to teach an eager young student.

"If you knew the gift of the Lord and who it is who says to you 'give me a drink' you would have asked him, and he would have given you living water."

Living water? Who was this man offering living water? Free-flowing water that purifies. Mara's heart fluttered around an ember of excitement.

"Sir, you have nothing to draw with and the well is deep." She prepared a cup for him.

Now Mara's heart raced at a sudden revelation. Rain. Living water that feeds fresh flowing streams. Only a prophet like Moses can call forth living water from a rock in the desert. Only a prophet like Elijah can call down rain from a cloudless sky.

"Where do you get this living water?" Was this the Promised One who was supposed to be like Moses? Mara's hands trembled, the water quivering in the cup. "Are you greater than our father Jacob, who gave us this well and drank from it himself?" Mara handed him the cup.

The stranger raised it to his lips and looked over the brim, meeting her eyes. "Whoever drinks of this water will thirst again, but whoever drinks of the water I shall give him will never thirst. But the water I shall give him will become in him a fountain of water, springing up into everlasting life."

Though he was not comely, there was something compelling about this man's face. Something she had never seen before. Something she sensed she would never see in another. Mara's eyes locked with his, and she had no wish to be freed.

An unexplained wave of joy washed over her.

He speaks with the authority of a holy man. But he speaks in riddles. Yet he seems to want me to sift his meaning.

Mara's mind worked to unravel the riddle. Only the Creator is the author of life. Only He can promise eternal life. She seemed to reach for a reward dangling just before her face, but she could not take hold of it. She shook her head and shrugged off her vexation.

All this talk of eternal life was beyond her, but the daily chore of drawing water was not. "Sir, give me this water that I may not thirst nor come here to draw."

How often had she wished she would never have to draw water from the well again. Never have to watch the village women turn away from her. Never have to face her need for acceptance. Her need for HaShem and His provision.

"Go call your husband and come here."

Why must she bring a husband to obtain living water?

Drawing water was woman's work. "I have no husband." Mara cringed at the bite in her tone.

"You have well said *I have no husband,* for you have had five husbands and the one who you have now is not your husband. You have spoken truly."

Mara looked at her feet. *He knows me. He knows all my lies. All the darkness in me. He knows all I have ever done. And all that has ever been done to me.*

Her mind raced against her heart. *Yet he honors me by speaking with me.* Who is he?

Is this the man who called the Jerusalem temple a den of thieves? Perhaps he will restore the Samaritan temple on Mount Gerizim. *I must know. I will test him.*

"Sir, I perceive that you are a prophet. Our fathers worshiped on this mountain. You Jews say that Jerusalem is the place where one ought to worship."

"Woman, believe me the hour is coming when you will neither on this mountain nor in Jerusalem worship the Father. You worship what you do not know, we know what we worship for salvation is from the Jews."

Mara's heart sped and its wild beating leapt into her ears. Everything she had been told was true. The Magi from so long ago worshiped the child they found in Bethlehem. He was to be called King of the Jews. Ruth said the Magi followed the star because in their scroll it was written, *I establish the tribes of Jacob ... as a light unto the nations, to be My salvation until the end of the earth.*

The prophet drank deeply. "The hour is coming and now is when true worshipers will worship the Father in spirit and in truth. The Father is seeking such to worship Him. God is spirit and those who worship Him must worship in spirit and truth."

Father. This man must be the one who called the Jewish

temple his Father's house. He seemed to speak with the spirit of Moses. Will he heal the breach between Samaritan and Jew?

Mara's mouth went dry. Had she had just drawn water for the Taheb? The Messiah?

"I know that Messiah, the Christ, is coming." Her voice was quiet, but her words were sure. "When he comes he will tell us all things. All truth."

"I, who speak to you, am He."

Mara's vision clouded and her legs felt weak. The stranger claimed to be the harbinger of all Truth. Was this blasphemy?

Mara's mind tried to unknot the mystery.

But if his claim was true, it was not blasphemy.

Mara knelt. She did not understand but she somehow trusted that he spoke only the Truth.

She wanted to kiss his feet but did not dare. She wanted to ask for forgiveness, but she was not worthy to ask anything of him.

My sheep hear my voice, and they know me.

This voice, his voice, was the one that spoke to her soul for all these years. And she heard it again now.

Each day you draw water at this well. Alone.

Each day, I have seen your loneliness and your pain and your sorrow for your sins.

HaShem had sent his Promised One to meet her face to face. And she was not worthy.

I came through Samaria just for you.

Your sins are forgiven. Go, and sin no more.

"Sir, please stay. I will go and tell everyone I have found the Promised One."

He smiled with such gentleness, such acceptance, such love.

Go and spread the good news. For this you were born.

A warmth flooded Mara's veins. He had exchanged her unworthiness for a wellspring of undeserved worth.

Just then a group of Jewish men came to the well with packets of food. They must be his disciples. She overhead them whisper amongst themselves. "He speaks with a woman alone?"

"And a Samaritan?"

Yet no one admonished him. Or asked him why.

Always ask all of your questions. Questions will strengthen your faith, not weaken it. Seek and you will find.

She went to take up her waterpot. But it would slow her.

The stranger raised a hand, blessing her. *Mara. Leave the waterpot. I will be here. Waiting to water the flock you bring to me with living water.*

Mara started to run toward Shechem, but suddenly stopped. He knew her name. She turned back. "Sir, how are you called?"

"I am Yeshua the Nazarene."

Mara ran fast and hard toward Shechem. She came to the center of the village. "I have found him." Breathless. Voice weak. She braced her hands on her knees, chest heaving.

No one had heard.

Spotting the cymbal in front of Abram's house, she picked up the striker and tapped a light, joyful rhythm. Not the clanging, desperate rhythm she had pounded when Samuel was in danger so long ago.

Doors opened. People leaned out.

"Come and see. I have found him." Mara lifted her robe higher and ran, telling all she saw, "I have found him."

She would run to the high priest. Johakim had been watching and waiting since the coming of the Magi.

Footsteps pounded behind her. She looked back, the villagers were following.

Mara arrived at the gate of the House of the High Priest.

The villagers surged in front of her. Mara shouted. "Come out. Come out. Come out."

The high priest, in a simple linen robe, hurried outside. "What has happened?" His voice was steady. A shepherd calming his frantic flock.

Mara pushed through the crowd. "I have found him." She could not stand still. She spun around and her feet skipped like a bride leading the village women in a wedding dance. "Make haste. Come with me."

It was Johakim the man, not the high priest, who studied her face. She caught the spark of understanding ignite in his eyes. "The Taheb? The Promised One?"

"Yes. I have found him." Mara's tone filled with certain pride.

I am never lost. You were the one who was lost.

Mara's stomach tightened around a twinge of dismay. "In truth, I have not found the Promised One. He has found me."

She wove through the crowd. "Come and see a man who told me all I ever did. My good deeds. My lies. My secret sins." She smiled, touched hands, tugged robes. "He knew of my five husbands. My sorrow. My regrets. My repentance."

Mara looked into the eyes of the women. "This prophet also knows all that was done to me. He did not shun me. He spoke with me when you would not."

The women looked down. Not shunning her, but shamed.

"He has lifted my curse." Mara approached the high priest, took his hand, and drew him toward the gate.

Snatches from the crowd came to her ears.

"She seems in her right mind."

"Changed."

"Freed from her sorrow."

Mara beckoned to them. "Come. Consider for yourselves. Could this be the Promised One? The Christ?"

The high priest opened the gate. "Lead the way. I will follow."

Mara dashed off, desperate to see Yeshua again. Desperate for the others to hear his Truth.

"Where are we going?" Abram's voice carried to her.

Mara shouted over her shoulder, "To Jacob's well." Only a few were able to keep pace with her. She came over the rise and halted. Nearby, the Promised One was sitting on the boulder, teaching his disciples clustered at his feet.

"Do you not say, there are still four months then comes the harvest." He waved his hands toward the fields. "Behold, I say to you lift up your eyes and look at the fields for they are already white for harvest."

The field had just sprouted green, but droves of villagers cut through the new-planted grain. Their light tunics were white in the sunlight. White ripened wheat.

Suddenly Mara understood. The people of Shechem were his harvest.

The Promised One looked toward her as if she were the only one there. "One sows and another reaps, but they both rejoice together." He motioned for Mara to sit at his feet.

She took her place of honor. "Look. I have sown the seeds and brought them to you that you may reap."

The high priest stood with the villagers dressed humbly, not as high priest, but in plain linen, as any other man.

The Promised One turned to the crowd. "Why are you here?"

"This woman, Mara, is changed." Abram lifted his hands, "Praise HaShem. The shackles on her soul have been released."

"Yes Abram, Mara was a daughter to you and Ruth. You

have watched her suffer. And yet, you never lost hope that your son Samuel was alive."

Abram's eyes opened wide with wonder.

"And you praised HaShem when Samuel returned to Shechem dressed as a Greek."

Abram knelt. "Truly only a Prophet of the Lord can know these things."

Mara helped Abram rise. "The Magi came through Shechem many years ago. One gave my mother a rare gold coin. He said that the one to whom it belonged would see the Taheb."

"Show us the coin." Tobiah pushed toward her. "Give us your proof." He stretched out his hand.

"I gave it to Samuel when he ran for sanctuary." She reached into the leather pouch around her neck. "But I found another in Seth's harp-sack and hoped the promise was restored." She lifted the coin and showed it to the crowd, then looked at Yeshua.

"Mara, I say to you, you never had need of a coin to know me. For you have always heard my voice."

Mara wept into her hands. Free-flowing tears. Living water. "Whether it was a deed beneath the cool, midnight moon or a deed beneath the searing, midday sun, this man has seen and told me all I have ever done."

The high priest walked through the gathering and bowed to Yeshua. "Long ago, I spoke with the Magi. I saw the star of great wonder. Tell me rabbi, where were you born?"

Mara heard both hope and a test in the high priest's tone.

"The Magi testified of My Coming. Johakim, you know where I was born as surely as I know of your plight with Judith and Jareb."

Johakim's face turned the color of a whitewashed tomb. He dropped to his knees.

Sounds of surprise and murmurs amongst the villagers grew louder.

"He knows the high priest without his robes."

"He knows names from past generations of the House of Johakim."

"He knows of a secret trouble."

Yeshua pointed to Johakim. "High Priest of Shechem, tell your people when and where I was born."

"You were born in Bethlehem of Judea." Johakim's awe-filled voice quivered with emotion. "At the time of the census of Caesar Augustus."

One disciple jumped up. "The prophecy says *O Bethlehem Ephrathah ... a ruler will come from you on my behalf.*"

Yeshua smiled, stood, and put his arm around the disciple's shoulders, the way one would restrain an excited child. "This is Simon."

Another disciple rose. "Yeshua was immersed and proclaimed by the Baptizer, the prophet I followed first."

"And this is Andrew." Yeshua put his other arm around him.

Mara sucked in a sharp breath. The Baptizer was beheaded by King Herod. The Promised One was to be King of the Jews. To survive a ruthless rival like Herod, Yeshua must step with great care. He would tread through a den of vipers.

The high priest stretched out his arms, gathering his people under his wings. "The sun is low, and we have many questions, much to learn." He turned to Yeshua. "Please, stay. Teach us."

Yeshua seemed to study each villager and he gazed at the high priest with such compassion. "I warn you, some of my teachings are hard."

"Hard to understand?" Worry flickered in the high priest's eyes.

"My words are simple but often hard to accept, and at

times even harder to live by." Yeshua's face shadowed with some unspoken sorrow. He sighed. A heavy sigh that seemed to shoulder the burden of the sins of those around him.

The high priest lifted his arms to the sky. "Let each one listen and choose what they will believe. Choose how they will live. For in the times of Joshua, was this not the valley of decision? Baal or the Lord?" The high priest knelt. "I will listen to the words of the Lord."

Slowly, the villagers knelt with their high priest.

"Let it be so." Yeshua raised his hand in blessing. "Tonight, we will sup and sleep in your courtyard under the Heavens of my Father. In the morning, we will reason together."

Mara's thoughts turned to Samuel.

My Beloved. Hasten home. I have found the Promised One. The Christ. He makes all things new.

39

Shechem

Mara

At first light, Yeshua sat on the cistern wall in the high priest's courtyard. His disciples settled the people in front of him on the ground, women and children to one side, men to the other.

The high priest, now in a rich robe and black turban, stood by his side.

Mara studied the gathering. The rumor ravens, whose squawks of sorcery put her life at risk, perched to her right. A simmering soup of rage curdled in her stomach.

Mara drew in deep breaths and chose the steep, rocky path of forgiveness. The Promised One said she was forgiven. If he in his righteousness would forgive her sins, how could she in her unrighteousness withhold forgiveness from any other?

The fluttering in Mara's chest grew. She must speak her truth so that each soul would know how the Promised One accepted her without condition. And that HaShem's love for her knew no beginning or end.

Yeshua's eyes seemed to call her to come out from among the other women. She threaded her way toward him like a scuttle weaving across her loom. "Yeshua knew the secret flaws I had woven into my life. I will speak them so you may believe he is Messiah." She stopped in front of Him.

"Even if they do not believe, does not the proverb promise that when you speak the truth, justice will be done." Yeshua gestured her toward his right hand. A place of honor.

The knot of fear that had long lingered in Mara's stomach was dislodged by a shiver of joy. "I was a young girl, barely on the cusp of womanhood, afraid of my betrothed, afraid of my father, and afraid for my Beloved." Mara confessed the herbs, the burning of her moonblood cloth, and her prayers for deliverance from Achor and Jareb, even if it meant their deaths.

"You."

Mara turned and met the scornful eyes of the alluring potter's daughter.

"You know herbs, maybe you also know poisons."

Mara kept her voice soft, forgiving. "This Prophet is my witness. I never once thought of poison or sorcery."

Yeshua turned to her accuser. "Woman, your tongue reveals more about your unclean heart than it condemns Mara."

The young woman shrank back, fear on her face.

Mara turned to the high priest and bowed her head. She placed her palms together. "My choice to take heathen herbs left my womb withered and cheated the House of Johakim of a rightful heir."

The high priest took Mara's hand and turned with her to Yeshua. "This woman has sinned, yet she has been sinned against and suffered much. Rabbi, what say you?"

"Justice must be tempered with mercy. Mara has repented and I have forgiven her sins."

Angry murmurs flooded Mara's ears.

"Blasphemy!"

"Who is this man to forgive sins?"

"Only HaShem can forgive sins."

One man picked up a clod of dirt. Another a stone.

"Stop." Abram took the clod from the man's hand and threw it on the ground.

Silence. A tense silence stretched. Silence balanced on the precipice of something profound.

Revolt? Repentance? Revelation?

"Who are you?" The high priest's voice quivered perhaps as much from his quest for truth as his fear to hear it.

"Who do *you* say that I am?"

The high priest's face paled. Not with fear. Not with revulsion. His eyes glimmered with something else.

The people stirred and looked at one another—confusion on every face. They mumbled and grumbled. Some rose, starting to depart.

"Quiet." The high priest's command cut off all debate. "Let us consider all that this stranger has to say. It was foretold that the Promised One would make all things clear."

Yeshua gestured to a spot on the cistern wall.

The high priest sat beside him. "I have a scroll that speaks of the Son of Man. This scroll has been much studied, much pondered."

"A copy of the ancient scroll of Dani-el was given to you by the Magnus, Balthasar of Babylon." Yeshua nodded. "And what have you learned?" Yeshua's tone was gentle yet probing.

"That I see the Truth only in part." Tears streamed into the high priest's beard. "What is needed to grasp the whole truth?"

"Your whole truth will set you free to see."

The high priest's face crumbled. "I must confess my secret, my darkest sin." His voice faltered on the word sin.

He turned to the villagers. "I held to the harsh letter of the Law for Mara but broke it for my beloved wife." The High Priest continued, his voice gaining strength. "Judith was defiled by a stranger in the same field where Achor accosted Mara. Under the Law of Moses, the high priest must marry a virgin. But we loved one another and I would not see her shamed. We married quickly and lay together, so we would never know if she had conceived a wicked man's child."

The villagers remained silent and still.

"With time, we both came to believe Jareb was the son of her defiler. He looked like him. He spoke like him. He had his depraved temperament. When Jareb demanded to marry Mara, I could have threatened to disinherit him, block his appointment as the next high priest. Yet, I did neither of those things."

Johakim took both of Mara's hands. "You scarred Jareb's hand and face. And for some unnamed sin sent Enosh away. HaShem used Mara to preserve the purity of the priesthood when I would not."

Yeshua rose and came toward Mara. She knelt and he laid his hand upon her brow.

"You are called Mara—meaning bitter. Yet your mother named you Tamara—meaning date palm which is sweet. Today, woman of Samaria, I give you a new life and a new name. Not Mara, not Tamara, but Shamara—meaning protected by the Lord."

Yeshua turned to the villagers and raised both hands over them. "The Magi found the King they sought and stopped here first. In the fullness of time, the people of Shechem will be among the first to believe all that I have done. For my work has just begun. My time has not yet come."

Yeshua had forgiven her sins. A fiery surge ran through Mara's veins and seemed to chase every shadow from her mind. HaShem had sent His prophet to meet her face-to-face.

Shechem

Three days later

Shamara

Mara, now Shamara, sat on the cistern wall in the High Priest's courtyard retelling her encounter with Yeshua at the well, three days past. The people never seemed to tire of hearing the tale.

She spotted Samuel coming under the courtyard arch. Sheer joy flooded her heart as it had when Samuel first wanted to marry her. She stood, stepped between the seated women, and dashed to him.

Samuel gathered her close. He stepped back, his eyes seemed to search her soul. "Something earth-shaking has happened here. You are no longer shunned, but sought-after."

"I have found the Promised One." Shamara took Samuel's hand. "And now I will marry you."

Several women clapped their hands and laughed loudly. Blessings buzzed around Shamara and Samuel like bees in a new field of flowers.

Shamara glanced behind Samuel. A young, beautiful woman holding a baby waited quietly at a distance. A wife waiting for her husband.

Shamara's heart raced, her stomach twisted, her vision blurred behind unspilled tears. Had Samuel taken a wife? She sniffed back her shock and humiliation and straightened her shoulders.

Shamara moved toward the woman but looked only at the baby. She reached out and the baby grasped her little finger. She looked back at Samuel "This baby ..." Her voice broke and she dragged in a deep breath, forcing her mouth to move past her hurt and surprise. "... your daughter?"

"Yes." Samuel took Shamara's arm and turned her toward him. "Truly, you will marry me?" Samuel's tone flooded with unbridled joy. "I will arrange for a proper wedding feast."

Samuel walked over to Dan. "Once Mara and I are betrothed, the shepherd's cottage and field will be your inheritance once again."

Dan clasped Samuel's forearm. "When you marry, you may stay at the cottage until your father's house is made ready for your bride."

"A thousand thanks." Samuel sounded pleased with the peace offering.

Misha, now the head of Daveed's family, stepped forward. "Mara will not marry you without means. She brought the Promised One to my family and all of Shechem. Half the profit from the field my father left her will be given to your House each year."

Samuel turned to Shamara. "And the profit will be hers to do with as she wishes."

"My Beloved is as generous as he is righteous." With means of her own, she would not be at the mercy and whims of a first wife—a beautiful, fertile, foreigner. A twinge of sadness pricked at her heart.

The baby whimpered. The rumor ravens turned their raptor eyes and sharp beaks, poised to pounce. Snatches of gossip rained down like orange cinders from a fire. Cinders that singed Shamara's heart.

"Must be Samuel's child."

"Enticing woman."

"Like the temptresses of old."

The slurs became more noisy and nasty.

"Bathsheba."

"Delilah."

"Eve, the first temptress."

The young woman cast Shamara a pleading look. The young beauty's dove-gray eyes were pools of pain on the verge of frantic panic.

Shamara raised a hand to the gossips. "Enough."

Johakim looked unsure if he should trespass into the matters of women. He put his palms together and nodded toward Shamara, ceding his authority.

Shamara took the hand of the young woman. "You must be weary and are welcome here." She pointed to Okpara. "Tell the servants to prepare my old chambers."

A servant girl led the young woman toward the house. She sighed, seeming relieved to be free from the scrutiny of strangers. The baby peeked over her shoulder.

"Wait, what is your name?" Shamara asked.

"I am called Yonah." At the sound of her voice, the baby smiled, a satisfied toothless smile. Samuel's daughter loved this woman. Yeshua would want her to learn to love Yonah too.

The potter's daughter stepped in front of Yonah and spit at her feet. "She looks like a Jewess." Jealousy and enmity dripped from every word.

The peace of the Promised One enfolded Shamara. "Have we not been abundantly blessed these two days past by a traveling Jew? A prophet who risked a journey through Samaria?"

The young woman looked as if Shamara's gentle tone had heaped hot coals upon her head. "You would yet marry Samuel?"

"The deepest desire of my heart has always been to be the

wife of Samuel ben Abram. You forget. I have been a content second wife. And now I will be a wealthy one."

She went to Samuel and took his hand. He shook his head, his face full of mixed emotions. Not one of which she could read.

He leaned toward her. "It is not what it seems. Beloved, I would speak in private."

"When you left Shechem, I thought only to be a concubine. Yeshua has freed me from fear. I will be a happy, humble second wife."

"*Second* wife?" Dex strolled into the midst of them. "I tend the ox and return to find you have made a mess of your homecoming."

He slapped Samuel on the back and laughed from deep in his belly—a man accustomed to sorting out squabbles. "I have known this man for years. Mara, you are the love of his life. And Yonah is not his wife. She is a palace servant who cares for his baby, Lyra."

Shamara's knees turned to wet wool. She sought Samuel's eyes.

He put a steadying arm around her waist. "I vowed I would never marry another." He drew her closer.

Johakim straightened and arranged his robes, suddenly waking to his role. "Samuel, who is your friend?"

"I am Dex, sent with Samuel to bring the baby and Yonah safely here."

"And Yonah?" The foremost rumor raven shook a finger at Samuel. "We have women in Shechem to care for a baby."

"Quiet, woman." Samuel's angry voice cut through the pleasant breeze. "I have brought messenger doves. Yonah has also been sent to serve as the dove keeper."

Samuel turned to Johakim. "Before the sun sets, I would be betrothed to Mara."

Shamara touched Samuel's hand. "The Promised One has given me a new name. I am now called Shamara."

Samuel turned. "Shamara, our betrothal will be a simple signing. But all here will be invited to the wedding feast."

She put a finger to his lips. "Remember the bride is not to know the day or the hour when her bridegroom comes."

"But she knows when his coming is near." Samuel picked her up by the waist and spun her around. "Look up. Tonight, the waning moon gives half its light. All of Shechem will share our wedding feast before the waxing moon shines half bright."

40

Shechem

Samuel

S amuel wiped the sweat from his brow and inspected the first room he and Ozri were adding to Abba's house. He spotted Mara rushing through the village, her face aglow, her copper curls slipping from her head covering. She entered the yard, looked at him, eyes shining blue as a bright summer sky.

"Here is a gift for our wedding day." She was breathless and blushing and beautiful.

Samuel opened the parcel. "A new kitel."

A double of the one he had ripped to bandage Theo on the road to Jericho so long ago. The kitel was flawlessly woven.

"Beloved, I will cherish this all the days of my life, but how did you have time to fashion this so quickly?"

"Yeshua told me to look in the wooden chest where your ima kept her unfinished work. Unbeknownst to me, she started a kitel for you, always holding fast to the hope that you were alive and would marry me when I was free. I merely completed what she started."

"Yeshua. A name that crosses the lips of many. Yet a name steeped in conflict." Samuel could not keep the uncertainty from his tone.

"If you had only seen Him, heard Him speak."

"Ozri tells me most believed him to be a prophet. Some believed he was the Taheb." Samuel's stomach tightened around a drab of doubt. "There were even some who wondered if he may be something more." His stomach wrenched and burning bile clawed up his throat. Surely this was blasphemy.

Mara took his hand. "Many suspect He may be more than we ever dared hope."

"How are we ever to know the truth regarding this Jew?"

"Yeshua said His time was not yet. We must watch and wait."

Mara's eyes sparkled every time she spoke the name *Yeshua*. Samuel did not know what to think, but he did know the name Yeshua crossed Mara's lips more often than the name Samuel. He swallowed an olive pit of jealousy.

Samuel

This was the night Abba had approved for Samuel to bring his bride to the wedding feast. He climbed down the bank and into the shallow mountain stream. Unlike the stone mikvah at the High Priest's House, the flowing stream was a natural ritual bath. The cool water swirled at his shoulders, and he dunked his head. All was in readiness.

His Beloved said Yeshua called all people to repent and

his disciples baptized them in the river Jordan. Samuel shook his long hair. He did not understand, but then no one in Shechem seemed to fully grasp the teachings of this new prophet.

Samuel climbed out of the stream and let the warm breeze dry his skin. He pulled the new kitel over his head, put on his best robe with a green thread at the hem, and laced on his fine leather sandals.

"Shamara awaits her bridegroom." Abba joined him, face beaming.

Samuel's ears bristled at *Shamara,* the only name his Beloved would allow. It pricked his pride she rejected even his name of endearment, *Mami.*

They walked to the House of the High Priest. Servants scurried in the courtyard, preparing for Samuel's return with his bride.

"My beloved Ruth's vision is being fulfilled. May HaShem grant you many seasons together."

Samuel kissed his father on both cheeks. "Please do not remind Ma—*Sha*mara of Ima's last hope for an heir. My Beloved is barren."

"As were the first mothers of our people." A patient smile crossed Abba's face. "In old age, Sarah bore Isaac. And in old age, Rachel bore Joseph and Benjamin. Yeshua has reminded us that nothing is impossible with the Lord."

At Abba's words, Samuel's heart overflowed with joy. But something more swelled in his chest. As a carpenter shaves away the flaws of a rough plank, Samuel shaved away each trouble in his life until he was left with an emotion that was smooth, exposed, raw. One he had not allowed himself to feel in a long time.

Hope.

Hope for a son.

A servant brought a stallion for the procession of the bridegroom and boosted him onto its back.

Samuel held up his hands. The merry-making men went silent. "Many thanks. Shechem has prepared the feast and festivities and flourishes I have always wanted to give my Beloved Bride."

Abba stood at Samuel's right. "A wedding worthy of a wealthy bridegroom."

Ozri blew a long blast on the ram's horn announcing the coming of the bridegroom.

Tobiah ran to catch up. Thankfully, he was clear-eyed and clear-headed. Abba said Tobiah was slowly returning to the loving friend he been before Mara's birth.

Samuel urged his mount forward, the men flocking behind him. He stopped outside the shepherd's cottage where his bride would be watching, waiting.

Samuel called out, his voice brimming with joy and pride. "Arise my love."

"I answer the call of my bridegroom." Mara's voice was strong and sure.

Abram entered the cottage and soon returned outside. "I vow the bride is none other than Shamara."

The men cheered. The women sang and the timbrels in their fingers rang.

His Beloved ran out to greet him. A circlet of gold coins banded her head covering and jingled with each step. Though her lower face was veiled, he could see his own joy reflected in her eyes.

Every virgin in the village had trimmed her oil lamp. They danced around Shamara like bees around their queen's hive.

Abba took the reins and Samuel moved back. Shamara's giggling attendants lifted her in front of him. She leaned against his chest and sighed. "My bridegroom brings me to the wedding feast, blanketed with his love."

Samuel put his arm around her waist and nuzzled her neck. "May we never again be parted."

Shamara

An impatient thrill danced around Shamara's heart. The wedding feast lasted for hours and surpassed all her dreams. Now, her marriage contract would be sealed before a host of witnesses.

Shamara glanced up at the star-filled night sky. The moon shone half-light, as Samuel had sworn. Her heart fluttered, filled with the joy of a blessing for which she had not dared hope. "I am my Beloved's."

"And my Beloved is mine." Samuel's eyes shone with what seemed to be disbelief and wonder. He sipped the wine. "I promise to provide, protect, and love you all the days of my life." He passed the cup to her.

"I promise to serve, honor, and love you all the days of my life." She sipped her wine.

The high priest lifted a cup to Shamara. "You are now a wife."

Abram lifted a cup to Samuel. "And you are now a husband."

"We will be glad and rejoice with you." The guests sipped their wine.

"Bless Yeshua. I have entered this covenant freed from fear and shame because He has cleansed my heart."

Samuel's face changed. His eyes dimmed and his gentle smile creased, hardening like new-formed bricks in the sun.

Shamara's throat tightened. "What troubles you, Beloved?"

"It is nothing."

Samuel's answer did not ring true. His tone carried some wordless worry. She drew him away from the others. "I once told you there should always be plain-speaking between us. Tell me how I have given offense."

"My thoughts are small-minded."

"Still, I would care to know what has troubled you."

"I am of two minds." Samuel took a deep breath seeming to order his thoughts and choose his words. "Because Yeshua freed your heart, you have become my wife. But must I always share your heart with this prophet?"

"Each day of my life, my love for you spans as far as the east is from the west."

Samuel's eyes softened and his smile gentled. "It is not your love for me that is troubling. It is your single-minded seeking of Yeshua's will that vexes me."

"Love swells our hearts. It does not shrink them." She touched Samuel's arm. How could she ever confess to Samuel that he held her heart, but Yeshua cradled her soul?

The flaps of the wedding tent were lifted open. Welcoming arms. Shamara looked back at the heavens. Clouds passed in front of the moon, snuffing its light. A shiver ran down her arms. *HaShem, may I never have to choose between Your beloved prophet and my beloved husband.*

Samuel took her hand, and they crossed the threshold of the huppa. Reaching, they each released a tent flap. At last, she was alone with her Beloved.

Samuel opened his arms. "Your eyes sparkle like topaz, like a stream in the sun."

She stepped into his embrace. "Like living water."

"You alone are my living water. And I will not share my

wedding night with the prophet even if he was sent from the Lord." Jealousy seemed to sharpen his tone.

Something flickered in Shamara's heart. Not anger. Not judgment. Perhaps disappointment.

He leaned close and caressed her cheek. Shamara felt the warm whisper of his breath beneath her veil. 'Let me uncover your face and unbind your hair." He released the veil and gently kissed her. "Your lips taste sweet, and your face is fair." Her head covering fell to her shoulders. "And copper is the color of my true love's hair."

He led her to the pallet strewn with flowers. "Come, let my arm be under your head and your ear at my heart." They lay side by side and Samuel gathered her to his chest.

The hum of his heart settled her soul. The rhythm of his heartbeat joined with hers. A rhythm of life. A rhythm of love that set their desire on fire.

Samuel kissed Shamara's brow. "Time cannot be stoppered in a bottle. Time stands still for no creature under the sun."

"Lord, teach us to number our days that we squander not a one." She reached up and pressed a finger to his lips.

"Even your lightest touch sends a rush of joy through my veins. You are my heart, my life, my home."

"Since I was on the cusp of womanhood, I have thirsted for you." She reached her arms around his neck. "Your arms. Your lips. Your love. Will you slake my thirst?"

She surrendered to warm waves of love and desire.

Samuel lifted her chin. "Our thirst should be quenched often."

Samuel lifted one of her copper curls and wound it around his finger. "Your hair still crowns your head. Such a fiery bramble." Samuel drifted toward a drowsy bliss.

Shamara stroked his hair. Troubles and time faded away.

May their lives and hearts and souls always be entwined like their braided limbs.

Samuel

It had been two months since Samuel's wedding. He wedged a stone into the rising wall of one of the new rooms he was adding onto Abba's house. Sweat dribbled down his neck and back.

Ozri pushed a hand-held cart, piled high with stones, toward him. "I would choose to work wood over stone every day of my life." He dumped the stones onto the ground. "Will Lyra live here?"

"Lyra is a slave and must stay with Yonah the Dovekeeper and live in the servant's quarters at the House of the High Priest. Even so, I will visit Lyra every day." Samuel jostled the last two stones into place. "How did Yonah fare during my wedding week?"

Ozri's brows drew together. "I have never heard what you have called Yonah's unbridled tongue." His face filled with confused concern.

"Nevertheless, do not speak to her of kings or queens or royal things. Rome does not take kindly to insult."

"Fortunately, there are no royal Romans in Shechem." Ozri grinned, all worry wiped from his face. "So, tell me, what other words should a man avoid with the woman who has snared his heart?" His tone was equal parts sober question and light-hearted jest.

Samuel took Ozri by the shoulders. "Never mention the prophet who was called the Baptizer. Never. Ever."

Something changed in Ozri's eyes. "But—"

"Better yet ..." Samuel stared hard into Ozri's face. "Never mention any prophet."

"But the villagers speak of the prophet Yeshua many times each day. Some tell the tales of their repentance, baptism, and renewal. Yonah has heard all these things and I have never witnessed any mad rants."

"Perhaps she will find peace here in Shechem, far away from Herod's court."

"Perhaps ..." Ozri flushed the color of a ripe pomegranate and pressed his lips into a tight slash.

"Perhaps what?"

"You will think I am foolish, easily duped."

"Tell me. I will withhold all judgment."

"Perhaps Yonah has been restored to her right mind."

A lump clotted in Samuel's throat. Ozri so wanted to believe Yonah was well.

Ozri looked down and wrung his hands. "Since Yeshua left there may have been healings."

"May have been?" Samuel threw up his hands. "An illness is healed, or it is not. Listen to yourself. Have you been robbed of your senses?"

"Not all healings are sudden. Since Yeshua left, some have noticed a slow, steady renewal."

Samuel nodded, battling the urge to belittle Ozri's hope.

"Remember the knots in my right palm, the in-drawing of my fingers? It worsened. I could not lay my right hand flat on a table." Ozri placed his hand flat against the wall.

Samuel turned Ozri's hand over. "The knots are much as I remember them. Who else has noticed a healing?"

"Your Abba has walked with a staff for many years, his shoulders stooped."

"He has aged since the passing of Ima. What could be more likely?"

"For the last week, Abram has felt his strength increase. This morning, he walked to the woodshop, standing straight, without his staff."

"Many burdens have been lifted from his shoulders. Maybe his strength and stance have been renewed by his happiness."

"The high priest says his night sight was fast fading. Now he can follow the flight of a bee at last light."

"These healings may not come from the power of the prophet Yeshua, but from the power of hope, alone."

"Consider Tobiah."

"I would rather never think of him."

"Strong drink has not passed his lips since the day Yeshua offered us living water."

"He must smell a chance to gain gold with claims he is healed." Samuel felt his temper rising, but he did not want to offend Ozri.

"Tobiah makes no claim of faith or healing, but admits he craves strong drink every waking moment."

"Then why does he not drown in his drink?" Samuel could not keep the sour snarl from his voice.

"Yeshua gazed into Tobiah's eyes and at that moment, Tobiah suddenly saw himself through the eyes of others. Greedy. Selfish. Besotted."

"That seems beyond belief."

"The truth about Yeshua will unfold." Ozri touched Samuel on the shoulder. "Only HaShem knows how long we must watch and wait."

Jealousy seethed in Samuel's heart. "No matter how desperately we 'watch and wait,' we will not force the hand of HaShem. Or hasten the coming of the Promised One."

41

Shechem

Three years since Shamara and Samuel's wedding

Ten years since Samuel fled Shechem

Shamara

S hamara stood in her small vegetable garden behind the rooms Samuel built onto Abram's house. She stretched out her arms and slowly spun, basking in the warmth of the sun and the feel of the air in her unbound hair. For a moment, a young girl again.

Since the coming of Yeshua almost three years past, Shamara's life had been filled with much peace, healing, and joy. She rejoiced in her marriage with Samuel and had come to accept that she would remain barren.

She stopped spinning. The only thorn in her side was Samuel's jealousy of Yeshua had sprouted into a root of bitterness. Samuel refused to consider that Yeshua might be the Promised One.

Tobiah walked by, smiled, and waved. A warm thrill cradled her heart. After so many years of suffering her father's cruelty, he was now clear-minded and loving. He continued toward the wood shop where he worked with Samuel and Abram every day. He passed little Lyra and Yonah hand-in-hand coming toward the garden.

Lyra began to skip. "I come and help."

Lyra, now more than three years since her birth, was the darling of the village. Everyone counted the days until the time of her redemption from slavery. She took her small water jar and sprinkled a row of cucumber plants.

Yonah sighed. "Perhaps today Ozri will return from Jericho."

"Every day you speak of his return. Even when he has just left." Shamara's tone was tender and teasing.

Yonah blushed and looked down.

"Ozri seems as fond of you as you are of him."

"I do miss him when he's gone for days, taking news of Shechem to the Jericho Inn."

"It is a blessing that Ozri also takes Samuel's new harps for Prima to sell." Shamara added water to Lyra's jar. "I feel I have come to know the blacksmith and his wife well since they always visit Ozri when he is at the inn."

Lyra ran to water the next row and Yonah smiled. "They delight in hearing stories of Lyra's happy life here."

"Ozri tells Samuel the queen's questions are always centered on you, not Shechem. Her last words to him are always, *Remember me to the dovekeeper.*"

"Yes. The queen is fond of me." Yonah's tone was flat, but her face looked troubled.

Shamara's hands went to her hips. "Who are you to the queen?"

"I am the keeper of shared sorrows and shared safety. I am the one she most hates, yet most loves—most fears, yet most protects."

"You talk in riddles. Samuel must know of these things."

"Samuel and I have driven all these things from our minds. Lives depend upon our forever-forgetfulness."

"Is danger lurking at our door?"

A look Shamara had never seen flickered across Yonah's face. The light in her eyes seemed to dim to a time in the past—then sharpen to the brink of madness.

"Terrible things happen to queens ..." Yonah rubbed her hands against each other as if washing them without water. "And terrified queens do terrible things."

Was this the madness of which Samuel had warned?

Lyra ran up to them and tugged Yonah's skirt. "Come watch me."

Yonah stopped dry scrubbing her hands and shuddered, seeming to wake from an ill-fated dream.

Lyra ran back to her row in the garden and gently pulled weeds from around a lentil vine.

"Well done, my child." Yonah's eyes sparkled like silver coins in the sunlight. "When Ozri returns, he will be so surprised."

"And proud." Shamara's heart quickened and she turned to Yonah. "Ozri will bring tidings of Jerusalem. I long for the day Yeshua returns to us."

"Will the Promised One be a kind king and bring peace?"

Yonah sounded so wistful—so wounded. "Yeshua brought me peace with myself and peace with HaShem."

Lyra looked up from her planting. "Is Yeshua coming?"

Shamara smiled at Lyra with the loving smile and heart of a mother. A faint flutter in Shamara's belly made her gasp. "We must watch and wait, little one." Another flutter. A flutter she had never felt before. "And we must hope and pray." Shamara glanced toward the crossroads. "Look at that dust cloud. I have never seen oxen move so quickly. Must be Ozri."

"Something has happened." Yonah wrung the front of her tunic, then ran to the road. Shamara picked up Lyra and followed.

Ozri stopped the oxcart, smiled broadly, and stood. "Samuel is summoned to redeem Lyra early. I will drive to the wood shop and get him. He and Lyra must journey to Jericho at once."

Shamara picked up Lyra, spun around, and laughed. She glanced at Yonah who looked worried, not happy.

Yonah turned to Ozri. "Why does the queen send for Samuel so soon?"

"I do not know, but there is much unrest. Zealots rail against Herod and his harlot Herodias."

Yonah hugged herself. "Samuel must go dressed as Didymus. Herod believes Samuel is dead." She muttered. "My former self is also dead."

Who was Yonah? Was her friend truly safe? Was Samuel? Shamara looked up at Ozri. "What shall we do?"

Ozri eased onto the seat and picked up the reins. "Plans are in place. Samuel will meet Prima outside Jerusalem where she will disguise him as Didymus."

"Lyra is my charge." Yonah took Shamara's hand. "If I travel to Jericho, lives could be forfeit. Terrified queens do terrible things."

"Here in Shechem, you will remain safe. I will go and tend to Lyra."

Shamara prayed that somehow Samuel would meet Yeshua. Surely if Samuel heard Him teach, felt His love for others, and witnessed His miracles, Samuel would come to believe Yeshua was the Promised One and share her steadfast faith.

Samuel

Two days had been needed for Prima to resurrect the Didymus disguise for Samuel. Now, he listened to the rumble of the oxcart's wheels past Jerusalem, past the Mount of Olives, and onto the road to Jericho. Shamara sat beside him, and Lyra slept on the hay in the back. His stomach boiled with excitement and fear. Excitement Lyra soon would be redeemed, no longer a slave to a treacherous queen. Fear that something unforeseen would thwart her path to freedom.

"Samuel, when you are worried, you reach to tug at a beard that is no longer there." Shamara laughed.

"Call me Didymus." Samuel's stomach twisted. "I despise this disguise, but it was a small sacrifice to take up my pagan remnants to redeem my daughter."

"Be at peace. You will dress as a Samaritan again."

Samuel squeezed Shamara's hand. "My brilliant Beloved. Your story that I am playing a Greek king guarding his secret little princess may keep Lyra from giving us all away."

Shamara nodded. "I hope any slips from Lyra will be taken as a childish fantasy."

Content in the quiet and the calm, Samuel drove on for several miles, Shamara's head resting on his shoulder.

The road narrowed and the crowd swelled, forcing Samuel to a halt. "Shavuot has finished, but people choke the road, not going home but toward Jerusalem."

Shamara sat forward seeming to search the teeming masses.

"Prima told me Jerusalem and Jericho are brimming with reports of Yeshua's works."

"His works?" A cord of jealousy wound around Samuel's heart. He edged the cart through a curve.

"Miracles. The people flock to Him, desperately hoping to see ... *or to be* ... the next miracle. The wonders never cease. The deaf hear, the lame walk, the blind see."

"These things cannot be true." A tight resentment pressed in Samuel's chest.

"Prima has seen these miracles with her own eyes. And has heard Yeshua forgive sins and cast out demons with her own ears. He speaks with the authority of HaShem."

Prima, like Shamara and so many others, must be under Yeshua's spell. Samuel edged the cart forward. "Every city and every generation has its charlatans and false messiahs." He could not keep the mocking from his tone even though hurt creased Shamara's face.

She grabbed his sleeve in the manner of a beggar seeking scraps. "If only you could meet Yeshua, I am certain you would see Him as I do."

Samuel balked at the slight needling in Shamara's tone. But then he glanced at her face—a slight frown, pleading eyes, and a mouth pursed tight with conviction. Shamara was not needling, she was desperate. Determined.

"Why is my opinion of Yeshua of such import?"

"Because I have chosen to follow Him. I would have us on the same path."

Her desire was a whispered prayer. Samuel wanted his answer to satisfy, but he could not reply with a lie. "I will allow that this Yeshua is a good man. A prophet even. I am certain of nothing more." The cord of jealousy cinched tighter around Samuel's heart and chaffed like a prisoner's shackle.

His wife was still so taken with this man, Yeshua, even

though she had not seen him for so long. His friends and father spoke of Yeshua each day—at the well, at the wood shop, and every time they broke bread. Samuel suspected Shamara thought of the prophet every waking hour.

"Samuel, would a good man, a true prophet, lie to His people? Would He feed His flocks of disciples from a field full of lies?"

Samuel squirmed under the scrutiny of Shamara's gaze. "A good man is not a liar."

"If Yeshua is not a liar, then do you believe He is a madman?" Shamara's voice and face carried the fervor of full-fledged faith.

A chill wormed itself across Samuel's neck. He remembered Salome's sudden raving madness. "No. The prophet's teachings are too lucid to be those of a madman."

"If Yeshua is not a liar, and not a madman, surely it follows that He must be who He says He is."

"He claims he is the Promised One." Samuel heard the uncertainty in his own voice.

"Beloved. Look at me." Shamara touched his cheek. "To those who really listen, He claims to be more ...

Samuel stopped the cart and dragged his eyes to hers, afraid of what he might read on her face.

"Yeshua told me all I ever did and forgave my sins. Only then, could I marry you." Tears filled Shamara's eyes and her sadness stabbed his soul.

Samuel looked away. A snake of jealous anger reared its head and struck. "Your Yeshua has not told me all I ever did."

"But you have not yet met Him."

"I do not chase after him looking for miracles as others do. Why should I believe what I have not seen with my own eyes?"

"Yonah believes in Yeshua, and she has been healed. Even though she has never seen Him."

Samuel bristled at the growing challenge in Shamara's tone "Enough talk of prophets and miracles. We have a more weighty worry. Prima has not sold the last harp I left with her."

"Do you have the silver needed for Lyra's redemption?"

"No. Not all. I was called to Jericho before the appointed time." He pointed to a sack at his feet. "We must somehow sell this harp on the street, even though it was meant to be Lyra's legacy."

"We cannot delay. The sands of time are sifting away. Danger must loom. Why else would the queen send for you oversoon?" Shamara reached into her robes and slipped a coin into his hand.

Samuel looked at his palm. His heart raced, his hand trembled. "The Magi coin. But ... how?"

"It is not the same coin, but one left for me by Seth."

Samuel could read Shamara's forlorn face. "I spent the coin left for you by your mother. I cannot take this cherished other."

"Seth is dead. And Lyra lives. Riches are never meant to be hoarded but used to bless others."

Samuel took Shamara in his arms and kissed her brow. "Blessed are you among women. You have sealed Lyra's freedom. May all your prayers be answered." Samuel snapped the reins and the cart jerked forward.

People pressed against the cart, moving far away from a group of maimed, foul-smelling lepers. He stopped to let the pitiful outcasts pass.

Lyra roused, and Shamara climbed onto the hay with her. Over the next several miles, Shamara fed Lyra bread and cheese and passed some to Samuel. She kept them both amused with stories of kings and fools and things with wings.

At the signpost for the inn, Samuel reined the ox. "We are here." He helped Shamara down, lifted Lyra, and set her next to the signpost. She traced the wheat carved on the sign. "Abba, did you make this?"

Samuel's throat tightened, his mind flooded with memories of the prison cell in Jericho, his trial, and the bite of the assassin's blade.

"Didymus."

Samuel turned toward the welcoming shout. "Dex."

His friend ran up the path and trapped him in the powerful hug of a blacksmith. "The crowds must have slowed you."

"Yes. But I trust we are in good time."

Dex spoke in his ear. "Now that you are here, Barid will send to Jericho for Herodias."

Behind Samuel, Sophia came forward and hugged Shamara. "We meet at long last."

Sophia's son clung to her robes, staring shyly at Lyra.

Lyra scuttled around Sophia's skirt and took the boy's hand. After a long, strong stare, they ran off to play in the barn. Sophia followed them.

Theo came out from the inn, leaning heavily on his crutch and flashed Samuel a heart-felt smile. "It has been too long my friend. I would hear all your news, but first I will feed and water the ox." He limped to the barn, the beast in tow.

Barid came to the door and waved them inside. "For nigh on ten years, Theo has kept constant watch for the priest and Levite who left him for dead."

Dex led Samuel and Shamara into the inn.

Samuel sat at the table across from Dex. "I see there is at least one cripple in Judea that Yeshua of Nazareth has not yet healed."

Dex shot Samuel a sharp look, then a flicker of sorrow crossed the blacksmith's face. "We have begged Theo to go to Yeshua. Some days He heals all who come to Him."

Samuel hid his vexation. Dex was under the prophet's spell too.

Shamara took a seat beside Samuel. "Does Theo not want to be well?"

"Not enough to lay down his vigil for vengeance. He refuses to chance missing the wicked holy men—even to be healed." Dex shook his head.

"Does Theo remember anything of his life before I found him?"

"No. But he has the skills of a highly trusted steward. Sometimes I wonder if he is afraid of what or who he might remember." Barid laid out a simple supper of bread, cheese, and wine. "Your rooms are ready."

Samuel took coins from his waist sack and placed them on the table "This should cover our food and lodging."

Theo called from the door. "Wait. Do not charge Samuel—he saved my life." Theo made his way to the table and handed Samuel a coin.

Samuel's breath hitched, his stomach twitched, and his heart leapt like a startled deer. "Is this ..."

Shamara looked at Samuel's open palm and drew in a quick breath.

Theo's face filled with pride. "Yes, it is the very same Magi coin Mara gave you so many years ago. I asked Barid to set it aside for me to earn back with my wages. He told me long ago how dear the coin was to you."

Samuel handed the coin to Shamara with tears in his eyes. Tears that matched those glistening on her cheeks. "Theo, bless you for this kindness."

Shamara lifted the coin and waved it gently toward Samuel. "HaShem rewards a righteous man double for his trouble."

"And my favorite Samaritan is a righteous man." Theo brought plates of figs and cucumbers and olives to the table.

Barid wiped his hands on a towel. "Theo, put an extra pot of lentil stew over the cookfire. Hundreds of travellers crowd the road."

Theo stared toward the road and stiffened. A clay plate dropped from his hand and shattered on the floor.

A murderous look on his face, Theo pointed. "I saw him."

Samuel stood. "Who?"

"The priest who left me for dead."

42

Jericho

Samuel

Theo picked up his crutch and hobbled to the door. "He vanished into the crowd, but I would never forget that face. I will track that wicked priest all the way to Jerusalem." He took his cloak and left.

Barid slammed his fist on the counter. "By the gods, it is Theo's due to accuse that priest. But Samuel, please keep Theo from violence. Keep him from death on a cross."

Samuel turned to Shamara. "Lyra's redemption ..."

"Leave the payment." Dex handed Samuel a waterskin. "Give Barid your proxy. On my life, Herodias will honor Lyra's liberation from slavery."

Barid pulled out a parchment. "Sign your makers-mark here. Go. I will record all that is needed."

Shamara prodded his elbow. "Beloved, go quickly before Theo is lost in the crowd or does something rash."

Samuel grabbed his cloak and rushed from the inn. A mysterious foreboding bore deep into his chest. He did not know whether he was racing toward the outworkings of the Hand of HaShem or torments from the Snare of Satan.

The crowds grew. What was drawing them? It was not the week of a feast. He had never seen such a river of pilgrims.

Samuel kept searching for Theo. Was he skulking in the crowd?

The golden roof of the Temple in Jerusalem glinted against the sky. *HaShem, surely it was not your will our Jew would be consumed by vengeance.*

There were so many cripples. Samuel spotted an uplifted crutch.

He ploughed through the masses toward the crutch and caught sight of Theo. He was just behind the unsuspecting priest who had stopped, blocked by the cumbersome crowd.

If Theo's blow landed, even if he did not kill the priest, he would never survive the sentence of a scourging.

Samuel leapt in front of Theo. The blow meant for the priest, landed between Samuel's neck and shoulder. A lightning bolt of pain ran down his arm.

The crowd surged, and the priest vanished again.

Samuel grabbed the crutch and wrenched it from Theo. "Do not throw your life away on a wicked priest."

Theo seemed to wither. "What am I to do with the hate that hardens my heart, poisons my mind, and smothers my soul?"

"Be patient. The Temple is close. It must be the priest's turn to serve. Bring his sin before the other priests. Let him live with the public humiliation of his hypocrisy."

They walked on. When Theo seemed calm, Samuel gave him the crutch.

After walking almost a mile, Theo tugged at Samuel's

sleeve. "Look. That wicked priest is not turning into the city gate. No one is going to Jerusalem."

The crowd pressed around them, forcing them along. Samuel helped Theo across a slick stone. "Everyone is turning onto the road to Bethany."

After another mile, the crowd moved off the road into a clearing. Those in front of them settled onto the ground.

"There he is." Theo pointed to the wicked priest winding his way through the crowd. He sat on a boulder near the front by a rabbi who was already teaching.

From a distance, the rabbi seemed the most ordinary of men. But this must be Yeshua. Crowds of this magnitude followed none other.

Theo's knees gave way, and Samuel barely caught him. Theo was white and quivering like a new-born lamb. He hissed. He might be taken with a fit.

"What is it?" Samuel lifted the waterskin. "Drink."

Theo knocked it away. "The Levite who sits by the priest is the second man who left me for dead." Theo's face grew red, and his voice grew loud, drawing the stares of those nearby.

"Shh. Kindly be still and sit down. We want to see and hear the Master." An old woman behind them smiled and sat on her cloak.

Samuel helped Theo ease onto his cloak and sat beside him.

Up front, near Yeshua, the largest disciple shoved the smaller one next to him. His manner seemed part jester, part bully. He turned to Yeshua. "Lord, how many times must I forgive a brother who sins against me?"

This must be Simon. Big man. Booming voice. The man who loved deeply, hated fiercely, and spoke freely—often before he thought. Shamara had told him about the disciples.

"Must I forgive as many as seven times?" Simon counted

six fingers for the crowd. He wiggled his seventh finger, a warning that his patience had worn thin.

The smaller man elbowed Simon and broke into a waggish smile that would melt even a tyrant's temper. Must be John. Shamara said John was water to Simon's fire.

Yeshua waited. Both men looked at him. "Have I not told you, you must forgive not just seven times, but seventy times seven."

Simon scowled at John and made a fool's face at the crowd. "The good news is that no one is beyond forgiveness."

John grinned and slapped Simon on the back. "Not even you."

Samuel laughed with the crowd, but Simon did not.

Yeshua put up a hand. "John, it is wrong to tempt a brother to stumble. Both of you must forgive your brother from your heart, or my heavenly Father will not forgive your trespasses."

People looked at one another. No one was laughing now.

Samuel glanced at Theo. He hoped his friend would forgive the priest and Levite and be set free from the prison of his poisoning hate.

Theo pushed up on his crutch. "I cannot remember my name, or my sins. So how can I repent?" Theo shouted and shook his fist in the air. He pointed toward the priest and Levite. "I well remember the faces of these two men. They have sinned against me. I will not forgive their trespasses."

People close by stared and glared and motioned for Theo to sit and be silent.

Yeshua looked slowly across the crowd. He seemed to see deeply into each soul. "Again, I say to you, forgive your brother, or my heavenly Father will not forgive you."

Then a Pharisee, a young lawyer, approached Yeshua. The man touched his own brow, lips, and heart as a sign of respect. "Rabbi, what must I do to inherit eternal life?"

"Tell me how you understand the Law on this point."

"Love the Lord with all your heart, all your soul, all your strength. And all your mind." The lawyer puffed out his chest like a rooster announcing the dawn. "And love your neighbor as yourself."

"Yes. Do this and you will gain eternal life."

The lawyer smiled the eager smile of a scholar. "And who is my neighbor?"

"There was a certain man ..." Yeshua paused, studied the lawyer, and gestured for him to sit.

"There was a certain man ... a man going down from Jerusalem to Jericho. But robbers stripped him of his clothes, beat him, and left him half-dead."

Theo cried out.

Samuel clasped Theo's shoulder and leaned close to him. "Many other bandits and many other men have travelled that road." Samuel, caught up in the story, looked back at Yeshua.

"A priest and later a Levite saw the man and passed him by on the other side of the road."

Theo gasped. "He knows. He truly knows."

A slurry of uncertainty soured Samuel's stomach.

The priest on the boulder buried his face in his hands, seeming shamed and repentant.

The Levite stood, spat, and left.

Samuel balked at the Levite's preposterous arrogance. Perhaps Yeshua spoke of these very men Theo accused.

"But a Samaritan came upon the man." Yeshua rose and searched the crowd. His gaze rested on Samuel.

Samuel's heart pounded, crashing within his chest. He held his breath, trying to hear past the thrumming in his ears. Yeshua must be speaking of him. Samuel, a hated Samaritan.

"When the Samaritan saw the man, he took pity on him.

He went to the man and bandaged his wounds, pouring on oil and wine."

Even from a distance, Yeshua's look seemed both probing and gentle. As if he knew Samuel too had been beaten and left for dead. As if he was waiting for Samuel to truly see, truly hear. Truly surrender.

Samuel took both Theo's hands and pressed them between his. "Swear to me, you never spoke these things to any man, woman, or child."

Theo whispered into Samuel's ear. "I was left for dead. Some of these things even I did not know."

"Then the Samaritan brought the beaten man to an inn." Yeshua was tall, His manner kingly, yet humble. "The next day, the Samaritan paid the innkeeper to care for him."

Some in the crowd spoke words of amazement and approval.

Yeshua turned to the lawyer. "Which of these three, the priest, the Levite, or the Samaritan, do you think was a neighbor to the man who fell into the hands of robbers?"

The lawyer looked flustered, caught in his own trap. "The one who had mercy on him."

"Go and do likewise." Yeshua spoke with such absolute, certain authority.

Murmurs of astonishment, anger, and confusion travelled through the crowd.

Yeshua had told the entire assembly all Samuel had done for Theo. A chill ran up Samuel's spine and sent icy fingers into his mind. *Yeshua knew all his sins, his doubts, and even his stubborn unbelief.*

Suddenly his doubts seemed washed away. Samuel's whole body quivered, and his hands shook. *Yeshua knew of Samuel's hopes, his prayers, and his love for HaShem.*

Prayers.

Samuel's own words to Shamara echoed in his mind. *May all your prayers be answered.*

Shamara had been praying for him. She said Yeshua offered his disciples the hope of eternal life.

Suddenly, Samuel was certain. Certain Yeshua was so much more than the Samaritans or the Jews had expected. Certain Yeshua was Messiah.

Yeshua raised His hands, dismissing the crowd with a blessing. "May the Lord keep you in the palm of His Hand."

The sun sank toward the start of Sabbath Rest and the people hastened home.

Samuel and Theo rose slowly, among the last to leave.

Silent, clinging to one another, still unsteady with wonder, Samuel and Theo walked toward Bethany seeking refuge for Sabbath.

Just ahead, Yeshua walked with His disciples.

"Master, what became of the man in your parable?"

One disciple was scratching a quill across parchment.

"The man has not yet found the will to forgive. The end of his journey is a matter of courage and is not certain. But woven through his journey is a golden Magi coin and a friend whose hem has a peculiar green thread."

Samuel could not believe the words he heard. *Had Yeshua known every jot of Samuel's life before it came to pass?*

Theo stumbled. "He knows me. My past and present and future. And also, yours."

Samuel, trembling, clung to Theo more tightly.

Yeshua glanced back, and Samuel looked more closely at His face.

A memory burned through Samuel's veins. "Theo, I know this man. He saved me from a fatal fall from a runaway camel. He saved me again when He told me to trade my Samaritan robe. But his kinsman called him Aryeh ben Judah."

"Lion of Judah." Theo's voice was hushed with awe. "That is not a name, but a title for our king to come. Messiah."

Samuel was sure HaShem brought him to this place to heal his unbelief. When Sabbath was complete, he would run and share his new-found faith with his beloved Shamara. Now, though it was his greatest desire, he did not dare speak with Yeshua.

The disciples continued to talk amongst each other.

"Matthew, always writing, ever the scribe."

Simon, taunting a friend again.

"I used to collect taxes, now I collect the Master's parables." Matthew had not taken the bait from Simon's hook. This one will be *The Neighbor.*"

"No." Yeshua stopped, turned, and met Samuel's eyes. "Until the end of the Age, this parable will be known as *The Good Samaritan.*"

An older man stepped up to Yeshua. "The sun is low. Martha has readied the Sabbath supper. Mary waits for you to light the candles."

Yeshua nodded to his host. "Please invite this Jew, Theo, and his friend to sup with us."

Samuel's heart raced, his soul soared. He would sup with the Promised One. The Taheb. The Messiah.

The older man bowed to Theo. "I am Lazarus." He turned to Samuel. "And Greek, how are you called?"

"I am not a Greek." Samuel's sight was blurred by free-flowing tears. Living water. "But ..." He turned to Yeshua and confessed his faith.

"I am now ... a certain man."

Author's Note

Yeshua of Nazareth is both a historical and religious figure whose life and teachings are recorded in the Bible.

A Certain Man is a story—a biblical novel that inhabits the space of the verse:

Jesus did many other things as well. If every one of them were written down, I suppose that even the whole world would not have room for the books that would be written (John 21:25 —NIV).

While I am neither a historian or a biblical theologian, I have a long-standing fascination with the study of the Bible and the history of first century Judea. My desire with this work is to create a tale that rings true to both scripture and history. My hope is the reader will be intrigued with the compelling times and teachings of Jesus and they may further consider the claims of His Story.

Where gospel scenes are included in *A Certain Man,* I have decided to closely paraphrase the NIV and NKJ translations for clarity of meaning and sound and syntax of first century language.

Author's Note

The pronouns he, his, and him become He, His, and Him when the character speaking or thinking begins to understand that Yeshua the Nazarene is more than the long-awaited Messiah, more than a deliverer, and more than a mere prophet.

The choice to write of this era presents unique challenges. Historians and biblical scholars often disagree, and the mountain of details and research to sift can be daunting. Any unintended errors are mine alone.

Blessings,
Linda Dindzans

For book club and discussion questions, references, and interesting extras, please see website: lindadindzans.com.
facebook: Linda Dindzans, Author
X: @lindadindzans

Acknowledgments

Most writers claim "it takes a village" to write a book. My journey to publication needed "a whole country".

Life with me can be a roller coaster..."I believe I am being called to retire from medicine and write fiction."

"Okay. How can we help?" I am grateful the Lord has given me an unflappable husband – Vince, and family – Andra and Greg Morton, Karlis and Karen Dindzans, and Viktors Dindzans and Lauren Krukowski. They have propped me up when I was discouraged and celebrated each small success. With much love and thanks, you are my Home.

I am blessed with friends, who refuse to let me take myself too seriously. These women lent listening ears and they know "laughter is good medicine" so they dosed me with heaping spoonfuls—Roz Diederich, Peggy Dixon, Suzie Edstrom, Barb Chasin, Karen Eyers, Cheryl Geurts, Valerie Hawkins, Monika Hoerig, Jackie Mortenson, Lee O'Daniel, Noemi Prieto, Linda Stolz, Deb Stone, Barb Tock, CeCe Wells, Joanne Woodard.

The Lord has gifted me with brothers and sisters in Christ. Heartfelt thanks to the Thursday night Bible Study: Gina English, Chris and Sylvia Paulsen, Julie and Michael Shuster, Ken and Lindy Zinkgraf, and to the women of the Alliance Bible Church Women-in-the-Word Bible Study... especially my early encouragers... Cathy West, Jan Elmendorf, Randi Koenig,

Hugs to my many patient pickleball friends who take me and my game "as is" and keep me moving and somewhat sane.

Many writers have impacted me over this 11-year adventure. Here in Wisconsin: Sarah Freymuth and Ian Bultman , the SE Wisconsin ACFW chapter—especially long-time friend Nancy Radosevich, early mentor Liz Tolsma, Barbara Britton, and Chapter President Laura DeNooyer. These writers help assure scripture doesn't get sacrificed for story.

Tons of thanks to my writing champions, critique partners and dedicated Beta readers... Susan Taylor-Boyd, Marilyn Malcolm, Nancy Martin, Michele Merens. Your love and insightful edits have polished my writing so I could join your ranks as published authors.

Writer's conferences offered early encouragement: At Writer's Advance Bootcamps from Cindy Sproles, Vonda Skelton, and Mike Dellosso who became my first writing coach. Edie Melson introduced me to Blue Ridge Mountains Christian Writer's Conferences that fed my hunger for further development.

Online groups have opened a new world for writers. In my quest to hone my skills, I have spent hundreds of hours @ margielawson.com. I am indebted to my fellow Enduro Immersioners who tackled the intense, advanced work with me at all hours, from all parts of the globe: Lainey Cameron, Jenny Hansen, Stina Lindenblatt, Monica Schroeder, Cassandra Shaw. Margie Lawson, a PhD psychologist and editor extraordinaire was the midwife for this story. She offered counsel for me to "dig deep" and psychological insights for my characters so their emotions would ring true. Without her, this book would not have been birthed. I look forward to the next project under her guiding hand.

Much gratitude to the Page 3 Posse for wise wordsmithing.

This group has hatched beach writer's retreats* and a facebook group *Writing with the ERASERS:* Starr Ayers*,Bonnie Sue Beardsley, Charlsie Estess, Sandra Melville Hart*, K. Denise Holmberg*, Caroline Powers, Sandra Vosberg and Deborah Sprinkle*. Deborah has been my guardian angel and introduced my work to Scrivenings Press. My deepest gratitude for your steadfast faith in my writing and me.

I thank God that He moved the heart of Linda Fulkerson to take on an unfinished work, provide me with a family at Scrivenings Press, a keen and skilled editor Amy Anguish and a careful line editor, Mike Ehret. The icing on the cake is Linda's riveting cover design.

Soli Deo Gloria.

About the Author

Linda Dindzans, M.D., is a speaker , writer, and retired ENT surgeon with a longstanding fascination with God's Word and commitment to in-depth Bible study.

She is grateful for this time to lay down her scalpel and pick up her pen as she follows a call to write. A published writer and educator, Linda has been a guest speaker at medical conferences, national and regional Christian conferences, and a facilitator for church and home Bible studies. *A Certain Man*, a tale of ancient Samaria at the time of Jesus, is her debut novel.

Linda and her husband, a fellow physician, have been blessed with three adult children, a son-in-law, a daughter-in-law, and three grandchildren. Wisconsin is home but they enjoy photography, birdwatching, and singing with choirs all across the world.

More Biblical Fiction from Scrivenings Press

New Star by Lana Christian
Book One of The Magi's Encounters

How far would you go to protect what you believe in?

Akilah, a highly respected priest-scholar in Magi society, considers all his astronomy discoveries well-deserved stepping-stones to a more fulfilling life. But the appearance of a new star challenges his priorities. As Persia totters on the brink of an undesirable king coming to power, Akilah declines a position that could turn that tide. Instead, he studies a star that doesn't appear in any almanac or religious writings. Except Jewish.

When he and his colleagues uncover a few Jewish prophecies linking the star to an eternal king, Akilah becomes the target of Persia's religious and governmental conflicts. Jailed for crimes he didn't commit, Akilah must rely on questionable resources to free himself and reach Jerusalem.

Persia's purists aren't the only ones bent on keeping their country free of Jewish influences. As dangers at home and abroad plunge Akilah and his colleagues into three countries' religious conflicts and circumstances beyond their imagining, Akilah realizes his knowledge of Jesus could potentially destroy Magi society and its power over Persia's official religion and government. Untrusting of his Council, a thousand miles from aid, and bound in a potentially career-ending contract, Akilah must decide how far he will go to protect what he knows of Jesus—and whether the cost of his belief is worth the risk.

Available September 24, 2024

https://scrivenings.link/newstar

Stay up-to-date on your favorite books and authors with our free e-newsletters.

ScriveningsPress.com

Made in the USA
Monee, IL
22 July 2024

61674074R00236